Christmas across Time

David Gillanders

Christmas Across Time

Dedicated to

My paternal grandparents

James and Margaret Gillanders

Chapter 01

Leo Lennox greeted Friday evening with an enthusiasm that confused most people. He rushed home from work to begin his labours on the house with a fervour that would be in keeping with a child on Christmas morning.

Christmas was still some weeks off and Leo had the entire weekend to work on the house without his day job clambering for attention. He enjoyed the work, but this particular house had something that set it aside from the other two houses he has renovated since his divorce.

He didn't have a problem with his ex-wife, Laura, and the kids staying on in the family home and he had an easy job back then persuading his old friend Mike to allow him to stay at his place until he sorted out something more permanent.

The something more permanent came in the form of a run down two-up-two down. He decided on a dilapidated hovel, more for the time it would consume than the money it would save. Working on an old house, he decided, would keep him busy and keep his mind of the things he lost through the divorce, like daily access to the kids.

Leo was happy to use a sleeping bag on the floor for the first few weeks and he had expected some initial back pain, although he didn't expect the enjoyment the work would instil in him. To take charge of a rundown old hovel and revive it with his own hands gave him a sense of pride equalled only by his kids.

When the work on that first house was complete, he decided to sell it and buy something larger to work on. Now he was on the third house, the most challenging with seven bedrooms. He used two of the rooms to store most of his furniture with the sale of the old house going through faster than expected.

Work on the first house was merely a distraction from the divorce, but this third house quickly became special to him and he was unsure he would want to sell it when the work was completed.

He experienced a warm family feeling when he first entered through the threshold, a strong surge of déjà vu, as if he had already known the house as intimately on that first visit as he had come to know the previous two after the time spent reviving them.

He checked up on the history of the house, the first owner was also the owner of a textile and leather manufacturing company, Mr Ronald Bennett, who bought the house in 1867 for his bride to be, and they took up residence six months after purchase.

The bride gave birth to a set of twins after five years of Mrs Bennett longing to begin a family. Felix preceded his sister Amelia by 17 minutes.

The year 1893 began like any other year. However, August arrived, and ended with Amelia and Felix becoming 21-year-old orphans after the death of their parents in what was known as the Midnight Storm, a powerful and destructive tropical cyclone, which struck New York City in August 1893 as the Bennett's enjoyed a long awaited holiday, leaving Amelia and Felix just nine days after their joint birthday.

Leo worked on the house all week after work and the weekend offered him Friday evening, all day Saturday and part of Sunday to get on with things without the usual distractions, then off to spend some time with the kids on Sunday afternoon.

The work of the weekend would be rewiring, which Mike would coordinate and they would both rip the old wiring out according to Mike's instruction and replenish with the new, again to Mike's instruction. Therefore, to greet Mike's arrival, Leo got two mugs and after spooning sugar and coffee into them, he sat down at what he referred to as the old left-behind table, due to it being there when he took ownership of the house and the previous owner's family not requiring it.

Leo could use the old left-behind table for various tasks before dumping it on completion of the work on the house.

He could have got on with some work while waiting, but he was anxious to look through some photos he obtained of the house, which dated back to the early 1900s, complete with occupants.

As he slid the photos from the envelope, the photo on top was of Amelia and Felix. It occupied the top prime position because it was the last one he looked at earlier and he had opened the envelope several times since getting it and always paid additional attention to this particular photo. He seemed uncontrollably drawn to it.

He heard a noise coming from the front door and rose to his feet. He set the photos down on the table and went to the kettle as Mike arrived in the kitchen saying, "You'll no doubt have the impression that I hang about outside until the aroma of coffee hits my nostrils.

Leo gave the kettle an additional blast of power and smiled as he said, "There won't be an aroma until I pour the water onto the coffee, but I think you have the timing down to a tee, old son."

"What's this?" Mike said, sitting down and lifting the photos. It was obvious what they were, so Leo didn't offer a response and carried on with the coffee as Mike looked through the photos. After pouring, Leo brought two coffees to the table and sat down.

Mike said, "I recognise the house, but who is the couple?"

Leo took the photo from Mike and said, "This is Felix and Amelia Bennett. They were twin brother and sister. A workmate of mine discovered these photos in a book at the library, took

6

and printed out these photos for me when he realised they were of this house. I have a small portable scanner, so I'm going to see if they will allow me to scan the original photos in the book, although these aren't bad."

"It's strange to see the house as it used to be over a century ago," Mike said, taking a deeper interest in the rest of the photos. Leo was happy to allow Mike to look through the other photos because it allowed him to view the photo in his hand with impunity. When Mike glanced over, he detected that Leo was captivated with Amelia, and appeared to be especially concentrating on her eyes.

Leo felt that Amelia didn't merely look familiar to him. He was positive he knew her and had spoken to her, yet he knew how impossible this was due to her having died before he was born, before his parents were born even. However, he accepted that we are all susceptible to a spot of déjà vu at times.

Being an electrician by trade, Mike had offered to rewire the other two houses and he decided he should also do this third one although it was much larger than the other two houses together. The electrical work was about the only thing Leo could not fully commit to alone and for legal and insurance purposes; Mike's help was a huge asset.

Leo works as a bus driver, but in his younger days, he began to serve his time as a plumber. Being solid and muscular, he detested the small areas he at times needed to squeeze into, so he never finished his apprenticeship, although he had gained enough skill to do the plumbing work in the first two houses, which revived his talents well for this third house.

In between his plumbing and driving jobs, he worked for a builder. While starting as a labourer mixing mortar for bricklayers one day and plaster the next day and called on when needed to do some plumbing, he refused the opportunity to return to plumbing full time and gradually rose through the ranks and became a skilled labourer. It all helped when he was married and bought a house, even more, when he bought the first of the three houses after the divorce.

Leo didn't enjoy the work with the building firm, but it was a job and it came with an acceptable wage. Neither did he enjoy working on his own house after getting married. Therefore, it later amazed him that he loved working on the three houses after the divorce! Maybe it was down to being able to do everything the way he desired instead of everything being dictated to him by a boss or a wife.

However, the building firm had no pull with him and he decided he would be much happier driving a bus. Its only drawback was it being shift work; although the stopping and starting times were daunting at first, it didn't in any way interfere with the work on the houses.

Mike reckoned a previous owner had updated the wiring sometime during the 1940s, and the fact of the house-changing hands in 1942 would back this, although it would have come in the middle of the Second World War. The new owner did what most new owners do when buying an old house, and even back in 1942, the house would have been 75 years old.

Mike knew they would not have added the original electrical wiring when they built the house in 1867. It would have come later, probably around the late 1880s, early 1890s, most probably, Leo decided, after 1893 when Amelia and Felix took over ownership after the death of their parents.

Mike reasoned, even though the age of the house is not a sign of the age of the wiring, he also mused that the age of the wiring was never a sure sign of safety or functionality. However, it was still 80 years since they rewired the place and it would be best to rip the lot out and update it all.

With seven rooms, it would be a big job, expensive too, but Mike would not want to live in a house with 80-year-old wiring and he would not expect a friend to either.

Midway through the evening's work, Leo accepted and paid for a delivery of Chinese takeout and called to Mike to have a break. Leo put sugar and coffee into two mugs, so it was just a matter of flicking the switch on the kettle and they were soon sitting at the old left-behind table and Mike said, "After this, could you get into the attic and feed some cable down to me for the up stair lights?"

8

"That won't be anything like a problem," Leo replied."I didn't think you'd be ready for that for a while, so we must be making good time."

"Is there a garage or workshop out the back that will need a feed?"

"No, a garage was added, but as you will have seen when you arrived, it was built at the side of the house."

"That's strange, there's an old feed that appears to be going out the back from the kitchen area. If we don't need it, I'll just ignore it. I think it's part of the original system anyway. Maybe they originally had a workshop or something out the back that required such a feed. It isn't a problem.

As they ate, Mike noticed that Leo's eyes kept going to the envelope of photos and he said, "There isn't."

Leo frowned in confusion and said, "There isn't what?"

"There isn't a sign in any of the photos of their being any kind of building out the back. I am assuming that is why your attention is on the photos. Is there much on the house at the library?"

"There's just that one book, but there might be more in the National Archives."

"The library might also have individual photos of the house that will be much clearer. Their newspaper archives on microfiche might be some help too if you are planning to do research. As for the people, like the girl that appears to draw your attention, you could look up a lot of stuff on old census records."

Leo pondered as if mentally deciding whether to continue the conversation and he finally said, "Actually, I have been researching ever since I got these photos. The girl, Amelia, was a writer and she died young." He looked studiously at the photo and continued, "She had a private room that she used for her writing and her brother was so distraught at her death, that he had it sealed to prevent anyone disturbing anything. That is not the case now because we have been in every room in the house."

Mike smiled and said, "Have you checked the layout from outside to ensure there are no secret rooms?"

"You jest, but I did. Laugh if you will, but I had to make sure. I even counted the windows outside and in and I have accounted for all rooms and space. Either the brother broke the seal or a new owner opened it all up again. It would have been amazing to see it as it was the last time Amelia used that room, though."

Mike frowned at Leo and said, "You speak about her as if you know her, mate. Anyway, it's a shame you don't have the blueprints of the house. I could give you the names of a few inspectors and assessors who might help. It would help if there was a house the same as it in the area, you could have contacted the owner."

"I don't see any point in all that," Leo said, after some thought. "If there was a sealed off room, I would have come across it by now and all the blueprints would show me would be there are seven bedrooms - well, eight originally, but one was requisitioned as a bathroom at some point."

"You said she was a writer, did she write anything that you could find in a book shop today?"

"I haven't been able to find anything, although I don't know which name she wrote under. She might have used a pseudonym, I don't know."

"That just gives you more research to do and it will all take time."

"Talking about research, are you still researching your ancestry?"

"Yes, I got loads of stuff on my great-grandfather who bears my illustrious name of Michael."

"Still not got too far, then?

"I have got beyond him, but I got a lot about him."

"How far have you got?"

"Michael's Father was Terrance and Terrance's Father was Michael. As the story goes, Terrance had an appalling life after someone he worked with accused him of theft in his first job and it took him a long time to sort his life out after it. According to my granddad, Terrance was in the job for less than a week. His boss fired him over the theft allegation and his mum refused to believe he was innocent. Soon after that, he left home. I guess he found it hard living with the knowledge of even his family not believing him and he later turned to the bottle. He ended up on the streets, but we Browns are plucky and resourceful and he pulled himself out of it all with the help of the one who would become his wife, Alicia-Jane."

Leo said, "With Terrance naming his and Alicia's son after his dad, Is this a suggestion Terrance repaired the family relationship?"

"Possibly, I'm still searching through the archives. Have you checked your lineage?"

"I know my grandfather had the name of Graham, but he died before I was born, so I never got to meet him."

"So, I've got further than you?"

Leo didn't respond verbally and raised a forkful of Chinese food to his mouth as he pondered.

Mike too raised a loaded fork to his mouth, tipped it in and pondered as he ate before saying, "There are usually some amazing stories attached to old houses like this, although we don't always get to hear those stories. It would be something if you could put your hands on some of her writing. Do you know what her brother did for a living?"

"No, although if I were to hazard a guess, it would be textile and leather manufacturer and he possibly took over the business when their dad died."

"They seem to have been an affluent family."

"I get the impression of moderate affluence, although I don't think they had a string of live-in servants. Their bank account didn't help in the end, though, because the parents still died at a reasonably young age just like Amelia."

Mike reached out for the photos and said, "As they say, a picture paints a thousand words."

The photo of Amelia and Felix was still separate from the bunch and sitting on the table. Leo's eyes fell directly to the photo. His hand reached to it and he picked it up for a closer look and decided the camera lens would reduce the true life and soul in her eyes that he could detect and he tried to imagine them in the flesh, as it were.

11

Mike took a sip of coffee and said, "Have you anything a shade cooler, mate. The dust under the floorboards has given me a slight thirst.

"There's a bottle of coke. I meant to get a few beers, but forgot in the rush home from work."

Mike sighed and said, "I'm afraid I'll have to sack you for forgetting the beer. Get your coat."

Leo took a sip of coffee and allowed his eyes once more to fall on the photo and in particular on Amelia.

Leo called into the cemetery. He had already contacted the office and got the section, block and grave number details. This just proved to make it possible to find Amelia's grave, though, but still far from easy and it took a while. However, he did find it. It was wedged in between her parents' grave and that of her brother Felix and Felix's wife who passed away three years after him.

The three graves appeared to have had a visitor recently, suggested by flowers. However, Leo had also brought a fresh bunch to place on Amelia's grave and felt slightly guilty that he didn't show the same thought for her parents and brother.

He noticed that Felix's wife passed away in 1942, and this agreed with the information he had on the house, which changed hands in 1942.

Felix passed away in 1939, so either he unsealed Amelia's room before his death, or his wife unsealed it after his death. The time was unimportant, and Leo would never get to see the room anyway - at least not as it was when used by Amelia. He would like to know which room it was, though.

Rather than relying on memory for the details on the tombstones, Leo got his phone out and took some photos, moving in close for the epitaphs, and further away to get all three graves together. He then put his phone away and it was much too cold to sit on a nearby bench, but he wanted to stay a while. It seemed to him like spending some time with Amelia.

As he often does at a graveside, he found himself trying to penetrate visually through the soil to view the object of his thoughts, mentally using the image from the photo, rather than attempting to visualise her as she was at that moment. He even spoke to her as though she was there in person. He was sure she would hear him, but he was equally sure he would not hear her.

He heard a voice; it was the voice of a man. The man was quite a bit away, but the silence of the cemetery made his voice travel further than it perhaps normally would have and he appeared to be devoid of hope. He uttered this in the words of him having "nothing left to live for."

Leo was unsure of whether to pity the man or take out anger at his selfish speech because his mind was not so much on his wife, but on his personal pain at losing her.

The man appeared to be in his fifties, so possibly had kids and grandkids, yet he claimed he has nothing left to live for. Of course, Leo has only known divorce, so maybe it was different for him, although he was sure that divorce could be as severe as death with the grief every bit as hard to deal with.

Leo had deeply loved his wife Laura and it was a shock when she asked for a divorce. It was not her fault and she had not met someone else. She just simply allowed herself to marry someone with whom she was not fully compatible. Marriage was a reflection of her need to be cared for after a life with a tyrant for a Father, rather than a desire to join with another person and become a single entity, a family.

At first, it was just like a death, although Leo working on the first house helped him through the darkest of those early days and as time lengthened, the pain eased until he looked on her as he would look on an old friend whom he no longer has much interaction.

The kids are a different issue, of course. However, without Laura, there would not be any kids.

As Leo walked through the cemetery towards his car after a long visit, he saw a familiar woman with head lowered at a grave. It was Mike's wife Phoebe. She appeared to be crying. Leo was sure this was the grave of Phoebe's twin sister. He was not positive, but he knew her sister had died long enough ago for the tears to be unexpected.

He went over to her and could see that she has indeed been crying and he said, "Phoebe is everything okay?"

Phoebe was startled and had not realised Leo was approaching, so his presence at her side was a shock and her initial reaction was to step back and then she realised who it was and she said, "I'm sorry, Leo. You know what it can be like visiting this place."

"Is Mike not with you?"

"No, I came alone."

Knowing Phoebe didn't drive, he said, "I'll wait for you and when you're ready, I'll give you a lift home."

"That won't be necessary, Leo. Thank you for the offer, though."

"No, I'm sorry, Phoebe, but there is no way I'm going to leave you here alone while you are so upset. I would never be able to look Mike square in the face again. I'll wait for you in the car, it's just across the way," and he gestured the direction with his hand.

Phoebe could see that Leo was determined not to leave her here alone and she nodded her head and said, "Thank you, Leo."

Leo said, there is only one way in and one way out, so you will not escape me." He smiled as an indication to her that he was not being fully serious and she said, "I'll just be a moment."

Leo went to his car and switched on the engine to get the heater to circulate heat around the interior, he pondered on putting the radio on but decided against it, and he waited until he saw Phoebe and he waved to let her know where he had parked. She waved back, he opened the passenger door for her, and she got in and put the seat belt on.

Before driving off, Leo said, "Look, Phoebe, I consider Mike to be my best mate. You know that. You must also realise that this being the case, I could never ignore his wife being as upset as you were at the graveside and I know you were not grieving your sister because she has been gone many years and I'm sure today is not her birthday. What's the problem?"

"Mike doesn't want anyone to know just yet, but I'm sure he will tell you everything when he gets his head around it."

"Get's his head around what?"

Phoebe wasn't sure she should tell Leo, but she felt she couldn't contain the silence any longer and she said, "His firm has been on the decline and they have made his job redundant. He was offered part time work at another firm, but he needs full-time work, Leo."

"I understand perfectly. I'll, of course, keep an eye out for him and if any spark jobs come up in the bus depot, I'll let him know. Are you okay for money? I could let you have a loan."

"We're fine for now, thanks."

"Mike has been taking only mates rates for the work he has been doing for me, so I'll have to revise that and I'll get it sorted out right away."

"Please don't, Leo. That is why Mike didn't want you to know. He knew you would try to correct things from your wallet and he doesn't want that. Please don't do anything and please, please don't tell him you know."

"I can't stand back and do nothing, especially with Christmas being so close."

"We have everything sorted out for Christmas and it would embarrass Mike so much to have to rely on you for help and support. You know how proud he is."

Leo nodded his head and said, "Yes, I know. Be assured I'll not mention it to him, but be also assured that I'll find a way of proving my friendship to the stubborn fool and remember that I'm there if and when you both need me."

The kitchen with its early 1900s floor and wall tiles was overdue some work. While Mike suggested they didn't need to remove the old tiles, Leo was a perfectionist who was taking great pride in the work he was undergoing. He said, "Removing them would result in a much better job, but rest easy, mate, I'll do it alone. Mike was happy to allow Leo to rip out the tiles alone and so with the plan that Mike would return and connect a new double-gang outlet at the tiled area, Mike remained at home watching TV and Leo got to work on the old tiles.

Leo was tempted to tell Mike he was not up to ripping the tiles out and so offer to pay Mike for doing it. However, he knew Mike would see through this and would somehow guess that Phoebe had mentioned the redundancy. Therefore, Leo felt forced to carry on as if he didn't have that conversation with Phoebe at the cemetery.

However, if Mike doesn't mention anything by the New Year, Leo will assume Mike's bank account has dried up and he will force Mike to accept his help despite the pride he knows Mike has. He was sure Phoebe was being honest when she said they had Christmas sorted and he was sure Mike would get a redundancy settlement that would get him through the first months. However, when those first months have lapsed, Leo will then come into force.

For now, though, he decided on ripping out the wall tiles first and he didn't get too far along the first wall until he decided he might have been a shade hasty in his decision because it was extremely hard work and his arm ached swinging the hammer.

"Look on it as a work-out," he told himself, but he didn't bluff himself and he pondered on interspersing the work with other labours. However, he decided it would be best to get on with it and get it out of the way, so he chipped away at another tile.

It was good when an entire tile left the wall with just one hammer blow on the bolster, but this happened very little and he thought about Amelia as a distraction. He wondered if she would have seen the tiles. Perhaps Felix decided on the tiles after her death. Leo decided an expert could probably suggest the date of the tiles production and that would give him an indication, although he was sure they were an early 1900s addition.

He got to a section of the wall that appeared to be a stud and not solid brick and mortar structure. The tiles came away from this section much easier, but he could not think why the builders would add a section of a stud wall to a solid building.

He was unsure builders from 1867 would even build a partial stud wall and he could see no reason at all for it. Stud could be a cheap alternative, but it would not make sense to build the majority of the wall with brick and mortar, then a small section with stud. The answer lay behind the tile and wood. He quickened his pace to get to the answer.

16

Leo shone a torch through the opening he had created by pulling some boards off. The beam of the torch quivered as his hand trembled. He could not believe the sight that met his examining glare and he was unsure what to do. A large part of him was tempted to push on, but the more methodical and reasoning part of him urged caution, hold back if only to regroup mentally.

He rushed to his mobile phone on the left-behind table. He paused to consider, he had no desire to send any wrong signals, but he knew what he saw irrespective of his problem in believing it. He knew the first thing he needed to do was calm down and to this end, he breathed in deeply through his nose and out slowly through pursed lips and he made his way out of the house.

His hands still trembled as he swiped the screen of his phone and tapped. Mike quickly answered and said, "Leo, don't tell me, you've seen the error of your ways and have decided ripping out the tiles is too much work. I understand, mate."

Leo took a couple of breaths and fought to retain calm before saying, "Mike, we have known each other for a very long time and you will know that when I ask if you could come over here, I'll have a very sound reason. That being the case, could you come over here, mate?"

"Yes, of course, but why?"

Leo showed some panic as he said, "Don't ask why!" He quickly forced calm to return and added, "Sorry, I have come across something that I'm having a problem with. Could you come over here now with this being the only information I can give you on the phone?"

"I'll be there as soon as I can, mate."

"Thanks Mike. I might not be in the house, but I'll not be too far away. I'm in the garden now and will probably stay here for a while."

"It sounds serious, but as I said, I'll be there as soon as I can. Take it easy, mate."

"Thanks again, you're a real mate, Mike."

Chapter 02

Mike didn't know what to make of Leo's phone call, and he felt it impossible not to worry as he got into his car. As Leo had mentioned, they had been friends a long time. He was sure it would be a matter of most seriousness with it warranting a phone call asking him to go to the house. Of course, going to Leo's house was not a problem. For a friend like Leo, nothing is a problem to Mike and he did it happily despite the lack of information.

This is what friends do; they are there for each other when needed. Leo had been there for him several times when needed. Over the years, they have developed an unbreakable friendship that doesn't need to rely on information before deployment and Mike knew if he needed him, Leo would not need to know why and will merely ask when and where.

Mike was worried, though. With Leo speaking about waiting in the garden, Mike had the impression of there being something to fear in the house, perhaps a ghost, Mike decided. It could be a burst pipe and Leo had left the house rather than get soaked, but he (Mike) was an electrician. Who in their right mind would call an electrician to help with a burst water pipe? It must be a ghost, he deduced.

"Why me," Mike said in a whisper to himself, his face contorted and forehead furrowed in a worried frown as he went up a gear and wondered if he should not instead go down a gear or even stop the car. He knew why him, though. Who better to call than a friend in an emergency?

Mike doesn't know a lot about ghosts, other than they are manifestations of people who have died. He knows a few things about dead people and if they move or speak, it's best to keep a reasonable distance from them, like several miles or even a continent if possible!

Mike doesn't believe in ghosts, but he greatly fears them and he doesn't care if it's a contradiction to fear something that you don't believe exists. He used to join his elder brother in ghost stories under the light of their torches while awaiting sleep to take them to a new adventure. He reckoned whatever would meet him at Leo's house was real, though, and not a mere story designed at frightening. It came with its own level of fear, without the pen of an author and it came with the reality of - well, not believing in ghosts or the supernatural in general reduced what it could be the reality of, other than the reality that he was already terrified.

He has never seen a ghost, though, and he doesn't have a great desire to start seeing them now and he pondered on phoning Leo again to ask exactly what the problem is that forced him out of the house to wait in the garden! He could tell from Leo's tone of voice during the phone call, though, that Leo had a problem expressing it in words over the phone and needed to face him to express all.

Leo was standing at the gate when Mike arrived, and he raised a hand to acknowledge Mike's arrival. Mike fought to appear calm and collected as he climbed from the car and went to the gate.

"Thanks for coming, mate," Leo said.

"Not a problem, but I can't think what good I'll do and you should have called Ghostbusters. Which room is it haunting and why didn't I see it when I was laying the cable?"

"Are you assuming I called you here to show you a ghost?"

"What else would install in you the fear to get out of the house?"

"I just felt I needed some fresh air, the house is a bit dusty after chipping tiles for the past few hours."

"You didn't come across a ghost? That sure is a bag full of acceptable words. To be honest, I was a bit worried, worry bordering on terror!"

Leo pondered before saying, "I suppose, in a way, I did come across a ghost, mate. At least, the ghost of the life works of Amelia."

"Amelia? You mean the girl who lived and, if I dare say, died here?"

Leo nodded his head and began to walk toward the house. Mike followed with no small amount of caution. As they entered the hall, Leo said, "I should have listened to you and tiled over the old tiles because they were well adhered and while the odd one came off with ease, it was a mighty job chipping most away until I got to a section of the wall that was no more than wooden stud."

"Stud," Mike Echoed, furrowing his forehead in a confused frown.

"Stud," Leo confirmed. "I thought it was strange with the rest being brick and mortar, so I had a closer look, it looked like the stud wall was covering what originally was a doorway, and when I pulled it down, I discovered the doorway."

"So, they blocked off a door that was never used?"

"No, they blocked off a door that Felix intended not to use again."

When they reached the area, Mike could see that there was an entire wall complete with tiles and he wondered if Leo had thought of a way of persuading a gullible friend to help to chip them away. However, Leo ignored the tiled wall, lifted a torch and shone it on through the hole in the wall that he had earlier created by pulling the stud wall down. When Mike looked, he could see a staircase leading down from where the kitchen doorway had been, into a cellar.

Mike shrugged his shoulders, remaining unconvinced of any importance pertaining to the stairway until Leo aimed the beam of the torch further down and it illuminated the area at the bottom of the stairs with furnishings covered in dustsheets.

"It's Amelia's study, Mike, where she did all her writing and it appears to still be as it was the last time she used it."

"This is amazing!" Mike said. "At least we now know what the electric feed was for that appeared to be going out the back. It was obviously going to this cellar. Would you like me to rig up some temporary lighting to give a better view of everything?"

He pondered, and quickly added, "Of course you would, and that will be one of your reasons for calling me here. What do you plan to do with everything? It could all be worth a lot more than the actual house."

"I am not in the position of deciding what to do with it, but I do know I'll not sell it. It belongs to Amelia. I'll need to begin by looking for a direct descendent."

"You now own the house, so any contents left in it belong to you. That stuff could be worth quite a few quid, mate, all over a century old and all, I assume, in mint condition. You would be a fool to hand it over to a stranger who, after all this time, would be as connected to this girl Amelia as I am to the butler at Buckingham palace."

"Do you even know there is a butler in Buckingham palace," Leo said. "I would feel like a grave robber keeping it. I'll leave all that stuff to Burke and Hare, chum."

"That is very frivolous but Burke and Hare were not grave robbers."

"What were they?"

"Just a couple of bygone idiots who murdered people and sold the body's, mate. This is a sample of what can happen when you don't pay attention to your history teacher. You need to listen to me as well and get onto Christie's, Sotheby's or maybe even eBay."

"You didn't listen to your history teacher either and simply watched the film. I would rather get it to its rightful owners."

"You are the rightful owner. You bought this house, lock, stock and cobwebs. Besides, do you realise the work and time it would take to find a direct descendent of this Amelia girl? It's not hard to guess that she died childless, so there will not be a direct heir anyway and you would need to search through her brother's descendants."

"If that is what I'll need to do, then that is what I'll do, Mike. Conscience would not allow me to sell the stuff."

Mike tapped Leo on the shoulder and said, "You are a good and honest man, but I feel it all legally belongs to you and you should at least speak to a solicitor and find out who legally owns everything. However, if you are happy with making it all available to the family, then good for you, mate. I just hope the government doesn't claim it if you can't find a direct descendent."

With the cellar properly illuminated, the dustsheets removed and the furnishings polished, Leo sat down on the chair that Amelia would have sat on when writing. The writing desk boasted three drawers down the left side, a drawer in the middle and a cupboard to the right side, each containing personal items belonging to Amelia. There was an ink well on the right side of the desktop, so Leo guessed Amelia was right-handed.

The ink well contained only a dry residue of ink, more a stain really and Leo surmised they didn't add things like biocide to ink back then. The nib on the nearby pen was also dry, although there appeared to be some ink blotches on the ink blotter block beside the pen. However, he lifted the pen, knowing the last person to have held it, apart from when he lifted it earlier to polish the desk, would have been Amelia.

On the desk before him was probably the last piece of writing she had worked on. It didn't surprise him that it was unfinished. Neither did it surprise him that this knowledge made him feel extremely sad, to the point even of grieving her absence.

Leo found it difficult to accept that everything before him was exactly as it was the last time Amelia sat down at this very spot to do some writing. Well, it was not all the same. The atmosphere was different; it formed 100 years after Amelia's death.

He wondered why she chose a cellar for writing. There were no windows, no way of looking out into the world for inspiration. Perhaps that is why she chose it. She might already have had her inspiration in her mind and heart and needed to cut the outside world from her sight and concentrate on a world of which she was the creator.

He lifted the manuscript and flicked back to the first page and saw that she wrote under her own name and not a pseudonym. He began to read and he allowed the words to submit his mind to Amelia's world as it encouraged him through the threshold of her imagination.

Mike had long gone when Leo finished reading. He decided it would be good to complete it, but Leo was not a writer and didn't know anyone who could offer an end to Amelia's story that would do it justice.

He placed the unfinished manuscript down on the desk and rose. There were other manuscripts and several items that he assumed were personal to Amelia. He decided not to browse through anything else. He would need to check the drawers in the writing desk to compile an inventory of Amelia's office and personal effects for the family, assuming he can find a direct descendent.

Leo already knew that Amelia died young and never married or had children. However, as he continued the work on the house, he dedicated what time he could to research during the following weeks. It all revealed the information that her twin brother Felix went on to Father two children, a son and one daughter. The son left the UK bound for America in 1925. All mail home spoke of his business doing extremely well until a telegram reported his suicide to the family as The Wall Street Crash took effect in late 1929 and his business crumbled and left him without the will to go on.

The surviving daughter, named Anna, was married in 1926 and she planned that her honeymoon would be a two-week stay in Florida. In the early 1920s Florida was the fastest growing city in America and its sunny beaches was an enormous attraction to

Anna. Departure time was noon and this fitted in perfectly with the wedding commencing at 02:30 the previous day.

The wedding proved to be a perfect day, enjoyed by all and intoxicants freely consumed, with the groom, John Hall, becoming highly inebriated and spending the first night of married bliss in the doghouse.

The plan was to rise at an early hour in the morning and board the pre-booked Parisian taxi. This was not taking into account things like John's hangover and his inability to separate himself from the bed or later the water closet. The Parisian taxi proved to be much more comfortable than the Hansom cab it replaced several years earlier, but it failed to diminish the threats and promises made by Anna on her first full day of married bliss as she encouraged her new husband to speed things up a shade.

They finally got on their way, the combustion engine soon caused a nauseous state to descend once more on John, and it arrived with the need to call on the driver to stop and allow him to get out and breathe in some fresh air to clear his nauseous state.

The Parisian taxi remained still and quiet and the driver remained patient while John found a suitable place to leave his latest deposit, but Anna was far from pleased and was even less pleased when a further stop resulted in them being so late they had to turn back home.

John Hall then spent some time in hell until Anna read in the Daily Mail that the Great Miami Hurricane had struck, resulting in the devastation of the hotel in Florida that was booked to accommodate them during their honeymoon stay.

This news earned John a hug and had he not have suffered so outrageously with a hangover, they might have been numbered with the hundreds who had died and would at the very least have had an awful honeymoon with all the memories it would impose on them both for the remainder of their lives.

Due to John's drunken stupor preventing their honeymoon break away and possible loss of lives, John and Anna went on to produce four offspring, two boys and two girls. They had a further two who didn't survive, although the surviving four all married and had children numbering twelve in total and the combined offspring of the twelve, numbering thirty-two. This thirty-two would be Leo's task from which to concentrate on and jointly they would be or would represent the rightful heir/s of the content of his cellar.

Mike still suggested that Leo legally bought the house and everything within, so everything in the cellar legally belongs to him. He asked if Leo would search out a legal heir to take possession of the left-behind table. However, Leo was determined to find the rightful owner.

They decided to run an electrical cable into the cellar, although this would not begin until the completion of the upstairs rooms to enable them to move all Amelia's stuff into one of the bedrooms to await collection.

Leo felt saddened when moving her stuff out of the cellar, but stored in one of the rooms would protect it from any damage that could occur during the work. This led to the problem of mail, it was accumulating with letters for the previous owner, and some addressed to the present occupier.

He didn't know why the previous owner had not given a change of address and had his/her mail redirected to their new address and as the house had been idle and empty for a long time, there was quite a lot of mail and he set about obtaining a forwarding address. He failed to find one and discovered instead that the previous owner died.

With some mail, it was simple and there was a return address at the back of the envelope, so he simply wrote "no longer at this address," and dropped them all into the post box for return. As for the ones addressed to the present occupier/owner, he felt justified in opening them but left them to the side for when he had more time. There remained several letters addressed to the previous owner and without a return address. He decided to drop them off with the estate agent and asked if there is a way of preventing future mail for the previous owner from arriving.

Again, Mike made a suggestion and he proposed Leo should open the mail and dump any that had no importance. That could be dangerous, though, with it being illegal to open mail addressed to someone else. While this was Leo's third house, it was the first time he had a problem with the previous owners' mail still arriving and he decided he was much too busy to allow it to become a concern and he would go through the remaining mail (addressed to present owner/occupier) sometime after Christmas.

For now, after falling behind on the house due to ancestry and various other internet searches, he needed to turn his concentration back to the job of turning a house into a home. He also needed to think about what to get the kids for Christmas and had not realised how close it was now. His last thoughts on Christmas came with the knowledge that there was loads of time. Having his mind centred on Amelia's things quickly changed that, though and he was swiftly now running out of time.

With now knowing that Amelia wrote under her own name, Leo set out to search for her work. He could easily guess she would not have had anything published recently by virtue of her being dead for over a century, so he decided to begin his search in second-hand bookshops, but none of the booksellers he met had ever heard of her. Google was not a lot of help either.

However, he could plan his next move while getting some work done on the house and the next job was to take all the doors off and have them dipped in acid or a caustic-based liquid to remove all traces of paint, varnish, wax etc. He was sure that underneath over one hundred and fifty years of history there would be a set of amazing doors. He would also clean off and polish the brass work of hinges, handles, hand plates and kick plates.

One of the kick plates, in particular, would need some work with a file, because it had a rough edge that caused an injury to Leo and he required a plaster, so he went in search of his J.T.R. bag. J.T.R. is a title he awarded the bag and it stands for Jack the Ripper. Mike bought it for him one Christmas, more as a joke due to Leo's fascination with the famous Victorian killer. It's an old leather doctor's bag. Leo loved it then and still loves it now and he keeps everything medical in it, so it's in effect his first aid bag.

Thoughts of Mike drew Leo to the problem of Mike's redundancy and he had to seek a way of helping that Mike could not reject. Phoebe was right in that he was a proud man, so Leo would have to be as cunning as the proverbial fox.

Leo realised it was getting close to Christmas when he began to feel pain at the onslaught of an ear infection. He has had an earache at this time of the year before, but a quick visit to the doctor the last time resulted in a prescription of antibiotics. That cleared it and he was sure he should be over it by Christmas.

According to Mike, Leo could save time in going elsewhere than to the doctor and simply include some Umcka in his shopping list.

"Umcka," Mike told him, "is a herbal form of antibiotic that will offer the same help as the stuff the doctor will prescribe. It's also apparently good for other ailments."

Leo pondered on Mike's previous advice on opening the mail, which would get him into deep trouble due to opening someone else's mail being illegal. He became unsure, so he decided on a Google search on Umcka. It appeared to be what Mike claimed it was, so that will save him a trip to the doctor's surgery and most likely a long wait in the queue once he gets there.

He needs to go to the supermarket anyway; otherwise, he would starve, so Mike's advice has, at last been useful! To be on the safe side, Leo decided to get two boxes, or bottles, whatever it comes in because it might not be as strong as antibiotic. If he doesn't need them both, it will not do any harm to have one stored in his J.T.R. bag for any time he does need it, if the use by date permits it.

Leo had the coffee ready for Mike's arrival to complete the work on the rewiring, this time mostly concentrating on the cellar. With it being as it was when Amelia used it, it was not easy for Leo to drill out a channel to run the cable with a length of conduit inside the wall. Nevertheless, it offered a neater finish than running it through trunking on the outer wall.

Leo had planned to finish off with plaster the following day. He was pleased with the job, and he wished Mike's advice could always be as sound as his electrical work, Umcka notwithstanding. However, the work was coming on great guns. He celebrated another completed phase by ordering Chinese for them both, and it arrived just as Mike switched the electricity on to the cellar.

"Have you any plans for it yet," Mike asked as they sat down to eat.

"For what, the cellar do you mean? One idea might be to pack in my job and open up a B&B with having seven rooms and the cellar could serve as my office."

"So, you've definitely decided not to sell this one? If you were serious about a B&B, I would advise you to add an en suite to at least some of the rooms, the larger ones. To be honest, though, I cannot see you making seven beds every morning and washing and ironing the sheets, pillowcases and duvet covers for them."

"That would be where staff members would play a part," Leo said and he raised a fork full of Chinese cuisine to his eager mouth."

"Taking on staff is a huge responsibility, mate."

"It would be better than yours truly doing all the work alone. I would do the maintenance, of course, but I would need a good man alongside me plus a hard-working woman to make the beds and clean the rooms. It's a pity you already have a job, but maybe Phoebe would consider a career in hospitality?"

"What you need is a wife."

"You know I had one of those and had to let her go."

"A wife would work without a proper wage and she wouldn't demand twenty-one days holiday every year. It might be worth thinking about."

"It wouldn't have to be my wife and could be your wife. The problem is if she was my wife she would be entitled to half of everything if I ever had to sack her."

Mike laughed and said, "Have you never heard of a prenuptial agreement?"

Leo's mobile interrupted the conversation and the Chinese meal to announce a call. He looked at the screen and said, "You'll not believe this, but it's Laura."

Mike rolled his eyes and said, "First you neglected a prenuptial, and then you allowed the direct debit to lapse on the maintenance payments."

"Hello Laura, what's the problem?" Leo said into the phone.

Mike carried on with his Chinese meal as Leo listen dutifully for a while before saying, "Okay, I'll be there as soon as." He swiped the phone to end the call and said, "It's Peter, he's in pain and cannot sleep. He needs some medication. Where did I leave my J.T.R. bag?"

"She could get everything she needs at the all-night chemist, mate."

If Leo heard him, it was not obvious and Mike carried on with his Chinese as Leo scurried about in search of his J.T.R. bag, found it and then rushed out of the house.

Mike sighed peevishly.

Chapter 03

Mike was upstairs and came downstairs when he heard Leo returning. He said, "All sorted?"

"All sorted and treated," Leo said.

Mike said, "I left your Chinese in the microwave. It was cold, as food tends to after some time, and will need a fresh nuke, mate."

Leo said, "Was I away that long?"

Mike sat down at the table and said, it takes 20 minutes to get there if the traffic lights behave, how long do you think Chinese stays hot, mate?"

Leo paused at the left-behind table and said, "Hours if we could get on with some stuff and then travel back to when it was first cooked. Sorry I was away so long, mate."

"No hassle, Marty, but don't think Doc Brown is going to heat your Chinese up, you can press the button yourself, mate."

As Leo went to the microwave, he said, "I listened to an interview on the radio on the way back. It was a bloke who claims to have been caught up in a time slip."

He set the time on the microwave and hit the start button. As he did this, Mike said, "I've heard of this, it happens a lot in Bold Street in Liverpool, doesn't it?"

"So they say, but this one happened close to here. He said he was walking down the street when it went very quiet. Then, when he looked around, he realised he was in the 40s. It was the same street, but as it was 80 years ago. He spoke of going into a shop and the shop he spoke of actually existed in the 1940s."

"Claims like this have been rife for decades, mate. There is the suggestion that the Bold Street ones have something to do with the underground railway or something. I think it has more to do with sad people trying to get their 15 minutes of fame."

Mike sat down at the table and added, "However, if this is you trying to change the topic from you staying away ages, it's not for me to tell you how to run your life, mate. Anyway, you didn't tell me how Peter is after your medical dash?"

Leo took a step to the table and tossed his car keys on top of said table, went back to the microwave while saying, "Peter is fine, mate. He had a dry throat which he imparted to Laura as pain and she assumed it was tonsillitis, as women do."

Mike looked at Leo's coffee, rose and said, "I'll get you a fresh coffee." He lifted Leo's cup and added, "I know Peter is your son, but you really shouldn't jump every time Laura cracks the whip."

Leo smiled and said, "I guess this is you not telling me how to run my life, mate. I only ever go when one of the kids needs me. I might no longer live in the same house as them, but I'm still their dad."

"Laura's boyfriend took on the role of stepdad, so he should have gone to the chemist. Did you leave your medical bag there?"

"No, I left it in the car. Tony was out and not answering his phone and Laura decided Peter needed pain killers and she could not leave the kids on their own or even take them with her to the chemist."

Mike filled the kettle and flicked the power button before rinsing out Leo's cup and his own cup and he put coffee and sugar into both and said, "They would have been fine in the car."

"With her thinking Peter had tonsillitis; she decided it would be best to keep him in the house. Tony was using the drill earlier and it seems Peter sucked in some dust from it."

Mike smiled as he took the milk from the fridge and said, "Trying to work a ticket for a few days off school?"

The microwave pinged to announce the fact of Leo's Chinese having completed the reheating process and Leo took it out, carried it to the table, sat down.

Mike, after pouring two coffees, placed Leo's coffee on the table and said, "Your coffee, sir. Would you like me to call the wine waiter for you now?"

Leo mixed the rice in, scooped a small amount up along with some sauce for tasting purposes, and raised it to his mouth and after a taste said, "It at times is not the same when reheated, but this is not too bad."

"It might help when not allowed to get too cold. My putting it into the microwave for you no doubt had a lot to do with it by removing it from the cold air." He took a sip of coffee and added, "When you finish, could you push the rest of the cable down to me in the cellar? I'll have my coffee up stairs while I finish off up there."

"That doesn't come under the heading of even a small problem. Just give me a second to down this."

Mike lifted his coffee, went up stairs and Leo reached across the table for the envelope of photos and from it took the photo of Amelia and Felix. He spread the other photos out on the table, but held onto the photo of Amelia and Felix, set it beside his plateful of Chinese and glanced at all the photos and then carefully perused every inch of one half of the photo of Amelia and Felix as he continued his Chinese.

The beginning of the third week in December saw some colour and Christmas cheer come to the living room of Leo's new house. Work was far from complete on the house, but he knew he would need to put a tree and some decorations up to please the kids, otherwise, they would not visit him, despite their presents now being bought and in the house to put underneath the tree.

Leo was not enjoying the festive cheer and was with Mike as they checked each room and decided which was large enough to add an en suite and Mike was deciding how to bring the cable through for each to add electricity for the electric showers that Leo had chosen.

Mike took some measurements with his steal rule and scribbled some markings on the wall. He said, "I am assuming, as with the last two houses, you will be doing all the plumbing work despite the size of this place and the possibility of adding the odd en suite? That is, if you stick to the idea of turning the place into a B&B."

"Of course, there is no sense in paying a plumber when I can do it gratis."

"I hope it all works out for you, mate, but I have to say, a B&B would be the last thing I would struggle with."

"It might not be a B&B; I might go for a guest house, Mike."

"Oh, there's a difference, is there?"

"A B&B usually has five or fewer rooms. By taking over the cellar as my room and office would leave me with seven rooms. I was thinking about the living room being used as a kind of bar/communal room and I'll sell beer and spirits. I'll have to look into how the licensing laws work on that, though."

"For a start, the size of the cellar would better accommodate the bar and you could easily throw in a pool table and dartboard for your mates. You know less about this caper than you need to know and you have zero experience in hostility."

"Do you mean hospitality?"

"It will be hostility if you get it wrong and agitate the punters, mate. Realistically, you are blind, deaf and dumb to things like food, hygiene and safety in the kitchen."

"A bar in the cellar would be a bit daft for a handful of punters. If I decide on a guesthouse, I'll have to provide an evening meal, otherwise, just a fry, toast and cereal for breakfast will do. If I go for the smaller B&B, any punters who want an evening meal can phone the nearest fast food delivery."

"Don't rush in where angels need therapy, mate."

"After Christmas, I'll seek professional advice on any legal matters such as leasehold restrictions as well as tax, including VAT.

Mike laughed and said, "You need professional help, more than advice, mate. Have you any idea of the costs of running a B&B or guest house?"

"I have more than an idea of how much it will cost to get the place up to a standard that will be approved. Planning permission may not be required if I use half or less of the bedrooms. I could offer a few double rooms all with en suite facilities and keep the remaining rooms on hold."

"Do you want my advice, mate?"

"Forget the whole thing?"

"No, you appear to be drawn to it as a way of handing in your notice with the buses, mate. If it were yours truly, I would try the smaller option of the B&B with three rooms first and see how that goes. If it goes well, then you could open the other rooms later on. This way, you could use the cellar as a bar and have the pool table installed. It's a fair size, and possibly too large for a few punters as you said, but if you got licensed, you could open it to the public as well as guests, although you would need to look into the legal side of this. You will need a dining room, though, even if you just do breakfast."

"I would need to take on bar staff, mate. I know what you used to be like pulling birds, but what are you like pulling a pint?"

Leo and Mike entered the kitchen and Mike sat down at the table while Leo flicked the switch on the kettle and got two mugs before saying, "Tea or coffee?"

"I'll have tea for a change."

"Good call. I'll have the same. I've been drinking too much coffee lately." He got busy with the sugar and tea bags.

Mike turned his attention to the laptop sitting on the table. He touched the keyboard and a Microsoft word page came up on the screen. Mike turned the screen away and said, "Sorry mate, I didn't realise you would have some personal stuff on the screen."

34

"It's okay; it's not really personal, at least not private. It pertains to my online search for information on the house. Have a look, it's nothing private."

Mike nodded his head and turned the screen back to face him for a browse. "How is it all going?"

"Not bad, although a bit sad. I've discovered that Amelia died on Christmas day."

Mike browsed the contents of the screen until Leo placed a cup of tea in front of him and he lifted it and took a sip.

"You said it was nothing personal, yet you appear to be taking this girls death in a personal way, mate."

"It's a shame that people had to die back then with illnesses that are easily curable now."

"What did she die of?"

It began as heavy flu and progressed to pneumonia. A course of antibiotics would probably have sorted it all out and cured her. Unfortunately, they didn't have antibiotics back then. Just a few weeks ago I was able to get the medication from the supermarket that you had recommended. It might have cured her."

"If only you could post some to her through the time barrier."

"Yeah, if only. She had her whole life ahead of her and that life was cut short."

"Out of our control, old son," Mike said and he took a sip of tea before adding, "Have you begun the search for any descendants to get rid of that stuff of hers you have stored upstairs?"

"I got so far and then the work here began to demand my time. There are times when I could use a few extra hours in a day, mate."

"You will have them if you pack your job in and go all out on that B&B idea of yours. It's a huge risk, though. If it goes belly up, you will be out of work, my friend. Have you anything decent in the way of holiday entitlement that you could fall back on to start things off until you could work out how well or poorly the B&B will do?"

Leo felt guilty that Mike had lost his job, yet was worried about him losing his. He had to reject such thoughts, though, and he said, "That's not a bad idea, Mike. Yeah, I could take all my holiday entitlement and then maybe even go on sick report for a month or two. The last time I was at the doctor's, he quizzed me about low mood with living on my own, so I probably would not have a problem convincing him I was depressed and he would give me a sick note."

"He might decide that being off work will add to your phantom downer. Anyway, it would be better than packing your job in, so you should give it some thought and decide on a sure lie that will get you a sick note, although you'll be claiming that you are unable to work while working flat out here."

"Yeah, I wouldn't want to do anything criminal and get thrown in prison. It would be hard to start up and run a B&B from a prison cell. I think I'll take my remaining leave and then tell my boss that I am not on top form and hit him with a sick note for a month or two."

Leo paused for thought before adding, "I think my employment contract says he will have to give me full pay for a certain time. Then I think he will reduce it to half-pay. I could perhaps do a deal with him and instead of going sick; he could allow me to take an extended holiday at my own expense. That would save him a lot of money and would keep my job safe should I need to return. At least, I would not go to prison."

"Don't make a move without thoroughly looking into everything. Anyway, did you get that mountain of post sorted out?"

"I took some of it to the estate agent and told him to deal with it. A lot of it had arrived before I signed for the house. I have a batch still to sort, all addressed to either the present owner or the present occupier. I am the present owner and occupier, so that allows me to open them, although I have more important things to do first."

"You could delegate some of it. Rather than witness my old mate running himself into the ground, I am willing to take half of them and sort them out for you. They'll no doubt mostly be nothing more than promotions and offers anyway."

"I suppose if I asked you that would make it all above board with me being legally entitled to open them. That would be a huge help. Are you sure you don't have a problem with it?"

"I'll get them before I leave. I have loads more free time than you."

"That would be great, thanks mate! However, are you forgetting it will be Christmas in a few days?"

"No, I didn't forget and sorting them out will give me something to do because it can get a bit boring on Boxing Day and I'll go through them then. Forget half of the pile; I'll sort them all out. It'll help you and give me something to do on Boxing Day."

Leo placed some freshly cut flowers into a vase at Felix's grave, he then placed some Christmas roses at Amelia's grave and tidied and cleaned both graves. Many people once believed that it was a sign that the fallen had found peace if the flowers rooted into the ground and grew. He had never met either of them, but it was his fervent hope that they both found peace.

People might see it as strange him visiting and leaving flowers at the graves of people who he had never met, but he feels he knows them by living in the house where they grew up. He gazed through the earth, mentally penetrating the grass and soil, even the wooden coffin, or what if anything was left of it, and could see Amelia's face as it was when she was very much alive and well.

He could well understand the grief that caused Felix to seal the cellar and have it remain the way it was when Amelia last used it. That act told Leo how much Amelia meant to her brother and he could understand the devastation Felix felt at Amelia's death because he was feeling a whisper of it as he looked down at the grave and mentally spoke to her. The words he spoke didn't come from his mouth, they came from his heart, no one else would hear the words he sent to her, and no one else has ever heard the same words spoken to them by Leo. His words were for her and her alone.

Leo was happy to close the door after entering the house. He needed to spend some time alone with his thoughts and he flicked the switch for the hall light to illuminate his way. As it was Christmas Eve, he decided not to do any work on the house and would simply pour a drink and contemplate. He would like a roaring fire in the living room but had to make do with the central heating radiators without a flame between them to gaze into as he sipped his drink.

A single sip was all he tasted and he failed to create a desire for a second sip, so he placed the glass down on the small table to the side of his armchair. He turned his chair a shade to view the Christmas tree, perhaps not a perfect replacement for a glowing fire, but certainly much better than a radiator.

He had a few invitations for Christmas lunch, but turned them all down and decided it would be better to spend his time over Christmas planning the future and he wondered where he would be next Christmas and what changes there would then be to his life.

He intended still to be in this same house, although he felt he could not boast of another day let alone another year. If Ebenezer Scrooge could be visited by three ghosts on Christmas Eve, Leo realised that one could visit him, the one known as the angel of death. He could see that to plan for next year or even next week was folly and we can barely plan with any assurance for tonight.

The main thing now was he had given all the presents to those he bought Christmas presents for and had received presents from those who had presents for him. The important ones in all these exchanges were his kids.

His phone pinged and he lifted it from the small side table and swiped the screen. It was a text from Mike to say he would be busy transmogrifying into Santa later for the kids, so will send his greeting now and he wished him a very happy Christmas and an amazingly perfect and peaceful new year. Leo smiled and got his thumbs to work on the screen to respond and send the greeting back to Mike.

He then placed the phone on the side table and rose, walked to the kitchen and then down to the cellar. The cellar was cold because he had not installed the radiator's there yet and had planned to plumb them in after Christmas. However, the lights were functional thanks to Mike's hard work.

He could easily remember where Amelia's desk had earlier been and he imagined her sitting at it and writing. It came easy to him because he had imagined this many times and it became much easier with the knowledge of the words she had written in her last story.

He heard the ringtone coming from his phone in the living room and it pulled him out of his reverie. He didn't rush to the phone, though, and made his slow way up the stairs, almost cursing the phone for dragging him away from his thoughts of Amelia. Even though he refused to hurry and the seconds were rushing past, the phone continued to shriek out its ringtone and he was surprised at the determination of the caller because most people would have hung up and tried again after a moment.

He lifted the phone and saw that it was Laura.

"Leo, it's Peter again and he is not playing for time off school because he has finished school for Christmas! I have tried phoning Tony, but getting nowhere and –"

"Slow down, Laura, what is the problem with Peter?"

"It's his ear. He is in abject pain with it and I am out of painkillers. I meant to get a stock in for Christmas, but with one thing and another, it slipped my mind."

"It's okay, I have my bag here and I always keep it well-stocked in pain relief. I'll bring enough over to keep the smile on Peter's face throughout Christmas."

"Please be quick, he's in agony!"

Leo had neglected to turn the car radio off when he got home, so when he switched on the engine, Boney-M quickly filled the car with the sounds of Mary's boy child. Leo was not a fan of Boney-M, but he let it go because he knew it was almost at the end of the track and he slipped the gear stick into first.

As he suspected, he had not travelled too far when the voice of the DJ faded the sounds out with the words "That was Boney-M and later in the studio, we will have an interview with Professor Donald Fairview who will be telling us about a supernova expected to be seen tonight in the skies above us. The professor will explain how the actual star of Bethlehem 2,000 years ago, might have been a supernova exploding its glory into the cosmos. For now, though, we have another Christmas golden oldie with Wham and last Christmas."

Wham was more than Leo could bear and he switched the radio off. He was calm as he drove to Laura's house and he could see nothing to get into a panic over, despite sensing panic coming from Laura, so she was worried, although he reasoned that is normal power for the course with women.

Leo is not a doctor, but he decided it could be an ear infection. Like himself, Peter has had a few ear infections. Paracetamol should do the job of easing the pain and he asked Laura to go to the bathroom and run some hot water over a face cloth, ring it out and allow Peter to hold it to his ear.

Leo said to Laura, "I had an earache a few weeks ago and I have stuff in my bag that might help, but with Peter's age, I'd rather a doctor made the diagnoses and decided on the medication, but Paracetamol should be fine until you can get him to the doctor."

Laura nodded her approval and agreement. After some time, Leo was happy that the Paracetamol appeared to be kicking in and Peter assured him the pain was easing.

"That's good," Leo said. "Just relax and try to get some sleep because Santa will be arriving very soon and I think I had a glimpse of his sleigh in the sky as I drove over here."

Leo looked up at Laura and added, "What time will Tony be back?"

"He will probably be having a drink with workmates, so I'll expect him when I see him."

Leo turned his attention back to Peter and said, "Your ear doesn't appear to be inflamed, although I'd need a doctor's torch to be certain. However, if it flairs up again, your mum will soak a flannel in hot water and rinse it out for you. I'll leave plenty of Paracetamol and I'm sure you'll enjoy Christmas just like any other year, although you will have to get to sleep soon before the big man in red arrives. Mr Ho-Ho will not be far away."

Laura said, "When Mike gave you that bag, I thought it was a silly idea, but it has come to the rescue so many times with the kids. Thank you, Leo."

Leo took some tablets from the bag, handed them to Laura and said, "Always happy to help ease my kids' pains." He bent down, kissed Peter and said, "You be a good boy for your mum and have a brilliant Christmas, son. I'll have to go now, but I'll phone you in the morning, and no fighting with your sister."

Peter nodded his head. Leo looked to Laura and said, "You can stay here with Peter, I'll let myself out. Have a good Christmas."

"And you," Laura said.

"Happy Christmas, dad," Peter said.

Leo put his hand to the handle of the bedroom door, looked back and smiled. "Have a magical Christmas, son. Goodnight." He opened the door and left, closing the door behind him.

The landing light was on, although it instantly dissolved into darkness as Leo closed the bedroom door. His first step down the landing echoed strangely, he could no longer feel carpet underneath his foot, and it came down onto wooden floorboards.

He felt for the light switch, it felt strange and he flicked the switch on and off, but to no avail. He carefully made his way down the stairs in the dark to the solid wood front door. That was strange because Laura didn't have a solid wood front door, she had a PVC door with a large pain of glass and under his feet, he could feel what he took to be unpolished cement or concrete and gone was the smooth feel of Laura's hall tiles under his feet.

He opened the door to a building site. Close by a man sat just inside a small portable hut with a glowing fire on the outside, just in front of him. It was as if Leo had been tossed back in time one hundred years to when the house was first built and as yet unoccupied and the man in the hut was a watchman, paid to guard the site. There was no sign of the fence or gate, or even the garden and Leo quickly sought a reason to give the watchman for him being inside the house.

He decided he could make a run for it, but reasoned it was bad enough the man having to work on Christmas Eve night without having to give chase to him. Instead, he went over to the man, struggling to come up with an excuse that the man would accept, while also trying to figure out what was happening and how he came to be outside the house during what appeared to be the time of its construction.

41

As Leo approached, he realised the man was sleeping and he could easily just walk on past. However, he stopped, cleared his throat loudly to force the watchman to open his eyes, and he said, "Do you mind if I warm my hands at your fire?"

The watchman leapt to his feet and his eyes fell on the leather bag in Leo's hand and he said, "Doctor, sorry, the glow from the fire can get hypnotic and it caused me not to see you coming."

"Relax," Leo, said as he sat his bag down on the ground, "I just wanted to wish you a Happy Christmas and to ask where I am because I appear to be lost."

"This street doesn't have a name yet, but I understand they plan to keep it in line with the name of the area and it will have Balfour in it somewhere, after the prime minister."

"That confirmed Leo's thoughts and suspicions because the name of Laura's street is Balfour Way and, as the house was in construction; he had, as he assumed, been thrown back 100 years in time to the early 1900s.

Chapter 04

The layout of the streets was much the same as in his time, but the gas lamps failed to illuminate as clearly as the electric lamps. However, the gas lamps presented the streets with a cosy comfort that electric lamps failed to offer. There were very few cars on the road and Leo had been walking for quite a while and had yet to see his first automobile.

The road he travelled had a bus route in his time and he decided it would probably be the same in this time, only it would be a tram route now. It didn't matter because he was aware of it being old currency back then. He reckoned a tram journey would possibly cost about a farthing or a halfpenny and he didn't have either. Therefore, while it was a long walk from Laura's house to his house, it had to be what they would once have referred to as shanks' mare or the old plates of meat. To put it in a 21st century term, he would have to walk. The last tram was probably long gone anyway.

He was sure this was Christmas time as it was in his prime timeframe, although he was not sure which year. He knew Laura's house was built sometime in the early nineteen hundreds, but he could not be more accurate, although he assumed it would be somewhere between 1902 and 1905 with the street being named after the prime minister, as the watchman said, because this was the time duration that Arthur Balfour was prime minister.

The experience of thrusting through time should be scaring him, but he was calm and it all felt normal to him. He could not understand it, but he doesn't fully understand the Internet yet and this lack of understanding doesn't stop him from using it and enjoying it. His main thought processes gathered around the possibility of this being a time before Amelia's death. If it was, he had a possible cure in his bag that might prevent it from happening.

It was cold, and being in the car with the heating on when going to Laura's house, he didn't bother with a coat and he wore just a pair of dark chinos and a thick wool pullover. He hoped this fashion would blend in with the fashion of the time and, although he was sure that, despite the leather medical bag and the watchman mistaking him for a doctor, he didn't have the appearance of an early nineteen hundred's doctor. However, it was possible that an emergency call-out would have doctors even back then, or now, arriving dressed casually.

He was hopeful that people would accept his wardrobe as normal in this time, although it was still on his mind that he might look ridiculously out of time.

Much of the surroundings were familiar to him, though, although much newer, like the houses having the same brickwork, but with wooden window frames and no double-glazing anywhere.

He hadn't seen a telephone kiosk, so he had to assume they were not available for public use just yet. It would not matter a lot if there had been one, though, because he didn't have anyone to phone or a relevant coin to make a call. He also noticed that the rooftops of the houses all had chimney pots, but not one of those chimneys had a TV aerial mounted to it or a satellite dish anywhere near.

It was late and all the shops closed, although he felt drawn to a shop, or more accurately, to a poster in the shop window, which read, *"We would like to thank all our customers for their generous patronage throughout the year, and wish you all a very merry Christmas and a happy and prosperous 1905."*

If the New Year will be 1905, that would suggest it's now 1904. If it was late Christmas Eve night as in his prime time, Amelia will have suffered flu of late and will now have developed pneumonia. He held the leather bag close to his chest and tapped it. Within it, lay what he hoped would be Amelia's cure and he realised that he now had the potential of meeting her and offering her the medication.

He didn't have a clue how he would bring this about, although he had to remain positive and reject negative thoughts and replace them even with clichés such as "where there's a will, there's a way."

He continued to make his way along the darkened streets. He was aware of the fact that he was not in London, but he was in a time just twenty-two years after Jack the Ripper did, what the people then would refer to as "his dirty deeds." Lurking in the shadows of most towns and cities are those with a similar mentality to Jack, at this time when poverty still abounds and the workhouse was still the only answer.

He spotted a man in the distance. The man was coming toward Leo and dressed in a manner that suggested a lack of affluence in a cloth cap, jacket much too thin for the weather and a scarf around his neck and across his mouth.

Leo immediately turned his mind to the time and he decided he had left Laura's house at roughly eleven-thirty and had been walking at least thirty minutes, and he decided against the possibility of the hands of the clock in an altered state by being in a different period.

He was unsure when the clocks were first set forward and back one hour, but he was sure it was only between March and October, so it would not affect the present time he was in, which he decided, might still be Christmas Eve night closing in on or having arrived at Christmas morning, 25 December.

He was sure the time would be close to midnight and he wondered why anyone would need to walk the streets at such a time at Christmas. Perhaps the man was having Christmas drinks with friends, but the lack of a stagger suggested to Leo that the man was sober. "Sober as a judge," some would say, although Leo was not convinced that judges remained sober at all times and he decided most would probably have a bottle or two stashed away in their private chambers.

Normally, Leo would smile at the suggestion of a judge with a secret stash of booze, but he was wary of the man and that took precedence and he considered crossing the road. He decided against this, though, because it would suggest fear and signs of alarm would do more to bring on an attack than it would to avoid one.

He had to rise above it all and show himself as being fearless, so he pushed his shoulders back and formed his facial expression into a stern glare that showed no fear. As he neared him, he could see that the man was glaring psychopathically at him and wondering what evil deeds had him walking the streets at such an hour at Christmas.

They passed each other with their expressions warning the other to stay away and neither spoke, but both sighed in relief as they passed and could hear the other walking on. Both were too scared to look back and just carried on their journey, one leaving his girlfriend home and wishing he had brought his bike. The other leaving his son's bedside to enter the twilight zone. With it being so soon after Jack the Ripper did his dirty deeds, the medical bag in Leo's hand didn't reduce the man's fear.

As his journey progressed, he thought about Peter. He was sure Peter's ear problem would quickly resolve itself with the tablets he left, but he could only hope his son would be blissfully unaware of his dad's disappearance in the landing just outside his room.

His car will probably have remained parked outside Laura's house and that will be a puzzle, although she will probably surmise that it would not start and Leo merely decided to phone for a taxi and get the car towed to a garage sometime after Christmas. She might not even notice it because she will have no reason to leave the house and Tony will probably be too drunk to become aware of it when he gets home.

Leo had made the same journey many times during the past weeks, but walking gives a better understanding of the distance between Laura's house and his, even though in this time, it will be Amelia and Felix's house. However, the distance between the two houses is a reflection in many ways of the distance now between Laura and him.

When Laura first asked for a divorce, it was devastating and he felt his life had ended. It was similar to the grief of death. Now, he could see that it was the best thing for them both and, while Tony can at times fall short of being perfect, he is good for Laura.

Leo is aware that Mike thinks Laura is using him every time she calls and he goes running with tablets and such. However, he is grateful for this extra time to speak to the kids and assure them of his love and he will always go to them when they require him – or perhaps that will no longer be possible from the year 1904 coming into 1905. That was a worry that he had not thought about until that second.

He might never see his kids again. They will not know what became of him and the story will be he simply disappeared after leaving Peter's room. He had to force thoughts like that out of his mind and accept there must be a reason for what is happening to him and everything will work out in the end.

Metal horseshoes on cobblestone had a sound all of its own and it didn't appear to be very safe for the horse as the metal tended to scrape and slide along the cobble at times. Most horse riders drove or rode with care and didn't push the beast too much, though, so all was fine. Still, the clip-clop of the horse's hoofs on the cobblestone was eerie, somehow ghostly with echoes of evil goings-on in the shadows.

Daylight was still some hours away from making an appearance by the time Leo got to what he had come to refer to as "home." He saw a man with a long pole and he guessed it was the man's job to use his pole to tap bedroom windows and waken the people to begin their day.

The rapper up was in full employ until the early 1950s when alarm clocks became more reliable than their early counterparts were, although he can only assume the rapper-up must have had a good alarm clock. He had just a few addresses on his list this morning, so his days' work would be short due to it being Christmas morning.

Another man would probably come along with another long pole and it would be his job to douse the street lamps and kill off their light. That would not be until later when the brightness of the new day would no longer need the light the street lamps offered.

Leo wondered if the milkman would make his rounds today, or would he have Christmas day off? He also wondered if he would do his rounds aboard a horse-driven cart with a milk churn and fill the customers' vessels with milk and charge accordingly, depending on the amount of milk the vessel held or the amount the customer required. Leo was not sure, but he would witness the answer a few days later when he spotted the milkman's horse pulling a cart laden with bottles.

Leo had plenty of time to dwell on milkmen and lamp dousers because he had arrived at the house, but he could not go any further because it was still early. The drawn curtains and blinds served as a suggestion that Felix was still sleeping if he could get any sleep. Amelia's worsening condition would probably remove any desire or need for sleep with Felix, but it would still be unkind to go wrapping on the door at such an hour.

Leo could see it was Christmas and it could have been any year, but he was convinced it was the year 1904 due to the note at the shop. He didn't have his watch and he had left his phone in the car, placed it on a phone cradle on the dashboard and connected wirelessly to the onboard blue tooth. That meant he had no way of knowing what the time was. However, he had been walking quite a while since leaving Peter's room at approximately half eleven.

His sore feet suggested he had been walking several hours, but it was impossible to tell with any accuracy. He could assume it was still the middle of the night, though, or the wee small hours.

The knocker up would have known the time and Leo should have asked, but where was the town crier when needed? Should there not be a man walking through town and calling out the time at intervals, Leo wondered. Maybe that was back in the time when the highwayman would cause a threat as he waited in the shadows; ready to pounce on a rich person going home after an evening of joviality.

A hot beverage would be appreciated and Leo would not care if it was tea or coffee, as long as it was hot. Tea came to the UK in the 1660s so some of the milkman's milk was probably used for the early morning cup and he could do with some of its refreshing warmth.

Coffee was also around in plentiful supply in 1904. The first coffeehouse in the UK opened in St. Michael's Alley in Cornhill, London in 1652. Therefore, sipping coffee is an older pass time in the UK than sipping tea. That would be a surprise to many of the UK's tea drinkers.

The traditional breakfast of 1904 was very similar to the traditional breakfast of Leo's prime time. However, he could not have any because, even if he could find a cafe or inn open that served breakfast so early on Christmas morning, he had only modern currency and not a ten-shilling note or a half-crown on his person. It's a good job he didn't have a ten bob note because they didn't go into circulation until 1928 and the 1904 public would frown on it.

Standing about with his eyes on the house didn't do much in way of warming him up and he would get slightly warmer by going for a walk and so he decided to go for a walk although his feet were already aching from his earlier traipse across town.

He went by way of Mike's street, although Mike's street would not be there for many years. Leo amused himself with the thought that it was advantageous that Mike's house was not there yet. Had it been there would be a tree blocking off the front door, or at least where Leo guessed the front door would be due to judging the distance from a wall, which he could see in 1904, and remains in prime time.

There were signs of life coming from some houses, caused no doubt by eager children awakening to the reality that Santa had been. This was a more affluent part of the city and the story might not be the same in the slum areas. However, each household would have its own private Christmas customs and traditions and his mind drew back to Christmas when he was a child back in the 1980s/90s. He remembered his sister being mad keen on troll dolls and he got Mr Frosty.

He got many other things, but he could not remember them so they must not have been very exciting, although he remembered his main present one year was a bike. He secretly wanted a BMX even though they had been out for many years and seen as past their sell-by date to many of the kids, but he always wanted one.

After a few hours riding his new bike, though, he forgot all about the BMX and grew to love the one he got that Christmas.

Leo made his cold and hungry way back to the house and still the curtains and blinds remained closed. It took a further hour for them to open and allow the day in and Leo rapped the door. He was nervous. He had not rehearsed what to say and decided it would be best to keep it to what came to mind at the time and when the door opened he had his first sight of Felix and Leo froze in that he opened his mouth to speak, but nothing came out apart from an "err."

Felix's eyes fell on the leather medical bag and he said, "Doctor, good morning. Doctor Brown said he would delegate his best as a replacement for the Christmas period, but we were not expecting to see you without us telephoning to request it. Please come in."

The name Doctor Brown got Leo thinking with Brown being the surname of his best friend Mike and he wondered if this doctor from 1904 could be an ancestor of Mike. Mike had spoken recently of his ancestors, but Leo could not remember any of them being a medical doctor. The name Brown is a common one, so Leo decided this doctor most likely had no relationship to Mike.

Leo stepped into the hallway. He was familiar with it at this time due to the photos, but he could see that the photos didn't do

50

it true justice and he reached his hand out to Felix and said, "I am pleased to meet you, Mr Bennett. My name is Leo."

Felix accepted Leo's handshake and said, "Ah, the fifth sign of the zodiac. You must have been a summer baby. As you appear to have given your Christian name, please feel free to address me as Felix. Your hand is like a block of ice!"

Leo realised he would need to lie, so he said, "I'm afraid a wheel came off my carriage and I had to walk most of the way. I apologise that I didn't have time to dress more appropriately. I was eager to get here because I have a new medication that I feel will greatly help in miss Bennett's full recovery."

"Doctor, that is wonderful," Felix said with much excitement.

Leo took the bottle of Umcka from his bag as Felix showed him up the stairs. Amelia was awake when they arrived in her room and Leo became instantly besotted and he had to force himself to remember that he is just a visitor from another time and had no way of knowing how long he will remain in this time period.

Felix said, "If you remember, Amelia, Doctor Brown told us he would be spending today with his family and he said he would delegate the best there is to replace him, and the good doctor has arrived with new medication for you." He turned to Leo and said, "You will need something to warm you up. Have you had breakfast yet?"

"I wanted to get here as soon as possible with the new medication, so, no I'm afraid I skipped breakfast."

"Do you prefer tea or coffee?"

"I take both, but prefer coffee, although there is no need to go to such trouble."

Felix said, "To a man bringing such hope, nothing can be seen as trouble, sir, so coffee and a cooked breakfast coming up."

Felix left the room and Leo turned his attention to Amelia. He could not believe he was in the same room as her and he said, "My hands are cold, so I'll not examine you and I can imagine how you are feeling, so let's get on and see how quickly this new medication takes to work."

Amelia said, "Thank you, doctor."

"Please, call me Leo."

51

"I could not do that. I can imagine how hard you had to work and study to become a physician and to address you in a way other than doctor would be an insult to you."

Leo could detect that Amelia didn't much feel like talking. To say what she did, indicated to him that addressing him correctly was important to her. Leo was amazed just to be in the same room with medication that had the potential of saving her life. Therefore, he simply smiled and nodded his head to indicate his acceptance and understanding.

Leo arrived in the kitchen as Felix finished off preparing breakfast and the first thing Leo noticed was the absence of the tiles that he worked so hard in removing. He had previously assumed that they would have been a later addition to the kitchen, and their absence proved how correct his assumption was. He was pleased he didn't have them peering at him.

Felix put a well-filled plate on the table and invited Leo to sit down. Leo said, "I was not expecting this and there is no need."

"There is a huge need," Felix said. "You skipped breakfast and left yourself open to the elements to come here and help my beloved sister get well and the least I can do is provide a hot and filling breakfast to warm you up and revive you ready for the day ahead. I wish Amelia would eat something, but her appetite has been very weak of late."

"Hopefully that will change when the medication kicks in."

Felix placed his own breakfast on the table and sat down. "Kicks in? I am afraid I am not familiar with this phrase."

"Sorry, Felix, are you sure it's okay me calling you Felix?"

"By all means, please do."

"When I say kick in, I mean for it to begin its function of seeking out and destroying the virus that caused your sister to become ill."

Felix nodded his head and pondered before saying, "I don't know what it is, but I feel good about you being here, Doctor - Leo. I have been terrified that I might lose my beloved sister. However, I have strange and strong confidence that you will do her good and will bring her through this. You must be an angel to rise especially and not allow a broken carriage wheel to deter

52

you as you ignore the elements and hunger to tend to my beloved sister. This has earned my fullest respect and gratitude. I must admit that worry had faltered my appetite, but now I feel I could clear this plate in a second. Your presence here, Leo, has filled me full of confidence and I don't know how this could be, other than you must be an amazing doctor."

The more Felix spoke, the more embarrassed Leo became because he was not the amazing doctor that Felix was praising and he merely was in the position of having future medication.

He said, "Your praise should go to the ones who developed and perfected the medication I brought. Would you permit me to remain here? With it being a new medication, I feel I should administer it personally and keep its effect under constant observation."

"By all means, Leo, please consider my house as your home. Martha is not here at the moment, so I shall personally prepare a room for you, should you need to stay overnight with you not having transport to get home, although I could return you home in my automobile, if you wish. "

That was a huge worry sorted out for Leo, as he didn't have a great desire to walk the streets for a second night.

Felix added, "You don't have a change of clothes or bedroom attire with you. Obviously, with it being Christmas, everything has closed down and if you are unable to get home and collect an overnight bag, I would be happy to help rectify this, if you don't mind wearing some of my things. We appear to be the same size and build and I assume you take size nine in a shoe? I have at least one pair that I have not worn as yet and I would be happy if you could make use of them."

Leo didn't expect Amelia's medication to have an immediate effect and she looked haggard later when they checked. He didn't have much in the way of record of her condition from the original history to make any judgment, but he knew she died on Christmas day, so he was hopeful if she could get through the night she would make a full recovery.

He took comfort and assurance from the fact that he could remain there until her recovery was complete because he had nowhere else to go and didn't have any money for a hotel room. Therefore, had it not been for Felix's kind gesture of a room, he would have been open to the mercy of the nearest Salvation Army centre.

Felix had neglected to arrange for Christmas and therefore didn't have anything on order. Leo completely understood this and struggling with the worry Felix had over Amelia would remove any desire for a huge Christmas dinner with all the trimmings.

Family members and close friends, knowing he would not leave Amelia, offered to deliver a meal for them both, although he asked them not to and said Amelia would prefer them to remain at home and enjoy the day. Leo was happy with that and it meant they would not be asking him loads of questions.

There was loads of food, but no turkey or trimmings and neither Felix nor Amelia was in the mood for turkey and trimmings anyway. Leo would have found it hard to work through a huge dinner too, so Felix and Leo were happy to sit down to a plain meal after Felix took a meal up to Amelia. He later returned with it un-touched.

With being there, Leo was in the position of dispensing Amelia's medication personally and this reduced the chances of Felix having the bottle in his hand and being open to the fact that the glass bottle is so flexible and less solid than glass would normally be.

It also had a childproof lid, so Felix might have experienced problems attempting to open it. Leo could have told him the bottle and the lid were both plastics, but that would be the same as telling someone of Leo's time that sudanianasium particles compiled the substance of the bottle.

Leo realized he needed some cover stories and he decided on one for the bottle. He informed Felix, "It's experimental glass that will not smash if dropped." *Why not*, he thought. The medication was claimed as new and could be experimental so why not also the bottle?

Leo insisted on washing, drying and putting away the lunch things. Leo knew they would not spend their time watching TV as most people do on Christmas afternoon, because 1904 had not witnessed the arrival of the television set and most families would possibly gather around the piano. It would be a further eighteen years before the UK would witness its first radio broadcast.

There is a demand in prime time that TV reduces the joys of a family conversation. Leo and Felix were happy to join in conversation and Leo was aware of the many points in which he could trip up and he even pondered on telling Felix the truth.

Leo took a bathroom break to have a quiet think. He does a lot of thinking while sitting on the toilet, although the toilet is normally inside the house and not in the yard with the cistern way above his head and a chain hanging down with the wooden chain handle striking him on the left ear.

He mentally walked back into the house, sat down and said, "The truth is, Felix, I am not a doctor at all. I am a bus driver, which means I drive a tram of the future that an engine will pull along as opposed to horses. I live in this very house in the future and am renovating it. I uncovered Amelia's room in the cellar more than a century after you sealed it off from the world. Somehow, I was permitted to travel back to this time with medication that has the potential of saving Amelia's life."

As he sat on the toilet contemplating his words, he could see how Felix would receive it.

When Leo returned to the house, a man was waiting to greet him and the man stood up when Leo entered the room. Felix too stood and said, "Leo, allow me to introduce you to Doctor Davies. It appears doctor Brown might have double booked him to come here."

After realising, what the truth sounded like after uttering the words in the outhouse, Leo didn't have any words of explanation left and decided the game was probably up and he expected Felix soon to ask him to leave.

Leo shook Doctor Davies' hand and Doctor Davies was the first of them both to speak as he said, "Mr Bennett has been telling me that you are here under the direction of Doctor Brown. I am confused because I know the entire list of doctor's in local practice, but you escape me. Might I ask where you studied and to whom you studied under?"

Leo struggled for an answer, but he didn't have one and Doctor Davies said, "I am afraid, Mr Bennett, you have been hoodwinked into accepting an imposter into your home to care for your sister."

Chapter 05

Leo could not deny being an imposter in that he was not a doctor. However, he had a good and legitimate reason for being there and he knew if asked to leave, Amelia might not receive the medication and she would possibly die. He reasoned the medication she had already taken might delay death for a short time, but she would need to continue with it and Leo was confident Doctor Davies would refuse to administer it.

Leo said to Felix, "Would it be possible to speak to you privately?"

Doctor Davies said, "Such would fail to receive my approval, Mr Bennett."

The doctor's words to Felix had the opposite effect to what the doctor intended and Felix directed Leo to the kitchen with the nod of his head and he said, "We will not be long, Doctor Davies."

When they got to the kitchen, Felix said, "Normally, what I have so far heard would force me to expel you from this house with great force and speed. However, I saw something in you and can still see it, so I must allow you to explain and convince me of your motivation."

"Thank you. It's true I am not a doctor, which is why I preferred you to address me as Leo and not with the title of Doctor. I must appeal to you for permission to remain here to continue administering the medication to Amelia, or at least allow me to show you how to administer it. The medication is not new or experimental and has been for a long time proven to cure ailments such as Amelia has and I assure you it offers the only hope possible of defeating this illness."

"How can you know your medication will cure her while traditional and conventional modern medication will fail?"

I have seen the results of using just traditional medication from this time, Felix. I am not from this time. I don't know how but I received some kind of temporal time displacement, a time slip you might say. It has given me the ability to bring and use medication from the future and this medication has been proven time and time again and without it, I would have great fears for Amelia's survival beyond this day."

"Are you saying I will lose her today?"

"I hope to prevent it with this medication."

"How could you possibly have access to future medication, Leo?"

"By the same means that I have access to information such as the demise of Amelia having such a profound affect on you that you will seal her study in the cellar."

"How did you know about her study in the cellar? I locked it off when Amelia became ill, and you could not possibly have gotten in without my knowledge. However, you are possibly correct and I would have huge problems with seeing it and would possibly seal it off to retain everything as Amelia had it. How could you know, though?"

"The same way that I know in several years you will meet and marry one Brenda Paterson, although that is so long in the future that it will not convince you because you will not have met her yet. However, you will meet her and you will marry."

"And you can save my precious sisters life?"

"Not I, the medication I have can save her."

"You could not possibly know by conventional methods, and no one knows, but I have admired Brenda Paterson from afar for some months. I have not made an advance towards her, though, because I fear she will turn me down."

"She will not turn down your marriage proposal, so I suggest, next week when Amelia is up and out of bed and fully recovered, you should either arrive at Brenda's doorstep with a bunch of flowers or have a bunch delivered to her with a note."

"I don't think she would be interested in someone like me, Leo. It would be nice, much more than nice, but I cannot envisage it happening."

"It will not happen if you don't make it happen. I can understand your reluctance, but you will eventually collect the courage you need and you will one day be married and have children with her."

"That would be amazing."

"It will happen and you are wasting time wishing for it to happen because nothing will ever happen by us thinking about it. We need to be active and go out and get the things we desire." Leo paused for thought as a vague memory came to mind and he said," Before Christmas, were you in clandestine negotiations with a man by the name of Norman Summerville?"

"Those negotiations, as you said, were clandestine, Leo. This being the case, how could you possibly know about them?"

"How I know is unimportant, Felix, although you must be aware that this information will become available in the future."

Felix moved to respond and Leo raised a hand to urge him into silence and said, "Please give me a second, Felix. I am drawing from a vague memory and need to concentrate."

After a moment, Leo nodded his head as though in agreement with his memories and he said, "You postponed your talks until the New Year due to Amelia becoming ill. I understand, though, that you are suspicious of Mr Summerville's reasons for demanding a clandestine nature to your negotiations and am I correct in assuming you are inclined towards rejecting his offer due to this?"

"Now you appear to know what I am thinking, Leo. Yes, I am considering a rejection of his offer. Do you have the ability to read my mind now?"

"No, just the ability to search through Google and if you could travel one year into the future, I would guarantee you would regret such a decision. It will not greatly harm your company not to accept Mr Summerville's offer and you will be no worse off next year than you are now. However, I can assure you that you and your company have a lot to gain by considering his offer more favourably."

Felix pondered and then looked deeply into Leo's eyes and said, "Is everything you are telling me true, Leo?"

"It's as true as the accuracy of history and memory allows, Felix. Everything I have said is compelled and guided by complete and utter honesty."

Doctor Davies sat twiddling his thumbs impatiently. He took out his pocket watch and glanced at it, sighed peevishly and returned the watch to the pocket of his waistcoat. He quickly stood up when Felix and Leo returned. Felix said, "I am so sorry to have wasted your time, Doctor Davies. I have entrusted my sisters' health issues with my friend here and he has my blessing to continue treating my beloved sister privately."

"As you wish, Mr Bennett, although I foresee a need to return when this imposter fails to deliver any obvious promises he made when you left the room with him. Good day, sir."

"Good day to you too, also, thank you and please allow me to show you to the door, Doctor Davies."

Leo put the medication back into his bag after administering Amelia's latest dose. He had not struck up a lengthy conversation with her yet because he decided she would not yet be strong enough mentally or physically for it. She appeared to be just the same as she was the first time he saw her, but he didn't expect an immediate change and he was happy still to be there to aid in her recovery after Doctor Davies visiting and announcing him as a fraud.

He, of course, was a fraud, but a well-meaning one who had Amelia's well-being at heart.

He wondered if the doctor would report the issue to the authorities. It must be illegal to pose as a doctor and administer medicine to a patient. Faith healers don't normally have any kind of degree or training in medicine, yet they treat patients in a way, so maybe it's legal, and he never claimed to be a doctor and that was Felix's assumption. If he ever gets back to his prime time, he will look it up on Google, but at least for now, he will contend himself in the fact that he was sitting at Amelia's bedside and permitted to continue administering the medication that will, he hoped, get her through her illness and back to full health.

He told her it was fine for her to close her eyes and sleep if she so desired. She so desired and so she closed her eyes and Leo could see how weak and exhausted she still was in the way her eyes closed and he detected that she fell into an almost immediate sleep.

He was tempted to take her hand and hold it as she slept, but refrained due to realising how this might look should Felix walk in, or Amelia should waken. It would be innocent enough, but it was enough to simply be in the same room with her and watch over her as she slept.

He wondered how much of any conversation she could pick up when awake and was sure it would be little at times due to obvious drowsiness, although there were also times when she appeared to be alert, like when she refused to address him as Leo and insisted on Doctor.

He wondered if she would remember him when she recovered fully. The memory might be hazy, he decided. By then, he would have no reason for staying at the house and he would need to work out a plan of sorts, otherwise, he could face homelessness and he was sure this would not be a pleasant experience in any year, let alone in 1904.

His only alternative after here might be the workhouses because he had no means of buying food or shelter. Felix was a kind and thoughtful man. He would no doubt grant him financial assistance, but Leo could never allow that and he already felt guilty living there with free room and meals and even wearing Felix's clothing.

He had no way of knowing how extended his stay in 1904 will be, but he had to consider a job, although he reasoned Boxing Day as a bad day to start a job search and no one would be hiring today. When the wheels of industry begin to turn once more, though, he will get out and seek a job, although it might not be easy because he doesn't have any credentials or form of ID. On the hopeful side, the national insurance scheme will not begin until 1948, so he didn't need to worry about that.

Felix arrived, offering a courteous gentle rap on the door before opening it and entering. "How is she now?" He asked in a whisper.

"Much the same and sleeping will help her build back her strength. I feel, though every hour brings her one hour closer to a full recovery and I'm very confident now that she will be fine, Felix."

"I have no way of thanking you to the extent deserved. I could sense that God sent you the first time I set eyes on you when you came to the house. It seems a long time ago, but it was just yesterday morning."

"Yes, sorry I arrived so early."

"Nonsense, you are our Christmas angel, Leo. Angels don't work by the clock."

"My ex-wife would vouch for the fact that I am no angel, but I'm happy to be of service and I'll stay here only until Amelia is well and I'll reimburse you for everything when I get my affairs settled."

There is nothing to reimburse. I owe you a huge debt of gratitude and I have a feeling I'll be in debt for the remainder of my life, so huge is the bill."

"You owe me nothing and we will both celebrate when Amelia has recovered. However, in case I am called away unexpectedly, I need to leave Amelia's medication in your capable hands."

Leo took the medication from his bag and handed it to Felix as he said, "The instructions are simple. However, you will notice the bottle differs from any you have before held. It's made from a futuristic substance which we call plastic and it's much lighter than glass and doesn't have the same capacity to breakage. However, the lid might prove problematic to you, so would you like to open it?"

Felix took the bottle from Leo, turned the lid until it clicked and attempted to pull it off. Nothing happened and he gave it another turn. The same happened or didn't happen and he frowned at Leo.

Leo smiled and said, "Lids were made like this to prevent children from opening them and taking the medication inside. You will need to push down on the lid before turning it."

Felix pushed down firmly on the lid, turned it and smiled victoriously as it came away from the bottle. He said, "This is ingenious! There is always a risk of children thinking a medication bottle contains a treat and would take the content in detriment to their health. You truly are from the future!"

Leo smiled and said, "It took a childproof plastic bottle to convince you of this?"

Leo decided on a walk to get some fresh air and stretch his legs. He was finding nothing to do all day was hard because he was used to driving a bus for several hours and then rushing home to get to work on the house. When he looked out through the window earlier, it appeared to be sunny. He assumed it would not be too warm, but sunny was good for Boxing Day. However, the sun had given up the ghost when he decided on his walk and he could feel the possibility of rain in the air.

He was dressed warmly in hand-me-downs from Felix, so he could not complain and he was much warmer than he had been during the journey of the previous day, which probably began around 11:30 pm. He decided he looked ridiculous in 1904 clothes. There was the possibility that he would need to get used to it, though, because he could not see an obvious way of getting back to his own time.

This reality brought a deep sadness because it arrived with the possibility of never seeing his kids again. They would not know what became of him and even their wildest guess would not have him going back to 1904. In travelling over one hundred years to bring medication that would save Amelia's life, he might have given up all rights to his own life in his original time.

Kids were out playing with their new toys, some already broken as if to mock the belief that they don't make them like they used to. Many Mothers were busy preparing Boxing Day lunch, which can often be as grand as Christmas Day lunch.

It was strange walking through an area so familiar to him, past houses of friends and relatives, while not knowing a single person. As he did the previous day when close to Mikes house, or where Mikes house will eventually be. He passed by the site of his sister's house. It was not there and will not be there until sometime around 1980.

The difference between his sister's house and Mike's house was in the fact that nothing existed close by as a marker to where her house will one day be, although they'll build Mike's house close to a wall that still exists in Leo's prime time. Therefore, Leo didn't know if there was an obstacle blocking his sister's future doorway by not knowing where her doorway will be.

He decided to visit the cemetery, soon if possible. He has several family members buried there and it would be nice to visit at a time before their burial. It would be even better to be able to visit a time when they would still be alive, although that, even if it were possible, would not be without complications.

Once more his mind centred on the real possibility of never seeing his kids again. He was finding that hard to deal with, although it was all beyond his power to change. He wondered what power brought him to this time. Was it a hole in the fabric of time and he slipped through it? It's strange that he arrived on the perfect day and with the perfect medication to help Amelia.

He decided, if he would ever get back to his own time, his prime time, he would probably need to get back to Laura's unfinished house if he could even find a way past the watchman. He didn't have a great desire to walk there as he did from there. However, he knew he could do if he needed to.

He came to a row of houses that he didn't recognise from his time. They were of recent construction but perhaps became a target for the Luftwaffe during the war. Of course, in his time they would be over one hundred years old anyway, so might have outlived their usefulness.

He passed by an advertisement for Vim, pasted onto a gable wall. He was vaguely aware of Vim as a scouring/cleaning product from the 1990s, but had not realised it goes all the way back to 1904/5.

It was nice to get out and stretch his legs, but it was also nice to get back to the heat of the house and Felix had given him a key so he didn't need to disturb anyone when he got back and he simply let himself into the house. Felix was relaxing in the living room, enjoying the heat from a hot air system, 1904's answer to central heating, and he immediately enquired as to Leo's walk and Leo sat down and discussed the day's events with him.

The fact of it now being Boxing Day reminded Leo that Mike promised to sort out the letters on this day and Leo wondered how he was getting on with them. His line of vision took in an artwork on the wall opposite and he said, "I am puzzled at that picture. Did you not have a picture of a lady in blue looking out to sea in that spot?"

Felix frowned and gazed at Leo as though attempting to look through his eyebrows and he said, "I much prefer the one of the lady in blue, but a friend painted this one and I could not refuse when he gifted it to me. The lady in blue is in the loft and will be returned when I am satisfied I have displayed my friends work for a reasonable time. I'll not even ask how you knew about the lady in blue, though."

"It can be challenging when attempting to be kind to a friend's endeavours, although I quite like his work and he has a talent."

"Yes, he is a talented artist, although I prefer to choose that which I put in display in the house and would have preferred him not to gift it to me because, while it's technically fine, it's sadly not really to my taste."

"That is often the main problem with a gift from a friend."

"It was my fault because I complimented him on it."

Leo smiled and said, "Compliments can often be mistaken as a hint or an outright request. We often need to be more careful when paying compliments and consider the kind nature of the one to whom we offer a compliment. I would even suggest we should be less complimentary in our compliments if that is not a contradiction."

Felix frowned and smiled. "I think I follow your reasoning. He had a desire to please me and assumed with me complimenting the painting that I would enjoy owning it. I attempted to pay him for it, but he would not hear of it."

"I can imagine how you would have felt at paying for a painting that you didn't fully appreciate. It's not easy to replace something you love for something you must tolerate and I think I would have sought the ultimate compliment that would have taken the painting from me like it's so pleasing to the eye that it makes the other paintings appear to be third rate."

Felix laughed and then frowned in thought before saying, "I could still use that ploy, Leo. However, to redirect our conversation, you mentioned Amelia recovering within a week. Is this still your prognosis?"

Leo was confident of the medication offering swift recovery with Amelia now having passed the day of her death. He said, "One week is normally enough time for recovery, although she might still be weak and possibly have other symptoms, albeit, while remaining, they will be nowhere near as severe and debilitating. With some people, it might take a month or so, although Amelia is otherwise strong and while she spends a lot of time writing, she is also active."

"How would you know this?"

"Google."

Felix frowned and said, "I am not aware of Google, although you will not know a lot about her unpublished writing because she keeps it very private until it's published. However, do you know what she is working on at present?"

Leo smiled and said, "I have read it, Felix. As she likes to keep it private, I'll speak to her about it when she has recovered enough and she will be able to assure you on how accurate or otherwise my memory of her work is."

Felix smiled and said, "She will not be happy about that. To her, someone seeing her manuscript before publication is likened to someone seeing her room before it has been tidied and she likes to go over everything and make changes and alterations to tidy it up before even allowing her literary agent to read it."

"Oh dear, that suggests I might be in trouble when she finds out."

Felix said, "I think that will guarantee you will be in trouble when she finds out." He smiled, rose and added, "I'll just nip up and ensure that she is comfortable. Could you put the kettle on while I am away?"

Leo rose and said, "Certainly, tea or Coffee?"

"Tea for me and whatever you are having. I apologise for asking, but I strangely see you as a member of the family, Leo."

Felix went upstairs and Leo felt good about Felix's last comment as he entered the kitchen with a smile. Gas powered cooker, it was quite modern for 1904 and Felix had it installed to replace the old coal-powered Rangemaster stove even though the Rangemaster had the dual saving of heating the water and cooking food. It also heated the room quite well. However, there was now the gas cooker and Leo smiled as he filled the kettle and put it on one of the rings to boil. He was aware that if he did this to his kettle at home, the kettle would melt, therefore the smile.

He got two cups and would have to make the tea in a teapot due to the lack of tea bags making it hard to make it with the teabag in the cup. He spooned tea into the teapot and he put the teapot over the spout of the kettle to allow the steam to enter the teapot when the kettle had boiled. He didn't know why people used to do this, but he saw it in a film once and decided there must be a reason for it.

As Felix chose tea, Leo decided to have tea as well and he would need to remember the tea strainer. He had never used one before, but Felix used it. Therefore, at least Leo knew what to do with it and he merely needed to rest it on the cup and pour the tea through its wire mesh to allow the mesh to prevent the loose tea from getting into the cup. He knew from the experience of his last cup that the mesh didn't catch all the loose tea.

He planned this time to leave a small amount of tea at the bottom of the cup and so remove the possibility of taking a mouthful of loose tea, which can quickly make a person violently throw up, or at least give the feeling of needing to violently throw up.

Of course, the same can happen with tea bags if the bag bursts.

Felix returned. He appeared to find it hard to speak and when he attempted to utter some words, tears flowed from his eyes and he had to sit down at the kitchen table. Leo felt his entire being flow out of him as he looked at Felix. He was almost too scared to ask, but he forced out the words, "Is Amelia okay?"

As though in a dreamlike state, Felix looked at Leo and slowly shook his head.

Chapter 06

Leo had the sensation of blood flowing out of his entire being as Felix shook his head in response to his question on Amelia being okay. There was the dual sensation of needing to run up the stairs to Amelia's room and not being able to move with the exiting blood flow rendering his legs useless and there being no one to tell him it was all in his mind and his blood was still running as normal through his veins.

Felix slipped into a dazed reverie of thought and had to force himself out of it and address Leo's worries and he said, "Sorry, I guess emotion got the better of me, Leo. I have been so worried about Amelia and now I know that thanks to you, she will be fine. She spoke to me while I was in her room and she told me she was hungry and asked for something to eat. That means she is getting her strength back, Leo, does it not? I so needed her to eat something. She asked for boiled egg and toast.

"Why the tears?"

"They are tears of relief and joy, my friend."

Leo felt ability returning to his legs and he scooted up the stairs two at a time and stopped when he reached Amelia's room. He needed to rush in, but the simple rules of etiquette held him back and he lightly tapped the door and heard Amelia's voice utter the words, "Come in."

She was sitting up in bed. That was the first time he had witnessed her sitting upright. She was still obviously unwell and pale-skinned, but much healthier looking than she had appeared earlier. Leo had the desire to rush to her and embrace her, but that would puzzle her, perhaps even scare her. She greeted him with a smile and said, "Doctor, I thought I remembered hearing that you would remain here until I got well. Was I as ill as my brother appears to assume I was?"

Leo sat down on a chair at the side of the bed and said, "Yes, I am afraid you were. How do you feel now?"

"I still feel pretty awful, but my head doesn't swoon when I sit up. I realised how ill I was when I tried to sit up previously. I could not manage it and I woke up a couple of times feeling extremely hot and perspiring quite heavily. Perhaps this was the effect of fever."

"Perhaps, although it appears to have helped," Leo said. He had so much to say to Amelia, yet had to leave it mostly unsaid for now, although he felt it would be fine to say, "You had us quite worried."

He could imagine that if Amelia had been as some of the women he had known, they/she would have responded with something similar to, "Sorry if I put you out, but you should try it from my side, chum." Of course, there would have been more than a hint of sarcasm. Amelia, however simply whispered "sorry" and smiled apologetically. He was tempted to crack funny, but he was not sure she would appreciate his brand of humour.

He was also tempted to reach out and hold her hand in his, but he fought this urge as well and said, "The weather has been cold, but dry, so if the rain holds off for a few days; it will do you no harm at all to go for a short walk. You will need to wrap up warm, though."

70

"That would be nice. Richard and I often go for walks down to the river."

Leo mentally recoiled and the question reverberated around his head, *who is Richard*? He had not thought about it before, but it would be natural for someone so beautiful to have someone special in her life and he was confident Richard was not the name of the family dog because Amelia and Felix didn't have a dog.

Yes, there was no reason for there not to be a Richard. He had not seen anything of this Richard and if she meant anything to him, he would surely be with her during her time of illness and there should be flowers from him, placed in a vase at the side of her bed. Maybe this Richard is not important to her and is just an acquaintance that she goes for the odd walk with or possibly is a friend or neighbour's dog and she enjoys walking him.

Three words to Amelia would have this answered, but he felt now was not the time to ask her *who Richard is*. A better question might be *where can I find a gun*? It's strange how we can feel so full of Christmas joy one minute, and then filled with doom and gloom the next, especially when away from your kids and have no assurances of ever seeing them again. How quickly depression can fall and he had to retain a balanced countenance with the odd smile emanating from it. He now regretted suggesting a walk.

As always, when life lies in tatters all around him, his mind turns to the important things in life and he said, "Felix said you asked for egg and toast, so can I assume you are getting something off your appetite back?"

"I have not had anything to eat for a few days, so I am sure I'll have room for it. I asked for a single egg, but I would wager Felix will bring two."

"He has been worried about you not eating. Is Richard a friend?"

He didn't mean to ask that; it just came out in an uncontrolled blurt. However, the blurt was out and he could only await her response and hope Richard is an old uncle or something, yes, he could live with Uncle Richard taking her for a walk to the river.

71

She said, "I suppose you could say Richard is my sweetheart. 'Richard the Lion heart,' he refers to himself as."

Leo had a different name for him, but that will remain his secret for now and he could only take refuge in the fact her saying "I suppose." There is a lot of non-committal and insecurity in that word suppose. It could be Richard is a child. Many women refer to a certain child as being their sweetheart. Leo could ask more probing questions, but he could see she was not strong enough for an inquisition, so he decided to move on to something else and he said, "Apart from walks to the river with Richard, what do you normally do for relaxation and exercise?"

"Much of my time is spent writing, but I do enjoy Equestrianism."

"So, when you are not sitting at your desk, you are seated on a saddle?"

Amelia laughed. It was the first time he had witnessed her laughter and he liked it. He didn't mean to crack funny and was not expecting the laughter, although it was nice to witness.

She said, "You will think of me as being idle in always being seated."

"Not at all, you have your walks to the river with Richard."

"Yes, I do. I have lots of exercise although, perhaps I need to walk more and I had not realised before how many hours of the day I spend in a seated position."

"Now you have transferred to semi horizontal."

Amelia laughed again and it was like music to Leo until she appeared to have problems breathing and he urged her to lay back and relax, asked her if she would like a glass of water or anything. She said she was fine and would have a nap after the egg and toast.

She caught Leo by surprise when she said, "I was sure I was going to die and I think Felix thought this too."

"Well, you are very much alive, so enjoy it."

"I remember you administering the first dose of medication and something told me this would cure me and I know I have you to thank for my life."

"No, you owe your life to the amazing people who developed the medication. I merely brought it to you.

After some time, they became aware of Felix reaching the top of the stairs and seconds later he entered with a tray in his hands and Amelia smiled at Leo as with her eyes she directed his attention to the two eggs instead of the one single egg she had asked for.

The tray was complete with feet. Felix dropped the feet and locked them before placing the tray before Amelia, and he sat on the edge of the bed. He ran his fingers through Amelia's hair to comb it back and away from her forehead and said, "You scared us. Do not ever do that again."

"I have no immediate plans to, Felix," she said. "You should not come so close, though, in case you catch my condition."

Leo pondered on suggesting Felix should wash his hands, but he decided against it for now in case it offended Amelia and she saw it as Leo's way of calling out "unclean!"

Felix bent down at the side of the bed and said, "I'll take your chamber pot away and empty it for you."

"Do not dare," Amelia demanded, glancing coyly at Leo.

"Okay, I'll do it later."

Leo moved towards the door and said, "I'll go and allow you to eat in peace. It's really good to see how you have improved."

"Thank you," Amelia said.

Felix said, "A telegram arrived from Richard." At the mention of Richard, Leo stopped at the door and looked back at Felix.

Felix continued, "I should have brought it up to you, but apparently, he has finally managed to make a booking and will be sailing on Wednesday 28th. That means he will be home for the New Year."

Leo had heard enough and left the room.

Most companies began business again the day after Boxing Day, which was Tuesday, and Leo decided to visit as many of them as possible in search of a job. He knew the driving license was in use even though it didn't come with the need for a driving test. Therefore, he would possibly need to show a valid driving license for a driving job, and he was sure they would not accept his license as being valid with it having a futuristic date and made of a strange substance and not at all like the yellow document of the time. He didn't have it anyway and it was in the glove compartment of the car outside Laura's house back in prime time. In 1904/5, a driving license was valid for just one year anyway and he would need to apply for a new one each year.

Felix had earlier informed Leo there had been a slump in work in the building trade, despite them working on Laura's house and surrounding streets. However, there were good employment opportunities in mining. It was dirty work and came with obvious dangers, though, and he heard they were hiring due to an accident there before Christmas when five workers lost their lives with several others injured.

Leo decided to attempt other avenues first.

Felix had been quite a while in control of his dad's business and had hinted at offering Leo a job there if he so desired. However, Leo decided Felix had been over-kind as things stood and he refused to abuse that kindness by further relying on it and Felix for a job.

He was without luck on the first three days of his job search. However, realising the problems before him with unemployment, he decided to cast caution aside and he went to the colliery. He reasoned the vacancies that rose before Christmas might no longer exist, but he had run out of other ideas in a very short time.

He remembered hearing a very old song that went *Don't go down in the mines, dad.* He also remembers someone jestingly adding the words *there's plenty of coal in the yard.* Coal or no coal in the yard, some people had no alternative and off he went with zero interest, mostly given the fact that he had zero experience. However, he gave his details.

When he gave his address, someone in a smart suit, Mr Clive Weatherford, overheard and asked if that was the address of Felix and Amelia Bennett. When Leo responded in the affirmative, Mr Weatherford asked other questions and invited Leo to wait. Leo later learned that the man had phoned Felix and Leo came away with the name of Mr Ronald Cooper whom he had to report to on Monday 2 January 1905.

He was almost back at the house when he realised they had not given him a starting time, just a date, but Felix was able to determine this and also the fact that his work would not be in the mine and would be in the offices. Leo, with some reluctance, was willing to go down the mine, but would be quite happy working slightly above the surface of the earth as opposed to beneath it!

Amelia was in fine spirits when deemed well enough for a short walk by Doctor Brown, who examined her and was extremely pleased with how far she had progressed through her illness. She expressed the desire to go to the park. Felix reminded her that Richard will be setting sail, but they had no idea what time his ship would dock. However, Felix assumed he would not dock until late afternoon or evening time.

The park was approximately the same distance from the house as the river and Leo was happy not to go to the river with the memories it could entail with Amelia of Richard. She was overjoyed that the doctor deemed her fit enough to take freedom from the house and Leo had not relied on Felix making it a threesome, although that was fine and Felix's presence boosted the conversation and kept it off the subject of Richard.

They were happy to walk at a slow pace, which they allowed Amelia to dictate and she stopped to accept the good wishes of neighbours. Slightly further on, they were stopped again by another well-wisher and while the park was a mere few minutes' walk away, it took quite a while to reach it with the slow pace and the well-wishers and Amelia was exhausted at being on her feet all this time.

She was still obviously unwell and not strong enough to stand about talking to well-wishers and was more than happy to sit down on a bench when they reached the park.

Leo could see that Amelia was extremely popular and he understood well-wishers desiring to stop, but he suggested they could not allow a reoccurrence on the way back.

Felix said, "It might be a good idea for me to bring the automobile here when you are ready to go home, Amelia."

Amelia said, "That would be excellent, but might we feed the ducks in the duck pond first?"

"We may do anything you wish," Felix said.

"Feeding the ducks would be good for you and the ducks, Amelia," Leo said.

Amelia laughed and said, "You are such a hoot, Leo."

That was the first time Leo had noticed Amelia addressing him as Leo and not doctor. He liked it. He had been serious and he had been avoiding explosions of humour because he realised what he decided was funny, other people might see as an annoyance and he decided they might not appreciate his style of humour in this timeframe.

However, Amelia was displaying some of the characteristics of someone who enjoyed a good laugh, so he considered he might have to review the above. He decided to perhaps slip into humour gradually and suss out her sense of humour properly as he went along.

There weren't a lot of people at the park due to the weather with it being cold enough to keep many people away, but not cold enough to freeze the duck pond adequately for ice-skating. Leo decided the park was a safe place for the kids to play with their new Christmas toys, especially bikes, although he was aware that there were not too many cars on the road anyway.

He noticed a lack of penny-farthings, too, and in photos, he saw of them, the riders were dressed in clothes of this era, or close to it. He decided, they had not come out yet or possibly kept in the shed or garage until the weather improved, possibly the former due to the lack of automobiles enforcing a shortage of garages.

He brought up the subject with Felix, who informed him that they were popular for about ten years, but have not been used for approximately the same time and he purchased one fifteen years previously and it was now collecting cobwebs in the garden shed. He offered it to Leo for a fun ride, but Leo decided the seat was slightly too far from the ground for him and he was sure he would break his neck trying to climb on board or disembarking.

Amelia enjoyed throwing food for the ducks and some other birds came along for a nibble, so she cast part of her bag full into the duck pond and part on the grass.

After Amelia had finished feeding the ducks and other birds, Felix decided to go for the car and prepare it for returning her home when she was ready to leave the park.

Amelia said, "I would like to go for a walk around the park before leaving. Would that be possible?"

Leo held back a response and decided it would be more fitting for Felix to reply to it and Felix said, "If Leo doesn't disagree, I would not find variance in it either, although I'll not need to mount a search when I return, will I?"

He smiled at Amelia.

Amelia returned his smile and said, "I'll return to this very spot, so if I am not here when you get back, just wait for me at this point."

"Enjoy the walk, both of you," Felix said and he walked off in no obvious hurry. Leo and Amelia stood up and Amelia indicated walking in the opposite direction. As they began to walk, she took his arm. Felix looked back and saw them walking off in the opposite direction and he didn't have an obvious problem with Amelia taking Leo's arm. Leo certainly didn't have a problem with it and he pondered on what a lovely day it was.

With not having a TV or any form of a film projector, Leo thought opening up a conversation on this might be good as they walked along, so he said, "Many people find entertainment with music and have a piano that the family can gather around. However, you don't have a piano, so how do you normally pass the time and what entertainment do you have during the evenings? We struck on this a few nights ago, but I would like to continue on it to know you and Felix better."

"We do have a piano and Mother used to play it. She was quite an accomplished musician. However, when she passed, it did lay unused and we felt it best to remove it due to the memories it forced every time we saw it. We have a gramophone for music, though. Do you play?"

"No, I began lessons as a child, but it was against my will and I got to the stage where I refused to take another lesson and my parents agreed to allow my ending the course. I wish now that I had kept it up. My brother too gave it up after a short time. My sister stuck with it and she is very good, although she dumped the piano and got a keyboard."

"Just the keyboard alone, Is it possible to get a tune from the keyboard without the hammers and strings?"

"Keyboard is just a name she gave to her new instrument and it's similar to an organ, not a huge church pipe organ, but a small one. You spend a lot of time writing, though?"

Leo quickly realised his mistake in mentioning a keyboard and he hoped that getting onto the subject of writing would exile his mistake to the forgotten pages of history.

Amelia said, "I do. I also like to read, as does Felix."

"I remember you mentioning equestrian sports, do you have a horse?"

"No, sadly, we don't have room for a stable, although I have the use of a remarkable beast at the stable I have access to. I am hopeful they will allow me to keep a horse there when I purchase one."

"So, you have considered buying one?"

"Yes, to enter events, it's much better to own your horse and be its only rider. That way rider and horse can get to know each other well. I am not the only rider of the horse I use and I am sure it's perplexing for him having various riders with various weights and styles."

"I would imagine that knowing a horse as closely as its possible will allow you to second guess his actions and moods quite often, become one with each other?"

Amelia faltered on the path and clung to Leo, Leo put his arms around her to steady her and he said, "Are you okay, Amelia?"

"I felt slightly woozy, light-headed and the sound of your voice came as a distant call. I apologise profusely, Leo."

Leo helped her to the nearest bench as he said, "You must have felt faint and will need to rest for a second." He cupped both his hands around her hand as they sat down on the bench and, as Felix did previously, he removed one hand to use as a comb to sweep her hair back off her forehead and he could not help saying, "You are so beautiful, Amelia."

He immediately realised he should not have said that and he rose and added, "I apologise. It must appear that I am attempting

78

to take advantage of your weakened state. Allow me to take you back to await Felix's return with the car."

Amelia had a confused bearing as she rose partway to her feet and had to sit down again and said, "May I have one moment please Leo?"

"Certainly," Leo said, unsure she even deciphered his words of a moment ago, with them coming during the moment of a weakened and giddy state that most certainly appeared to leave her somewhat vague and unsure.

When she felt ready, she smiled at Leo and said, "I feel much better now. Perhaps we should walk back to where we arranged to be upon Felix's return."

They both stood up and again Amelia took Leo's arm and they strolled back in the direction from which they had come. Amelia said, "You spoke of finding me beautiful and I have to say that I find you extremely handsome, Leo. However, I must say that I still view you as my physician and will need some time to come to terms with the fact that you are not."

This told Leo that she had heard and understood what he had said to her. It also suggested that she was not rejecting him for this Richard person and would need time to work out her emotions, which was understandable.

He said, "Please take all the time you need and feel free to ask anything you wish of me. The main thing, for now, is you making a full and speedy recovery and if I can help this along in any way, I would feel it an honour. As the protagonist in your latest book said quite poetically, 'be it a fleeting glance or an immeasurable vision, know that my heart beats at your decree and awaits your decision.'"

Amelia frowned at Leo and said, "How could you possibly know that? Felix assured me he has had my writing room locked off ever since I took ill and no one will have had admission to read my book."

Felix knows and I told him I would discuss with you pertaining to the content of your book. I had planned to wait until you were fully recovered, although you have hastened that hour, so allow me to give a full synopsis and you can judge how closely I read it."

"I cannot understand how you could have read it at all, Leo."

"I read it in full in the future, although without the ending. Now you are designated the time to complete your work and, if I may say, thrill your reading audience."

"I can discern from your words that you read my book after I had died without completing it. I understand and I know you are not an angel but are outside of your time. I understand it all and I accept it all and I value your input in what is not only my recovery but also my survival and I would accept it an honour to discuss my book with you after hearing your synopsis."

Leo presented his synopsis of Amelia's book as they walked back towards the duck pond and he continued as they sat down on the bench to await Felix.

Leo then gave his opinion on it and Amelia knew he had read it all and it made her eager to get back to it and complete it, partly because writing was in her blood and she loved it, but partly also to allow Leo to finish the story. She would not like to get through most of a book and not get to read how it would end and she was eager to allow Leo to finish the book.

She didn't like the knowledge that he had read it in its raw state and would like to have polished it up beforehand. This is why she doesn't allow anyone to read her work until it has been published or is ready for publication and she would normally write it and leave it for several months before going back to polish it up.

This would take a while and she could not even tell Leo how it would end because she didn't know herself. She at times developed the ending long before coming to it, but on this occasion, she created at the desk and the words came to mind and directly onto paper. As she explained this to Leo, she spotted Felix arriving. He was not alone and Leo didn't recognise the other man, but he could quickly hazard a guess that it was Richard and his heart sank into his borrowed Oxford Brogues.

Amelia remained seated, but Leo rose and it was not until Felix and Richard were level with her that Amelia stood up and Felix said, "Richard was standing outside the house wondering where we were."

Leo didn't like what met his eye in Richard. He saw a tall, athletic man that women would drool over and he didn't like it at all. On top of that, Richard wore a suit from Anderson & Sheppard of Savile Row. That meant he was obviously not short of a few bob and certainly would not drive a bus for a living.

Leo could have sworn he saw the sheen of a sword glistening in the sunlight at Richard's side as he came forward, took Amelia's hand and kissed it. What he did see was the sun bouncing off a Cartier watch and he disliked the man even more. Richard said, "My heart expounds with joy at your recuperation and I can only apologise for not being here earlier."

Leo decided he should now walk off into the moonlight and not look back. He decided if Richard was his opposition, it would be likened to a single fighter in the ring and he (Leo) would be wasting his time even adorning his boxing gloves.

Chapter 07

Leo decided to keep to his room for the remainder of the day with the excuse that he was not feeling one hundred per cent. He had no desire to be in the same room as Richard because that would allow Amelia to see the huge difference between them both. He felt it best not to allow her to see his failings in measuring up to Richard with Richard obviously being everything any woman could ever want and him being an out of time bus driver with a growing love for a woman who died a century before he met her.

He paused and was not sure if that word love had come from his thoughts.

However, he could not deny that he saw something special in her eyes from her photo. After meeting her, he saw something special also in her heart and he decided Richard was not good enough for her. She deserved much more than either of them could offer.

He felt it strange that Richard merely kissed her hand and didn't put his arms around her. He had such a desire when he first encountered her, although he had fears of worrying or scaring her because he was a stranger to her and she assumed he was her doctor. However, Richard had taken her for walks to the river and she deserved a bit more affection than a kiss on the hand.

He rose to his full stature and while it didn't reach the heights of Richard's stature, he determined that he would not hide away from Richard and would go down the stairs and face him like a man instead of cowering away in his room.

Cavalleria Rusticana was playing on the hand-cranked gramophone player when Leo entered the living room. The Christmas tree was still in pride of place, decorated as a way of cheering Amelia up when she first began to feel unwell. Amelia sat on an armchair at the side of the fire with a blanket over her knees, Richard sat on an opposite armchair and Felix sat on a sofa in between them both and faced the glowing fire.

Leo didn't think much of the music, but the room was cosy despite Amelia having need of a small tartan knee blanket and he sat down on the settee next to Felix.

"I'm pleased you could join us, Leo," Felix said. "I trust you are feeling better."

"I feel fine now, thanks," Leo said.

"I hope you are not picking up that horrible illness I had," Amelia said.

"I don't think so," Leo said.

Richard didn't speak.

Leo decided to force Richard to speak and get to know the kind of man he was and he said, "Was the crossing in any way rough, Richard?"

Richard frowned and said, "The crossing?"

"Yes, crossing the ocean in the boat."

"Oh yes, I see what you mean. Sorry, Leo, no, it was surprisingly calm for the time of the year. Had it not been for my worries about Amelia, I might even have enjoyed it."

Leo had expected a basic response of a few words. He was not at all happy that Richard appeared to be a pleasant man. He detected an accent that didn't belong to his attire and Cartier watch, though, and would be more in keeping with Leo's upbringing outside of the silver spoon race. Leo said, "Were you away on business or pleasure?"

"Business, I am afraid. It was planned for me to stay until March, but I had to come home when Amelia became unwell, although getting home at Christmas is not an easy task."

Felix said, "I thought you would not make it back until the New Year, but it's good that you are here now and we will all ring in the New Year together, unless you have other plans, Richard."

"I have no plans at all, Felix," Richard said.

"Will Evelyn be joining you at any time?" Amelia asked.

"Evelyn?" Leo said, taking a sudden interest with the hope that Evelyn was Richard's girlfriend or possibly even his wife. Nevertheless, disappointment was swift and came with Amelia's response.

Amelia said, "Evelyn is Richard's sister, Leo. I was hoping she could join us."

Leo was determined to remain undaunted and he said, "Do you often socialise with your sister, Richard?"

Richard said, "I try to when I can due to her husband being killed some years ago in the South African war."

"She will have to come here and spend some time with us," Amelia said. "I do so love the chats we have together."

"As does Evelyn," Richard said, "I have not had the opportunity to speak to her yet, although I'll be staying with her tonight so I'll invite her if that is fine with you both?"

"That would be more than fine with us, Richard," Felix said. He turned to Leo and said, "Evelyn and her husband were married just a few months when her husband was killed in the Boer war, so they didn't have any children. That is a shame because children would have been such a blessing for her."

Leo was slightly confused at Richard saying his brother-in-law died in the South African war when Felix said it was in the Boer war. Richard didn't appear to be surprised that Felix called it the Boer war, so Leo could only surmise it must be two names for the same war, although he had heard of the Boer war while the

84

South African war was new to him. That might be down to the failure of his history teacher, though.

"It will be good for her to have friendly faces around her," Leo said. "It cannot be easy for her living alone."

Felix smiled and said, "I can sense a party in the planning stages."

Leo smiled and said, "You should invite Brenda Paterson, Felix."

Felix's face adapted a slight crimson glow and he forced a smile but didn't respond verbally.

"Who is Brenda Paterson," Amelia asked, gazing with suspicion and smiling.

Leo looked to Felix to encourage a response from him and Felix adapted an awkward stance and said, "Miss Patterson is just a lady I know."

Leo said to Amelia, "If he can summon the courage, she might even become your sister-in-law."

Amelia gazed wide-eyed and said, "Felix, you must invite her. Where do you know her from, does she reside close by? I want to know everything about her!"

Richard said, "I know a woman by the name of Miss Brenda Patterson. She works for me, if it's the same lady. Does she live at Boundary Heights, Felix?"

Felix sighed deeply and then smiled before saying, "Yes, Richard, I do believe she lives in that direction."

"She does the books for me and now that I am home, I will need to speak to her."

"I need to meet her, Amelia said. Could you bring her here, Richard?"

Richard pondered and said, "If neither of you has an objection, I could ask her to come here with me, but what reason could I give her?"

"You said she does the books for you, Richard," Amelia said. "You could bring her here to check Felix's books."

"I have an excellent bookkeeper," Felix said.

Leo said, "I am sure if he is upfront and honest, he would not mind if you got a second opinion on his work. Okay, he might assume you don't trust him, but we can work around that."

Amelia said, "If my shy brother is overwhelmed and cannot talk to her at first, I'll tell her we have decided the books don't need her expert eye after all and I'll invite her to stay for dinner – no, I'll insist she stays for dinner as our way of apology."

Richard said, "Although it sounds underhanded, I'll pay her for her time."

Felix said, "Underhanded? Does this not seem wrong to anyone else? If it must happen, I'll pay for her time, Richard, but it was generous of you to offer. Thank you."

"Do not get nervous, Felix," Amelia said, "Just take deep breaths and look forward to a wonderful evening."

On arriving in the kitchen, Leo noticed the door to the cellar was unlocked and slightly open. Felix arrived in the kitchen soon after Leo and he noticed the door too and said, "Ah, I see Amelia is getting back to work. She must feel her health continues to improve. That is good."

"It surely is," Leo said. "Does she normally take her meals down there, or does she come up for air on occasions?"

Felix laughed and said, "If she gets a rush of ideas, she has been known to stay down there, but she should come up for her main meal of the day and I'll just slip down and see what she would like for breakfast."

"I'll get things started up here until you get back."

Felix tapped Leo on the shoulder and descended the staircase to the cellar and Leo filled the kettle and switched the gas on the stove. He didn't put the frying pan on and decided to wait and see what everyone required first.

However, a cup of tea always starts the day off well and he was sure he would require three cups and he put milk into the milk jug and sugar into the sugar bowl, put the tea into the teapot and got the tea strainer ready.

After a while, the kettle boiled and he poured some of its boiled water into the teapot and looked towards the cellar door, but there was no sign of Felix or Amelia coming up for breakfast.

He carried on with the tea, looking again towards the cellar door and Felix finally appeared and said, "She wants just a cup of tea and toast and will have it at her desk. I tried to persuade her to come up here and have a proper breakfast, but when could a man ever persuade a woman to do something against her will?" He laughed.

Leo lifted a knife, prepared to slice some bread for Amelia from a loaf, and said, "Maybe one day someone will discover a way of producing pre-sliced bread. They might also develop a method of baking a loaf of bread in a tin pan and referring to it as a pan loaf."

"Is this based on what you know, or what you surmise?"

Leo responded with a smile and said, "Amelia must be feeling much better with having the desire to catch up on work she has missed."

"I would much rather she relaxed and took it easy, but she is happy down there working. She told me about her conversation with you pertaining to her latest book yesterday at the duck pond. She said you have a wonderful understanding of what she was attempting to say in her storyline."

"She is an excellent author. Have you read any of her work?"

Felix got the eggs out from the larder and said, "Boiled, poached, fried or scrambled?"

Leo could detect from Felix's failure to answer the book-reading question that he had not read any of Amelia's books and the fact embarrassed Felix. Leo was aware that an author's family doesn't always read his work and he was sure that if his sister wrote a book, he wouldn't read it.

He said, "I'll have my eggs done the same way you will be having yours done, Felix. I'll be in a position to contribute financially when I start work next week."

"That is not worthy of the worry you must be awarding it. I know you worry by the fact that you feel forced to mention it as you do. You have well earned every crumb we award you, so please don't think about it and please know that I am still grateful and will be eternally grateful for you coming here. I strongly believe I would be preparing to bury my sister now had you not arrived with your wonderful medication from the future. Poached egg and toast?"

"That would be perfect. Thank you. Would Amelia abject if I bring her breakfast down, or would you like to take it?"

87

"I think she would be fine with you taking it, considering you have already read her book."

Leo smiled and when the toast was hot and toasty, he buttered it, put it on a plate and lifted a cup of tea.

When he first saw the cellar, it was with one hundred years of dust and everything looked different now, much newer and cleaner, even in comparison to as it was after Leo had cleaned everything in prime time. "Breakfast is served, madam," he said, placing the toast on the desk at Amelia's left side and the tea on her right side.

"Thank you, Leo," she said. Would you like to read the end when I have it finished?"

"I would love to. Can I ask how long you have known Richard?"

"Many years, Felix knew him before me as Richard's father died at the same time our father died and as Richard worked for Father then and Felix took over the running of the business, they saw a lot of each other and Felix offered advice and other help when Richard started his own business."

She took a sip of tea, and then continued, "I didn't know Richard despite him and his Father working for our Father."

"Both Richard and his Father worked for your Father?"

"Yes, although I had known Evelyn a long time and we had a lot of our education at the same school. Felix began to run the business when Father died and Richard's Father died Just a few days later and Felix visited Richard to offer his condolences and to give an assurance that Richards' job was safe, although Richard had other plans, of course. Do you have a reason for asking this?"

"No reason just interested. You obviously must like him after knowing him five years?"

He can be very quiet and withdrawn and is not open to shows of public emotion, which is why he greeted me yesterday with a mere kiss on the hand. However, he is an extremely passionate, kind and loving man and I trust you will get to see this as you get to know him, Leo."

"I was beginning to see that last night. If I can be bold enough, to be honest, I would have to admit that I didn't like him initially and determined him as being cold towards you. However, as we spoke last evening, I found myself beginning to warm to him. Anyway, I'll have to get back up to the kitchen and help Felix with the rest of breakfast. If you would like anything in addition to the toast, just call up and I'll bring it down to you."

Felix was busily engaged in poaching eggs when Leo returned and Leo got busy with the solid brick of bread to make toast for them both. Felix said, "Just one slice for me, but cut it thick. I enjoy thick bread toasted with the butter melting through it."

Leo rested the blade of the knife on the bread and said, "Will this suit."

Felix waved a hand to indicate Leo moving the knife out a shade for a thicker slice and when Leo reached the desired thickness, Felix raised his forefinger and Leo was not sure if the finger was Felix's way of reminding him to cut one slice or was perhaps the 1904 equivalent of a raised thumb.

Nonetheless, he sliced through at the spot indicated and then sliced through again at the same thickness and said, "I am also quite partial to a thick slice with the butter melting through it."

Felix said," Amelia is getting stronger every day."

"She will need to finish the medication to ensure she doesn't have a relapse. Switching to Richard, can I ask what business he's in?"

"Leather, He owns a tannery. It's much more than a tannery and comprises several sub factories, more a complex. He imports all manner of animal hide from several countries and they go through the tannery, and then sent to the various sub factories, some to be fashioned into handbags, belts, halters, saddles, shoes, that kind of thing. He went into business shortly after his Father passed away. He worked with us back then as a Girdler. After beginning to export, he decided it would be a good idea to expand production to Europe. He has been extremely successful here and I heard he was making good ground with the European market, although I don't know how that will go now."

"He should expand to America. They go big guns over there for leather saddles and holsters, etc. Can I ask what a Girdler is?"

"A Girdler is simply a belt maker, Leo."

Leo assumed it would be a maker of girdles, but he decided it wouldn't be prudent to voice this and he had no desire to dwell on it and he said, "What about your business? No doubt you will be missed at the helm?"

"Amelia comes first, Leo. I can see that I'll be able to return to work soon, though, now that Amelia is getting back to her writing. Poached eggs almost ready, how is the toast coming along?"

"Just about ready, this burner toasts it very quickly."

He took the two thick slices of bread from the stove and buttered them, then he put the butter into the larder and he noticed Felix kept his meat fresh by placing it on what looked like a concrete shelf in the larder.

He decided this was a good idea in the absence of a fridge because concrete has a high thermal mass and will keep meat fresh for quite a while. However, keeping meat fresh during the winter is not as problematic as keeping it fresh during the summer, although not having a freezer would rule out bulk-buying meat.

Leo looked out through the bedroom window and could see Amelia and Richard in the back garden clearing a small amount of freshly fallen snow away. Amelia scooped up a small amount into her shovel and sent it in Richard's direction. In retaliation, Richard scooped up a hand full of snow, pressed it into a ball and lobbed it at Amelia.

Fool, Leo thought, *does he not realise that Amelia is recovering from a serious illness*? He was tempted to open the window and discharge some verbal abuse at Richard, then he saw Amelia preparing to throw a snowball and to prevent her, Richard shot forward and took her in his arms, trapping both her arms, but releasing them when they began to kiss and Leo came away from the window.

He decided it was not healthy for him to watch someone he cared for being with someone who could not treat her the way he would. He could see there would be more pain than joy in staying in 1904 and he was greatly missing the kids and he decided he was perhaps ready to return to his own time and attempt to forget Amelia.

Going back now would leave him without a way of repaying Felix as he had planned, but he had already offered some advice pertaining to Norman Summerville and their clandestine discussions. This would make a financial difference to Felix over the coming years. He sat down and put more advice to paper that he reasoned would benefit Felix financially, so this would repay him for everything.

He had an explanatory note prepared, so he would not be merely disappearing and Felix will be aware of everything when he reads the note, although Leo knew he will miss Felix's friendship.

He gathered his wallet, car and house keys and enough 1904 money to cover the tram fair to Laura's house. He put the keys into his JTR bag, but left all medication behind for Felix's use.

He thought about the journey back from Laura's house should the force that brought him to this time not return him to his prime time. That was negative thinking, though, and he reasoned he would need to be positive.

There would still be a watchman keeping watch over things, even though there would not be any building work done. All the builders' tools and equipment would probably remain on-site and it would need someone to protect it from a would-be thief. That would leave Leo needing to formulate a plan for getting past the watchman.

If it was the same man, he could use the fact of finding him sleeping the previous time and promising not to tell his boss if, in return, he would ignore him entering the empty and unfinished house.

Of course, there was a greater possibility that it would be a different watchman because he reasoned there must be at least two due to one man not being able to keep watch twenty-four hours per day, seven days per week, especially during Christmas.

The trip from Felix's and Amelia's house to Laura's house was much quicker and easier than the trip from Laura's house to Felix's and Amelia's house had been because most of it was by way of a horse-drawn tram. Horses earned their bag of oats in 1904, although this one had the privilege of pulling its tram mainly on level roads and it didn't have too many steep hills to negotiate and the local garden enthusiasts didn't have too far to go for a bucket of organic fertiliser for their garden.

Everything was much the same as it was when he made the reverse journey on Christmas morning and he noticed the shop, which had the notice in its window to wish their customers a Merry Christmas and a Prosperous New Year. The note was still there, even though the shop was now again open for business.

He arrived in 1904 at the same time he left his prime time (Christmas Eve night at around 11:30), give or take just over a century. He reasoned the return journey would be the same.

He would need to think of a reason to offer Laura for his sudden appearance in the landing when he gets back to his own time. Leaving was fine because he was leaving the house anyway, but how will he explain his return? He could claim that, as a loving Father, he was worried about his son's earache, although that would not explain how he got in through a door that Laura always kept locked.

Leo had his leather medical bag, so he could say he had left the bag behind and needed to return for it, although that again would not explain how he got through a locked door without a key. Besides, Laura would wonder, if he left the JTR bag behind, why she didn't see it in the days since Late Christmas eve when he left.

He could arrive back unseen and unheard and be able to slip out without anyone noticing. That was his best hope. Of course, he decided he might return at the exact time of his disappearance on Christmas Eve at around 11:30. If that proves to be the case, he could simply walk down the stairs and out through the door without worrying if he was heard or seen, as long as he was not seen materialising in the landing. Then again, if he did, he would just need to deny it because such a thing would not be possible and most people seeing such a thing would accept they must have imagined it.

The journey took a lot longer than it would normally take him by car, but horsepower was still much quicker and much more comfortable than manpower, although he had the last few hundred yards to travel on foot.

He arrived back at Laura's house over a century before it became Laura's house and he could see the watchman's legs protruding from the hut toward the heat of his fire just outside the hut. He could see an old teapot on top of the fire, so the watchman was brewing a cup to help keep out the cold, or perhaps it was his lunchtime. Leo was not sure what time it was, although he reckoned it would be about 3:00 pm, a bit late for lunch. However, a watchman can have a tea break at any time.

Outside the house at the other end of the timeframe his car would be waiting and he had the keys in his JTR bag and could get back to his own life and leave this painful life behind. He was pleased that he was able to do what he had set out to do in bringing the medication to Amelia and he could only wish her a long, happy and peaceful life.

He had the desire to also wish Richard a long happy and peaceful life, but this was not easy given the fact Richard destroyed the hopes Leo had arrived with.

When drawing up level with the watchman, Leo saw that he was asleep. It should not have surprised him with this being the way he had found him the last time. It appeared to be the same watchman and it appeared he had put the teapot on for a cup and dutifully fell asleep while it boiled away.

Leo reckoned the handle of the teapot would be scorching hot, so he lifted a nearby rag to protect him from a burn, lifted the teapot from the burning ambers and placed it on the ground. He didn't wake the watchman and simply walked on and tried the door. It was unlocked, so perhaps the watchman uses Laura's house for filling his teapot with water.

He entered the house and closed the door gently so as not to disturb the watchman in his slumber. He looked up the stairs before putting his foot on the first stair tread. He knew what the next fourteen steps would entail, but after that, he didn't have a clue and would be happy enough just to get away from the pains of 1904.

Chapter 08

The foolish thoughts that can enter his head at the strangest times never fail to amaze and entertain Leo. He had just climbed five stairs when he had the idea of writing something on the bare plaster walls. This would mean he could tell the kids about it when he travelled back in time by using their house as a time portal and to prove this, he could go to the section of the wall and scrape the paper off it to reveal the message underneath.

Of course, Laura might object to him destroying her wallpaper and this might have one of those paradox things connected to it anyway. However, it would light up the kids' eyes for a while and mesmerise them for a season, as they would become enthralled in his story.

The fact of Leo turning his mind to the kids suggested that he was becoming excited at the possibility of soon seeing them again. For appearance's sake, unless he arrives back within a short time of leaving, he could go outside, and then knock on the door with the reason that he had called to see how Peter's ear was.

He was still saddened at the realisation that Amelia belonged to Richard, but it would be good in other respects to get back to his own time. He left her desk and other stuff in an empty bedroom, but it probably will no longer be there. Having survived in this new timeframe, Felix will have had no need to seal off her cellar study and Leo had already witnessed her getting back to her writing. Therefore, she will have got full use out of everything.

She will also have finished her book, and possibly several other books. Leo was not sure he would have the wherewithal emotionally to read anything now. It would merely serve as a painful reminder of what he had lost, or at least didn't gain.

However, he expelled all that from his mind as he arrived at the bedroom door and wondered how this would work. Will he just need to open the door and pass through and into the room to be back in his son's room in prime time, or will he need to go inside and come back out in the same manner he did on Christmas Eve?

If he is back in prime time when he enters Peter's room, he could merely claim to have neglected to tell him to ring him if he needed more painkillers. It would be normal for him to leave only to return with the information he forgot to give, even if Peter didn't need it and Laura would phone him anyway if Peter needed additional pain relief.

He probably told Laura to let him know if she needed more tablets, but she would not be suspicious of him telling her twice.

He paused when he put his hand to the door handle. He would probably never get back to 1904, so if he had anything he needed to do in this time, he needed to do it now or accept he would not do it at all. Writing on the bare plaster walls would be silly, almost as silly as going back to Amelia's house and taking his last possible opportunity to take her into his arms and kissing her. Once he goes through the door that will be the end of it, with nothing more to do other than to get on with his life in his prime time.

He turned the door handle and walked in through the doorway. He was then in an empty room nearing the end of completion. He closed the door, then opened it again and walked back out and was then back in the landing of the uncompleted house. He tried again, still no difference and no sign of his prime time or his kids.

He felt a sense of panic rising from within. He had no desire to remain in 1904 and watch as Amelia and Richard carried on with a relationship that he could only dream of having, and he now had a deep desire, even a deep need to get back to his kids. Would fate be so cruel to bring him here with the medication that Amelia needed to save her life, and then leave him stranded with no way back to his family and friends!

He had quickly made a good friend in Felix and was even beginning to warm to Richard. However, he had nothing here to remain for in comparison to what he had waiting for him in his prime time. He tried going through the door again, and again, but he just went through a door and it had no effect on time displacement.

After his second long walk from Laura's to Felix and Amelia's house, he had to rap the door because he had left the keys Felix gave him with the other stuff for Felix to find. It appeared Felix had not been to Leo's room to find the things and the note and other paper work he had left, so at least he would not need to give a long and drawn out explanation of anything and Felix accepted his story of going for a very long walk, which he had with having to walk back.

As Leo entered the house, he saw one of Amelia's books in Felix's hand. Could it be he had started reading her work? Leo was sure Felix would enjoy it because Amelia is a rather exceptional author and there was no sign of her so he assumed she was back to her cellar and was busily writing. Either that or she had gone for a walk or something with Richard. He decided it was possibly fortunate he didn't steal a farewell kiss from Amelia now that he was back with no way of reaching prime time.

He decided that when he starts work, he would use part of his wages to pay for a room, so he would have to look out for something. Felix will possibly suggest he could stay on at his place as long as needed, but it would be hard remaining under the same roof as Amelia, especially with Richard at oft times frequenting the house.

Of course, Richard will be going back to win over Europe and expand his business and he didn't take Amelia the first time, so it was more than possible he would leave her behind this time as well.

Leo felt a surge of hope at the reminder of Richard soon going back from whence he came. He returned due to Amelia's ill health and now that she was making a full recovery, nothing was preventing his return to Europe and that would put things back to the way it was before he got back.

Some people would call Leo a love rat for making overtures at another man's woman during the other man's absence. Leo would agree it's not a nice thing to do, but leaving her for such a long time is not a nice thing either and if Richard can abandon her, Leo decided that gives him the right to attempt to win her over. It was not a matter of the old cliché of all being fair in love and war and was more a point of one man's failure to treat a lady as she deserves, which will cause another to make up for the deficit.

Leo decided it would help take his mind of things to do some work and the only work he could find was a bit of cleaning and dusting around the house. Felix informed him that he normally had a lady who came in and did the housework, although when Amelia became ill, he decided the lady would take a holiday in case she should catch the illness.

Felix added it was not proper for a man to wear a pinafore, although Leo needed to keep busy.

During the cleaning, Leo had a look in some unused rooms. One was the old nursery, unused for many years and still home to Amelia's dollhouse, Felix's rocking horse and much more. The next room he went into was set up for use with a bed, wardrobe etc. He cleaned and tidied in there and then went back to the nursery. It was good to see the things that gave them pleasure and he remembered his dad putting his toys into the attic and then filling a skip when the attic needed cleared for new draught-proof insulation going down.

Leo quickly grew weary of cleaning and he decided to slip down to the cellar and see if Amelia would like a cup of tea or coffee. "I would love a cup of tea," she said.

"Coming right up," Leo replied and ascended the stairs. He looked through to Felix in the living room, still reading Amelia's book and asked if he would like tea or coffee. Felix wanted coffee, so Leo decided to have the same and it was two coffees and one tea. He normally prefers coffee, but with loose tea floating to the bottom of the cup, this made his preference even more of a preference because he was used to draining his cup and the secret with tea, it seemed to him, was to leave the last mouthful and therefore prevent getting a mouth full of tea leaves.

He took Felix's coffee into him and this left him free to carry his coffee and Amelia's tea down to the cellar and perhaps discover what Richard's plans might be now for the European market. However, when Amelia saw the coffee in his other hand as he placed her tea on the writing desk, he could detect her gentle sigh, which told him that she wanted to get some work done and didn't have time for a chat.

Therefore, he said, "How silly of me to bring my coffee down. I cannot stop, so enjoy your tea and feel free to call out if you need anything else."

"Thank you, Leo," she said and Leo ascended the stairs much sooner than he had hoped he would.

He was almost tempted to go back to the kids' old playroom because he was getting extremely bored. A good film would pass ninety minutes or so, but where do you get a DVD let alone a player in 1904.

There was neither radio nor TV, just a gramophone player and he didn't like Amelia and Felix's collection of gramophone records. There was just one thing left and he asked Felix if he could borrow a book. He found in Felix's book collection, an 84-page Science Fiction book published by William Heinemann in 1895 entitled The Time Machine by HG Wells. He decided, perhaps he could compare some notes.

The chef arrived early to begin the preparations for the dinner and he had arranged for a staff of one waitress to arrive and this would allow Felix and Amelia to relax and enjoy the dinner with zero hassle to them, also to Leo who would otherwise have felt he should offer a hand.

Felix was nervous, not about the dinner, but because he was aware that Brenda would be coming, or at least invited with the feigned purpose of checking Felix's business books. He got even more nervous when he heard someone at the door and realised it would be Richard with his sister Evelyn and Brenda.

Amelia went to the door to greet them with a smile and an apology that the problem they had discovered in Felix's books was no longer a problem and she added, "However, we will nonetheless happily pay for your time in coming here and we would love you to stay for dinner."

"Before Brenda or Evelyn had a chance to respond, Richard said, that is extremely kind and Miss Patterson would love to stay."

Miss Patterson would possibly have declined the invitation due to not knowing Amelia. However, she felt she had to go along with Richards acceptance due to him driving her there and her not having a way of getting home that didn't entail waiting for the next tram and walking a quarter-mile. She didn't put up an argument when Richard encouraged her to remove her coat and enter the living room where a blazing fire was waiting to greet them.

An extremely coy and nervous Felix arrived in the room and Richard said, "Ah, Felix, come meet Miss Brenda Patterson. Brenda rose as Richard added, Miss Patterson, please meet Mr Felix Bennett."

Felix reached out to take Brenda's hand. He was unsure of whether he should shake her hand or kiss it, but he settled for the former as he said, "It's a pleasure to make your acquaintance, Miss Patterson."

"Ditto," Brenda said. She gazed at Felix for a second before adding, "You are a local businessman, are you not, Mr Bennett? I remember your Father who ran the company before you took over. He was a wonderful man."

"That is very kind of you to say." They both sat down on a sofa to chat and Richard decided his work was complete for the evening. He moved to Amelia who was in discussion with Evelyn, although he could see they were fine without a third person. He was happy to see Leo arriving in the room.

Leo would have preferred not to spend the early part of the evening chatting to Richard, but what could he do. He noticed that Amelia was happily engaged in conversation with Evelyn and he decided Evelyn might be like a spare wheel later in the evening when Richard and Amelia get together, and he hoped they would not pair him off with her, although he decided they probably will.

He offered a week smile as Richard arrived beside him and said, "I think this evening will be a tremendous success, Leo."

"It looks like Felix has settled down anyway," Leo said, "Let's hope it all works out the way we would all like to see it working out and Felix discovers lasting happiness."

"Miss Patterson is a wonderful woman, just as Felix is a wonderful man and they make a wonderful couple."

As Richard spoke, Leo could see Amelia and Evelyn coming over to them and he could see his earlier thoughts were correct. This enraged Leo slightly and he saw it as part of a plan to force him and Evelyn together. He was fine with some matchmaking with Felix and Brenda because their union is history and this was simply speeding it along slightly.

However, if lined with a thousand other women at that second, Evelyn would have to settle for second place at best, because Leo could no longer deny that his heart belonged to Amelia, even if her heart belonged to Richard, and his only desire now was to get back to his own time and the kids.

Amelia said, "Do you not think Felix and Brenda appear to be hitting it off splendidly together? How could you have known, Leo?"

Leo smiled and said, "That which is meant to be can become obvious to those with an eye and I would suggest that you have brought together a man and his wife, or I should say his future wife."

Evelyn said, "Are you some kind of clairvoyant?"

Leo smiled and said, "No, I'm a time traveller."

Leo's words brought Amelia back to while she was recovering and discovered that Leo was from a different time. She assumed this was an illusion, but now she was not sure. She felt now was not the right time to discuss it. She laughed; her laughter enticed Richard also to laugh.

Evelyn frowned and then decided Leo must be joking. When she saw Amelia and Richard laughing, she laughed too and said, "Seriously, though, Amelia was telling me how it was your idea to bring them together, so you must have an amazing insight on people."

Leo said, "We all do at times and we should take the opportunities presented to us instead of running away from them."

"I agree," Richard said, not realising that Leo was directing his remark at him for running away from Amelia to work in Europe. He added, "We might be lucky in getting a second chance. However, second chances are very rare and we must grasp that which will make us happy or spend our remaining days regretting our mistakes."

Leo realised he could not argue with Richard because such things tend to spoil what otherwise would have been an excellent evening. However, he found what Richard said to be hypocritical in the extreme. He had begun to slightly warm to Richard, but this recent helping of verbal claptrap was making huge changes and coupled with the obvious matchmaking, Leo decided he should excuse himself and leave the room for a while until his temper simmered in case he lost the ability to contain it.

He said, "Please forgive me, but I need to check on something. I'll return as soon as possible."

Leo left the room and Felix looked over at Amelia and frowned. Amelia took the frown to be a silent query as to why Leo had left the room. She shrugged her shoulders at him, he rose with Brenda, and they both went to where the others had gathered in a cluster.

Amelia decided on the seating arrangements and she decided to dispense with the normal etiquette of Felix at the head of the table and herself facing him. She also decided it would be a mistake to have it boy girl with the seating removed at the head of the table at each end because this would place one girl and two boys at one side and two girls and one boy at the other side.

Therefore, she decided to dispense with the head of table positions and have all the boys at one side of the table and all the girls at the other side. It was not perfect, but at least it would have a boy facing a girl.

Richard would sit facing Amelia; Felix would sit facing Brenda and Leo would sit facing Evelyn.

The table was set up in the dining room before the guests arriving. The table normally sat eight persons, so leaving out either head-end made the numbers fit perfectly with a Christmas plant upon a table-high plinth at either end of the table with candelabra placed on the table at either end.

Normally, after the meal, the men would gather for brandy, cigars and a chat about football or rugby, depending on preference; and the girls would retire to discuss the finer points of sewing and knitting depending on preference. It was decided, though, to dispense with normal formal arrangements with everybody mucking in together to discuss as mood directed.

It all began with the chef arriving in the room and saying, "Ladies and gentlemen, your meal is ready. Could you all make your way to the dining room, please? With the announcement completed, the chef went back to the kitchen where the waitress was waiting and ready for his instruction and Amelia explained where everyone would be seated.

It was then that she realised that if she had used the two ends of the table, she could then have had a boy/girl at each side with a boy/girl at the ends of the table. Amelia had asked for a few moments for everyone to relax before bringing the food, although the men especially by now were hungry and would be happy to dive straight in.

The best thing about small numbers for a dinner party is, the food doesn't get cold for the last person to be served and the waitress could quickly deploy this with speed. When serving the men, there would be a heavier load, due to the instruction being to fill the men's plates slightly higher than the women's with men generally having a larger appetite.

No one complained about portion sizes and they were soon eating, chatting and enjoying the evening and the company with the waitress remaining on hand should the men require a top-up on anything pertaining to food.

At the end of the meal, Richard used the handle of a knife to tap his glass as he stood up. This would normally indicate the fact of a speech looming in the air, so everyone fell silent and awarded him full attention.

He began, "Those of you who know me best, will know I have often delivered speeches at business conferences and such, however, you will also know that I am an extremely private man who would never divulge desired, feelings or emotions in public, not even to an audience of friends and family."

He smiled at Felix and added, "I should say that I would have kept the chef hidden and would have claimed this meal as my work. It was perfectly the most delicious meal I have tasted in a long time. However, toasts to the chefs' culinary expertise later."

He cleared his throat and continued, "I left here two months ago to open and establish a European branch to the company and, before I left, I made myself an assurance that I would commit upon my return. The shocking news I received before Christmas changed things and I knew that I had to return before my chosen hour. On Christmas Day, I had the most awful feeling that I was too late. However, I was thankfully not too late and I can let you all know that I intend to delegate the European work to someone else, someone with no other commitments, and I intend to stay here and see the completion of the building of the house that has been ongoing in my absence."

Leo could see where this was going and he was tempted to rise and exit, yet he knew he could not embarrass himself and others in this way. He forced a smile, put a hand around his glass, and prepared to raise it to his mouth at the appropriate time.

Richard pushed his chair back, stepped around the table and turned to face Amelia. He smiled at her and said, "I might be accustomed to public speaking, however, you know Amelia I would never publically announce my love for you, yet I do it now in front of family and friends. I have loved you so much for so long and the feelings I had on Christmas day have convinced me that I have no desire to spend another day away from you for the rest of my life. Therefore, while I'll not embarrass you by getting down on one knee -"

From his pocket, he took a small ring box, smiled and added, "No, I will embarrass you, myself by getting down on one knee."

He lowered his left knee to the floor, opened the box to reveal the ring, smiled at Amelia and continued, "I have had this ring for quite awhile and it's only now that I dare to say, Amelia Bennett, will you do me the absolute honour of becoming my wife?"

All heads turned expectedly to Amelia.

Chapter 09

Leo flopped down onto his bed with the thought that overall it was quite an eventful evening. He wondered what else was waiting to surprise him in 1904, a year when 7 months previously, George 5th took over the throne from Edward 8th, Arthur Balfour was in power in Downing Street and Ernest Mangnall was team manager of Manchester United at Old Trafford.

Leo was confident the trinity of King, Prime Minister and temporary demigod would not know the sadness raining down at that moment. His thoughts of them attempting to pair him off with Evelyn was wrong. However, this didn't lessen Leo's desire to go home. He needed to see the familiar faces of his kids.

He had determined himself to man up to it all and step back from womanly pursuits such as crying. Men don't cry, they simply bite on the proverbial bullet and get on with life. Nor do men sulk or engage in self-pity, although with two out of three being an acceptable measure of strength with most people, he allowed a tear to run down his face just this once.

The problem was, it didn't arrive alone, its brothers and sisters arrived too, and his face quickly became saturated.

It appeared he didn't have a return ticket and when he embarked on the journey to 1904, it might have been a permanent transfer, a perpetual relocation rather than a temporary visit. He will go back to Laura's house periodically until the first owner takes ownership of it, but he didn't expect anything to change and he would need to arrange an agreement with the watchman. It was Leo's only hope, although he didn't have any confidence in it.

He was pleased that Richard realised his folly of abandoning Amelia for several months in the line of business. It was good that he was making a success of his business, but there are things of more importance and Amelia was high up on that list and, in fact, she was at the top.

Leo respected Richard for taking hold of his ambitions and putting Amelia first. With this now being the case, Leo will be happy to step back and cease being a hindrance to Richard and will instead offer his support to him.

It still hit Leo hard when Amelia said "yes" to Richard's proposal.

There was also the matter of Felix and Brenda. Leo could see the insecurity peeling away from Felix's facade as the evening progressed and relaxed confidence replacing it. Leo could easily see that until that evening, Felix had spent his time worrying about what Brenda thought of him and he neglected to consider his competence and potential.

He was worried about not being good enough for Brenda and this forced Leo to consider the possibility that Felix might have been hurt in the past and had possibly lost out in love to such a degree that it forced the opinion that he didn't deserve Brenda and that Brenda deserved someone much better.

Now they had each other before fate originally deemed it.

Evelyn appeared to be a nice enough woman, but Leo was pleased that his former thoughts of his new friends attempting to force her onto him had no real anchorage in reality. He would have appreciated their reasons, but his circumstances would not allow it.

Now that he accepts he will never win Amelia, he will commit a few surgical strikes on his heart to repair the damage and will then set his mind to finding someone. He gave up on love after losing Laura and he turned his mind to work on the houses. It will have to be different this time because he has spent too much time on his own.

Things will have to change whether or not he gets back to his prime time. If he does get back, He will sell the house because his heart will no longer be in it. Starting at the beginning of whatever timeline will be his prime; he will concentrate on building his life from the ashes of this foretaste of hell and will search out someone with whom to grow old.

Unlike he surmised Felix to be, Leo doesn't believe his new friend doesn't deserve love. Everyone deserves it and everyone eventually finds it unless he or she gives up and commits to live the life of a hermit. Even Hitler had Eva Braun and somewhere on this planet, we call earth, there will be someone waiting for Leo in either timeline.

Still, when he lay back in bed and closed his eyes to beckon sleep, he saw Amelia in his mind's eye and he decided it might be a long night.

Morning arrived, the last morning of the year. Come midnight, the world will celebrate the arrival of 1905, but it was hardly new to Leo with it arriving a century in the past, although he could hardly wish people a Happy Old year. Therefore, he would treat it as a New Year, one that will usher in new hope while all the old failures would disappear with the Old Year.

He will start in his new job on Monday 2nd January 1905. With the job and the New Year, came a new way of life and an old determination not to allow the past to drag him down. He could see how blessed he was in coming to this time and already having the friendship of Felix to rely on and it was with some excitement and anticipation that he asked Felix how it went with Brenda – "Miss Paterson."

He found it difficult to adapt to the more formal ways and language of 1904/5. The informal would often pop its head up and cause heads to turn when the correction of Miss Paterson didn't arrive with the needed speed, although Felix was fine and knew the differences in Leo and other men was because he was out of time and so slightly out of step with others.

Felix was beginning the preparations for breakfast, but he stopped when Leo spoke and smiled widely before saying, "It went extremely well Leo, and I can only thank you for the devious yet wonderfully kind manner in which you brought Miss Paterson and me together. She was nervous at first, which took my mind off my own nerves, and I spoke mainly with the hope of putting her at ease. We were both able to relax, though and enjoy the dinner and it was something of a surprise that Richard made that proposal. Can I ask how you feel about it?"

"I feel fine. I was angry with him going away for months and expecting Amelia to be waiting for his arrival back, but last night I could see that he genuinely thinks a lot of her and she deserves that. Her happiness is the main priority and I could see last night that Richard could make her happy, so I'm happy with everything."

"That is an extremely benevolent attitude, Leo, and it shows your true character. It is my fervent hope that you too find someone soon. You didn't appear to appreciate the arrival of Miss Brooks?"

Initial confusion struck Leo by the name Miss Brookes, although he then realised that Felix was referring to Evelyn. He admitted that he had manipulated the circumstances surrounding Brenda being at the dinner as much if not more than anyone had manipulated Evelyn being there. However, a thing will always seem different when someone else assimilates it.

Leo could detect that Felix was not at all peeved at having Brenda thrust on him and he could see that Felix realised his well-being and contentment were of utmost concern in the scenario.

Leo said, "I don't doubt that Evelyn is a lovely woman and I truly desire her to find happiness. However -" At this point, Leo had to be careful due to any argument he put forth having the potential to come back at him and echoed by Felix. Leo didn't attempt to hide the fact of being the main collaborator in bringing Felix and Brenda together and, therefore he could easily appear to be slightly if not wholly hypocritical in his assessment. With this quickly entering his thoughts, He added, "I am not highly deserving of her and she will find someone more worthy."

"I think you are very deserving and worthy, Leo. You have referred to having an ex-wife and I think you have a desire to settle down and Evelyn might be a good choice, but she must be your choice. Now, what would you like for breakfast?"

Leo was aware that factory workers in the early 19 hundreds had to work 16 hours per day. At the colliery, he would not be a factory worker, not even a miner. He would be an office worker and he was so surprised at the sudden and dramatic turn of events from the appearance of him having no chance to being offered a job on the spot, that he didn't think to ask about hours of work or things like pay structure.

He thinks these things got a mention, but shock from the offer rendered his mind in a bewildered state and he didn't take in a lot of information. He has no experience in office work, but that was the job offered after the boss spoke to Felix and he could only think that Felix must have something on this new boss to force him into such a dramatic turnabout. Maybe Felix is a 1904/5 Mafia Don on the side and the softly spoken kind gentleman's demeanour was a shrewd subterfuge to hide his true gangster nature.

No doubt, the fact will reveal itself over time, Leo decided, drawing back from his jovial and mischievous thoughts as he entered the living room to find Amelia deep in conversation with Evelyn. He prepared to apologise for the interruption and decided to leave immediately.

Amelia caused a delay when she said, "Leo, perhaps you can help us."

If ever a single sentence would imprison a man and make him succumb to the woman's will, it was that one and Leo felt forced to remain and he declined an ear.

Amelia continued, "Richard and I have decided to partake of that time-honoured tradition of exchanging gifts on our wedding day and I was wondering if you could offer any suggestions."

Leo's first thought was on women knowing how to make a man suffer; his second thought suggested it's an honour that she should ask him given the fact that she hardly knew him. Amelia, with appropriate hand gesture, invited Leo to sit down and he sat facing them and said, "Is it not a bit early for deciding on gifts? Richard only just proposed last evening and I don't think you even have a date set for the wedding yet."

Amelia said, "I like to get things like this decided and out of the way early."

Evelyn said, "What would you like to receive as a wedding gift, Leo?"

Leo's mind said, "Anything as long as it doesn't come from you," although his lips said, "I would deem the giving and receiving of rings as being the only gift necessary."

Amelia said, "Really? You don't agree with the bride and groom exchanging gifts?"

Leo thought it was fine for those of wealth, but it would put an additional burden on most of the people he knew and it was an unneeded additional burden and it spoke of the difference between them with Amelia raised in middle to upper-class standards and him being working class.

He then realised that he might have made a goof by referring to rings in the plural when in 1904 it was always ring in the singular. Women hadn't taken to getting the new husband a wedding band in this time period, but he was relieved neither Amelia or Evelyn appeared to see anything amiss in his mention of rings in the plural.

He could see that Evelyn, as was her brother Richard, grew up in working-class standards, even though Richard had worked through that and into affluence. However, he felt he had a great need to be careful because Amelia might not understand the concept of a gift in terms of it being a financial burden.

He said, "I think that a glimpse into the heart of my intended would greatly out weight the value of a purchase or a betrothal dowry and I would place more importance on perhaps an extension of wedding vows where bride and groom should, in turn, tell the other what they most love about each other."

Evelyn said, "My late husband and I didn't exchange gifts, although we did something similar to what you just suggested, Leo. It was not part of the wedding ceremony and was something we had agreed to share privately together."

Amelia rose and said, "I'll consider this, Leo. Thank you. I need a cup of tea, so please carry on chatting together while I go and put the kettle on for us all."

Amelia left the room with such swiftness that it failed to leave Leo the possibility of suggesting an amendment to her plan. He felt trapped but had to remain with Evelyn. He was unsure if this was a deliberate ploy on Amelia's part, but the possibility of it being a deliberate manipulation told Leo that he would need to be extremely careful before anyone began to ponder on there being a double wedding.

He felt as if he was caught on the hop and didn't have much time to think and so he could blame that for the fact that his first utterance was of second-rate quality as he said, "Do you prefer tea or coffee, Evelyn?"

The second he had asked it, he regretted it because he could see how desperate it was, the act of a man abandoned and at the mercy of the woman, with the brain slipping into malfunction, leaving him open to mental dominance.

Evelyn said, "I do enjoy the odd cup of coffee, but I much prefer tea. It's nice to have a cup of tea and a chat with friends."

Leo reasoned that Evelyn mentioning friends in the plural was her way of drawing Leo into her small group and imprisoning him. For the sake of his mental stability, he needed to find disagreement, not to the extent of argument, but simply not allowing Evelyn to dictate the conversation along the road of her agenda and he said, "I prefer coffee, but the occasional cup of tea is nice."

He was sure she would accept this because it was the truth and she would know it was the truth if she had paid any attention the previous evening when he had a few cups of coffee. He didn't know how to react to the situation, though, when she lowered her head in sadness and said, "My late husband preferred coffee, but often suggested tea, possibly because he knew I preferred tea."

Leo was unsure if the sad demeanour was a female ploy to force the man to soften and go to her with the view of comforting her in her apparent sadness. If it was a ploy, it was working because he felt his attitude alleviating and he had the desire to go over to her and attempt to comfort her. The thought struck him that he was being silly thinking it was all a female ploy and she appeared to be genuine in her sadness.

However, the stakes were high and his freedom might be on offer, so instead of moving the few feet to her, he remained where he was and said in an understanding and sympathetic voice, "I can see the pain is still relatively fresh, but it will ease with time and you will find happiness again. I am sure your husband would want this, he certainly would not want you to be so unhappy."

She looked up and forced a smile and Leo could see her eyes were moist. The moistness spoke of it being a real pain and not a ploy and he wondered why she had not reached for her handkerchief until he realised there was not a handbag or any other such lady's bag in sight, so she might have left it elsewhere and therefore didn't have a handkerchief.

History demanded that the Scott Company would begin to sell disposable tissues in 1907. This couldn't come quickly enough for Leo and against his better judgement, he went over to her. As he made the journey, he took a hanky from his pocket. He was sure he had not used it to blow his nose and it should be clean, but he glanced down at it to be sure, and, happy with its hygiene level, handed it to her. He then decided she deserved some privacy without him leaving the room and he turned to look at the picture on the wall that Felix's artist friend gifted and he wondered when Felix would gather the courage to put the picture of the blue lady back.

Amelia arrived with a tea tray and didn't see as being sensitive Leo having his back to Evelyn while she cried and he admired a portrait.

Amelia went to Evelyn. She could then tell from Leo's demeanour and Evelyn's reaction that Leo had not behaved in a manner that would call for her to go to the gun cabinet, which was good because they didn't have a gun cabinet.

"I apologise," Evelyn said and she dabbed her eyes, blew her nose and offered the hanky back to Leo.

Leo said, "That's quite all right, hold onto it in case you need it again."

Amelia put her tray down, looked at Leo, and then at Evelyn and Evelyn said, "I was discussing tea and coffee with Leo and, I am afraid, it reminded me of –"

Evelyn could not bring herself to end the sentence; but she had said enough for Amelia to get the essence of what the problem was and she hugged Evelyn and said, "I understand your pain, but it will ease with time and you will find happiness again."

Evelyn looked directly at Amelia and said, "That is what Leo said."

Leo was in a dilemma in that there were three cups and one was for him. However, he had even less desire now than before to remain in the room with the girls. He felt he was surplus to requirements anyway with Amelia now taking on the role of comforter. Amelia hugging Evelyn had the result of opening up the floodgates and the tears returned, with added tears now coming from Amelia, and Leo's line of vision took in once more the painting on the wall as he sought the most acceptable reason for leaving the room.

Stranded in a room with two weeping women was not the way Leo had desired to see out the old year of 1904 and he pondered on what 1905 will offer him.

Monday 2 January 1905 was the day Kanno Sugako was hanged for her part in the plot to kill Emperor Meiji of Japan. It was also the day Leo began work in his new job at the colliery. Leo had to gleam the news about the hanging from the newspaper. The radio was still some years away and the colliery had no modern electronic devices other than the old faithful telephone. There was not a phone on Leo's desk, though.

Leo learned his working hours would be 50 per week, which was less than he had heard others had to work, but was more than he was used to. The wages would be £135 per year, although it came with the promise of rising substantially after the first year. While this wage kept him on the level of working class; it could probably enable him to raise a family without financial strain. He worked out that £135 per year would get him a gross weekly wage of £2.13s per week.

He didn't have a lot to do on his first day and he found it quite boring. He quickly found his way around and got to know the people and the work, but this didn't include the mines and miners.

He saw the miners as being the real workers, but it appeared others viewed them in the same way as apparatus, machinery. They were of no real importance other than doing their job, but of no concern other than financial should they break down or fail in any way through injury or death to produce the coal that paid everyone's wages.

Of course, this might have been an improper impression Leo had picked up from some office staff.

Midway through the day, Mr Clive Weatherford stopped by to ask how Leo was finding his first day.

"Like a tram driver in a colliery or the proverbial duck out of the water, to be honest," Leo said. "I feel inadequately qualified for the work."

Mr Weatherford nodded his head and said, "You'll soon pick things up. Most people feel this way on their first day, but I have high hopes for you and Mr Bennett has assured me you will surpass yourself in a short time."

"Is it due to you knowing Felix that you offered this job to me?"

"I value his opinion and he convinced me that you are the man for the job. He values you and credits you with his sister's recovery from her recent illness."

"However, if I may be as bold as to suggest, none of that sets me ahead of anyone in office work."

"Mr Bennett referred to you as the doctor and he informs me that you are vastly informed and highly experienced in medicine. We need men like you who can double as first aid workers when there are injuries in the mines. We don't always have time to get them to hospital and I came up with the idea while chatting to Mr Bennett that we could train some of our people to deal with medical emergencies and perhaps save a life or two."

In Leo's prime time, several companies train several staff members in first aid, although he was sure this would be unheard of in 1905 and Mr Weatherford could become a pioneer. It appeared Felix mentioning Leo's gift in medical matters gave Mr Weatherford the idea, but Leo knew he was not as adept in medical matters as Felix appeared to believe.

As the conversation expanded, Leo learned that Felix contacted him after witnessing Mr Weatherford's son receiving grievous injuries when a horse, spooked by a sudden and loud rumble of thunder, trampled Mr Weatherford's son into the cobblestone. Mr Weatherford worked, so he was unable to claim the same medical care for his son that someone in the workhouse could claim. However, there were still voluntary hospitals for those who were affluent enough to dodge the workhouse, but not affluent enough to pay for private hospital care. Mr Weatherford was in this bracket back then with his wife having given birth to their third child and him still an office junior.

Mr Weatherford's son's injuries were so severe and his overall condition so critical that the volunteer hospital could only make him comfortable, but he needed the kind of care that demanded large sums of money. Those large sums of money came from Felix, who after witnessing the horse cutting the boy up, had a great need to help and money was an easy way of saving a small life and ending such parental worry.

This, in turn, gave Mr Weatherford the compulsion to push himself on at work and rise through the ranks to earn capital of such to ensure him the ability to repay Felix. It was easy repaying the money, but he felt he could never show his appreciation fully for the gift Felix presented in returning Mr Weatherford and his wife their son. Mr Weatherford was certain his son would have died and, while it took a long time, he eventually recovered in full with just a few scars in places that didn't show.

When Mr Weatherford realised how overwhelmed with gratitude Felix was at Leo, he understood it because he had felt it for Felix and he had to give Felix that small piece of joy by offering Leo a job. He didn't realise, neither did Felix, the pressure this would put on Leo, who felt out of his depth, and

115

unable to return the expected level of office or medical expertise that he had never claimed, but that people had somehow assumed he commanded.

What now, Leo thought as Mr Weatherford walked away after their talk. He accepted he could never win Amelia, and he knew he could never excel as expected at the Colliery. The future was looking black and bleak. Thinking about Mr Weatherford's son was resulting in Leo missing his own son and his daughter even more and he had a huge desire to leave the office, walk down the road and just keep on walking until he could walk no further.

He would then allow exhaustion to take over and he would collapse and go into a final unconsciousness with his last dream.

Chapter 10

Leo was happy to see the end of his first day at work. He got on well with his colleagues and his boss, Ronald Cooper. Mr Weatherford too was fine, but the work didn't suit Leo and he has always been more active. Even driving the bus, he would have lots to occupy his mind, but he found sitting at a desk extremely boring and not having much of a clue what the job entailed didn't help.

However, he will carry on and earn his £2.13s per week. It will give him a way of paying back his growing debt with Felix and, while in effect it was less than the amount he gave each of his kids each week for pocket money, it will give him a means of buying clothes and other necessities.

He met Martha upon his return from work. Martha is Felix and Amelia's housekeeper. Felix decided to give her an extended holiday due to him taking time off work to care for Amelia. He was aware of Amelia's condition being contagious and was worried it would transmit to Martha. Therefore, he took over Martha's duties. She had an entitlement to a Christmas holiday anyway and with Amelia almost back to normal, he was happy to see Martha arriving back.

Martha, Leo reckoned, was in her mid-fifties, so he was confident they would not try to match him up with her as they tried with Evelyn. She didn't wear what Leo deemed the normal attire of black and white of a domestic in the early 1900s. She wore a dress reaching almost to the ground and buttoning up from the waist to the chin with full-length sleeves and had the appearance of corduroy with light blue and off white stripes running vertically throughout, apart from the waistband which ran horizontally, with a deep pocket at each side.

She might have had an apron and a head covering to complete the ensemble, but if she had, she was not wearing either when Leo arrived.

Without a head covering, Leo could see she was going grey, although he knew from the experience of other women not to mention this small fact. He mentioned his aunt's grey hair once after she took three cups of tea off a tray and placed them on a coffee table. She then placed the tray on Leo's head with no lack of force and complained about the dent he left in it.

Laura laughed and he regretted bringing her to meet his old grey-haired aunt. He was just following instructions, though, so he introduced her and suffered the headache for the rest of the day. Of course, one day was nothing when later compared to the headache he suffered at the hands of Laura.

Blond, if he feels forced to mention Martha's hair, he should refer to it as being blond. Of course, she might then think he was patronising her and will whack him with a tray, so he looked around and was pleased to see there was not a tray in sight, although she had not at this time brought the tea through yet.

He shook her hand and said, "I'm pleased to meet you, Martha. Have you been here long?"

"I began in service to Mr and Mrs Bennett when Master Felix and Miss Amelia were still children."

"Oh, I see, so that will make you the family retainer?"

Martha lifted the poker from a companion set at the side of the fireplace and turned to Leo. Leo stepped back. Martha said, "I suppose you could say that."

She turned back, poked the fire and added, "I cannot allow you men to get a chill. I'll go and brew some tea now."

She left the room and Leo smiled as Felix entered. Leo said, "I thought she was going to whack me with that poker for referring to her as a family retainer."

They both sat down and Felix said, "Martha is an amazing woman and we see her more as part of the family than a family retainer."

With Leo sitting to the right of Felix, his line of vision took in the picture of the blue lady on the wall and he said, "Ah, you have returned your preference to its rightful place?"

"You have excellent powers of observation, Leo. I much prefer this artwork and I decided to take the risk of insult by returning her to, as you said, her rightful place."

"The art we display in our homes can be personal to us. A professional creation can leave us dispassionate, but the right one will touch us. I understand you putting up with the other painting for so long, but when relaxing at home, we should have that around us, which contents us and is soothing and pleasing to the eye. Is Amelia in her workroom?"

Felix smiled. He said, "Is it by accident that you asked about Amelia directly after referring to that which contents and is soothing and pleasing to the eye?"

Martha released Leo from the necessity of a response as she arrived with two cups of tea on a tray. She said, "I have had such a long holiday that things might have changed, but I still thought it best not to ruin your appetite so close to your meal, so I have brought just the usual tea and nothing to nibble."

"Tea is fine on its own, Martha," Felix said.

Leo smiled, but didn't make a verbal comment and would refrain from verbal comment until Martha had returned the tray to the kitchen. He was beginning to see a lot of his aunt in Martha, and it was not just the grey hair. There was strangely a strong family resemblance and Leo pondered the possibility of her being an ancestor.

It was possible to have ancestors in the area because he was born and raised not far from the house, as his parents were. It would be amazing, he decided, if she proved to be a great aunt or similar. However, with Martha being in her mid-fifties, he decided he should perhaps hyphenate the great with another to make her his great-great-aunt. He would keep that to himself in case it warranted a tray on the head, although, in terms of calendar years between them both, she would be well over one hundred years older and then some. He did a quick mental calculation and, considering her being 55 years of age now, he worked out that she would be celebrating her 165th birthday in his prime time.

"Good first day at work?" Felix asked, pulling Leo out of his thoughts and calculations.

It appeared that Martha did just about everything about the house and cooking the evening meal was just one of her tasks. However, Felix told her to sit down with Amelia at the table while he and Leo served the meal. Leo could see that Martha was looked on more like an old friend and she easily fell into conversation with Amelia. Leo assumed that Martha would be dining with them given the fact that she had earlier set the table for four persons.

Leo sniffed the air in the kitchen and said, "Full marks for aroma," he raised a lid and added, "I'll mash the potatoes." He pierced one with a fork. "They seem to be done to a tee."

"Martha is an excellent cook," Felix said.

"Does she not have a husband to get home to and cook for?"

"Sadly, no, as with Evelyn's husband, Martha's husband was killed in the Boar war. That war took many good men from us, Leo. He was 47 years of age at the time and held the rank of sergeant."

"I assume that as Martha has worked for you for many years that you will have known her husband and I am assuming she came to work here before getting married. Can I ask Martha's surname?"

Felix frowned at Leo. He was confused as to his desire to know a surname he said, "Collins."

Leo could not remember the name Collins being included in his family ancestry, but he could see that the horror of war had visited many in this time after the Boer war. He knew war would

120

take many more in the great 1914-18 war and more yet again in the 1939-45 war. He could never mention such things to anyone in this timeline, though. Instead, he asked, "Can I ask what Martha's maiden name is?"

Felix stopped, frowned in thought and said, "Collins. When you asked the first time, with you referring to a time before Martha was married, I assumed you were requiring her maiden name, Leo. I was just a boy when Martha was betrothed."

So, could you tell me her married name, Felix?"

"Sorry, of course I can. She is Martha Lennox."

Felix didn't realise it, but Lennox was also Leo's surname and the sound of Felix saying "Lennox" plunged Leo into deep thought.

After the meal, Leo excused himself and went for a walk. He decided he had a lot of thinking to do and he thinks better while walking. The air was cold, but he had Felix's long and warm winter coat to protect him from the elements. It would be a family member's birthday the following day, 3rd January, but as they had not been born yet, it would hardly matter now, although they might wonder in prime time why Leo had failed to send a greeting. He doesn't normally send birthday cards, but he would usually send a text or a similar greeting.

Laura always tended to birthday cards and Christmas cards and Leo simply failed to get into the swing of such things and tended to let it slip. He would also send a New Years greeting text close to midnight on the last day of the year. It might appear suspicious that he didn't this year and Laura and the kids might have noticed his car still parked outside their house.

However, as he previously reasoned, they will have assumed it failed to start and Leo called a taxi and, as he locked it before going into Laura's house, it will not appear suspicious. Suspicions might arise, though, should someone phone him about the car without receiving a response.

He didn't go for a walk to think about the car. His mind fell on Martha and her surname would suggest she is a long lost ancestor. He wondered if this would change on her getting married for a second time. Of course, his family are not the only

121

Lennox family in the area, Martha might have no connection to him, and he didn't have Google to look deeper into it. Looking up census records would not help a lot because they will end at 1904, or the closest census to 1904, which would be 1901 and he would need to follow Martha's descent a bit deeper into the 20th century.

If he had some knowledge of his ancestry, he might have a better idea, but it all starts and ends with his aunt whacking him on the head with the tray. She was his dad's sister, so will be a Lennox and possibly directly related to at least Martha's husband.

This line of reasoning might only be relevant, though, if Martha had kids and he could find that out with a simple question.

He didn't have the impression that Martha had a family and so she would have been alone when her husband fell in active service during the boer war.

It was dark long before Leo decided on his walk and the light of discovery failed to make any difference because there was none. Leo decided to leave further thoughts on Martha until he could ask questions or had internet access. Deciding he will have received a 100-year telegram from the Queen or King before even dial-up arrives commercially; he reckoned he might never get to Google some information on Martha.

He called into a shop. He was partial to toffee and the toffee King at the time, according to an advertisement board, was John Mackintosh. Therefore, Leo purchased a pennyworth of Mackintosh's toffee. He slipped a chunk of toffee into his mouth as he left the shop and then slipped his hands into his coat pockets and made a mental note to buy a pair of warm men's gloves at the first opportunity.

Why is it, you could walk for hours without a problem and the second you put a slice of thick, buttery toffee into your mouth, someone stops for a chat? It was Evelyn and she said, "Hello Leo, are you on the way to Amelia and Felix's house?"

Leo found it hard to reply with a mouth full of toffee and he pointed to his mouth and smiled awkwardly as he continued to clear his mouth as quickly as possible. It would take quite a while to get through such a large chunk of toffee, though, and it would be extremely rude to spit it out. He reached for his hanky and used it to cover his mouth while he slipped the toffee, unseen by Evelyn, from mouth to hanky and finally said, "I apologise profusely, I bought some toffee in the shop and –"

"Don't give it another thought," Evelyn said, cutting in. "You should have continued. I enjoy toffee myself."

Leo produced the bag of toffee, opened it, offered it to Evelyn, and said, "Would you like a piece?"

"Best not," Evelyn said, "Otherwise I'll have the same problem talking as you just had."

Leo realised the wisdom of Evelyn's words and he laughed and said, "So you would. That was silly of me. Anyway, now that I can answer, no, I'm not going there and I'm just taking a stroll. I take it you are going to the house to speak to Amelia?"

"That was the intention, but a walk sounds lovely. Would you mind if I joined you?"

Leo did mind and he would prefer her to go on to the house and leave him to walk and think without her beside him. However, what could he say or even do other than smile and tell her to feel free to come if she wished? She did wish and they set off together.

Leo felt awkward. He normally sees a walk with a girl as a way of getting to know her with a romantic view with no damage to his pocket. He had no romantic interest in Evelyn and he had to mentally struggle before any kind of subject worthy of discussion came to mind.

He noticed Evelyn had her hands in a toasty looking fur hand muff, although he didn't know it as a hand muff and referred to it as a hand-warming thing as he commented on how warm it looked.

However, it did look toasty and warm and he had just his pockets and it no longer seemed the right thing to do having his hands in them while walking along with a lady.

"I normally wear mittens in cold weather," Evelyn said. "However, this was one of my Christmas gifts and I thought I should try it out."

Leo decided it gave women an unfair advantage in that they could be holding a weapon like a tea tray and no one would know. Okay, maybe a tea tray would be a bit large to hide inside the muff, but he was happy with the idea that it was unfair, although he kept this thought to himself and simply said, "You have to take whatever measure of protection you can against the weather."

He could have added something about it being the skin of a dead animal, but he decided that the fur trade would not have the same reputation and repulsion in 1905 as it has in some parts of prime time and instead, he said, "It's a natural heat retainer, so it must be warm."

She said, "With it being open at either end, it might not offer the same protection during high winds, but my hands are quite warm."

She partially took one hand out of the muff, and then pushed it back inside and for a second; Leo thought she was going to take hold of his hand in hers to allow him to feel how warm it was. As it was, a small gust of wind had blown her hair into her eyes and she was going to use the hand to brush it back, but another gust of wind solved the problem and she could keep her hand inside its protective wrapping. It would not have happened if she had not forgotten her new hat, although she might have needed to go running after a blow away hat, so maybe everything worked out for the best.

Leo said, "I'm assuming your brother Richard will be at Felix's house later?"

"No, he has to go over a lot of issues with someone and he said it will take right into the small hours. I think it is his European replacement. He will be sailing in the morning, as far as I can gather, and Richard wants to ensure he goes fully equipped mentally."

"I can see the importance in sending him fully briefed on everything because a lot will depend on his performance and Richard must have enormous trust in his abilities."

"I don't understand the business side of things, but it will leave Amelia alone with Felix spending some time with Brenda this evening, so I arranged with Amelia to spend an hour or so with her."

"If you should be with Amelia now, please don't let me hold you back?"

"We didn't arrange a time and I left the house early because Richard was away and I was bored on my own."

Leo was slightly disappointed in her answer with it depriving him of alone time for thoughts and plans, but he refused to allow his disappointment to show and he said, "It must have been extremely boring for you while he was in Europe all that time?"

"It was, but he can't stay at home to entertain me and allow his business to dissolve. He must put the business first, at least until he gets it to where he desires it to be. I was surprised he deputized someone else for Europe and I can only assume Amelia taking ill caused him something of a mental jolt and forced him to review his plans and put her before the business. This is good and it shows how much he cares for her."

Leo had to agree, but the conversation was not going to the place he required it to go. He required it to end to allow him to carry on with his thoughts, but he struggled with deciding on an alternative subject for discussion because so many subjects were not right, such as the death of her husband in the Boer war. Most of what he knew about her was not open for discussion and he had already caused her some tears and desired to avoid doing that again.

He could understand how bored she must have been when she was alone with there not being any TV or other form of home entertainment. It's fine for a family and they could do things together, but what can a woman on her own do to pass an evening? He decided to ask, so he said, "Can I ask how you normally spent the time while Richard was away?"

"Much the same as I do now that he is back. When he is not working, he is normally with Amelia, so I find myself alone quite often anyway. However, while it would be selfish of me to throw myself at the mercy of others by visiting people often, I enjoy reading and that gets me through quite a few hours. I also enjoy crochet work and knitting. I would love to be musical and play the piano, but I am useless, tone-deaf, I am afraid. I am also useless at writing to the level of Amelia and I think she is amazing. I would love to have her talent and ability, but I have to stick to just reading, I am afraid."

"I agree with you and Amelia is an amazing author, although I say this having read just one of her manuscripts and it was unfinished, I'm afraid. But she has a huge talent."

"She allowed you to read one of her books before it was finished?"

"She didn't so much allow me and I'm afraid I read it without her knowledge. I was unaware of her preference of finishing and polishing before allowing even her literary agent to browse through it."

Evelyn paused for thought before saying, "last week, Amelia referred to you as her doctor, now it appears you are not a doctor and are Felix's friend. Was she experiencing a delusion as she fought fever at thinking you were a doctor?"

Leo could easily give a simple "Yes," but he felt he had to be honest without giving too much away and he said, "No, she was not delusional. I came with medication, I kept it in a doctor's medical bag, and this gave her the impression that I was a doctor."

"So, you are not a doctor and are a friend of Felix?"

Leo could not claim to have been a friend of Felix from before Amelia's illness because he met him for the first time on Christmas morning. However, they have since bonded as friends and he felt it was both acceptable and truthful to say, "I am blessed in having such a valued friend, as I can see you also are with Amelia."

Before Evelyn could make a verbal response, Leo added, "There's a coffee house. Let's get a hot coffee to warm us up a shade."

"Could I have tea?" Evelyn said as they hurried along.

Leo was unsure if they would have tea in a 1905 coffee house, but he decided Evelyn would know better than he would and he said, "Sure you can."

Within seconds, they were sitting down and already feeling the heat from a coal fire nearby. Leo was tempted to go to the fire and turn his back to it and so introduce his posterior to its warming glow, but he satisfied himself with unbuttoning his coat as Evelyn removed her muff to leave her hands free to unbutton her coat. Close by was a coat hanger and Leo took Evelyn's coat and was hanging both coats up as a server arrived.

Leo set down and said, "The lady will have tea, and I'll have coffee if that is okay." He then looked at Evelyn and added, "Would you like something to eat?"

"No, thank you," Evelyn said.

The coffee shop was less than thronging, most people would be at home enjoying or having within the past hour, enjoyed a meal after a hard day at work, and so the coffee house was quiet, perfect for a young couple to chat and get to know each other. Leo immediately decided it might have been a mistake, but he was cold and the thought of hot coffee was too alluring to ignore and he was beginning to find Evelyn's company more enjoyable than he would have imagined anyway. However, with there being a break in the conversation as they took their coats off, a new subject for conversation would need an introduction.

Leo said, "Can I ask if you work, as in having a job?"

"Yes, I work, although not for my brother. I like to keep my independence."

"Good for you. What do you do for a living?"

Evelyn looked away coyly and said, "Do you think it might snow?"

Leo could detect that he had asked a question that Evelyn preferred not to answer and she appeared to be slightly embarrassed over it. He pondered on a job that would embarrass her into silence and quite a number came to mind, although he could tell she was not the kind of woman who would fall for entrapment in most.

As Leo decided on another new subject for conversation, Evelyn turned to him and said, "I am a domestic worker, Leo. It's the lowest rung in the ladder, but I got the job without anyone's help and, while my brother has offered me much more working for him, I like to work at a job that I got by myself and not through being Richard's sister."

She then once more averted her gaze and looked away as though with shame.

Leo said, "I'm a bus driver back home."

Evelyn looked back, frowned and said, "A bus driver?"

"Yes, a bus it's similar in function to a tram, only it's propelled along by an engine, what you might call a horseless carriage."

"You drive a horseless tram? Does it work in the same way as Felix's motor vehicle?"

"Yes, it's exactly like Felix's car, only on a larger scale. Therefore, I'm a tram driver back home. There is nothing grand about that and it pays me a wage that I can live on. It's the same with your job, it might not be grand, but it pays a wage you can live on and that is all that's needed from a job."

"I agree. People like Amelia look on me for who I am and not for what I do for a living."

Leo realised he had given her too much information and he should not mention any of this to anyone, but he was fed up with deceit and needed to be honest. Evelyn didn't seem to suspect anything out of the ordinary anyway and he needed to let her know that he didn't look down on her chosen occupation.

He desired her also to know that he is from humble stock and only got a rung up the ladder with the office job due to Mr Weatherford having such deep gratitude to Felix in needing to pay back in a small way with the job.

The tea and coffee arrived, they thanked the server, and as they lifted their cups, Evelyn said, "Would you have a problem with me asking you a personal question, Leo?"

Leo took a sip of coffee and it was fortunate he took his sip before he said, "Certainly, ask anything," because Evelyn's next words might have caused him to choke on his coffee.

She asked, "Are you a time traveller?"

Chapter 11

It appeared to Leo on seeing Martha setting the table for four and then going to the cellar to speak with Amelia that she must be joining him, Felix and Amelia again for a meal before going home. This suited him well, it would allow him the opportunity to talk to her because there was not much opportunity during the day with him at work, and by the time he got home, Martha had almost finished her days' work and had almost completed the last task of the day with preparing the evening meal.

Felix arrived home a few moments after Leo, Amelia was still in her workroom in the cellar, and Felix invited Leo to join him in the living room while Martha came from the kitchen and brought tea in for them, and took a cup down to Amelia. "I think five should do it," she said to Felix before going down to the cellar and Leo assumed this meant the dinner would take just a further five minutes to complete the cooking process.

"Did you have a good day," Felix asked?

"Yes," Leo replied. "I'm getting more familiar with everything and this makes it all a lot easier and more enjoyable."

"That's good. I knew you would settle in quickly and if you ever face any problems that cause you a desire to work elsewhere, there will always be a place for you with me. This is not a charity reach out, it's simply me recognising your potential and having a desire to utilise it."

Leo smiled and said, "I would love to work for you, but would have a huge problem taking a wage for it."

"You wouldn't be working for me, you would be working with me and I am sure you would deserve your wage. Mr Weatherford told me he is more than pleased with your performance so far, so I'm sure if you have the desire, you will go far with him."

Leo guessed that Clive Weatherford would give such impressions out of loyalty to Felix, but he did find the second day more pleasurable than the first and he was more confident now that he would be able to handle his workload."

Felix heard Martha coming up the stairs from the cellar and called out, "Martha, I'm sure you've been on your feet all day. Come in here and sit down. I'll see to the rest of the dinner."

"I'll give a hand like last night," Leo said.

Martha popped her head into the room and said, "I'll just get my tea first, Felix."

When he heard her in the kitchen, Leo said to Felix, "Does she always have a meal here before going home?"

"It would be unfair her cooking our evening meal and then going home and having to cook her own, so she joins us most evenings. It would be nice to see her settled with a male companion, but until then, Amelia and I enjoy her company. Amelia was telling me that while I was with Miss Paterson, or I should say, Brenda, last evening, you arrived back from your walk with Evelyn at your side?"

"Yes, we met while I was out for a stroll and she was coming here. We stopped off at a coffee house and she asked –"

Martha entered with her tea and Leo cut off his conversation with Felix to say to Martha, "Has Amelia decided to stay down there?"

"She said she will be up shortly," Martha said, she sat down and added, "She is just clearing the clutter away from her desk first. You know how she dislikes arriving at a messy desk, Felix, and the best way to avoid this is to tidy things up before leaving it."

Felix rose to his feet, tea in hand, and said, "I think it's time for me to do my small bit in getting the meal onto the table."

Leo rose and said to Martha, "I hope you don't take it personally that we leave the room so soon after you arrive?"

Amelia arrived and said, "I shall entertain Martha while you men tend to the meal, now off you both go."

As Felix set his tea down and lifted what Leo took to be an oven glove, Leo could recall once hearing or reading that a baker with the surname of Mitt developed the oven glove in Texas back in the 1870s. Leo was sure this was a joke, so he checked it out and was surprised to discover it was a fact.

Felix adorned the oven mitt and retrieved a pie from the oven. Leo moved close and sniffed the air just above the pie as Felix placed it down on top of the table.

"It smells delicious," Leo said. "Whatever you pay Martha, it's not enough."

"I agree, Leo. Her crust is amazing and I could eat it without the filling. However, in its entirety, it's a culinary triumph. Nonetheless, I think you were about to tell me something that Evelyn had asked just as Martha arrived in the room and interrupted you?"

Leo transferred his attention to a boiling pot of potatoes and lifted a fork to pierce a couple to test them as he said, "Evelyn asked if I was a time traveller."

"I trust you responded with a small fabrication. I prefer honesty at all times, but on this occasion, honesty could cause more problems than you could handle with comfort."

Felix took a joint from the oven and reached for a carving knife to carve it up and Leo emptied the water from the pot of potatoes and looked for something to use for mashing them.

Leo smiled and said, "Are you suggesting I should lie? You surprise me. I just laughed as though I could not possibly take

131

such a comment seriously. However, how could she even suspect such a thing?"

Felix looked directly into Leo's eyes and said, "I assure you, she didn't hear anything about time travel from me. I cannot explain it, though. I'll question Amelia, but I don't think she would have given any clues."

"I believe you and I apologise if I gave the impression that I suspected you had said something to Evelyn, but it has baffled me how she could pluck such a question out of the air."

"Did you not ask her?"

"No, I got off the subject with great speed, Felix."

Leo paused to ponder before adding, "The other day when she asked if I was a Clairvoyant, I said, 'No, I'm a time traveller.' I'm sure you reasoned I was joking, though."

Felix stopped carving and frowned in thought for a moment before saying, "She might have mentioned it to Amelia when they spoke last evening."

"Don't broach it with Amelia. She might not be strong enough for an interrogation session so soon after her illness."

"I would, of course, have been discreet and sympathetic to my sisters' illness."

"I know, you have been an amazing brother to her and I know you would not have said anything to stress her out, I mean to cause her stress. I'll ask Evelyn. I should have asked her last night, but it came as such a shock that I had problems thinking with any kind of coherence."

"Richard will be here later and if Evelyn has been worrying about time travellers in the vicinity, she might have mentioned it to him."

Leo continued in thought as he mashed the potatoes.

Felix said, "There appears to be another matter on your mind, Leo."

Leo smiled and said, "You are beginning to know me a little too well, Felix. You know a lot about me, but you don't know my surname. It's Lennox, the same as Martha's surname. I think she might be an ancestor."

"Ah, that will be why you questioned me on her surname. Do you have the means to check this in your own timeline?"

132

"Yes, with one hundred per cent accuracy, Felix, thanks to the discovery of D.N.A.."

"Is this D.N.A. used in conjunction with your Google?"

"It's a science thing that I would need to know more about to help me explain it better." He smiled and added, "I could explain it after five minutes with Google, though."

"It sounds like this Google has a built-in information base?"

"The internet is itself an information base. Its introduction to the world was or will be at the end of the century as The Information superhighway. Google is one of the search engines it links to and you just type in your requirements, and it searches its database and gives you the answer almost immediately. It also connects people via email in a similar way that the telephone does. You could send a message with photos to a person at the other side of the world, and they would receive it almost instantly."

"This is one of the reasons why I accept you are of the future. No one in this time could dream up such, Leo – not even H.G. Wells."

Leo produced a mock proud smile as he finished off mashing the potatoes and said, "H.G. Wells, he's just an amateur."

They both laughed and then Felix put a halt to his laughter as he looked over at the potatoes' Leo had mashed and said, "Oh dear, Amelia requested we should refrain from mashing the potatoes this evening and would have them whole with a knob of butter."

Leo looked up in shock and said, "You're joking!"

Felix smiled and carried on carving.

In the early twentieth century, workers never see the light of day with it being dark when they go to work and dark when they travel home at the end of the day. This was almost true in Leo's case, although he can look out through a window when he forgets what daylight looks like. Unlike the ones who work in the mines. There are no windows in the mines and the coal miners must have the most dismal job of all, he decided.

Before arriving in this time, he would have argued that the chimney sweep has the worse job imaginable, but at least they get to see the light of day, although it was different for their junior, often just a child of barely twelve years of age. It was worse during the black sooty days of the seventeen and eighteen hundreds when "climbing boys" of all ages ascended and descended the larger and wider chimneys of the affluent to get to the areas where their brush could not reach. At times, they found themselves sold to the task like a slave by a needy or greedy parent, often to ensure the survival of other members of the family.

Leo decided he was lucky to have a job in a brightly lit and comfortably heated office. Even though he was not enormously suited to the work, it didn't impair or reduce the number of years he hopes to live and the level of health he hopes to maintain, with lungs free from coal dust and his body from the oft-times fatal accident.

However, as Leo's first week progressed in his new job, it got less boring as he found his way through the paperwork. While it didn't diminish his thoughts of other things like not seeing his kids, or the black hell others in other occupations had to endure, it gave him a means of paying Felix back for his kindness.

He assumed his pay would be monthly and it was a pleasant surprise that he received a wage on the first Friday without even the need of a lying week. It meant he could begin immediately to pay for his keep and allow himself the pleasure of a Saturday stroll to the local.

"Are you going for a walk, Leo," Amelia enquired when she saw him suited and booted for the outside weather.

Leo didn't want to tell her he was going to the pub and it suddenly seemed vulgar in the presence of one as innocent as Amelia. He quickly thought and prepared a lie to cover up his iniquitous desires for a pint, but decided honesty should prevail.

He replied, "I thought I should test the local ale in a quiet and comfortable establishment. Would you care to join me?"

He was more surprised than Amelia was. If he had thought about it, he never would dare to invite her, but he didn't think about it and the words just slipped from his unguarded mouth as honesty prevailed. Then he hastily pondered and added, "If you feel up to it."

"I am not as fragile as you men appear to think I am," she said. "I would love to join you. Could you give me a moment to change into something more protective against the weather?"

She would be bored hanging about the house all day, Leo reasoned as he sat down with the knowledge of women changing always takes quite a while and he might as well spend this time seated. He pushed out an evil smile as he thought about Richard bored mindless at his sister Evelyn's house. He should not gloat because boredom had visited him in great measure and will do so again; with their not being much in the way of home entertainment in 1905.

He lifted a book and glanced at the cover. It seemed to be about the Pankhurst sisters and Women's Social and Political Union, or W.S.P.U.. The book was entitled *Deeds, not words* and Leo was confident he had never before come across this book. He guessed it belonged to Amelia and he didn't realise she would be into this kind of thing, although she was a woman, so why not.

Leo didn't have as long as he surmised to wait until Amelia arrived suitably dressed with much wool and fur to battle the elements. Leo was aware that it was not his birthday, although also aware that it felt like his birthday, Christmas and the summer holidays all rolled into one glorious walk and for the next hour or so, Amelia would be all his.

As they walked away from the house, Leo said, "Are you a suffragette?"

Amelia frowned and said, "I would be in the position to address that more fully if I knew what a suffragette was, Leo."

The word suffragette hadn't been introduced to the vocabulary of the populous yet and Leo had made his first blunder and he said, "It's women's suffrage. I saw your book about the Pankhurst sisters from Manchester."

"Oh, I see. Emmeline got me interested in the work and I became friendly with her daughter Christabel, who is also a member along with her two sisters."

"I would suggest you take care, Amelia. Disruption and some civil disobedience might be the order of the day now, but I have a feeling they might get slightly more militant as time goes on. I don't mean they will take to the gun and bomb, although there might be such a campaign for a couple of years from 1912, instigated by the Women's Social and Political Union. I'm sure you wouldn't get into that, but they will expect you to become militant in a very un-ladylike manner. However, you will be pleased to know the result will be women getting the vote and one day in the far off future they will win full equality with men and enjoy the same wage for doing the same work as men."

Amelia smiled and said, "The prophet Leo has spoken. The same pay structure as a man for doing the same work would be an amazing breakthrough."

Leo knew it would take seventy years for equal pay to come fully into force, so he decided not to dwell on it and he said, "We should all be paid for the quality and quantity of our work and not on anything else. Nonetheless, you might already have equality as an author and get paid as a writer and not as a woman, so how is the book coming on?"

"I should have it completed in a short time, then I shall put it away and forget about it for a time before getting it back onto my desk and polishing it up. However, as you have already read more than three quarters of it, I'll do something I have never done before and will allow you to read the final couple of chapters before it goes into hibernation."

"I'll look forward to that."

"Firstly, though, you must tell me how it happened that you read it. Felix has told me it's all innocent and without guile, so there will not be a reason for non-disclosure.

Amelia smiled in a cheeky, cunning way at Leo and he returned her smile and said, "That would be an even longer story and I'll relate it one day, but sadly, you are not ready for it just yet."

"I was once told I was not ready for Lydia Becker."

Leo found a direct comment on this hard to come by because he didn't recognise the name, Lydia Becker. All he could muster was "Oh, so you are a Beckerite?"

"Firstly you introduce me to the word suffragette, and now Beckerite? I am learning an entirely new language with you. Lydia is truly missed."

Leo was guessing Lydia Becker was involved with the suffrage movement. Amelia's obvious sadness and speaking of missing her suggested she had possibly emigrated or died. However, Leo decided to steer the conversation in a different direction and he said, "You seem much stronger today and appear to have completely defeated your illness."

"I feel wonderful and having Richard back home has been quite a tonic."

Speaking about the amazing Richard was not the direction in which Leo desired the conversation to go and he said, "As he will be busy this evening, have you had any thoughts on how you will pass time?"

"Yes, Evelyn and I have decided to get the train to London and go to the New Theatre. A new play has opened, The Scarlet Pimpernel."

Leo nodded his head and said, "They seek him here, they seek him there, Those Frenchies seek him everywhere. Is he in heaven? Is he in hell? Where is that damn elusive Pimpernel?"

"You appear to be well informed on the Pimpernel. Have you read the book?"

Leo didn't achieve the level of surprise he had aimed for and amazement should have emanated from Amelia after his quote. However, he was merely showing off and ended up receiving a valuable lesson.

Amelia continued, "While on the subject of books, have you had time to peruse the one I recommended, Nostromo by Joseph Conrad?"

Leo was troubled in that an honest response might hinder the conversation he was enjoying with Amelia because, after reading less than a chapter, he realised that Nostromo was of the communist persuasion and didn't fit in with his views. He was fine with others not sharing his views, but he was also fine with him not sharing there's and he was at variance with almost everything Joseph Conrad had alluded to in the opening chapter. Leo plundered the depths of his mind in search of a response that Amelia would not take as an insult, or furthermore as an attack on her or her views.

"Do you have any plans for this evening," Amelia asked.

"Felix will be with Brenda, so it looks like I'll be alone."

"Why not come with us?"

If Amelia had suggested him going with just her, Leo would have grasped the opportunity firmly, but he was not so keen on being the only man on a female evening out. Evelyn being there made it an easier decision than otherwise would have been the case.

He said, "That's very kind of you, but I wouldn't dream of interrupting your evening with Evelyn and I can only say I hope you both enjoy the production."

"You will be alone all evening."

"I'll go across town and see if the time portal is open." Leo quickly realised he should not have mentioned the time portal even in a joke, and he quickly said, "The time portal is a gentleman's club."

Amelia raised her eyebrows and said, "Where gentlemen go to get away from their lady folk to a place where a lady would not be permitted entrance?"

"Well, I wouldn't be permitted to attend one of your suffrage meetings."

Amelia smiled and said, "You could go, but men simply would not understand the program."

It was not as tiresome returning from what would one day become Laura's house, because this time he had money in his pocket and he jumped on a tram. He wondered more than ever if he would see the kids again. Mike will no doubt have tried to make contact and will be wondering what had become of him, might even have informed the police.

He could forget his plans of taking some time off work to get the B&B established. With not returning to work after Christmas, he possibly no longer had a job - at least, not in prime time. He still has his job in 1905, though, so at least he would survive if he continues to fail to get back to prime time.

He cut short his tram journey. He had no real desire to sit in an empty house, so he went to the pub. Amelia wouldn't be with him this time and he might not know anyone there, but at least there would be faces and noise and people are normally not averse to talking to a stranger in the pub after they have had a few.

The Saturday evening entertainment was not to Leo's taste and it was not only the first time he had heard *Always leave them laughing when you say goodbye*, but it was also a first for everyone because it was the first time the singer had performed it. Before beginning, he announced that George Cohan wrote it in the year just past, 1904. Leo wished he had written it in the year to come, 1906. That way he would not be listening to it now.

The old song and awful singer notwithstanding, Leo decided to stay for a while, although, not long because, even though there were quite a few people, it felt no different from an empty pub. Rather than his former thoughts being the case of everyone being talkative with the alcohol, the fact remained that everyone was with someone else, apart from him.

The man next to him seemed friendly, but how could he strike up a conversation when the man was out with his lady. He was sure the man's wife or girlfriend would not appreciate Leo monopolising the airways around them with his conversation.

Leo took his time over his drink and left without ordering a second one. The streets seemed eerily quiet after the noise of the pub and darkness had descended. It only needed a cloud of smog to give the appearance of an old Jack the Ripper film. That would not have been a problem for Leo because he was fanatical about the Jack the Ripper theme, and has been since he went on a Jack the Ripper walk through the streets where Jack did his dirty deeds, although the modern cars and double-glazing spoiled it immensely. This year, 1905, offered a much closer backdrop to the original Whitechapel of 1888.

It was seventeen years after Jack the Ripper and the top hat and tails was mostly retired and stored for wedding hire. This fact might have expanded Leo's surprise at seeing a formally dressed man alighting from a Hansom safety cabriolet or cab. Leo had noticed that the man had to pay his fare to the driver via a small hatch in the roof of the cab before the driver released him from the cab. He decided modern taxi drivers could learn something from this to help them deal with fare dodgers.

Leo's attention was drawn by the man's bag because it was similar to the one Mike had bought him one Christmas, so it was obvious the man was a doctor and was visiting one of his more affluent patients, judging by the house.

Leo said, "Good evening, Doctor Brown."

The doctor stopped, looked and said, "Ah, its Mr Bennett's friend, is it not? Good evening, sir, are you out for a walk?"

"Yes, doctor Brown. Amelia and her friend, or soon to be sister-in-law Evelyn has gone to the theatre and Felix is spending some time with Miss Paterson."

Doctor Brown frowned and echoed, "Miss Paterson?"

"Yes, she's the new love interest in Felix's life."

"Good for Felix, and not before time, I should add. Miss Bennett has made remarkable progress. Might I ask if you have further stocks of that amazing medication?"

"I'm afraid not, and I have no way of getting any more at the moment."

"Such a shame, but I wish you a pleasant evening as I have an ill man to help recover to full fitness."

"Of course, good night, doctor Brown."

"Tell Felix I shall call in and see Miss Bennett soon. Good evening."

Leo walked on as Doctor Brown went up the drive to the house. As they spoke a moment before, Leo could hear the horses' hoofs scraping and clicking on the cobblestone as the driver took the Hansom cab to its next passenger. Leo deduced from this that Doctor Brown foresaw his attendance with the ill man as being a long one by virtue of a short visit making it more sensible to ask the driver to wait.

Replacing the sounds of the horses' hoofs, the clickity-clack of a pair of man's size thirteen hobnail boots echoed through the darkness of the evening. The man appeared to be extremely fit and agile, muscular too. Leo didn't fear for his safety, though, because clutching the man's arm was a woman.

He could tell, even from a distance in the dark that she was a woman, due to the long dress she wore, which protruded out from the bottom of her heavy winter coat. Therefore, she was either a woman or one of the world's first public transvestites.

140

Either way, he decided he was safe and he walked on and pondered on what to do when he got back to Felix and Amelia's house. He could listen to some music, but he knew he would not enjoy that. Neither would he enjoy reading the book Amelia had loaned him. He could borrow one of Felix's books, though.

If he even had his phone and a pair of earphones, he could listen to the MP3s he has downloaded to it. He could listen to them without the earphones, but the sound would be rather tinny if he had his phone, although it was in the car in prime time.

Most things were in prime time and, if he needed to, he had no way of proving he was from the future and only had his house and car keys and wallet in 1905. His bankcard could not exist in 1905 because it was plastic and plastic; even in its early form of Bakelite was not about in this time. However, would that be enough to prove he was from the future?

It didn't matter anyway, he decided, because those who matter believe him and he doesn't need proof.

A book would have to do and he would browse through Felix's collection for a suitable form of entertainment.

As the couple drew closer and the lamplight shone down on them, the man said hello to Leo and Leo said, "Good evening." He then turned his attention to the woman to give her an equal salutation when the lamp fully illuminated her face. It was a face he recognised, a face he saw every morning when he woke from his slumber during his years of marriage. He could not understand it, and neither could he deny that the woman facing him on the street in 1905 was his wife Laura!

Chapter 12

Leo was pleased to see the end of the day, a day that marked the beginning of his second week working at the colliery. The work didn't tax his mind, but he was happy to get away because there were long spells of idleness and he had too much time to think about the kids. It was just a couple of weeks since he wished them a Happy Christmas and administered medication to his son Peter. He felt guilty because he spent most of the visit with Peter and just looked in quickly on his daughter Lydia.

Will that be their last memory of their dad?

He didn't have a choice, and he accepted it was important to get the medication to Amelia, although it's also important to be with his family again and thoughts of them being so far away in time made it a very long Monday.

His first Monday was equally long. Maybe he was experiencing Monday morning blues. It felt worse than mere blues, though. It felt more like full-blown depression. He decided this was probably normal giving the circumstances of possibly never seeing his kids again, and he reasoned he might experience these same emotions every Monday because projects at work seemed to come slowly to him on Monday and this, in turn, made the hands of the clock move slowly, which gave him more time to think.

He decided it could become a vicious circle which he would defeat by Friday only to be presented with a new portion of hell the following Monday.

As was becoming the norm, Leo helped Felix plate-up the meal that Martha cooked while Martha and Amelia chatted in the living room. Leo realised that when Martha was not there to do the cooking and cleaning, etc, Felix always did it. That was understandable when Amelia was ill, but he reasoned she was now well enough to do more than sit on her bum in the cellar writing. Felix didn't seem to have a problem with it, though.

Beef expertly prepped and perfectly cooked helped Leo forget the day he had as he sniffed the air and said, "It smells like we're in for another treat, Felix."

Felix said, "It's all the more acceptable after not having had such aromas' to enjoy all weekend. I didn't get to talk to you much over the weekend. Did you do anything special? Amelia told me she invited you to the theatre."

"I couldn't go due to her desiring a friend's night out with Evelyn. I would have felt like a gatecrasher."

Felix frowned and said, "A gatecrasher? Amelia and Evelyn would both have been pleased for you to join them. It was a last-minute decision to go, so you would not have interrupted a long-standing appointment."

"It would have looked odd, though, Felix, going to the theatre with two women."

"Should I tell the ladies to make it just Evelyn next time?"

Leo frowned up through his eyebrows at Felix and sharpened the carving knife on the honing steel and Felix laughed. Leo placed the honing steel down and picked up the meat fork to hold the beef steady while he carved it and Felix got busy mashing the potatoes.

Leo said, "Oh, your mashing the potatoes, not having them whole with a knob of butter?"

Felix smiled and said, "Ignoring the possibility of Jack the Ripper in my kitchen with a sharpened carving knife in his hand, did you enjoy the weekend, considering you were alone for it after stubbornly refusing to go to the theatre?"

Leo smiled and said, "Sad individuals can always find their own entertainment, Felix. I just remembered, I met Doctor Brown and he asked me to tell you he will call in and see Amelia soon."

"Amelia is now almost back to normal, but it will be nice to have a chat with him. It's a pity it was Doctor Brown you bumped into and you didn't meet a lady."

"I did. I bumped into my wife Laura shortly after speaking to the doctor. It was not actually my wife and I think it was her great-grandmother. I could not tell the difference, though. I have never seen her great-grandmother, but I saw a photo of her gran and I remember thinking how alike they were and perhaps they got their looks from the woman I saw. It gave me quite a start."

"Did you have a conversation with her?"

"No, she was with a huge bloke with muscles. He seemed pleasant, but his size forced me to move swiftly on after saying hello."

Felix laughed.

Leo continued, "Laura's great-grandfather was a boxer and if the one I saw was the same, I had no desire to become a temporary punch bag for him. It looked like he was wearing his boxing gloves, but it was just his bare hands, they were massive and I'd hate to be struck with one."

Felix stopped mashing the potatoes as his laughter took on a higher volume and he gripped onto the worktop for support as Leo sighed and sliced through the beef.

Leo was relaxed in the living room with a book when Amelia and Evelyn returned after a walk to the baker's shop. Amelia said, "Enjoying your book, Leo? What is it?"

Leo turned the front cover toward Amelia to allow her to see the title and she said, "Ah, Extracts from Adam's Diary by Mark Twain. I have read a few of his works. I remember reading his

144

Adventures of Huckleberry Finn when I was much younger. I found the strange southern dialects he used to be quite confusing, but I enjoyed it. Is he still alive?"

Leo sniggered and said, "Well, it appears he was last year because this book was published then."

"He must be close on eighty years of age," Evelyn suggested.

Leo had to remain silent on the matter, but he was aware that Mark Twain died, or will die, in his seventy-fourth year in 1910. He nodded his head in agreement with Evelyn, though, because he had previously mentioned to Amelia things that he could not possibly know and he reasoned that giving detail pertaining to Mark Twain's future demise would be a bit much, even with Amelia knowing something of Leo being out of his own time.

Amelia and Evelyn had already taken their coats off before entering the room, so Evelyn sat down close to Leo and Amelia said to Leo, "We got some delicious pastry at the bakery. Would you care for one along with a hot cup of tea?"

Leo remembered Amelia making tea once before, but it was such a rare event that he had to accept and he said, "Please, that would be lovely."

Evelyn prepared to rise, but Amelia put out a hand to stop her and she said, "Sit where you are, Evelyn, you walked all the way here before we went to the baker's shop, so you must be exhausted. I shall get the tea."

Amelia left the room and Leo felt the need to close his book and place it on a nearby table. He could not help thinking this was a deliberate ploy by Amelia to force Evelyn and him together and he was far from happy about it, but he had to be gracious and he thickened his graciousness with a smile at Evelyn. After all, he had said "yes" to the tea, so lesson learned.

Evelyn could only respond to Leo's benevolent grin with an embarrassed and coy attempt at a smile. She too was suspicious of Amelia's motivation and it appeared to her too that Amelia was attempting to get her and Leo together. Perhaps the way she had previously spoken to Amelia about Leo forced Amelia into this obvious subterfuge with the tea. It embarrassed Evelyn to the heights of her needing to rush out of the room, but the same

145

embarrassment held her where she was with her coy smile and she averted her gaze away from Leo and aimed it at the floor.

The silence became awkward and Leo knew he would have to say something, anything. Asking if she had read any of Mark Twain's work would be silly, though. She had mentioned him, so obviously was aware of him and had probably read something in the course of her reading experience because Mark Twain will have been writing for a good chunk of her life, if not all of it.

"Did you enjoy your walk to the bakers' shop?" Leo asked. He instantly realised that this was as silly as asking if she had read Mark Twain. It was too late, though; the words had left his mouth and entered Evelyn's ears.

"Yes, I quite enjoyed it," she said.

Leo nodded his head and plundered his mind for something else to say. It would have helped if Evelyn had given a longer response and ended it with a question for Leo to respond to. He found his last discussion with her much easier, but he didn't have the feeling then of her being thrust onto him. He said, "I never got to ask you how you enjoyed the theatre. The Crimson Pimpernel wasn't it?"

"The Scarlet Pimpernel," Evelyn said, correcting Leo.

Leo knew it was scarlet and not crimson, but he was attempting to lighten the atmosphere and form a smile on Evelyn's face. It didn't work and she remained without a smile, after looking up briefly, set her gaze back down to the floor before she looked up once more, and directed her gaze in to Leo's eye line.

She took a deep breath to compose herself and said, "I have to apologise, Leo. Amelia's motivation is obvious and you are as embarrassed as I am.

That had the effect of taking the awkwardness right out of the conversation and Leo sat forward and said, "You have no reason to apologise and you certainly have no reason to be embarrassed with me. You are correct, though, and I was embarrassed, but I know Amelia is acting out of the command of her heart and means well."

Evelyn responded, "She is a good woman, political views aside, and my brother is blessed in having won her affection, but

146

I can see you have no interest in me and she should not attempt to force us together in this manner."

Leo had zero desire to insult Evelyn by agreeing that he has no interest in her because it was not true. He did have an interest and he decided who would not because she was quite pretty in many respects. However, he was visiting from a far off time and was unsure of his future in this time.

Leo said, "You are an extremely pleasant woman and have no need for Amelia's strategy and I'm surprised you haven't been scooped up by a man before now. However, fate will direct both of us to whomever it may be we are to share the remainder of our lives with."

Evelyn held her gaze on Leo as a tear slipped from her eye. Once the tear arrived, she directed her gaze once more to the floor. Leo is normally strong-willed, but seldom at the sight of a tear and it forced him to rise from his armchair and go to her. He took a hanky from his pocket, crouched down before her, took one of her hands in his and gently dabbed her eyes with the hanky, and said, "There's no need for tears."

This was the second time Leo had need of a hanky for Evelyn, although he was aware of a huge change from this and the last time. At the other time he handed the hanky to her and turned his attention to the painting on the opposite wall, while this time he was right in the war zone and looking directly into her tear-filled eyes and wondering why he seemed to have this effect on her.

"I'm sorry," she said.

"There's no need for apologies either. Would you like to go for a ten-mile run?"

Evelyn frowned in confusion at Leo and echoed "A ten-mile run?"

Leo smiled and said, "Not after you walking all the way here from your house and then to the baker's and back. I was joking about the ten-mile run and said it to remove the need for tears and it seems to have worked. If it hadn't worked, I might have felt the need to tickle you."

Evelyn smiled and said, "How strange, yet how effective." She laughed and added, "You are quite unlike anyone I have ever known previously."

"You said that without actually knowing me. If you would like to get to know me, perhaps you would care to join me for an evening of entertainment or a meal?"

Leo had not meant to ask Evelyn out on what she could only perceive as a date and he didn't know what made him ask, but the words were out and he could not recall them and could only await her response.

The response was not immediate because Evelyn initially had to deal with a certain amount of surprise bordering on shock. However, she finally said, "Yes, I would love to join you."

Lying on top of the bed and looking toward the ceiling, Leo could not work out why he had asked Evelyn out. He had no desire to take her out, but his actions often border on the ridiculous when attempting to cheer a disheartened person up.

His desire to cheer Evelyn up had resulted in self-depression and he decided he needed something in the way of medication and he wondered if some good and kind person in medical science had formulated Diazepam yet.

He didn't have a problem with Evelyn and she would be quite a catch for someone, but not he, Leo decided. He arrived at this time with Amelia on his mind and he cannot simply change this due to Amelia not being available to him. He would like to see Evelyn find someone special, but that someone was not him and he would have to treat their evening out as being friends getting together for a one-off occasion and he would certainly not strive for a repetition.

The question remained of where he could take her. A meal would be nice, although perhaps over intimate. Cinema, he concluded, would consist of a viewing of still photos in a flick that would give the impression of animation but without audio. That might be an amazing experience for someone from 1905, but for him, it would be boring in the extreme.

He pondered on the merits of an evening of musical entertainment, but the music was as much a backward glance in 1905 as cinema and he had already sampled enough from Felix and Amelia's gramophone collection. The only thing left was the theatre, Evelyn had already seen the latest production with

Amelia, sitting through a repeat would not be very exciting for her, and he didn't think he would enjoy it either.

He could take her for a walk, but that would smack of his youth when he didn't have any money to take a girl out and he was sure that walking the streets in the cold would not inject her with a lot of enthusiasm. He had to backtrack through the list and the only real option was a meal in a choice restaurant.

Leo could not help noticing how good Evelyn looked as the host showed them to their table. Leo had hired a Hansom cab and had picked up Evelyn at her house and it was dark, so he had not given Evelyn much eye time until then. He decided she was pleasing to the eye, though, so much so that he was displeased that it was 1905 and he felt cheated of the joy of showing her off to his prime time friends.

The host pulled a chair out for Evelyn and Leo waited until she had set down before himself sitting down facing her. It reminded him of the dinner at Felix and Amelia's house when he was seated facing her and her brother Richard was seated facing Amelia and went round to her side of the table to propose marriage. That one act ruined the meal for Leo.

The host said, "I'll send the waiter to you when you have had time to get settled. Enjoy your meal, sir, madam." Leo thanked him and the host left.

Leo said, "I almost left my wallet in my overcoat. That would have caused a problem or two when paying for the meal. I wonder if they would have dragged me into the kitchen to wash the dishes."

Evelyn laughed and said, "I am sure they would have allowed you to go to the cloakroom and get your wallet."

"So, you're saying you wouldn't have offered to pay?"

Evelyn blurted out an accidental additional laugh and covered her mouth with her hand, looked around and said, "Excuse me, Leo, how embarrassing."

"Laughter is good, it means you're relaxed and prepared to enjoy the evening. Do you have a preference for wine?"

"Not really, do you?"

"No, should we just order house red?"

149

Evelyn pondered before saying, "I don't have a strict preference on the label, but could we have white? Red wine doesn't always agree with me."

"I see, so you tend to get into an argument with red? White it will be then. I was going to have beef, but will have chicken to go with the white."

"Now I feel guilty. Please feel free to have beef, I'll have red wine."

Leo smiled and said, "I hadn't decided on beef and will peruse the menu before deciding."

"I said it before and I'll say it again, you are quite unlike anyone I have ever known previously."

"I hope you mean that in a nice way."

Evelyn smiled and said, "Perhaps."

Leo smiled and said, "You are unlike anyone I have ever known."

The waiter arrived and said, "Would you like to order now, sir?"

Leo didn't expect him to arrive so soon at their table and if he had paid attention, he would have noticed that they have not even had time to look at the menu. He didn't have a desire for himself or Evelyn to feel they should rush in their choice of meal, so he said, "Could you give us five minutes to have a look at the menu?"

The waiter said, "Certainly, sir, please let me know when you are ready to order."

Leo was not at all happy with the waiter thus far, but for Evelyn's sake, he would not make an issue out of it.

He said, "They must have double booked and will need this table soon. Therefore, take your time." He smiled mischievously at Evelyn and she smiled back in the same manner.

The first taste of the meal took the waiters earlier hurried approach out of Leo's mind. He was highly pleased, although he kept his pleasure to himself. He thought that spending an evening talking about the meal would be boring for Evelyn, so he chewed it into something his stomach could better digest before swallowing and then he said, "How long have you known Amelia and Felix?"

Leo's timing was less than perfect because he asked his question while Evelyn also tested her teeth on the meal and she chewed with as much feminine grace as she could muster until she was able to swallow and offer a response of "A very long time. I was at primary school with them both."

"I get it, with them being twins; they would be the same age and so be in the same class."

"It was a small school, consisting of one room and it had various age groups."

Leo had to remind himself again that he was in 1905, and things can often be different in this time from prime time. He knew there were schools as large as those in his prime time, but there were also many small school houses and the kids would have been issued with a slate as opposed to a family of jotters, exercise books etc.

He said, "Would I be right in assuming your brother Richard attended this school too?"

"Strangely, no he didn't. He was born before me. He had begun his education before we moved to a new house. Our parents didn't wish to disrupt his education, so they decided he should stay on there while I went to a school closer to our new home. Fortunately for Richard, while his school was further from our new house than mine, it was not impossibly far and he was able to walk there easily."

"Were you friendly with Amelia while at school?"

"Not really. We didn't get friendly until later. It was when we both lost parents. Felix and Amelia's Mother and Father both passed away. Shortly after this, our Father passed away. My Father and brother Richard worked for their Father and Felix came to the house to offer his condolences and to tell us he understood our heartache because his Father and Mother had just passed away also. He wanted Richard to know that his Father (the company owner) dying would not affect Richard's job, but Richard had already decided to start his own business."

"Very successfully," Leo said, although he was learning more about Richard and that was not the object of the questions, so he added, "When did you begin your friendship with Amelia."

He realised it might be a mistake to centre the conversation on Amelia and he would need to change that or face the possibility of Evelyn getting the impression that he would prefer to be with Amelia.

Evelyn said, "It was not until Richard and Amelia began a relationship together. Richard introduced us and Amelia told him that we were at school together."

"Taking Richard and Amelia out of the equation for a moment," Leo said, "Can I ask about you? What kind of things do you enjoy doing, places you enjoy going to?"

Leo's question took Evelyn unawares and she appeared confused for a moment, and then she smiled and said, "I like the simple things in life like going for a walk and I also enjoy going to simple places like the countryside to ramble through nature."

Going for a walk was one of the things Leo decided against for that evening out and he was intrigued in her mentioning it. He said, "So, a nature ramble would be a double ganger for you by combining your dual loves of walking and the countryside. It must get lonely, though, going for a country walk."

"I don't know what a double ganger is, but going for a walk alone could be lonely, it can also be idyllic because the countryside is so tranquil and beautiful. It's always nice to have company, but not essential."

Leo was beginning to feel extremely relaxed and at peace with the world. Not having any contact with his kids was still on his mind, but he was enjoying Evelyn's company. He decided it might not have been a one-time fluke that he also enjoyed her company the last time. What surprised him more was the fact that he would like to experience this again.

It felt natural for him to say, "Would you mind if I accompanied you during your next country walk?"

Once more, Evelyn appeared confused and she said, "Me, you want to go for a country walk with me?"

"Yes, I realise the weather can be less than perfect at this time of the year. However, it would be fun and we could choose a part

152

of the countryside that was close to a coffee house or similar where we could get a hot beverage."

"That sounds lovely, Leo. I would love to go for a walk with you."

Leo was not sure that Evelyn would be familiar with the term "it's a date," so he said, "It's arranged, then. I'll pick you up tomorrow. With it being Saturday, I'll not have to go to work, so we could leave early for the countryside to prevent having too much of our walk in the dark."

"That would be best. The countryside can be scary in the dark."

"Leo set his knife down on the plate, reached his hand across the table to Evelyn and touched her hand. He would have held her hand, but she was holding her knife and fork, so he just touched her hand and said, "Don't allow the darkness to scare you; I'll be there to protect you."

Evelyn placed her fork on the plate and Leo took her now empty left hand in his and gently squeezed it as he smiled at her and she smiled back.

He could not believe the situation, but he had decided to allow the evening to proceed naturally and at its own pace. It appeared he might not get back to prime time and what he had was all he would have and it was obvious he could not have Amelia, and part of him was happy with this because he was beginning to think that she was not the woman he thought she was.

In primetime, he saw Amelia as a sweet innocent woman and he was attracted to that. However, on arriving at this time, he has come to realise that there is a huge expanse between them in many ways, from her affluent upbringing to her political persuasion. Most of his thoughts on her remained as they were and he would enjoy having her and more so Felix as friends, but he could see now that it could never develop as more than a friendship with Amelia, and not because she had Richard.

He released Evelyn's hand and they continued their meal.

He was not happy with Amelia manipulating the situation the previous night and leaving him with Evelyn, but the tear Evelyn shed was like a revelation to him and he realised he was punishing her for the actions of others and that was wrong.

It was never his intention for her to cry and, while she will cry again, he will try to ensure he is not responsible for her tears and while she is happy to spend some time with him, he will be happy to spend some time with her, as friends, just friends. If his stay in this time is prolonged and that friendship should grow, then he would accept that.

He must also accept that her brother Richard is not such a bad person and is quite likeable and perhaps there is another pending friendship there.

He cannot understand Richard leaving for several months to work on spreading his business when it was already large enough to sustain him through life. However, that is ambition and everyone has a right to push themselves on. It was not for Leo, but Leo had to accept that not all wheels spin on his axle and everyone has the right to be different.

He was aware that Felix would enquire as to his apparent change of mind and change of heart. It's everyone's prerogative to make changes in all things and, while on this occasion, he is sure that Felix would be pleased; Leo knew that he doesn't need to set out to please anyone.

He has a life to renew and make work while at the same time getting over the loss of the life he has come from. He realised he is not the first person ever to lose contact with his children and sadly will not be the last. Nevertheless, while he realised that he might have had Evelyn thrust on him, he was fine with it now and he realised this would be his life now and he must make the best of it.

Chapter 13

Leo returned from another failed attempt to get back to prime time.

He wasn't confident of success anyway, neither was he sure the timing was good with his plans of a country walk with Evelyn, but going to Laura's house and speaking to the watchman filled some time.

He set about helping Felix prepare lunch.

He assumed Amelia would be in the cellar getting through some writing, but Felix informed him that she had gone with Richard to speak to the Church Vicar and discuss wedding arrangements, work out a day that would be suitable for church and the happy couple. However, with it being a Saturday, the vicar was unable to discuss it and gave them the appointed time of seven of the clock on Wednesday evening at the vicarage.

Seven of the clock sounded strange to Leo. He was used to it being announced as Seven O'clock and he reasoned the O' must be an abbreviation for 'of the' just as with O at the beginning of a name meaning grandson of as in many Irish names such as O'Brien and O'Neil.

Therefore, Leo reasoned that perhaps it only applied to grandfather clocks at they're not being too many grandson clocks about. His latter thoughts were in jest with the hope of taking his mind off his disappointment at another failure to see his kids.

He didn't mention to Felix that he had arranged to go for a walk in the country later with Evelyn. Neither did he tell him that he enjoyed an evening out and a meal with her the previous evening. He was not yet sure, how it would go and was worried his newly found attraction to Evelyn might be in way of a rebound situation from his former affection for Amelia.

As it turned out, Evelyn mentioned everything to her brother Richard and Richard relayed this information to Amelia as they returned from the vicarage, and Amelia in turn relayed it to everyone at the lunch table. Leo became somewhat embarrassed, although everyone else seemed somewhat pleased and Felix found it fitting to rise with glass in hand and award a toast, which embarrassed Leo further.

After lunch, Leo helped Felix with the washing up, during which he expressed his thoughts on Evelyn and Felix assured him that she was a wonderful woman who deserved some happiness after the horrors of losing her husband so soon after they married. Leo could see she had amazing inner beauty as well as being outwardly pleasing to the eye. He shared with Felix his reasoning for avoiding her previously.

How could he even think about beginning a relationship while his heart belonged to another? When that changed, his sole desire was to get back to prime time and then there was the feeling of being pressurised into it and Felix accepted part of the blame in this and admitted that his heart might have overruled his mind on the matter?

Leo could not hold this against Felix because he had acted in like manner pertaining to Brenda and he could only see the outcome and paid scant measure of thought to everything else. It worked out perfectly, though and Felix became far removed from complaint.

With the lunch things washed, dried and put away, Felix and Leo both bounded up the stairs in haste to prepare and when Leo entered his room, he went immediately to the note he had left there. It was becoming his practice when attempting a return to prime time, that he leaves the note on the bed. It will inform Felix of everything. He preferred not to tell him before leaving because he has no idea when or even if he will ever be able to leave this time and go back to his kids.

The note is his way of saying goodbye and Leo knew there was sadness ahead. If he doesn't manage to get back to prime time, he will have the sadness of never seeing his kids or friends like Mike again. If he does make it back, he will have the sadness of never seeing his new friend Felix or others like Evelyn again.

He stopped to ponder on Evelyn and was unsure. Perhaps he should be honest with her and tell her everything, although he was sure she would not be able to understand or accept it. He had no desire to allow her to draw close to him, though, only for him to find a way back to prime time and leave her behind in the same sudden manner in which her husband left her when he dies in the war. It was unfair. She deserved to know.

He decided to tell her everything. He also decided to write a second note when he gets back and will leave both notes together the next time he attempts a return to prime time. It might not be a perfect way of saying goodbye, but it was all he could do with him having no idea when or even if he would be leaving this time.

Felix offered Leo a lift in his horseless carriage and rather than dropping Leo off at Evelyn's house, he decided to loan Leo the automobile on the understanding that Leo would later pick him up at Brenda's house.

It felt strange to Leo to have to start the engine from outside the vehicle. He went to the front with the starter handle, but Felix informed him that he needed to start it at the side, so he brought the starter handle round the side of what he discovered was a 1901 Wolseley and, with enormous pride, Felix informed him it boasted a massive ten-horse power engine. His smile remained until Leo informed him that his car back home has a 170-horse power engine.

Felix instructed Leo on switching on the fuel, then opening the bonnet to prime the engine by pulling out the needle valve and holding it until fuel came through. He then needed to pull out, then turn the decompressor, and then open all of the 12 oil outlets. With this all done, he simply needed to turn the starting handle to a reasonable speed, switch on the ignition, and then turn the decompressor back to its original position.

Leo was tempted to inform Felix that he merely needed to turn a small key in the ignition of his car back home. However, he decided not to share this information in case it created some envy after witnessing the expression on Felix's face when he told him his car has a 170-horse power engine.

With the engine now lit and running, Felix and Leo were able to climb aboard; Leo drove as a way of allowing Felix to witness his ability to master the beast.

The countryside failed to present its usual green splendour due to a fine frosty coating, like a fine sprinkling of icing sugar over a Christmas pudding. Rather than impair the beauty, it enhanced it and somehow took the chill out of the air, so much so that Leo and Evelyn left their heavy coats, gloves and scarf's in the car when they went for their walk.

A robin visited them, adding a deeper Christmas atmosphere and they stopped at a wall to admire it until it flew off. They both desired a camera to capture the scene and they agreed it would make a perfect Christmas card. Leo decided his would be superior because he could take a colour photo. While colour would not matter with the white surface of the ground and the sprinkling over the trees, it would capture the full colourful enchantment of the robin.

After the robin flew off, they continued their walk and Leo had a strong urge to take Evelyn's hand. Perhaps it was the Christmas atmosphere set in all its fullness by the robin. Perhaps it was the romance of the walk, surrounded by the natural splendour of the countryside.

He decided to experiment with a quick test and he allowed his right arm to hang loose as they walked along and as his heart began to race, he moved his hand and allowed it to touch Evelyn's hand. He decided if she moved her hand to avoid contact, he would remove his hand away, but if she allowed her hand to remain after the touch, he would gently slip his hand around hers.

He was mindful of being in a time of virtue, not very long after the time when he would have needed to invite a chaperone on their walk to ensure virtue remained. He saw it himself when Richard, after several months apart, greeted Amelia with a kiss on the hand. To Leo, holding a girls hand was an innocent act, but how would a girl react to it in 1905? The desire was overwhelming, though.

He looked over his left shoulder as a way of offering a reason for his right hand to move. He could not believe or understand how nervous it all made him, and he felt a gentle feathering as his hand brushing against her hand. He prepared to offer an apology in case it offended her and after a few seconds of his hand gently touching her hand and Evelyn not making any comment and not moving her hand away, he slipped the expanse of his much larger hand around her small and feminine appendage.

"Excuse me," Evelyn said, "could you tell me what you are doing?"

Leo snatched his hand away from Evelyn's hand and said, "I'm sorry."

Evelyn smiled, took hold of Leo's hand and rested her cheek against his shoulder as she said, "You don't take a joke very well, do you?"

Leo felt Evelyn had smacked him with his own hand and he yielded to her greater sense of jovial banter.

Her hand felt smaller than it looked in the expanse of his hand and as she continued to rest her cheek on his shoulder, he was tempted to put an arm around her, but resisted due to the feeling he retained at her complaining about him taking her hand and he laughed that she could fool him so easily.

"He said, "You are a wicked woman. "I thought I had offended you."

Evelyn smiled and said, "It would offend me if you slipped your hand into my handbag, but holding my hand is fine, whether at a table while out for a meal, or enjoying a country walk."

Leo appreciated her response, it told him a lot about her, and it even suggested that she might be on his wavelength and they might get on well together. He decided that would be good if he could not get back to prime time, but not so good should a return proved possible.

He was still worried about beginning a relationship and having to leave. If he could get back to prime time, he would have to go because his kids meant everything to him and they would have to come first.

This thought helped him to make up his mind utterly about being honest with her. He could not string her along for some weeks, months or even years and then leave to go back to prime time. She deserved the truth. He decided this earlier, but now he felt it had to happen and it would then be her decision whether to carry on or dump him for a model built in the same timeframe as she.

He had to keep track of the path they were taking because they would later need to follow that same path to get back to the car. He knew some of the area, but most was new to him and one country path looks very much like another and in 1905, there were not a lot of roads in the city never mind the country and most of what there was were laid with a horse and cart in mind and were no more than dirt roads.

The original plan was a short walk and then back to the car and onto somewhere for a cup of tea and perhaps a bowl of soup to warm them up. Nevertheless, it was a lot warmer than they had imagined it would be and the walk continued further than planned and it was nice for Leo to walk along while holding Evelyn's hand.

It had been a long time since he held a woman's hand and it felt good. It was a long time since he had taken a girl for a walk too. Laura was the last woman with whom he enjoyed all this. His time since was eaten up by the three houses, and it felt like he had just begun to live again.

Mike would be pleased. He was always suggesting Leo should take a woman out and start living again. Leo wanted to because he missed female company, but it isn't easy to leave your heart open to more pain after suffering rejection from someone who took you for richer or for poorer, in sickness and in health etc. Besides, it took a long time for him to learn how to stop loving Laura.

For a reason unbeknown to him, Leo heard himself saying to Evelyn, "It couldn't have been easy when you lost your husband. Can I ask if you got him back for burial, or did they burry him over there?"

"Yes, you can ask and I'll tell you. I am afraid I didn't get his body back for burial and they buried him in a mass grave where he fell. We had a remembrance service for him, though. It helped, but it was not as helpful as I assume a funeral would have been."

"I'm sorry, Evelyn. The least the government could have done after he gave his life for his country, would have been to return him home for a proper, dignified burial. I'm assuming, with it being a mass grave, everyone who fell was buried out there?"

"I think so, although it might have been different for commissioned officers. Martha's husband is also buried out there."

"Felix told me he had died there, but not that he was buried there. I can imagine it being difficult for you to discuss such things, so, would you prefer if I chose something else to talk about?"

Evelyn glanced apologetically at Leo and nodded her head.

Leo said, "What are your views on football? I was thinking of going to see Manchester United versus Glossop at old Trafford on 21 January. Would you like to join me?"

161

Evelyn laughed and said, "A Woman watching football players? That would be quite a spectacle. Could I have a pie and a pint as well?"

Leo had been serious and didn't take into account the fact that women in 1905 didn't gather to watch football as they do in his prime time. He even knew of many women who played the "beautiful game," but the women of 1905 had a century of catching up to do. Evelyn assumed he was not being serious to get away from the seriousness of discussing her husband buried in a mass grave in South Africa.

"I enjoy tennis," Evelyn said. "I once watched Adine Masson. She is an amazing player, the first woman ever to win the ladies singles in the French Open."

"So, you witnessed history being made?"

"No, I saw her before her championship win. Richard paid for my sister and me to go. It was a year after my husband's death and was Richards' way of injecting some fun back into my life. I enjoyed it."

"I had assumed Richard was your only sibling?"

"No, I have two sisters, but Josephine is the only one who enjoys tennis. She got married and is living in Kent now, raising her two gorgeous daughters, my nieces."

"Does your other sister live close by?"

"Yes, at the cemetery."

Leo looked up swiftly and said, "I'm sorry. I –"

Evelyn smiled and interrupted Leo with a raised hand before saying, "No, Leo, she has not passed away. Her husband is, more or less, the head gravedigger or head groundskeeper or something of that description and they live in the gatehouse at the cemetery. They plan to move out of the gatehouse and into a place of their own and then to raise a family. The sooner the better, I say. The gatehouse of a cemetery is not ideal for raising children, especially now with darkness descending so early."

Mentioning the descent of darkness got Leo thinking that they should track back in the direction of the car because it would be dark soon. Finding the way back might be daunting, but much worse in darkness. He had enjoyed the walk, though, and he surmised that Evelyn had enjoyed it too. He felt they both have

162

come to know each other a little more and he was now looking forward to a cup of tea.

With the lateness of the day came a colder breeze from the north and if it got any colder he would feel the necessity to put his arm around Evelyn to offer her some body heat.

He had earlier deliberately parked close to a small establishment where they could retire for a cup of tea and continue their time together in more heat and comfort.

Darkness had fallen with a passion by the time they reached the car and, unlike the city streets with its gaslights, much of the countryside had no lighting at all. This didn't help with Leo having the responsibility of directing the journey back and he was beginning to think he had taken a wrong turn when they came to a recognisable feature and he knew they didn't have far to go, although it was with some relief that he soon afterwards spotted the car.

The tea was hot and refreshing and the seating was comfortable, so Leo was happy to take some time over his cup. Evelyn had no complaint about it either. They relaxed with the knowledge of there not being a lot of others would mean there would not be a need with the staff to request them to give up their table any time soon.

During the walk back, Leo had been thinking and he decided Evelyn possibly saw a lot of the sister that lived in the gatehouse of the cemetery, but not so much of the one in Kent.

He took a sip of tea and said, "Would you like me to ask Felix if I could borrow the car again and drive down to Kent to visit your sister?"

"I would love that. I saw her at Christmas, but don't get to see a lot of her."

Leo smiled and said, "In that case, I'll consider bringing you along."

Leo's wry smile told Evelyn that he was being less than serious, so she returned the smile and awarded Leo a kick and Leo said, "That is typical of a lady, to kick a gentleman with the table covering her unjust act from witnesses."

"Would you have preferred me to embarrass you by giving you a slap on the face?"

Leo laughed in appreciation of her response before saying, "Should I take your silence on the matter as a suggestion that you don't have the desire to visit your sister?"

"You may if you wish, but only if you dare to deny your inability to have heard me saying 'I would love that,' or should I take it as a suggestion that you are going deaf?"

Leo laughed again and said, "So you did. I think your physical and brutal attack soon after you spoke must have had a profound effect. I'll speak to Felix later, When would suit you?"

"I am not restrained by time, so any time that suits you will be fine."

Leo pondered on how good it would be not to have time restraining him and to have the ability to nip back to prime time, spend some time with the kids, and then come back to 1905. However, time had him trapped, a virtual prisoner unable to go back. If he discovered a way back, he would become a prisoner there and be unable to return to 1905. Time has its own rulebook and Leo had no control over it and could only accept what it offered him.

At least he appeared to be free within the restraints of time to move about in different localities as one belonging to this time. Of course, he had not tested this theory largely, although going to Manchester for the home game on 21 January would answer this question more fully than his assumption could offer.

It seemed he would need to go alone to Manchester with it not being etiquette at this time for women to shout from the stands of Old Trafford. He could invite Felix, but he had a strong assumption that Felix preferred rugby. He might go, more or less to please Leo, but Leo didn't want that.

Even though Great Britain had now entered the Edwardian era, Leo and Evelyn's surroundings had a strong Victorian flavour and Leo surmised the place had not even had a lick of paint in the last ten or fifteen years, with the furnishings greatly predating that. He was comfortable, though, as was Evelyn.

Like Leo, Queen Victoria was as one trapped in time since the death of her husband Albert. Part of the Queen died with Albert and it was forty years before she could properly live again and make way for her son Edward VII to succeed her to the throne and bring a fresh and vibrant realm to the monarchy after it being in mourning for that forty years.

Leo asked, "Apparently, Amelia is fond of horse riding. Do you ever go with her?"

"There is no fear of that. I did try it once and was fine for the first few seconds, but I looked down and it was such a long way to the ground and I had to ask someone to help me down from the beast. They are such enormous beasts. Have you ever ridden?"

"No, but the suspension on Felix's car is so poor that I feel like I rode a horse all the way here. Having solid tyres doesn't help either."

"Surely the tyres need to be solid to withstand and support the weight of the vehicle?"

Leo pondered and smile before saying, "I had not thought of that. Maybe one day they will discover a way of getting air into them, though, like a football, which appears to be solid, but is filled with air."

Evelyn smiled and said, "There are times when you appear to be full of air. I don't think air could support the weight of an automobile."

Leo offered an all-knowing smile and said, "You never know."

Evelyn offered Leo a small enquiring frown before saying, "You appear to think I am wrong and air will support the weight of an automobile?"

Leo widened his smile and said, "I can only repeat, you never know. Have you ever tested the amount of weight a ball, containing only air, can support? The air in a ball is contained in a small area, but if taken around the full circumference of a wheel in the same manner as a ball, within a rubber inner wheel, if you will, then do you not think it would withstand quite a lot of weight?"

"Is this a trick question, Leo? My brother Richard at times asks trick questions that have the appearance of a certain answer, yet the opposite answer is true. You have that same mischievous smile that he adapts when asking such a question."

Evelyn took a sip of tea and studied Leo for a moment, and then said, "Richard used to play rugby and I went on occasions

165

to watch. There was an enormous man who would not be very much shorter than seven feet tall on his team, a solid mountain of a man. He dropped onto the ball. I was sure his bulk and weight would surely burst the ball, but it took his weight with ease."

Evelyn paused to study Leo's reaction and offer a smile before adding, "A rugby ball is a different shape than a football, but they are both made, I believe, in the same manner. Perhaps if a wheel was encircled in a substance similar to a ball, with the air trapped in an inner section made of something similar to animal bladder with a tougher outer case similar to leather, then maybe it would support the weight of an automobile."

"You worked that out well and I can see the kind of mind that got your brother through to business success. You should have gone into business with him."

"I am not merely a silly girl without a brain then?"

"You appear to have an excellent mind, but I'll deny having said that if you repeat it to anyone else."

They both laughed and Leo pondered on the ability of her mind to understand and accept something of what he was about to tell her pertaining to how he got here and where he has travelled from.

He took a sip of tea, and then a deep breath and said, "I think it's time now for me to tell you about me, where, or more correctly when I come from. Felix is the only one who knows in full with Amelia being ware of some things. I would like you to Know."

Evelyn adapted a position that told Leo he had her full attention and without saying anything further, she awaited him telling his story.

"Okay, here goes," Leo, said. "I come from over a century in your future where, in Great Britain alone there are in access of 32 million people who own a car, automobile. We have aeroplanes that can take hundreds of people into the air at the same time and fly them across the entire ocean to anywhere in the world. In my time, I learned that your friend Amelia died on Christmas day and I was able to come here with medication from my time that swiftly cured her."

166

Leo stopped to gauge Evelyn's reaction thus far. She adorned a perfect poker face that any card player would pay a fortune for and Leo could not decipher how she was taking his news. Part of him regretted taking the conversation in this direction, but he decided she deserved to know the truth.

He remained unable to grasp whether she would accept it as the truth, the ramblings of a lunatic or the mind of a sadistic buffoon with an agenda against her. He took another sip of tea.

Chapter 14

Leo had assumed this third Monday at work would seem as long as the past two Mondays and his assumption proved correct. He was extremely pleased when it was time to leave his office and the colliery and make his way back to Felix and Amelia's house.

He was sure it didn't take him any longer than any other evening getting there, but the kitchen was inactive and it appeared owing to the stove being hot and empty, that the evening meal was on the table. Therefore, Leo surmised that perhaps Martha had been faster than normal getting through her days' work and saving Felix and him the job of finishing off.

Martha further surprised him by arriving in the kitchen with her coat on as he prepared to go through to check if Felix needed a hand.

Leo said, "Are you not staying for a meal?"

"I don't stay every evening and, as it happens, I have someone to meet this evening. Your meal is on the table and Felix awaits you there, so enjoy it and goodnight."

"Good night and have a pleasant evening, Martha."

Martha left and Leo went through to the dining room and could see Felix alone at the table.

"Everything is ready," Felix said, "so we just have to eat this evening."

"So I see," Leo said, sitting down. "Is Amelia not up from below stairs yet?"

"Amelia has gone with Richard. He picked her up a moment ago. He said he would take her to a restaurant for a meal after she made a choice."

"Choice," Leo echoed. "You mean he's going to allow her to choose the restaurant?"

"No, the ring, I should not know, but he secretly informed me of his plan."

"I hope they get there before the jeweller closes."

"The jeweller has agreed to show his range after the close of business for the day. Richard has arranged with him to call up stock from other shops and offer Amelia the widest selection possible. I am assuming there will be included rings that will make it well worth the jewellers' time."

"It sounds like there'll be a few dazzlers, but didn't Richard already buy a ring and give it to her on the evening he proposed?"

"Yes, but Amelia didn't see it beforehand. Richard wants her to see this selection of rings and possibly to make a choice from them. There will also be brochures with rings not included which she can view before making a choice."

Leo pondered on how it would feel to have that amount of money, but he would deny that it in any way made him feel even a smidgen of jealousy, although that would not be an honest admission because he could feel his nose slipping somewhat out of joint as he snarled at the news he was hearing. However, the snarl was to amuse Felix and he smiled and said, "Good for Richard."

"He was feeling guilty at not being here while Amelia was so ill, but he has to understand that a hugely expensive ring alone will not change this and he will have to buy me a gift also."

Leo had to look deeply to gauge Felix's jovial level, but the fact of Felix's laughter then made it obvious and Leo joined in with the laughter.

Leo began to load up his plate as he said, "I see Martha isn't joining us?"

Felix smiled widely. "She too is being taken to a restaurant and has arranged to meet Harold."

"Who's Harold?"

"Harold is Martha's man friend. They had known each other many years ago and since then, as you know, Martha lost her husband. Likewise, Harold lost his wife. Then they found each other. I do hope it works out for them both."

"It would be good for her. It will be good for us too if it means all this extra food for us."

Felix laughed and raised a loaded fork to his mouth, but stopped short of releasing it to the mercy of his teeth to say, "You were very quiet last evening when you left the automobile off for me at Miss - Brenda's house. No problems, I trust?"

"There is nothing that will hinder us from eating this meal. You must be worried, though. If Martha and this Harold get married, he might desire her to resign from her job here and you will have lost an amazing housekeeper."

Felix put the fork down and frowned. "I had not thought of that, Leo." He smiled and added, "The main thing must be her happiness, though, and I'm sure she will visit us from time to time. How did the walk in the countryside go with Evelyn?"

"We walked and we talked."

Felix frowned at Leo and said, "That is about all you can do during a country walk. Am I correct in assuming it didn't go the way you hoped it would?"

Leo nodded his head, Felix nodded his understanding, and both remained silent for a moment before Leo said, "I thought I should tell her everything about when and where I came from and I'm afraid she didn't appreciate my honesty and insisted on leaving immediately. She was furious and it was obvious she assumed I was belittling her intelligence because just before this I spoke about her intellect. It was complimentary, but overall she might have taken it in a way I didn't mean. I was merely trying to be honest, Felix."

"You were not very keen on her at the beginning, but I can see that has changed."

"It wasn't that I was not keen, Felix, I just didn't want to set out in a relationship in case a portal opened and I was ushered forward to my natural timeframe without being able to say goodbye to her or to explain."

Leo could see that Felix was less than convinced and Leo didn't have an answer for the fact that he didn't create the same impediment against Amelia.

Leo continued, "It appears now that there is every chance that will not happen and I'll remain here for the duration of my life. However, I know how I felt when Laura, my wife, told me she wanted a divorce. How much worse would that have been is she simply disappeared. I had no desire to put Evelyn through that, so I told her."

"You assumed telling her would allow her to decide if she could deal with such a thing, or, if not, to end the relationship with you before she got to a stage where losing you in such a sudden and uncertain manner would be unbearable for her?"

"I didn't expect her to react with fury."

"She is a woman, Leo. Women seldom react the way men expect them to."

Leo nodded his head with a mixture of acceptance and agreement in what Felix had said. "It isn't a huge deal anyway," he said. "I am no worse off than I was before we shared one another's company and a meal in a restaurant."

Leo's words failed to convince Felix, who could see that recent events had saddened Leo and Felix offered a hopeful smile. Then, as Leo's eyes fell on the plate before him, Felix pondered deeply and his eyes too fell on the plate before Leo as if it had become a magnet to their eyes.

Leo lay on top of his bed with his eyes transfixed on the ceiling and his mind in overdrive. He heard someone coming up the stairs but paid it scant attention. He assumed it was Felix and Felix had every right to walk up his own staircase. The steps were much too heavy for it to be Amelia, although if his mind had been in a more alert state, he would have realised that Felix had left and would be with Brenda at that moment.

He heard the rap on his bedroom door, but it was subconsciously and his thoughts carried on without the conscious realisation that the rap was begging his attention until a second rap on the door pulled him out of his trance like reverie and he sat up and called out, "come in."

Felix entered and Leo rose from the bed and said, "Sorry, Felix. Should you not be with Brenda?"

"I'll go back to her in a second. I hope you don't mind my interference, but I could never stand back and allow two people who are so obviously suited to each other to permit a silly misunderstanding to come between them. Therefore, I visited Evelyn and explained everything from my perspective and told her how your amazing medication from the future saved my darling Sister Amelia's life and not only returned her to all who love her but restored her to full health."

"What did she say?"

"Not a lot. She cried more than she spoke. However, why not ask her how she feels about it now. I'll go back to Brenda now. Evelyn is downstairs."

"Here? Downstairs here in this house?"

"Yes, at this very moment. She is nervous of the entire concept of you being here from a different time, but you have the power to help her to relax and understand it more clearly."

Felix opened the bedroom door more widely and beckoned Leo to go through it. Leo didn't speak and simply looked at Felix for a sign of what to expect. Felix too refrained from speech and simply rested his hand gently and encouragingly on Leo's shoulder as Leo went through the doorway.

Leo could hear Felix coming down the stairs behind him and out through the front door, but his mind was now on Evelyn and he found her standing in the living room with a hanky pressed to her face.

"There's no need to cry," Leo heard himself saying. It was almost as if someone else was saying the words, but he knew they were his words. He also knew they were his arms that were

172

around her and his hand that was drawing her head onto his shoulder. He gently rubbed her back with one hand and ran the fingers of his other hand through her hair as he said, "I thought I had lost you."

Felix closed the front door and smiled victoriously. He stood there for a moment, took in a deep breath of air through his nostrils, and released it slowly and satisfyingly through his mouth. He felt good. He had been seeking a way of thanking Leo for giving Amelia back to him and arranging for him and Brenda to get together.

He decided he had found a way to clear a small portion of the debt. He went to his automobile with the assurance that, after going through the various phases of starting up the engine, within the hour he would be on his way back to Brenda with some good news.

Leo was still unsure of what was acceptable to a woman in the year 1905. If he had been in his prime time, and with a woman from the same time, he would have put the lips on her by now, as he would jestingly refer to that first kiss. He decided he was being bold putting his arms around her, but was it appropriate to kiss her or should he put it on hold until their fifth or sixth date? He was unsure and didn't arrive in this time with a guide or a handbook on romantic etiquette.

He did know that he was now in this time three weeks and he had been back to Laura's a few times with no progress made to prime time. Therefore, he lacked the confidence of ever getting back and, while it grieved him deeply never to see his kids again, he knew he would need to endeavour to make this time his home and build new relationships here.

He felt a slight trembling from Evelyn at the beginning, but then she seemed to settle down and the tears had less intensity. Now he would have the problem of explaining everything when he didn't understand it himself and needed someone to explain it to him.

He left Peter's room on Christmas Eve night with the plan of going home and spending a rather lonely Christmas in a partially completed house. He probably would have spent most of Christmas day working on the house, but spent the first part of the day walking to it in a new time. It was worth it to be in the position of bringing medication that had the potential of saving a life and it proved to do just that.

Now he had to forge a new existence for himself in 1905 and he was happy it should now begin with Evelyn. Asking her out for a meal was no more than a rush of blood to the head and he has always had a problem with hastily made spontaneous actions, although this one turned out fine – well, it was fine before he told her his secret, although he was merely answering the questions she asked a few evenings previously.

He guided and escorted Evelyn to what others in the time refer to as a couch, but Leo has always referred to as a settee whenever he had one to make any kind of reference at all to it.

He sat down beside her and as he had already broken through the barrier of holding her hand, he took her hand in his and said, "I understand Felix told you a few things about me?"

She nodded her head.

"Do you believe the things he told you?"

"Yes, Felix is not given to having a fanciful imagination and he certainly is not given to lying about anything of such importance. He told me about the medication you brought for Amelia and the information you gave him about a business deal that you should not have known about. He had made up his mind not to, but you persuaded him and he already sees the value of your advice."

"I had the advantage of reading about it from a historic standpoint."

From beyond, they could hear Felix's automobile bursting to life and Leo smiled at the length of time it took him to go through the various phases, then realised it may be a long time until he will start a car with just the turn of a key in the ignition and his thoughts turned back to the kids. He had to push those thoughts to the back recesses of his mind. He will have time later to deal with them when he is alone in his room with no one to witness his heartache.

"There is a possibility," he said, "that I might be returned from whence I came in a similarly sudden and unexpected manner."

174

Evelyn nodded her head and replied, "There is also a high probability that we will be whisked off to our eternal reward, some before the dawn of another day, but we must still carry on our lives."

"That is an excellent way of looking at it. None of us can know when providence will change the direction of our lives or even end our existence on this earth."

They heard Felix driving away and Evelyn looked towards the window. While her head was turned and her eyes away from Leo, he had another one of his spontaneous reaction moments and he quickly leaned forward and kissed Evelyn on the cheek. She turned her attention back to him and he kissed her a second time. This time it was not on the cheek and the kiss lingered without her pulling away, pushing him away or slapping him on the face.

With the acceptance of not getting back to prime time and the kids, Leo put the explanation letters he had written into a drawer. He was now determined to get a place of his own and until then, he would leave the letters in the drawer after which, he would consider disposing of them.

He decided that being flicked back in time to this period must have been an outlandish fluke of nature and flukes like that don't normally happen more than once.

The work on Laura's house was almost complete anyway, the new occupiers would soon take up residence, and they would possibly have something to say about him arriving periodically and entering and leaving one of the rooms.

Of course, if he became the owner of the house, there would not be a problem and this would leave him perpetually open to the possibility of a return to prime time and the kids.

He closed the drawer, quickly pulled a coat from the wardrobe and took the stairs two at a time. Felix was passing through the hallway on his way to the living room when the dashing Leo grabbed his attention and he said, "My my, you are in a hurry."

As Leo buttoned up his coat, he said, "I need to go and see about a house. I shouldn't be very long."

With the glow of the fire illuminating the hut and the watchman in the darkness of the evening, the watchman busied himself brewing a cup of tea. He looked up when Leo arrived and said, "Ah, it's the intrepid doctor again?"

"I need some information," Leo said.

"If I can help..." The watchman said.

"I need to know who is having these houses built because I would like to buy this one."

"Hello," Leo said into the mouthpiece of the office candlestick telephone as he held the earpiece to his ear. "I would like to buy one of the houses you are having built at what I believe will be Balfour Way. Could I make an appointment to come and speak to you regarding it?"

Leo was sure the collier company would not allow him to make a private phone call, but he didn't have an option because he could not get to the estate agent's office before it closed without leaving work early. After listening for a moment, he said, "Yes, certainly, my name is Leo Lennox..."

"How are you on the theatre," Felix asked as Leo helped with the final presentation of the evening meal after Felix insisting that Martha relaxed in the living room as per usual with Amelia.

Leo frowned due to the question being unexpected and he said, "I haven't been to the theatre much. I went to the cinema a lot - that is moving pictures with sound – I also went to several live events, but not the theatre. I'm up for giving it a go, though."

"Amelia and Evelyn enjoyed the Scarlet Pimpernel so much that they have mentioned going back. I suggested another theatre and another production, but they would like to see this one again, so I can only accept they must have enjoyed it hugely. Anyway, I was thinking of taking Brenda, you could take Evelyn and perhaps Richard would like to take Amelia and we could book somewhere for a meal afterwards."

The Scarlet Pimpernel was not to Leo's taste, but he realised he would need to enter into the delights of the era and this was one of them, so he said, "Yes, I'd be up for that if Evelyn and Amelia don't mind sitting through it again."

"Wonderful! I'll order the tickets. It will be on Saturday 21 January."

"That's this coming Saturday," Leo said.

Felix stopped what he was doing and looked to Leo as he said, "Yes, does this date not suit?"

Leo had planned to travel by train to Manchester on that date and go to Old Trafford for the football match between Manchester United and Glossop. However, he knew there would be several more home matches before the end of the season, so, with a semi-fake smile he said, "It suits perfectly, Felix; It should be an enjoyable evening."

Leo pondered on buying shares for Manchester United. He knew that they would not always be a second division outfit like in 1905 and if he ever got back to prime time, shares in Man U from 1905 would be worth quite a lot.

He had to force his mind away from football teams and shares, so he looked earnestly at Felix and said, "I have a problem asking this, Felix. I obviously cannot stay here indefinitely, so will have to turn my efforts into finding a house. There is one I have been thinking about, although it's at the other side of town and they haven't completed the building work just yet."

Leo paused to ascertain Felix's reaction so far and Felix nodded his head and said "Yes," which seemed to Leo as Felix's' giving him the approval to continue.

Leo continued, "I'll need to approach the bank for a loan and, I'm not sure how banks work at this time, but they will more than likely need some kind of collateral or surety, which I don't have at the moment."

"You need not say any more, my friend," Felix said, sporting a huge smile. If you would like to use my bank, I'll introduce you to the manager. He deals with all my financial matters personally and has become a good friend over the years. He will work out something with you and I'll sign anything I need to. You will have the house you desire."

"I assure you I'll not miss a single payment and will aim to pay the bank back ahead of time."

"I don't need to know any of that and just need an address and a phone number and I'll arrange an interview and we shall have this all completed and signed very soon."

"Pending the bank manager saying yes," Leo said.

"No, if he doesn't say yes, there are other ways and wonders and you will have your house, although I am very happy with you continuing to live here. However, perhaps you are planning and thinking of when you and Evelyn will be married?"

"That isn't a plan yet. You will not have to worry about a house when you take the plunge because you have already got one."

"I only own half of this house. Father and Mother bequeathed it to both Amelia and me. However, Richard has commissioned the building of a house. Work began on it a few months ago, so I would assume they would live there. If this proves to be the case, I'll offer to give Amelia half the price of this house. I'll need to discuss it with her."

With that cleaned and tidied away, Leo turned his mind back to his previous thoughts and said, "I have been thinking of investing in some stocks and shares and –"

"Yes," Felix said with excitement, "you will be in a perfect position to know which will grow and which will crumble into dust. Please allow me time to make some enquiries for you."

Leo arrived at the bottom of the stairs, dressed and ready for work. Felix had already left and Leo had a look down the stairs to the cellar to wish Amelia a productive day with her writing. She was not there, so he assumed she was in the outhouse or was still in her room getting ready for the day ahead. She was normally at her desk from very early, but perhaps arriving home late the previous evening after celebrating the purchase of the wedding ring had exhausted her and she had decided on a later start to the day.

He decided to call up the stairs to her in case she was there. However, he would not call too loudly in case she was still asleep and he called, "Amelia, I'm going to work now. Have a good day and will see you later."

"Yes, you too have a good day, Leo," she called back from her room.

Leo left and checked the weather before stepping over the threshold. It was cold but dry, and he settled for that. Therefore, he stepped into the new day and closed the door behind him.

It was just a five-minute walk to the tram stop and he was beginning to recognise others who arrived at the tram stop at the same time as he. He had this far not got into a conversation with any of them, but he decided this might happen after another few sightings, especially with a couple who wished him a good morning and he wished them the same, without a conversation beginning between them.

It was dark as Leo made his way to the tram stop, agreeing with the old cliché of it being dark when leaving for work and dark when returning home. Daylight will later descend, though.

Many people will have already started work, some several hours earlier, some in his business at the colliery, would spend all their daylight hours down a black hole and would only ever see daylight on their day off, he realised how close he came to having such a job, and he felt blessed.

"Yo-ho, Leo", he heard someone calling out. He recognised the voice and when he looked across the road, he saw Martha, illuminated by the gas street lamps, waving and stepping onto the road to cross over and speak to him. He doesn't usually see Martha because she doesn't normally arrive at Felix and Amelia's house until long after he has gone to work, but she must have arranged or decided to come in early on this morning, perhaps to finish early for meeting Harold, he reasoned.

Leo didn't only see Martha, he also saw a pony and trap belting along at high speed, which would be better described as breakneck speed for a pony and trap. Even though Leo saw it, Martha didn't and suddenly seeing Leo forced her to neglect the early morning traffic, which was normally travelling too slowly to be a threat anyway and she stepped onto the road just as the pony and trap reached that same spot in the road.

Leo called out "Stop!" It was too late and he turned away, unable to witness such a scene, but realising the full horror as he heard a woman close to him screaming. When he looked, Martha was lying on the ground and the pony had its reins pulled back to halt it.

Leo had previously been telling Felix that Martha might be one of his ancestors. It was obvious to him that if he had not been there, she would not have attempted to cross the road to go to him, so this probably didn't happen in the original history of 1905 and, if related, it could have the consequences of effecting the lives of family members in prime time.

This left open the possibility that if Leo was a direct relative of Martha, how this affects her might affect him in that if she doesn't survive, he might not be born! Will he cease to be and just disappear when she draws her last breath?

Leo was oblivious to such thoughts and merely thought of getting to her with the hope of helping her. Others also ran over to her. Leo could see even from as far as the far side of the road in poor gas light that she was not moving. As he got closer, he could see blood coming from a head wound.

He remembered once hearing that the first-ever ambulance in the UK was pulled by a team of horses and was released in 1905 to bring the injured and seriously ill to hospital. He was sure, though, that it would not begin until later in the year. That would not be of use to Martha, she needed an ambulance now.

As Leo drew closer, he looked toward her breast with the hope of seeing it rising as an indication that she was breathing.

As he arrived close to her he quickly undid the buttons of his overcoat and used it as a blanket for her, then took his jacket off and slipped it under her head for a pillow. He then mentally chastised himself because he should first have checked her wounds and he pondered on tearing his shirt into strips and using it as bandages for her head wound, but decided his hanky would do, and for the first time in a long time, he closed his eyes and prayed.

Chapter 15

Leo and Amelia were in the hospital waiting area when Felix arrived. "What on earth happened," Felix asked.

Leo said, "She began to cross the road when she spotted me at the tram stop and a pony and trap arrived out of the blue yonder and struck her."

"It was my fault," Amelia said. "Yesterday, before leaving for home, Martha spoke of a place she wished to go with Harold. I decided there was no need to delay such an outing, so I gave her today off but asked her to come to the house early and I would prepare her by applying some makeup and doing her hair. I thought it would please her and it would be a nice post-Christmas treat for her." She glanced around and added, "I never dreamed it would result in her being brought here!"

Leo said, "It wasn't your fault, it was mine. If I had not been there, it wouldn't have happened and she would have gone on her way to the house and been pampered for her date with Harold."

Felix said, "Things like this can happen at any time without it being anyone's fault."

They all sat down and Leo said, "Apparently, a dog or a cat spooked the pony and before the driver could regain control, it was too late."

Felix asked, "Have you heard anything from the medical staff yet?"

Leo said, "I haven't heard a thing, not even the promise that they are doing everything possible."

"Have you been able to contact Harold?" Felix asked.

Leo said, "I don't know where Harold lives and have no way of contacting him."

Amelia said, "After I gave her today off, Martha arranged to meet Harold early and he will be wondering what has happened to her."

"Only Martha will know where we could contact him," Felix said.

"Excuse me," a nurse said, "Is one of you gentlemen called Mr Lennox?"

"Yes, that's me," Leo said as both men rose to their feet.

"Doctor Thompson asked me to invite you to go through." She motioned towards a corridor and continued, "If you go down that corridor, turn right, and then second on the left, you should find him there."

"Oh my dear Lord, that sounds ominous," Amelia said.

"How is Mrs Lennox?" Felix asked.

"I don't have any information," the nurse said. "I was just instructed to ask Mr Lennox to go through."

Leo said, "Thank you very much."

The nurse left.

"I'll go too," Amelia said.

"No," Felix said, "I'll go with Leo, It would be best if you waited here, Amelia."

"You may come with us if you wish," Amelia said to Felix.

Felix could see that Amelia was stern and static in her determination and he said, "Let us go and speak to the doctor."

"I don't like this," Amelia said as they followed the directions given by the nurse.

Leo said, "Is it normal for the doctor to ask to speak to the family, assuming he thinks we are family?"

"I am not sure," Felix said; "although I would assume he would convey most information through the nurse and the fact of him asking to speak to us suggests it's something extremely serious. However, I don't have a lot of experience in hospital protocol."

Leo said, "It might be best to allow him to assume I am related to Martha. We share the same surname, so it should not be a hard sell. If he knew neither of us is related, he might not tell us anything."

Leo was not surprised to see 16 beds, 8 at either side of the ward, but he expected at least some of the beds to have a curtain around them. There was not a curtain in sight, but there was a nurse and Felix said, "Good morning, madam. We are looking for the doctor who is treating Mrs Martha Lennox. Doctor Thompson is the name we were given."

The nurse said, "The doctor has completed his rounds, but Mrs Lennox was allocated the last bed on the right."

With that, the nurse left the ward and Leo, Felix and Amelia looked down the line to the last bed on the right. It was empty, with the blankets folded and resting on top of the bed with the pillows on top of the blankets.

"Felix!" Amelia exclaimed.

"Do not jump to any conclusion just yet," Felix said.

"Martha!" Leo shouted as Martha arrived from a doorway at the far end of the ward and began to hobble towards them on crutches.

They hardly recognised her with a bandage around her head, but Leo recognised the glare from the nearby staff nurse who appeared to take a dim view of him shouting in her ward. They hurried to her as she hobbled to them.

When they reached Martha, Amelia opened her mouth to speak, but Felix raised a hand to stop her and he said, "Assuming Martha is permitted to leave due to the fact that she is dressed, there will be time for questions later." He turned to Martha and added, "Instead of going back to an empty house, you will come home with us where we can care for you. I am afraid we didn't have any contact details for Harold, so we could not tell him about this. However, when you settle, if you could give me his address, I'll go and let him know. I'll also invite him back to spend some time with you. Now, where is this doctor? I would like to have a word with him before we go."

He turned to Leo and Amelia before adding, "Could you take Martha out to the automobile while I search for the doctor?"

Amelia said, "Did the doctor not wish to speak to Leo?"

"That's okay," Leo said with a smile, "Felix can deputise for me. let's get you to the Chugga-Boom, Martha. Did you know Felix could be this assertive?"

Leo, Amelia and Martha were sitting on a bench close to the car when Felix made his exit from the hospital and went to them. He sighed deeply and said, "The doctor didn't wish to speak to us at all. He merely instructed the nurse to tell you, Leo, to feel free to go through to the ward and collect Martha. She was mistaken on what she assumed the doctor had said."

Felix turned his attention to Martha and continued, "Anyway, it seems you have only minor damage to your ankle, probably caused by the pony kicking you. The doctor is happy that your head wound is also nothing that will require an extended stay in hospital."

Leo smiled and said, "I thought that unconscious thing was all a bluff, Martha."

Martha said, "I think it was more to do with the fact that I rushed out without breakfast and the shock of that great big beast coming at me possibly played a part. My head feels fine, though, and I don't know why they used this huge bandage."

Leo grinned mischievously and said, "You know how it is, Martha, a huge head calls for a huge bandage." He rose swiftly from the bench and away from Martha. Martha smiled and playfully threatened him with a crutch.

Leo, Amelia and Martha entered the house to the sound of Felix driving off. They stopped at the door to wave to Felix, then

184

entered and went through to the living room. "Take your coat off and get comfortable on the couch," Amelia said to Martha. "Feel free to put your feet up and would I be correct in assuming you would like a cup of tea?"

"I could make the tea," Martha said, as she rested her crutches against the wall to take her coat off.

"You will not," Amelia demanded. "You are going to rest and that is an order."

Leo smiled at Martha and said, "Enjoy it. Let us all pamper you for a few days. I'll hang your coat up." He took Martha's coat and Amelia directed Martha to the living room and the couch, and said, "I'll not be very long with the tea. What would you like to eat? You have been through an awful ordeal and I feel responsible."

Martha said, "It was my fault."

"No, I asked you to come early and you had no way of knowing there was a crazed pony on the loose. You might get bored sitting here; can I get you a book or something?"

"No thank you, Amelia. I'll have my knitting to keep me occupied when I get home."

"You will not be going home for a few days."

"I could go over to your house and pick up your knitting," Leo said as they arrived in the room. "I could also check on things for you, feed the cat and water the plants."

"I don't have a cat," Martha said.

"So, I won't get to kick the cat. Is there anything else that you would like me to bring back for you?"

Amelia said, "Soup and a sandwich are always good after such a horrific experience, Martha. Would you like a cup of tea, Leo?"

"I would love one, and then I'll have to get to work."

Amelia said, "You gave us quite a scare, Martha."

"I am sorry," Martha said. "It was a momentary lapse of concentration and I should have looked before stepping onto the road. However, there is nothing broken and the head injury is not serious, so I was lucky."

Leo said, "And then some. As the doctor seems to surmise, it appears the impact with the pony was slight, pushing you to the ground and you struck your head on the cobblestone, but I assumed the pony had come fully into contact with you."

"I maintain it was my fault," Amelia said to Leo. "I asked Martha to come here early." She turned to Martha and continued, "I am sorry, Martha. If I had not asked you to come so early, this would not have happened."

Martha said, "I am sure you would have suggested a different time if you had known this would happen. It's easy to plan with hindsight, so it cannot possibly have been your fault. Harold will be wondering why I didn't arrive at our agreed meeting place."

"I shall go to the kitchen now and prepare elevenses," Amelia said and left the room.

Leo said to Martha, "You know Felix will explain everything to him, so try not to worry. If you could let me have your house keys and a list of what you will need, I could call in after work, collect them, and see to everything for you. I am sure Felix and Amelia will not allow you to move too far from here until you fully recuperate and can dump the crutches."

Martha glanced at the crutches leaning against the settee and said, "One of the nurses loaned them to me. I don't think she was authorised, but she was very nice and sat with me for a long time. She said I reminded her of her Mother. Am I so old?"

Leo laughed and said, "She probably meant her sister."

Leo felt strange going into Martha's house with Martha not being there. He lit a candle. The house was neat and comfortable, just as he expected it to be. His eyes fell on a framed photo, and he looked closer. He assumed it was Martha's husband. Whoever it was bore a striking resemblance to Leo's Uncle John and he moved the candle closer to offer a clearer view.

He knew that Martha and her husband had no children, so there were no other pictures on view in the living room and this enforced the fact that Martha's must have been a lonely life. He could only hope that will change for her.

He had grown rather fond of the old girl and he decided she deserves some happiness. It was his fervent hope that she finds this happiness with Harold.

186

Amelia, Leo decided, tried her best with the evening meal, but she was not a great cook. She never claimed to be and apologised that it was not to the standard everyone hoped for and were used to. Felix was a good cook, but he had a business to run and this gave Martha reason to suggest getting back to work.

However, Felix was adamant it would be neither safe nor congenial for Martha to cook while hobbling about the kitchen on crutches.

Felix suggested, "It would allow Amelia to get back to her writing and for Martha to continue with the rest she needs if I put an order in at a restaurant and collect on the way home. If needed, we could heat it up in the oven before sitting down to eat."

Martha said, "That would be very expensive. The doctor said my foot should be fine in a day or two, so I should be able to cook tomorrow's meal."

Felix pondered and said, "I have to say that Amelia did well considering cooking is not her forte. However, we should wait until tomorrow to see if you could cope, Martha. I suggest if Amelia decides you are free enough of pain and can get about the kitchen without stress, you should carry on and she could help. Amelia could let me know by telephone if I should bring a meal home if it proves too much for you."

"That sounds like a plan," Leo said.

"Does that satisfy your need to get back to work?" Felix asked Martha.

"Yes," Martha said. "I feel a lot better already. Slightly sore, but it's nothing that would hinder me in the kitchen."

Felix said, "We shall try that and see how it goes. Would you like to invite Harold one evening, Martha? He appeared to enjoy being here with you earlier. Does he work?"

"He is self-employed," Martha said.

"Great!" Felix said. "We will be able to discuss business tactics."

Using a sawing action that would impress any butcher or even carpenter, Leo managed to cut through a slice of meat. He prepared to introduce it to his mouth but left it on the plate to work up to attempting the eating process. He looked over at Martha and said, "While I was at your house, I noticed the photo of a man whom I assume is your husband."

"No," Martha said, he was not my husband. He was my brother-in-law, my husband's only brother. My husband put that photo up on the wall soon after his brother passed away and I didn't have the heart to take it down, due to the amount the photo meant to my husband. My brother-in-law's name was Graham."

"Was your brother-in-law married?"

"Yes, unfortunately, he left behind a wife and a young son. His son has now married and they just recently were blessed with a son who they named Graham after the baby's grand-father."

Leo said, "He must miss his dad. Do you have any photographs of your husband?"

Martha nodded her head sombrely. "Yes, I do have a photograph of my Jack. I keep it on the bedside table and it's the last thing I see before dousing the lamp and the first thing I see when I rise."

"I brought a candle, because I wasn't sure how you lit your house."

Giving up watching Manchester United at home to watching actor's prancing about on a stage, with the male actor's appearing more feminine than the females, in a production of The Scarlet Pimpernel was enough for Leo to question his sanity. It was good that everyone could get together for a few hours, though, and the restaurant afterwards was inviting and he had been looking forward to that.

He was looking forward more to having a quiet word with Felix, though, pertaining to stocks and shares and he wondered how that was going.

Sunday began with him noticing a slight addition to his measurements, and it was taking slightly more of the belt to fit around his waist. Therefore, he stood sideways to give Evelyn a better view of his bulge and asked, "Do you think I'm putting on weight?"

"Not noticeably, at least not to me, but you would be more familiar with your girth than I."

"I am," Leo concluded, "I'm putting on more than I'm happy with."

"That must be down to Martha's cooking, and last night's meal after The Scarlet pimpernel would not have helped."

"I've had more of Felix's cooking since arriving. I do tend to pig-out on Martha's cooking, though."

"You'll have to ease off and fight all urges and temptations."

Leo smiled, gave Evelyn a quick kiss and said, "Not them all, surely."

"If I can fight off the urge to smack you, surely you could fight off the urge to overeat. Some exercise would not go amiss either."

"I get plenty of exercise. I walk to the table on my own every mealtime."

"Riding a bicycle might help keep the weight down. I remember Felix had one he could loan you?"

"He told me about that, it's a penny farthing and if I managed to climb up to the saddle without injury, I'd make up for it trying to dismount from such a height."

"If you are too scared to ride Felix's bicycle, perhaps you could attempt something a bit lower?"

"Such as..."

"Have you ever ridden a Velocipede?"

"I've never even heard of a Velocipede."

"It's more commonly known as a boneshaker."

"Leo turned away showing a lack of interest as he said, "You've been a lot of help."

Evelyn laughed. "I think what you need is a Rover Safety Bicycle."

"Are both its wheels the same size?"

"Yes, of course, and both wheels revolve."

"Does it have a wooden frame?"

"No, I think it's a metal frame and the seat is sprung for comfort."

"Does it have peddles and do you know what peddles are?"

"Yes, I do know what peddles are and yes it does have them, one on each side for turning the chain, which powers the back wheel. I have one at home."

"You didn't tell me you ride a bike?"

"I don't. It belongs to Richard. He bought it several years ago and he has not used it for quite a while. I am sure he would not mind if you made use of it."

"It would not harm anything to have a go if you're sure he wouldn't mind. Is it in your garage?"

"Garage," Evelyn echoed with a frown.

"That's right; cars are only just making a start in the world, so there won't be a lot of garages. Garages are places where men work on cars, but some people have them attached to, or built at the side of a house, for keeping the family car safe at night. It's like a large shed."

"Interesting, I have a shed, so therefore, yes, I have a garage."

"Okay, I'll give it a go, pending Richards' approval, of course."

Leo wheeled the bike from the shed and smiled at Evelyn as he said, "It doesn't have breaks, so I'd best not go too fast. How did Richard stop it?"

"I am not sure," Evelyn said. She pointed at a bar coming out from each side of the front fork and added, "I remember he used to put his feet on those bars, but I don't know why. Have you ridden before? It seems to require a while to master balancing on it."

"I have been riding a bike since I was a child. Don't worry, I've got everything sorted."

He drew his foot over the saddle to take up a riding position. With one foot on the right peddle and his left foot on the ground, he said, "Wish me luck."

"God's speed," Evelyn said and Leo pushed his right foot down and the bike began to move, although Leo felt awkward and was slightly wobbly and without full control of the beast. He peddled it down past the side of the house and out onto the road. Evelyn followed and watched from the front of the house. Riding a bike seemed safer in 1905 because there was much less traffic. However, Leo noticed that whether on a horse and cart,

190

bike or one of those new-fangled combustion vehicles, people appeared to cross the road as though it was completely devoid of traffic and his bike lacked a bell to usher them out of his way.

He came to a decline and put his feet up on the bars as Evelyn had told him Richard did. Leo assumed this would be to use his shoes as brake pads. However, the fact that it had his feet in direct line with the spokes seemed to rule that out and he decided the bars were for resting his feet on when he had no reason to peddle, such as when going downhill.

That still left the problem of how to stop in an emergency. He could stop in a non-emergency simply by easing off on peddling and allowing the bike to slow to a halt naturally. However, this was supposed to be a safety bike and he decided brakes would be a good safety feature.

As he went down the decline with his feet on the bars, the peddles continued to rotate and he decided they were one way only and didn't have a freewheel function, so the trick was not to ride too swiftly and just within the speed of the peddles traction to stop. He still decided brakes would be a good safety feature, though.

He saw a newspaper sign outside of a shop and crashed both feet onto the ground. His shoes skidded along the surface of the cobblestone for a few yards before finally forcing the bike to stop and, in so doing, while working out a quick way of wearing out the souls of his shoes; he might have discovered how to stop a Rover Safety Bicycle in an emergency.

The newspaper sign was heralding the score from the football match of the previous day where Manchester United beat Glossop 4-1 at Old Trafford.

He learned a lot as he rode around and when he got back to Evelyn's house, he realised a further lesson when he dismounted and attempted to walk to Evelyn. It didn't half hurt his bum and he walked like John Wayne with bowel issues.

"Did you enjoy your first ride on a Rover Safety Bicycle," Evelyn said.

"Despite the saddle being kind of sprung, the solid wheels leave a lot to be desired and I'll need a soft cushion when I sit down, but, apart from saddle sores, I enjoyed it and I'll probably get used to any discomforts there are."

"No doubt you could suggest some improvements to the makers?"

"Pneumatic tyres, gel seat covers, brakes, a bell, speed gears, although the design is good." After voicing this, Leo plunged into deep thought.

Leo took it upon himself to put the kettle on and make tea for himself and Felix. He had some thoughts, a possible proposition, which he will put to Felix and he decided a cup of tea could help and put them both into the right frame of mind for the discussion. Therefore, while the kettle heated the water to the boiling point, he got busy putting sugar into two cups and placing the tea strainer on top of one cup, ready for pouring the tea. He spooned tea into the teapot and put the teapot less its lid onto the spout of the kettle to allow the steam to enter the teapot and heat it before filling it.

He mentally went over everything he desired to say to Felix, with last-minute amendments and a redirection of his calculations, or how he would express those calculations to Felix, in the hope of perfecting his speech before uttering it, a speech that was becoming more to him likened to delivering a pitch to the board.

He felt slightly apprehensive as he took two cups of tea through to the living room, where he knew Felix had ensconced himself with a book. He didn't mean to interrupt Felix's time of reading, but the fact of Felix having taken his eyes off the page and looking up at Leo gave Leo a reason to speak and he said, "If you are mentally captured by the book you are reading, I could leave what I have to discuss until later. However, I thought you might enjoy a cup of tea."

"Tea would be lovely, take a seat," Felix said as he closed the book and set it down to give Leo his full attention. Leo handed Felix a cup and sat down with the second cup as Felix added, "I can see from your demeanour that you have something of importance to discuss. Would it pertain to your thoughts on investing in stocks and shares? I have someone making enquiries and -"

"No, I have something else to discuss, Felix."

Felix took a sip of tea and said "Excellent tea. What is it, Leo?"

"Thank you," Leo said. "It could be important. While I was with Evelyn at the weekend, I rode Richards bicycle and Evelyn suggested I might have some improvements I could suggest to the manufacturers. As it is, I have awareness of many things as they will progress through the years and could therefore suggest many improvements to what there is available today. I could start with you and, as you know, I was able to follow your business concerns and I have been putting many of my memories to paper and will get it to you when completed."

"I have already experienced how valuable your knowledge of the future can be and it has already given me much increase that I would not have enjoyed otherwise."

"It would be wrong for me to cash in on someone's hard work. For instance, I would not like it if I had been working on a problem for a long time and someone else arrived with a solution and tendered my hard work to the wastebasket."

"Very commendable, Leo, and I have admired your obvious honesty since you first arrived with us."

"I could offer advice, though, without diminishing someone else's work. For instance, I'll not jump ahead of great and noble inventors and pioneers. I believe that most things may have arrived with us at a time and via a person or persons preordained to establish them. However, there is a lot I could suggest to enable these original inventors and pioneers to complete their work much earlier. They will still be proclaimed and receive credit for their work, only perhaps sooner than history might otherwise dictate."

"I understand. You could become extremely wealthy with the knowledge you possess, but I can see that this is not what drives you. Rather than be the architect of change, you merely desire to instruct the architect and speed his work along a little. All I can say is, if there is anything I can do to help you in this quest, I'll gladly put myself and my business at your disposal."

"That's very kind of you, Felix."

"Not at all, Leo, I have a small amount of knowledge myself and I know the manner of man you are and where you come from. I also know that it's in my interest to now be silent and allow you to speak. Therefore, please feel free to relay your objectives in as detailed a manner as you choose. You have my utmost attention."

Chapter 16

Leo had been living in Felix and Amelia's house in access of four weeks when his first letter arrived. Felix had already left for work but had left the letter outside Leo's room. Leo collected it after his morning wash and shave. He pondered on whether to open it or leave it until he had taken his chamber pot out the back for the early morning flush out ritual. He decided to flush out his chamber pot first, with it being a job he didn't look forward to, although he was eager to read his letter.

He put the letter into his back pocket, collected his chamber pot, covered it with a towel, and headed for the outhouse, taking care to listen out for Amelia as he went. He didn't have a great desire for Amelia to witness him completing this early morning task, even though she will have to do it as well. Just about everyone in 1905 had it to do, apart from people like the King who would have had a servant to carry out this early morning duty for him if needed, although he probably had an indoor privy.

With the flush-out job completed, he left the chamber pot outside the outhouse with the towel still covering it and sat down on the WC to read his letter. He knew whom it was from before opening it. It was from the estate agent and Leo was eager to discover how things were going with the house. It was good news and other people who had been interested in the house had dropped out, leaving Leo's way clear to taking up the debt that came with it.

He punched the air in excitement and decided sitting on the toilet might not be the best place to begin plans for decor and furniture, so he put the letter back into the envelope and collected his chamber pot.

It was daylight when Leo arrived to view his new house, so he didn't need to worry about not having his electricity switched on yet, but he still flicked the light switch, which was silly because apart from there not being any electricity, there were no light bulbs in the light sockets. Nevertheless, it was his switch and if he had a desire to flick it, who could stop him?

He admired the light switch with its wood surround and the round metal switch with it's on and off lever. He could understand the novelty value it would offer someone new to electricity in 1905. He grew up with electrical power being as common as sliced bread and he had begun renovation work on his third house in prime time and they all had light switches in every room and even in the garage and shed. It still gave him an enormous amount of joy to flick the light switch, though.

As he and Evelyn looked around what will one day be Laura's house but was now Leo's house, he took note to get light bulbs for every room and additional ones for any bedside and table lamps he should purchase.

There was an open fire in the living room, as would be expected, and one in each of the three bedrooms. He decided they would require a lot of coal, but without central heating, how could he neglect to light at least the fire in the main bedroom an hour or so before retiring. He took a note to contact the coalman.

He had a measuring tape and he measured the floors and windows for carpet and curtains. The one he had in primetime was steal and self-winding. This one was soft and flexible but had a winding handle and it did the same job of measuring in the same manner, depending on the ability and eyesight of the user.

While Evelyn held one end, Leo checked the measurement and took a note in his notebook. He knew the numbers of rolls of wallpaper due to having decorated these same rooms a couple of times, but he didn't have a clue how many strips he would get out of one of these old 1905 rolls. He had to rely on guessing the number of rolls needed, although he would not tackle this job himself because he had seen wallpaper in this time and it required its edges trimmed and he decided it would need a professional painter and decorator and it appeared wallpaper hanging in 1905 was not for the DIY enthusiast.

Leo was surprised to learn that he could get washable wallpaper for the kitchen and bathroom if required. However, with the walls plastered with plaster from the 1900s, he decided he would have to leave it to dry out longer than modern plaster before papering and painting. This allowed him time to look up a good painter and decorator.

He hesitated before going into what will one day be Peter's room. He was aware of the shock it would cause for Evelyn to witness him disappearing. She was now aware that it had happened and that is how he arrived in 1904 from his prime time, but witnessing it would be a whole other roll of wallpaper and while he would take great delight in seeing Peter and Lydia again, he had no desire to leave Evelyn with such a sight.

Besides, he was growing fond of Evelyn. He was even thinking in terms of it being possible to set up home with her one day and perhaps even spending the rest of his life with her. The rest of her life might be completely different, though, if she witnessed him disappearing.

In many three-bedroom houses in 1905 UK, several families would clamber in together and some might take a dim view of Leo having a three-bedroom house all to himself. This might have the possibility of escalating his need to get married and would possibly deprive him of at least one excuse for failure in this direction. However, Felix and Amelia live in a much larger house without any obvious problem, so he was happy to allow time to tell how it would pan out.

He entered what will one day be Peter's room without disappearing. He went to the window and looked out into the

197

garden, almost completed and awaiting spring for the sowing of the grass seed. He was not an enthusiastic gardener, but it was unavoidable because gardens often go with a house and grass needs mowed and for this, he would need to buy a lawnmower. He would have thought he would have to settle for a push mower, which didn't inject him with any level of enthusiasm. However, He spotted a Jefferies petrol lawnmower in Felix's shed, so it appeared 1905 had already reverted to proper mechanised gardening, so it might not be too bad.

He was aware of there not being a fire in any of the bedrooms in primetime. He reasoned they would have become of no use after the introduction of central heating to the house. This was before he and Laura took over ownership. It always felt eerie being there, though, with the memories of the kids being pressed into his mind and he could almost hear them playing noisily in the rooms and running up and down the stairs like a stampede of wild horses.

He missed them deeply and the house brought his pain closer. He had no control over things, though. Peter's bedroom door seemed to have become a portal, but possibly just a one-way and one-time portal. However, should the portal ever open again, he will now be there to go through it and, he hoped, back to the kids.

Evelyn, in some mystic way outside of her intellect, felt Leo's pain. She realised the reason for it, and she slipped her hand into his and squeezed. She didn't say anything, but there was no need for words and he understood the gesture and forced a smile in her direction. She kissed him. It was a quick kiss, just a light peck on the cheek, but it sent a message to him that spoke of her understanding his pain.

Martha greeted Leo with a broad smile on his return from work. "Dinner is on the table," she said.

Leo said, "Would the fact of you having your coat on suggest you are not staying and will be spending the evening with Harold?"

"It would. I'll be cooking a meal for us both when I get home."

"After you have spent the best part of the past hour cooking for us? Go for it. How are you feeling now?"

"I am much better now and glad to have disposed of the bandage and crutches."

"Enjoy the meal and the company; I know I'll enjoy mine. Good night."

"Good night to you, too, Leo," Martha said and left.

Leo took off his coat and went through to the dining room where Felix and Amelia were happily eating. Leo was amazed at Martha's timing. When staying for the meal, she always has a small amount left to do, Felix would tell her to relax, and he and Leo would finish it off. However, when she is not staying for the meal, she has it ready for the table waiting for Felix to return home.

"Welcome home," Felix, said.

"Good evening," Amelia said.

Leo raised a hand in salutation and said, "I smelt this from afar and if it tastes as good as the aroma suggests, I think I'm in for a treat."

"You are," Felix said. "Good day at work?"

"Fine, although the office junior has decided to leave. He had an interest in the recent British expedition to Tibet and he decided to enlist."

Felix said, "I assumed you were the office junior?" He laughed.

Leo sat down and picked up a knife and fork as he said, "Try not to confuse young and youthful with inexperience, Felix."

Felix laughed louder.

"Oh dear," Amelia said, "If the schoolboys are getting their humour out to play, perhaps I should have my meal in the cellar." She smiled and added, "A military career will teach the boy a lot. When does he plan to leave?"

"At the end of the week," Leo said, scooping up some mashed potato and starting to fill his plate.

Felix said, "I was at one time considering a career in the armed forces. Father wanted me to come into the family business and Mother was noncommittal. I could tell, though, that Mother would have worried if I was caught up in battle, so I decided against it."

Amelia smiled and said, "Good for Mother, having the ability to force a change of mind without saying a word."

Felix said, "I received a letter this morning which I need to tell you both about. Back before Christmas, I commissioned a tiling company to tile the kitchen, but with your illness, Amelia, It failed to occupy a prime position in my mind. The letter was to inform me that a crew would be arriving on Monday 27th February. It will no doubt put the kitchen out of commission, so we will need to make other arrangements, although they advise that the work will take just one day to complete."

Leo was not surprised at the news, although he had assumed that perhaps Felix originally got the kitchen tiled merely to block off and seal the cellar door. He could not see it as being a problem for him because he would be at work throughout the day, although he looked at Amelia and decided she might have a problem with it.

Leo raised a loaded fork to his eager mouth and widened his eyebrows to silently suggest what he had tasted was good.

"This is most inconvenient," Amelia said. "However, while being disrupted by noisy workmen in the kitchen would not be conducive to writing, if it's just for one day, I could move to the furthest room from the kitchen, the attic. I could offer Martha a bonus for preparing it for me."

Felix pondered and said, "The attic has not been used in quite some time and will perhaps require a lot of work. I'll get someone to give Martha a hand and I'll help too if needed."

Leo said, "I'll give a hand as well, so that is that sorted out. Could I have a further discussion on all this later, Felix?"

"Of course," Felix said.

"Thank you. I should add that I spent my lunch hour doing some shopping and I ordered a few things for my own house."

"I hope you don't forget us when you leave," Felix said.

"There is no fear of that ever happening, at least not if I retain control. Besides, I'll have to keep in touch if only to pay back the money I owe you. How is the work going with Richard's house, Amelia?"

Felix waved away Leo's promise of paying him back as Amelia said, "It now has water and electricity. Therefore, Richard is confident it will be completed within one or two weeks."

Leo said. "The watchman used to fill his kettle at my house, so it has had water at least since Christmas, and it's now over a month since that, so one or two weeks might be slightly ambitious if you are accepting water as an indication of the completion date and you might be slightly ambitious, I'm afraid. I have also had electricity, despite it not being switched on yet."

"Perhaps, but I am not in a hurry, although Richard desires to occupy it soon to enable him to give Evelyn back her independence and privacy."

Leo nodded his head before saying, "Evelyn said she will miss him when he moves out."

Felix said, "Will you give up one of the houses when, or if, you get married, Leo?"

"I haven't considered that, but not necessarily," Leo said. "It might be possible to live in one and rent the other out. That will provide additional income and will pay off the mortgage."

"So, will you live in Evelyn's house and rent your house? That would save you needing to furnish yours."

"It hasn't been decided yet, but it's a long time off anyway."

Amelia smiled at Leo and said, "Felix is just attempting to arrange a reason for a party. He enjoys a party, does our Felix."

Felix browsed through his wardrobe, attempting to select evening attire that Brenda would approve. He looked back towards the bedroom door when he heard the knock and called out, "Come in."

Leo entered and said, "I won't keep you long, Felix. I mentioned at the table having a word."

"That's right, come in, Leo. I am assuming it was not for Amelia's ear, so is it about what you often refer to as your prime time?"

Leo closed the door and said, "That's exactly what it's about, Felix. It's looking very like I'll never get back to the kids."

"I'm sorry, Leo. I know you miss your children deeply and I fully understand how not seeing them must feel. There is always hope, though. Don't give up, my friend."

"I'll never give up hope, but I have to be realistic. I should say that I had - still have - a note left for you, which you will find if I ever get back to prime time. It will explain things more fully. I have also now left one for Evelyn and I would appreciate it if you could pass it onto her in the event of my disappearance."

"Of course I will, with great sadness, but it will be done."

"Thank you, Felix. I have a way of also getting a message to my kids and friends in prime time because the tiles you are planning to add to the kitchen, in my prime time, over a century from now, I was removing. It was while removing the tiles that I discovered the sealed off cellar because, in the original history, you had the cellar doorway blocked off and the entire area tiled over."

"That is right, I remember you mentioning it being tiled off, now I can better understand this happening with the room soon to be tiled, although thanks to you, we can now leave the basement open for Amelia's continued use."

"Would you permit me to buy club hammer and bolster and chip out a cavity in the kitchen wall where I can leave some documents and various papers to be found in prime time? I'll board the cavity up and prepare it for tiling."

"By all means, Leo, it cannot possibly harm anything if the wall will be tiled over anyway. However, will the wall be thick enough?"

"It's two bricks thick and if I remove brick from this side, it will leave me a cavity thick enough for papers. I would need a thin airtight container that would allow enough room to board it up and prepare it for the tiles."

Please, feel free to leave whatever you wish in the wall cavity you plan to create."

"Thank you, Felix. As I said, I'll need to make it as airtight as possible to preserve everything. Do you have any suggestions?"

"Not offhand, but I'll ask around."

"With a lack of plastic or suitable tin containers, perhaps a glass container would be best."

Felix pondered and said, "I'll check this out, although, I know a gentleman who owns a glass factory and I am sure he would be able to produce a flat glass container of document proportions with an airtight lid."

"That sounds perfect."

With Felix giving his permission, Leo went to his room and pondered on everything. Laura's house, which was now his house again, might become a problem. He reasoned the possibility of it remaining empty if the forces that control such things sent him back to primetime without him making any arrangements.

With him being the owner, no one else would have any authority to sell or even live in it, apart from the bank who he decided would have the power to sell it to recoup any outlay. This will only be a problem before he finishes off the mortgage payments, though, but it would not do anyone any good for the bank to take ownership and sell the house. However, he reasoned there might be a way around this.

It was in the interest of most people for Leo to clear this debt as soon as possible and to leave written instruction. There was a way to clear all payments soon, or at least have future payments dealt with in advance and Felix could be of help by introducing Leo to businesspersons in the area to allow him to pitch some ideas to them on improvements, using his knowledge of the future.

He could ask for a percentage from profits made from any improvements he may advise and he could set up an agreement within that to deduct mortgage payments from these percentage fees. That should stop the bank from getting their hands on the house and he could arrange beforehand to nominate Felix as executor of everything, treating it similarly to a Last Will and Testament.

Thoughts of it as a last will smack of doom and gloom. It even had the effect of ushering in a slight depression to his mood. However, he could not deny his departure from 1905, if it happens, will be similar to his death to those he leaves. They will be devoid of the hope of seeing him again but would be happy that he was going to a better place where he would be with his kids again because they knew how much he missed them.

Leo created what he deemed to be likened to a 1905 one-man corporate think tank, with ideas for several business concerns and companies on how and where to make improvements. If only he could slip back to prime time and collect his laptop, although he had access to a typewriter. Felix bought it for Amelia, but she preferred the pen and found it difficult to create while tapping on keys and found it much more natural with a pen in her hand. She was used to the pen.

Felix contacted several business acquaintances who could see the worth in many of Leo's proposals and several put Leo on commission. The number grew and Leo felt he should keep a notebook in his pocket during work hours, to enable him to scribble down any memories that would help any company to make improvements. Monday brought many filled pages in his notebook with him seldom being very busy on Mondays. He was sure the company would not tolerate this indefinitely, though, despite the loyalty Clive Weatherford felt for Felix.

As each person and company became more impressed with the input Leo offered to their business ventures, Leo's bank balance increased and as his bank balance increased, word of his advice and resulting achievements spread. He could not accept all those who sought his advice and he relied on what he could remember about certain business ventures in the future. He could advise some, but he decided not to due to reasons of improvement not being helpful.

He neglected to pursue earth-shattering changes because he was aware of how things can easily backfire and destroy hopes rather than inspire. However, it quickly became apparent that he might need to resign from the colliery at a future point in time to free up the time needed for what was increasingly becoming a business. As others prospered, Leo also prospered and he needed a decision of a maximum client base. It helped to discover a legal expert with whom he could work and whose legal advice he could trust.

With his legal eagle in place and giving advice, Leo drew out a five-year contract where he would agree on a percentage of the gains his advice awarded each business and he would receive this percentage for five years. This way, he would have an income for five years, after which, he should have enough capital to sustain him and he could then turn his attention to another business venture.

Things were looking good for the future.

Leo found a painting and decorating firm with proven capabilities and he commissioned them to carry out the work on the house. In primetime, Leo always did his own painting and decorating. However, not only was the wallpaper different in 1905 and needed the edges trimmed off, Leo simply didn't have the time to do it with his time already split between his job at the Colliery, advisement work within his think tank and forming a relationship with Evelyn.

He didn't like the wallpaper, not only the rolls he bought but also every other roll in the contractor's display. Evelyn thought it was beautiful, but the last time Leo saw anything similar was when as a child he went with his mates to watch the flattening of houses in a slum clearance area.

One of the workers mentioned the people who lived there didn't have a lot and would be much better off in the housing estate being built close by. Therefore, he saw the wallpaper as only being good enough for someone who didn't have the wherewithal to get anything better.

The range of wallpapers on offer to Leo comprised of various designs of 1905 or pre-1905.

"You will like it much more on the wall," Evelyn promised him.

He disagreed.

The owner of the firm informed Leo that, due to a rush in demand, they could allocate only one of their artisans to the work. Leo was fine with that. He finds when more than one is working on the same project; they often spend most of the day chatting or playing cards. One on his own, however, will get on with the job if only to relieve boredom.

During the first couple of days, Leo left the painter to get on with it. He left a note to inform the lone artisan that there will be a bonus if he completes the work with speed and to an acceptable standard.

After two full days work, Leo went along in the evening time to see how it was going. He knew the painter would have finished and gone home, so he would not feel Leo was checking his work. He didn't see it as checking and was simply curious because he may need to live with the results for a long time.

It appeared the painter and decorator was doing the work the way Leo himself would have done it and he had all the ceilings coated in distemper and all the skirting, doorframes, doors and other woodwork finished. Leo would prefer Acrylic paint for the woodwork, but Acrylic paint wasn't about in 1905, so it had to be oil based.

He had even begun to hang the wallpaper, although Leo reckoned there was still some day's work left. Leo was happy with the quality and speed of the work.

He was not happy with the choice of paint used on the ceilings, though, and he was aware that painters mainly used distemper in old houses because it covered cracks in walls very well, but this was a new house and the walls were without crack or blemish. Leo decided the firm must have got a job lot and was trying to use it up.

It was too late to do anything about the ceilings because they were finished. Leo decided to call in early the next day and have a word with the artisan and let him know he was not happy with the distemper. He could discover what he will use for paste before the completion of the hanging of the paper.

Leo had put off and excused himself from his first visit to Evelyn's house until Evelyn decided it was time to change this. There was no arranging a time and place to meet for Leo. The arrangement was simply for him to call round to Evelyn's house. This being his first visit, he wondered if she had electricity. In primetime, everyone had electricity, even if some didn't always have the wherewithal for payment and preferred to buy things of greater necessity like a daily twelve-pack and a bottle of inner warmth.

In 1905, though, not everyone had electrical power running to their home and he discovered this when he went to Martha's house. It would cost quite a lot of money to have a house wired and it would cause a lot of disruption and the disruption more than the cost would put many people off.

Richard would possibly offer to pay Evelyn's electrical wiring costs, especially given the fact that he was living there until his own house was completed. However, Evelyn might be one of the many who held onto her oil lamps due to the inability to accept the disruption a gang of bright sparks would create as they cut channels out in all the walls to bury their wiring.

The light flooded from the hallway onto Leo when Evelyn opened the front door to him.

Evelyn was not used to men calling to the house, apart from Richard. Small things like hitting her knee with the door as she opened it, spoke of her being nervous, or perhaps she lacked full control of her motor skills. She stepped back and invited Leo in and so it became Leo's turn to show signs of nervousness or lack of motor skills and he stepped into the hall and head-butted her. He meant to kiss her on the cheek but mistimed and misplaced his action.

He said, "I'm very sorry, I meant to –"

"Think nothing of it," Evelyn said, beginning to laugh. She then offered her cheek to Leo and said, "Second chance?"

Leo laughed and kissed her on the cheek before saying, "Everyone deserves a second chance."

Evelyn was unsure if she should invite Leo into the living room, or simply go in and allow him to follow. If she goes for the latter option, he might stand there and wait for her to invite him, so she decided to say, "Would you like to come through to the lounge?"

Leo frowned as he followed her. Even Felix and Amelia stop short of referring to the lounge, although he decided that she might be attempting to impress. He was aware of people having various titles for various rooms, though. His mum told him that his great-granny would refer to the kitchen as being the scullery, and to confuse the issue further, she would refer to the living room as the kitchen. He didn't know why this was, but he assumed it might be due to the living room fire in days of old being used for cooking.

He entered the living room. It was cosy with a warm fire glowing in the hearth and a filled coalscuttle at the side of it and a companion set at the other side. The flooring was linoleum with a large mat filling a large area in front of the fire and going back to the brown leather sofa with matching leather armchairs at either side.

In the corner, Leo noticed a gramophone player. It was silent. He was sure Evelyn's taste in music would be similar to that of Felix and Amelia and he was happy that such music should remain silent.

Evelyn noticed his attention on the gramophone player and she said, "Would you like some music?"

"Not just now," he said, remaining in a standing position and deciding he should remain like this until invited to take a seat. Evelyn suddenly became aware of this and she said, "Please, feel free to sit down."

Leo smiled and said, "I thought you were gonna leave me standing here."

He sat down on the left side of the settee and tapped the right-hand side to indicate that he would be fine with her sitting beside him. The settee would seat three people, so there was plenty of room for Leo at one side, Evelyn at the other and a mile of space in between them both. She sat down and allowed this space between them both to remain.

Leo pondered for a second before saying, "Evelyn, this is my first time in your home and I have to say, it's an extremely comfortable home and you keep it very tidy. However, I have to admit that, sitting here presents me with a problem."

"I am very sorry, Leo. What is causing you this problem?"

"Well, it began with the weather outside, although that was not the actual problem. The real problem came through wearing this very heavy and very warm overcoat to combat the cold outside and now, sitting in front of your warm and inviting fire, I feel I might melt at any second."

"Oh, I see," Evelyn, said, frowning in thought, "therefore, am I to think that you have become unable to remove your overcoat and would like me to become your servant and remove it for you? I have a rule in this house, if you are hot; you take off your coat, if you are cold, put coal on the fire."

Leo smiled and said, "That's two rules, but what if I need a kiss?" Leo said.

"You firstly remove your coat and you then can kiss it all evening if you wish."

"Are you telling me to take my coat off?"

"Yes, I am telling you to take your coat off."

Leo stood up and took his coat off and said, "The last time I was here, I saw just the inside of your shed when we got Richard's bike out. This is the first time I have been in your house, though, so I don't know where to put my coat."

"Did you not see the compost heap while you were out the back?"

Leo laughed. Evelyn rose, took the coat from Leo and said, "Men cannot do anything themselves."

Leo said, "We have women so we don't need to do a lot. However, could I stop you for a second?"

Evelyn stopped and said, "I advise you not to allow Amelia to hear you saying anything like that."

"Have me hung, drawn and quartered, would she," Leo said and he reached to the coat in Evelyn's hand and took from the inside pocket a small package and smiled as he added, "I'll need this for later."

As Evelyn left the room, she said, "Being hung, drawn and quartered would be a pleasure in comparison to what Amelia would plan for such a statement."

"I think you exaggerate," Leo called out after her as he left the package on a small table and sat down.

A moment later, Evelyn returned after hanging Leo's coat up, smiled and sat down, slightly closer on the settee this time to Leo. She could see Leo had left the small package on her small coffee table, but she didn't award it a lot of attention for fear of it making her appear nosey.

To show he didn't hold her in contempt for her closer position, Leo slipped his person closer to Evelyn and said, "It feels like this settee might be shrinking."

"Do you think so? Would it expand to its original size if I clapped my hand?"

"Do you not mean to clap your hands in the plural?"

"No, I mean to clap my hand in the singular against your face in the plural."

"Are you suggesting I have more than one face?"

Evelyn smiled.

Leo said, "I have two lips. You also have two lips. When I was at school, the teacher tried to convince me that two and two equalled four. He was wrong, though. Two lips plus two lips doesn't equal four, it equals a kiss. I can prove it."

"Can you?"

As Leo drew his lips closer to Evelyn's, she stood up and said," I think it's time for a cup of tea. Are you hungry?"

Leo stood and said, "I had something to eat not too long ago. Do you need a hand?"

"Since when have women needed male help in making tea? It's the man's job to relax, so relax."

Leo could see that his failed attempt at a proper kiss as opposed to a peck, was not in keeping with 1905 protocol and it was much too early. It's not always easy to remember the differences between women of opposite ends of the century, or of different centuries, as was the case. Therefore, he sat down to relax as instructed.

He glanced at the package on the table and pondered. He then looked over at the telephone. He thought she would have one because Richard would need it and he probably paid for it. He had not noticed it until that moment because it rang, unlike the notification ring tone on his prime time phone, but more like the clanging of an old bell.

"Would you mind getting that while I make tea?" Evelyn called from the kitchen.

Leo was pleased that Evelyn was at peace with him answering a private phone call and he was aware that some women would have dashed to the phone at all costs. He was happy to answer it if only to stop the annoying ringing and he lifted the phone, took the earpiece from the cradle, put it to his ear and spoke into the mouthpiece saying, "Hello." He listened and then said, "Could you hold on a second."

He pressed the mouthpiece to his shoulder to lessen the sound of his voice to the caller and called out, "It's Sylvia."

"Could you tell her I'll call her back later?"

"Hello Sylvia, Evelyn is busy right now, but she said she'll call you back later. Is that okay?" He listened for a moment and then said, "I'm not Richard, I'm Leo. Goodbye, Sylvia."

He put the phone back down and placed the mouthpiece on the cradle just as a rap sounded on the front door and he looked towards the kitchen and called out, "Would you like me to get that as well?"

"If you don't mind, Leo, thank you."

Leo reasoned he probably would not know the person, but he decided Evelyn would know them so he would be on his best behaviour and would not try to crack funny. Not everyone appreciated his form of humour, especially in 1905, and he was amazed Evelyn would risk embarrassment by first allowing him to answer the phone and now the door.

The hall light was still on with Evelyn neglecting to switch it off when they earlier went through into the living room. This meant Leo didn't have to grope about in the dark in search of the light switch and he opened the door. He saw the enormously wide smile first, then the bunch of flowers in the man's hand. The man immaculately dressed and fresh from spending a lot of time preparing, immediately lost his smile as he realised it was not Evelyn answering the door and he said, "Who are you?"

Leo said, "I think the more appropriate question lies in who you are?"

Chapter 17

"Is that Edward?" They heard Evelyn asking from the kitchen.

Edward looked past and beyond Leo and said, "Evelyn, I decided to take your advice and I'm going there now."

Evelyn arrived beside Leo with a smile and said, "Flowers, good idea! How can she say no to a man with flowers? Leo and I were about to have tea, can you join us?"

Edward gazed, wide eyed and excited at Leo, and reached out his non-flower holding hand, "You are the Leo I have been hearing so much about at work! I am extremely pleased to meet you!"

Leo Accepted Edwards handshake and said, "I take it you work together?"

"Yes," Edward said to Leo. He then turned his attention to Evelyn and said, "I can't stay, I just wanted to stop by and let you know that I have decided to do as you suggested and I have taken my courage in hand and will deliver these flowers to my love and hope she accepts my apology."

"I am sure she will, Edward. It was a mistake anyone could make and she will forgive you and it was silly you allowing fear of rejection to hold you back."

Edward said, "I must go now before I lose the courage to press on. I am Pleased to meet you, Leo, have a lovely evening both of you and thank you, Evelyn."

"Good luck, Edward."

Edward left and Evelyn said to Leo, "I'll explain all that as we have our cup of tea."

"I think I caught on to the gist of it," Leo said as he smiled and closed the door.

Evelyn went back to the kitchen and Leo went through to the living room and picked the small package up from the table. It was a necklace. He spotted it as he passed by the jewellers and he felt compelled to go in and buy it for Evelyn. It just remained for him to give it to her and he held it behind his back to hide it from her as she arrived in the room with the tea.

The house was not a hive of activity when Leo arrived and the painter had not yet shown up for work. He arrived close behind Leo, though, and was confused to find Leo there and didn't appear to know who he was, so Leo said, "Hello, My name is Leo and I own the mortgage on this house, which I suppose makes me the man who is paying your wages this week. It also gives me the right to ask why you haven't started work yet."

The painter shrugged his shoulders with the un-shaded light in the ceiling making obvious his worry as he gazed towards the floor like a guilty schoolchild with mischief having caught up with him and Leo laughed, slapped him playfully on the arm and said, "Just joking, mate. Don't worry, I won't tell your boss you were late."

The painter said, "My wife and I had an addition to the family and he kept us both awake quite a lot of the night."

"Newborn baby, congratulations on that, and don't let my weird sense of humour throw you. When was he born, you did refer to the baby being he, didn't you?"

"Yes, he's just over a week old."

213

Leo nodded his head and said, "Yes, they do tend to keep you awake at that age. I have two, a boy and a girl. I haven't seen them for a few weeks, though."

"I am sorry to hear that, Mr – sorry, I don't think I know your name."

"Call me Leo. What can I call you?"

"My name is Joe, Joe Lennox."

Leo went into instant compute mode as he attempted to make sense of what he was hearing. He reasoned that either Lennox was an extremely common name in 1905, or he might have stumbled onto another member of his family. He had to think fast, but he obviously could not tell Joe too much and to keep the conversation on a less than serious level, he said, "I'm pleased to meet you, Joe Joe Lennox."

"No, it's not Joe-Joe, it's just Joe, one Joe, not hyphenated."

"I'm still pleased to meet you just Joe, one Joe, not hyphenated."

Joe realised Leo was not being serious and he reasoned maybe the treatment wasn't having the desired effect, but he smiled. Leo reached out a hand and Joe Accepted it and they shook hands. Joe said, "I'm very pleased to make your acquaintance, Mr Leo."

Leo smiled and said, "Mr Leo, I like that, but make it just Leo. Anyway, I know of Martha Lennox who works for Felix and Amelia Bennett. Would you be related to her?"

"Yes, Martha is my aunt, my dad's brother's wife."

"Martha has a portrait on her living room wall of her husband's brother."

"That's right. That's my dad."

Leo reasoned he might be talking to a relation. He could not remember any with the name Joe, and he could only go back as far as Graham Lennox.

Using distemper for painting the ceilings was no longer an issue and Leo realised it would not be the painter's fault anyway. However, he decided to bring it up to grab some time to work everything out properly and he said, "I wasn't happy to see that you used distemper for the ceilings."

"Sorry about that. I can only use what they release to me from stores."

"I know it's not your fault, so don't fret about it. Everything remains the same for you, with the promised bonus at the end of the job if finished at a decent time and done to a decent standard. I was wondering what you are using for paste, though."

Joe gestured towards a cupboard and said, "It's in that cupboard along with the wallpaper."

Leo felt slightly foolish because he didn't think about looking in any of the cupboards and he went to the one to which Joe gestured. He already knew what the design of the wallpaper was because he chose it, so he checked the paste and was happy with it."

He turned back to Joe and said, "I think your boss probably got a job lot of that distemper and will use it on all jobs, but the paste looks fine."

Joe said, "Distemper is normally used on older buildings, not on a new house like this. I can only apologise."

Leo smiled and said, "You have to use what you're given to use and I'll be having a word with your boss about it. I don't in any way blame you, though. That aside, what's it like having a baby to care for at the beginning of 1905?"

"Hard, but I would not like to have attempted to bring up a child when I was young. We are in a new century and everything is modern now, not like it once was."

"Very true, Joe, can I ask the baby's name?"

"Graham. We named him after my Father."

Leo echoed the word "Father" at the same time as Joe and Joe frowned in confusion and said, "Sorry, you seemed to know whom we named the baby after."

"People often name babies after relatives. Fathers and Grandfathers are high on the pecking order."

There was the beginning of a possible tradition in the Lennox family of naming the eldest son after the grandfather, but Leo had said Father knowing that his elder brother received his Grandfather's name and it appeared that Joe might have begun this tradition with baby Graham by naming him after his Father, which, of course, was the baby's Grandfather. Leo missed out because he was born after his elder brother Graham. How could Leo tell Joe all this, though?

There was also a tradition in Mike's family to name the firstborn son after the Father and Leo understood this tradition to go back several generations to when Bartholomew Brown's wife gave birth. Bartholomew despised his name so much he made it known that he didn't wish it to be carried forward in the family. He felt so strongly on this that he promised, if any of his son's named their male children after him, he would come back and haunt them with a passion never before witnessed.

Therefore, when his son Theodor's wife gave birth to a male child, his chosen name was Michael.

Evelyn stepped slightly to the side to allow Leo room to pass her and enter the hall. Leo said, "I hope there aren't any love-torn work colleagues hammering on your door this time to let you know their plans for the evening?"

Evelyn smiled and said, "I don't think so."

She gestured for Leo to go through to the living room and followed him after closing the door. He could see she was wearing the necklace he had bought for her, but he decided not to mention this and they both sat down and Leo said, "How did it go with Edward and his girlfriend?"

"Very well and Edward arrived at work this morning with a huge smile, so I didn't even need to ask him. He was anxious to tell everyone, though."

"I got the impression that he hasn't had a lot of girlfriends?"

"Very few, he is normally extremely shy and is not as forward as he might have appeared last evening."

"I think he was on a mental high, maybe took something to calm his nerves before leaving the house. However, Edward to the side, is there anything you would like to do this evening?"

Evelyn feigned thought and said, "We could go skiing at Lassen Volcanic National Park, and then onto Duranbah Beach for a barbecue."

"Or," Leo interjected, "we could go to the park, feed the birds and then onto the coffee house."

216

"No, it's dark outside and the birds will have nested. I think my idea is much better with the places mentioned being in a different time zone and it not being dark there yet."

Leo laughed and said, "We could go to the pub for a quiet drink?"

"The last time I was at the pub, with my husband, a vicious fight broke out and I swore I would never go back to where angry men get drunk and take their temper out on anyone close to them."

"Did your husband get into many pub fights?"

"It was not my husband who was fighting, it was Felix."

"You jest?"

Evelyn smiled and said, "Yes, of course, I jest. I decided if you were going to give silly responses, I should do likewise."

Leo laughed and tickled Evelyn.

"Why did you tickle me," Evelyn asked.

"I hate laughing alone."

"Being tickled does not make me laugh, it makes me angry. Therefore, I would thank you not to do it again."

"Leo said, "I don't believe you," and tickled her again and she laughed, lifted a cushion and used it as a weapon to fend Leo off.

Leo took hold of both her wrists and pushed her hands behind her back and he said, "Now you are at my mercy and I am merciless."

Evelyn sighed and said, "You can be so childish at times."

"I can also be a thief," Leo said, and he kissed her and added, "See, I stole a kiss."

"As I said, childish, if I had the strength, I would bind you and have the police remove and put you into custody."

The sound of the front door opening caused them to sit up and put on the pretence of enjoying a sensible conversation together as they heard Richard saying, "It's only me." Richard then entered the room.

"I thought you were with Amelia," Evelyn said.

Richard looked closely at Evelyn and frowned. He put his hand to her forehead and said, "You appear to be slightly flushed. I hope you are not coming down with something." He looked at Leo as well and added, "You too, Leo. I do hope you have not caught that illness Amelia had at Christmas."

Leo smiled and said, "No, we're fine, just a bit hot after sofa wrestling and Evelyn not having the strength to tie me up and have me arrested."

"I see," Richard said, frowning. "Anyway, Amelia and I have decided to go to London and perhaps go to the theatre and on for a meal. Felix has already got something planned, but Amelia is getting changed and I decided to utilise this time by coming here to see if you would both like to join us?"

Leo looked at Evelyn to gauge her reaction and he nodded to her, she nodded back and he said, "That sounds like a great idea, Richard. We were both discussing what to do and where to go."

Richard smiled, looked to Evelyn and said, "Would you like to get changed?"

Evelyn rose to her feet and said, "Yes, I'll not be a second."

She quickly left the room and Richard sat down on the settee beside Leo. Leo said, "There isn't a lot to do around here of an evening, is there, Richard."

Richard said, "If you mean it can get boring, I would not know, Leo. I never allow myself to get bored and can always find something with which to occupy and entertain my mind. In my experience, only lazy people get bored."

Leo was already bored with the conversation and simply nodded his head, more as a sign of defeat than agreement. He had warmed to Richard but could not deny there can at times be a lack of spark within him, which he also realised, was the case with Amelia. He decided they were more suited together than he and Amelia would have been, so it possibly worked out in the best way for everyone involved.

He found Evelyn to be the opposite of Richard in many ways and while both being extremely pleasant, Richard was more subdued and extremely predictable, where Evelyn could be more outgoing and zany to the realms of weird and crazy, a bit like Leo himself.

The more time Leo spent with Evelyn, the more he realised he was in no way suited to Amelia and with this knowledge came a growing desire to spend more time with Evelyn. He enjoyed the fact that he could be himself with Evelyn and didn't need to adapt a psyche persona that didn't fit his natural mentality.

It was good that Richard arrived, though, because 1905 can be a boring time without his usual work on the house to get Leo through the hours.

He didn't relate boredom to laziness as Richard appeared to, he was used to rushing home from driving a bus for eight hours or so and then to work on the house for the next eight hours or so before giving way to eight hours of sleep and he would certainly deny being lazy.

However, having nothing much to do can zap the ability to get up and get on with things, although he would agree with Richard that an active mind could normally find another form of physical and/or mental occupation even when options become few.

Leo was ready for his evening meal after a busier than usual day at work and this time Martha joined them due to Felix inviting her man friend Harold. Felix insisted that Martha, after quickly changing out of her housekeeping attire and into something more becoming to the occasion, set beside Harold. Felix introduced Leo to Harold due to Leo having gone back to work when Harold arrived at the house the day of Martha's run-in with the pony and trap. "It's great to finally meet you, Harold," Leo said.

"Likewise, Mr Lennox, Harold replied."

Leo smiled and said, "Mr Lennox was my dad. Feel free to call me Leo."

"If I might ask," Harold said, hovering a pointed finger from Leo to Martha "are you related to each other? You have the same surname."

"Leo and I have discussed this, Harold," Felix said, "And we feel it's very likely, but there is no paper evidence to substantiate it."

"Of course," Harold said, "any relationship would be on Martha's husbands' side. However, many people share a name without sharing a relationship."

"To get off this subject and move on with something else, Leo said, "Can I ask what business you are in, Harold?"

"Nothing grand like Felix, I'm afraid."

"Believe me, Felix said, "There is nothing grand about raw textiles."

Leo said, "Maybe Harold was referring more to your bank account, Felix."

Harold smiled and continued, "I own a small hardware store in the north of the city. Actually, I co-own it with my brother."

"Might I ask what you're brother's name is," Felix said.

"My brother was named Marmaduke after our uncle."

Leo was of the opinion that Marmaduke was an extremely funny sounding name and he had a deep urge to laugh and had to suppress his urge though rather than cause insult."

Felix said, "I think I am correct that your surname is Hickinbottom and that would mean your brother is Marmaduke Hickinbottom. The warrant officer in Sir William Alexander Smith's Boys Brigade, that I was a member off as a boy, had the name Marmaduke Hickinbottom."

Harold smiled proudly and said, "Yes, that would be my brother."

"Therefore," Leo began with thoughts of saying to Harold *Therefore, that would make you Harold Hickinbottom*, which Leo saw as being even funnier than just Hickinbottom on its own. However, an unseen spirit from within suggested he should not take the conversation there and instead he needed to quickly think of something else to say and so he said, "I was in the Scouts." It didn't really follow him beginning with the word, therefore, but it was better than causing insult.

"What is or are the Scouts?" Amelia asked.

"The Boy Scouts," Leo said and then realised the Scout movement might not have formed yet in 1905, so he thought quickly and said, "It's a group of boys organised by Robert Baden-Powel, who was –"

"I have heard of Baden-Powel," Harold interrupted. Marmaduke often speaks of him as doing a lot of work with boys. I believe he still holds the rank of Lieutenant General in the British army and it's rumours that his work with boys will be sure to escalate when he retires."

To divert the conversation away from Baden-Powel, Leo said to Felix, "How long were you a member of the Boys Brigade?"

"I was not a member very long, Leo, from age twelve to fifteen."

Leo said, "Long enough, I would say."

Amelia said, "I think we still have your uniform."

Leo decided that one day a very large skip will be needed to remove all the junk Felix and Amelia appear to have accumulated and stored from all there old toys in one of the rooms, even down to, it now appeared, Felix's BB uniform. However, he neglected mentioning this and he said, "I have to say, this meal is yet another triumph, Martha."

"Yes," I agree," Amelia, said.

"You are a lucky man, Harold," Felix said.

"I agree," Harold said, smiling at Martha.

Martha smiled widely, although her smile bore a hint of embarrassment and she said, "It's just a meal, nothing special."

Leo said, "Don't be so modest, Even your quickly cooked lunches can be a veritable banquet to a man who was raised on baked beans and toast!"

Martha hemmed and hawed before smiling and saying, "I also do baked beans on toast."

Leo realised he might have made yet another mistake in mentioning baked beans because he didn't know whether or not they were available in the UK in 1905. However, Martha's response suggested she was aware of them. Living in 1905 was still not without its pressures for Leo, this thought brought him once more to thoughts about prime time, the kids, and not seeing the kids, and he missed them sorely. He will need to adorn a brave face and, while Leo would deny being two-faced, let alone having a face for every occasion, he managed to adorn his brave face with a smile.

Most things drew the kids to his mind and he missed them. He had to cover his heartache at not having a way that he could explain it and it saddened him that he could not be free with information pertaining to himself and his family. This was especially true of those who were possibly a part of his family such as Martha and Joe, plus those who could potentially become a part of his family, like Evelyn.

He could not deny that he was growing extremely fond of Evelyn and he was looking forward to spending some time with her later. He would like to buy a car because Evelyn appeared to enjoy going for a drive. However, to buy such an item, he would need to take out a second mortgage because a car would cost as much as his house and he still had to furnish it. The bank loan Felix arranged for him should cover that and the advice he was giving to business concerns far and near would more than pay for it. That would leave his wages for other things, but there probably would not be enough for a car, at least not for a few years when automobiles would go down in price.

As was customary, after the meal, the men retired to the living room to chat about men's things, leaving the women free to discuss less important issues. The women normally saw it as putting the world to rights. However, as there was just Amelia and Martha, they decided to leave most of the world for another day. They concentrated on the area around the local jewellers and Amelia asked if there was the possibility of wedding bells, and they manoeuvred well away from the men's hearing range for this.

Leo expected Felix to do some business in informing Harold of a range of leather ware that he could sell in the hardware store. Felix behaved, although Leo put him to the test by saying to Harold, "I would imagine the world turning to electricity will have reduced your sale of paraffin for lamps and you no doubt offset this by stocking other commodities?"

Harold glanced to his rear before saying, "Slightly, but paraffin is only one of the many items on sale and you should drop by some time and browse through our stock."

Felix might have denied himself the opportunity of some business, but not Harold and Leo smiled and said, "Actually, I'll do that because I'll need some things for the house."

Felix smiled as he reasoned that Harold glancing behind before replying suggested that Martha had pre-warned him about promoting his merchandise and he was checking she was not in hearing range before delivering his invitation.

Leo was more worried about the time and he had to excuse himself to get a quick wash, shave and change of clothes to spend some time with Evelyn.

With Leo realising that he might be held back slightly with Martha and Harold staying for the meal, he and Evelyn decided it would be best to meet somewhere, rather than Leo going to the house, due to them both agreeing on a walk to the cemetery.

Evelyn told Leo that she usually visits her sister at least once each week, but he realised this would not have been possible during the past few days considering the time they spent together. Therefore, they decided on a rendezvous point and when he got there, Evelyn was waiting for him. He greeted her with a kiss on the cheek, which slightly embarrassed her with it being in public, but it didn't stop her taking his arm as they walked on.

"I hope you didn't have to wait too long," Leo said.

"The briefest of moments," Evelyn replied. She glanced at Leo, smiled and added, "Are you nervous?"

"No, why, should I be? Your sister doesn't travel through the cemetery wakening the residents for a chat, does she?"

"No, of course not, but I would be extremely nervous if I was going to meet your sister for the first time."

"No, I'm not nervous. I am slightly apprehensive, though, and unsure of what to say to her. What's her husband like?"

"If I were to describe him in one word, that word would have to be weird, but he is very likable."

"That's six words."

"What is?"

"'Weird, but he is very likable' is six words and you said it would describe him in one word."

Evelyn nudged Leo with her elbow and said, "Weird is the one word, and the rest was just a follow-up, as well you know."

"What's his name, it's not anything silly like Marmaduke, I hope?"

"Why do you mention the name Marmaduke?"

"Martha, as you know, had her boyfriend over at Felix and Amelia's and he has a brother called Marmaduke and it was all I could do to refrain from laughing."

"Why, Marmaduke is a perfectly acceptable name. Anyway, my brother-in-law is called Ian William Enterrarlo, although he prefers Will to William and doesn't like Ian at all, so is I Will Enterrarlo."

"I Will Enterrarlo," Leo echoed. "What kind of name is I Will Enterrarlo?"

"Did you know that the translation of Enterrarlo, from Spanish to English, is Bury you?"

Leo frowned and said, "I Will bury you?" He laughed. What a brilliant name for a grave digger!"

Evelyn smiled widely, her smile acted as a light, and Leo said, "That's not his name at all, is it?"

Evelyn laughed louder and said, "His name is Ian William and he doesn't like Ian so is happier being addressed as William Anderson."

"I'm guessing your sister is Mrs Anderson?"

"Wow, I'm impressed with your powers of deduction."

"It's all very elementary, my dear Watson."

"So, I deduce you have experienced Arthur Conan Doyle's work?"

"No, but I read his book."

Evelyn frowned, and then laughed.

From behind and across the road, a man came out from an alleyway. They didn't see him, but they heard his footsteps in the otherwise quiet and darkened street, the metal heel and toe segs nailed to the underneath of his shoes clicking and scraping on the cobblestone like horses hoofs as he crossed over the road from the alley and was then directly behind Leo and Evelyn.

This was not the first time in 1905 that Leo came upon another person in an otherwise desolate street and he could feel Evelyn bracing up slightly, so he whispered, "Don't worry, it's just someone going about his evening's business and he is no doubt going home to his family, or is going to visit family, just as we are."

"That is all well and good, Leo, but they never arrested Jack the Ripper and he could still be free to commit his vile deeds."

"I'll protect you."

"Who will protect you?"

224

Leo won two gold medals at his last school sports day and both were for short distance sprinting and he reckoned he could outrun the man as long as he didn't throw a knife. Leo was not sure if he could outrun a knife, although it might depend on the velocity the man was able to muster in throwing it. Leo knew he could not leave Evelyn to fend him off alone, though.

Leo decided that Evelyn's broad hat, covering her Gibson Girl hair do, would not slow her down because it would no doubt fly off her head. Her Fine Vici shoes might be a problem, though. They didn't have the longest heal he had seen in 1905, but they were long enough to fall on the side of not being conducive to running at great speed. That might not be an issue, though, if Leo put himself between her and the man if needed.

He was confident it was just someone out for a walk and there was no danger, but he felt he should decide on a protective course of action. He didn't want to alarm her by giving instructions beforehand, but he decided it would not be a bad idea to quicken the pace slightly, not enough to alarm Evelyn, but enough to put some distance between them and the man.

Leo decided it was best not to look back, but he listened to the man's footsteps and when he and Evelyn increased speed, the man also increased speed. That didn't instil in Leo an enormous amount of confidence.

"Leo, I'm scared," Evelyn said.

"Could you quicken the pace and walk on alone? I'll fall back and see if he has any untoward intentioned."

"No, I'll not leave you on your own."

"He's probably just out for a walk."

"We will find out together, Leo."

They were in a long street without a turn off for a long way. That deprived him of the choice of making a few turns to see if the man followed them or walked on. He decided the man, if up to no good, was biding his time until a convenient spot presented a better opportunity, like another alleyway similar to the one from which he came. Leo could at least cheat him out of that plan and he pushed Evelyn's hand from his arm, quickly turned and went towards the man as he said, "Are you following us?"

"Don't Leo," he heard Evelyn say behind him, but he had made his choice and could not turn back.

"The man produced a late 1800s Smith and Wesson .32 calibre revolver and aimed it at Leo. To Leo, it was just a gun, like any other gun, and it caused him to stop. Leo heard a scream from behind. He knew it was Evelyn, but he could not see because his eyes were on the barrel of the gun as the man walked closer and Leo glanced back. He didn't want to back off because that would have brought the man closer to Evelyn.

"I need money," the man said. I want your money, your watch and anything else of value that you have."

"I don't have anything of value and I left my money at home because I didn't think I'd need it."

That was a lie and his wallet was in his pocket, but he didn't feel inclined to hand it over.

The man said, "Give me your valuables and you will live to walk away, refuse again and I'll shoot you and then take your valuables before taking whatever valuables your lady friend has."

Leo could hear a tremble in the man's voice and could see an even more eruptive trembling in the man's hand that was more obvious with the movement of the barrel with foresight at the front of the gun barrel protruding and exaggerating the movement. Leo was aware of the possibility of the man's trembling finger pressing unintentionally hard on the trigger and releasing a bullet accidently. The bullet could injure or kill him, but it could also injure or kill Evelyn.

As way of distracting the man for a second, Leo fixed his gaze beyond the man and slowly shook his head as if saying no to someone behind the man. Leo was beginning to think the man was not going to fall for it, when indeed the man did fall for it and looked behind. Leo lunged forward and grabbed hold of the man's gun wrist.

Evelyn screamed for a second time, the scream echoing through the darkness, but not bringing anyone to their aid and a shot rang out to compete with the volume of her scream, its thunderous bang sounding even louder set against the quietness of the evening.

Chapter 18

Felix and Richard stood in Evelyn's living room while Brenda and Amelia sat at opposite sides to Evelyn on the settee, each holding one of her hands and offering comforting words.

"I am perfectly fine," Evelyn was insisting, but neither Brenda nor Amelia believed her due to what she had suffered. They were judging her emotions on their own capabilities, though, without realising that Evelyn might be stronger than them. There were times when she didn't feel strong, but Leo seemed to give her the strength she needed when she needed it and she missed him from the room for the strength he offered.

Felix and Richard felt un-needed, like discarded candles from a birthday cake after they had been blown out and neglected by everyone who gathered around for a slice of cake while the candles would have served their function and would be as useful as a hearing aid to a blind man.

Richard asked if anyone wanted another cup of tea. No one did, but Evelyn handed her empty cup to him and said, "Could you leave my cup back?"

"Certainly," he said, taking the cup from her and looking to Brenda and Amelia with the silent question of whether or not they would like him to take their cups away too. They did and Richard juggled with the cups and saucers until he managed to stack the saucers together and was able to carry five cups with a finger through each handle and the fifth trapped by his thumb. Felix took his cup through to the kitchen, leaving the girls in a cluster on the settee.

As Felix and Richard returned, they heard the front door closing and seconds later, Leo arrived in the room, saying, "I thought he was never going to leave and let me get back into the heat of the fire. I'm glad I took my tea out with me, or it would be freezing now."

Richard took the cup from Leo and said, "I'll leave it in for you."

"Thanks, Richard," Leo said.

Felix said, "Did he give any idea of anything?"

Leo said. "He said they got a lot to work on with the gun and they were able to get a few good fingerprints. He suggested taking my prints at some time for elimination purposes, but I don't think that will be necessary because I didn't touch the gun and I grabbed him by the wrist and he fired into the air and got scared and ran off, dropping the gun."

"I thought you were really brave, Leo," Evelyn said.

"It could also be seen as silly," Brenda said. "You could have been killed, Mr Lennox."

Richard arrived back in the room as Felix smiled and said, "He prefers Leo, and hero's are seldom dissuaded with the worst outcome when facing such danger."

"I can only thank you, Leo," Richard said, "You saved my sister's life."

"No I didn't," Leo said. "After time to think, I can see more now than then that he wasn't dangerous and was simply desperate for money. He will know the reason, but I would suggest it must have been a strong one to push him into this because he was more nervous than Evelyn or me. He obviously saw it as a last resort."

"You appear to feel some sympathy with the man," Brenda said. "We have to remember that he threatened you with a gun loaded with bullets which automatically put both your lives at risk irrespective of his desperation for money. Granted, the money might have been to save the life of his child or something similar, but we need to remember that it was a loaded gun."

"How do fingerprints help," Amelia said.

"The police have been using fingerprints for a few years," Richard said. "No two people have the same fingerprints and they have a way of taking a person's fingerprint impression from something they touch and they can use that in court now."

Leo smiled and said, "It makes you wonder what they'll come up with next, does it not? Fingerprints will never be a patch on genetic profiling, though."

Brenda asked what genetic profiling was, but she didn't get an answer and Leo simply smiled at her.

Richard said, "I hope the police catch him soon because he failed to obtain the money he so obviously desired. That means he will quite possibly try again and he will no doubt be more desperate now and being more desperate must make him more dangerous."

Leo was pleased with the volume and quality of Joe's work. He had not expected him to have been so far on and could see that he would soon have finished the entire house and it would be ready for Leo to move in, although he still needed to buy furniture and odds and ends like curtains, floor covering, something to cook on.

He was also aware that the washing machine had made an appearance in 1905 and it had an electrical wringer to wring the clothes out, so he could forget about the washboard and mangle that someone suggested.

However, the information on the washing machine was not all good. When he went to the shop to look it over, he discovered that it had the potential of being a death trap. They placed the motor beneath the tub with the threat of causing a short circuit and a quite nasty shock if water dripped onto it. He decided to give it more thought.

Joe arrived for work and said, "I am not late, am I?"

"Not at all," Leo said. "Have a cup of tea before you start. I made us both one."

Leo handed Joe a cup and took a sip of his own before saying, "I had a look around and I have to say that I'm very pleased with the standard and speed of your work. It appears you will finish ahead of schedule. You will have your promised bonus and I'll tell your boss that I have had a warning to secure the building against burglars and I ordered you not to answer the door to anyone and not allow anyone into the house while I am not here. That will stop him coming out to check up on you and will leave you free to take the remainder of the time off work to spend with your son."

"I am not sure I should do that, Leo," Joe said.

"It's okay, you'll be safe. Your boss cannot discipline you for following my instructions and he certainly will not pay you any extra for getting the work completed early. He will simply send you onto the next job. I don't know him, but I know businessmen. Now, tell me about your family."

The discussion with Joe lasted longer than Leo meant it to and it left him late for work, although no one paid any notice to him arriving late and he saw a face he had not seen before, a fresh, youthful face, and he reasoned he must be the office junior replacement.

Leo decided to introduce himself and he said, "Hello, you must be the new kid on the block. My name's Leo pleased to meet you."

The lad frowned and said, "I'm not on a block, but my name is Terrance."

"Do you like Terrance, or would you prefer Terry."

"I don't mind, but my mates call me Terry. My mum doesn't like it and claims it sounds like something from the gutter, but she probably thinks I'm a guttersnipe anyway."

Leo laughed and he could see he was going to get on extremely well with young Terry and he pondered briefly before adding, "Your surname wouldn't be Brown, would it?"

"How did you know that?"

"Is your dad called Michael?"

"I get it, you know my dad. I suppose you will tell him any time I step out of line?"

"Not at all, Terry, what you do here will never be repeated by me outside of these walls."

Leo smiled and could see where his old friend Mike got his character.

According to Mike, Terry will be in this job for less than one week, will have an accusation of theft directed at him and will be fired. If he were a thief, then there would not be a lot Leo could do. However, he decided to keep a close eye on things for the following week.

Mike and the rest of the family would naturally argue that Terry was innocent, but he seemed like a decent kid to Leo, although even decent kids can stoop to theft if the need arose." Leo could use some additional information, though, like a description of the stolen item/s and who suffered the theft.

His mind went back to the house and he decided the work crew would have arrived by now to tile the kitchen. He pondered on this being different from the original history of the kitchen tiles where the doorway to Amelia's cellar was tiled. This would remove the need of a stud wall. Therefore, the stud wall will not be there in this new version of prime time.

He was confident that he would rip off the tiles in the same manner as in prime time and so, when creating his cavity; he made a small amendment to his plan. He decided on a different part of the wall, using his knowledge of the original history as a measuring rod.

After work, Leo called into the establishment of Millar and Perkins after Felix made it known that Mr Millar would like to speak to him about his advice on his business. It was not far from the Colliery and it would not interrupt the evening meal at Felix and Amelia's house. Felix had arranged the delivery of the evening meal and the caterer would most definitely not have the same perfect timing as Martha. They will be later in delivering it, so that would give Leo some additional time.

A young female junior showed him through to Mr Millar's office and Mr Millar said, "Thank you, A.J.. You may go home now if you wish."

"Thank you, Mr Millar," A.J. said. She smiled at Leo, he returned the smile and she left the office.

"So," Mr Millar said, indicating for Leo to sit down, "You are this enterprising young man I have been hearing so much about. Mr Bennett speaks very highly of you and considering the insight he kindly gave me on your advice, I tend to agree with him. You appear to have an amazing insight into where this business is heading and how to achieve its maximum potential. You have extreme clarity in your predictions. Am I correct in using the word predictions in describing your suggestions for the future?"

After sitting down and listening carefully to Mr Millar's opening statement, Leo realised he would have to be careful because he didn't want to be assumed as a Nostradamus of the early 1900s.

He said, "If you were to bump into something, it would not be difficult to predict it will topple over and if you throw a stone, it will not be hard to predict that it will take flight for several hundred yards before coming to rest."

Mr Millar smiled and said, "You are a clever man who has devised a means of working out percentages to an amazingly accurate level and you will not have the desire to give away your methods. I see myself as also being quite shrewd and perceptive. Therefore, I have a proposition for you, Mr Lennox."

Leo had not expected this. He didn't need to be everything Mr Millar thought he was to enable him to understand that when Mr Millar mentioned a proposition, he meant a business deal that would benefit them both and Leo gave him his full attention.

The tiles, all new and buffed up didn't excite Leo because he had seen them before, they caused him a lot of work, and he would still have a full wall of them in prime time to remove. He had to make complimentary remarks, though, and he praised the tiler's in keeping their promise of completing the task in one day. They completed the job to the extent of buffing them up to remove white efflorescence marks that had gathered when dry.

He looked along the wall where he had punched out a cavity and it was all flush and there was no sign of there being a cavity or any other difference in that section of wall and Leo knew it would remain intact through two world wars until he arrived in prime time to remove them.

This might become something of a paradox and with there no longer being a sealed-off Cellar, Leo in primetime will not come across it when he chips off the tiles. Therefore, will the time slip still take place when he leaves Peter's room on Christmas Eve in what will be the new future from this timeframe?

He pondered on the possibility of not being teleported back through time. Will this compel him to live the remainder of his life from the present time of 1905 while; in a parallel reality will live as was originally meant in prime time without travelling back? That would put two versions of him living a full life in two separate realities of a multiverse and this became too much for him to grasp.

He had just one question about this – is it possible for one person to split in two and live two lifetimes? If so, then it must be possible that in the cemetery he visited, when finding Mikes wife crying at her sisters grave, that he would be in a grave close by. It must also be possible that prime time Leo will eventually see this grave, although he would no doubt put it down to being just someone from the past with the same name as he.

The caterer arrived with their meal and Leo said, "Wouldn't it be a good idea to make food deliveries like this a common thing and we would simply need to phone in our order and have it delivered?"

"It would be very expensive," Amelia said.

Leo knew the reality of this and he said, "We could escape colossal expense if it became commonplace. If enough people ordered delivery, they would be able to reduce the prices to the same as eating out with just a small addition for delivering it."

Felix said, "Am I right in thinking you speak from experience, Leo?"

Leo smiled.

It was Leo and Evelyn's first walk together since the man with the gun and Evelyn was nervous. Leo too was apprehensive, but he hid it well. They were not in the same area and had decided to leave it for a while before visiting her sister. This helped her to regain her confidence before walking through that particular part of town again, although the need to visit her sister was not as great because her sister visited Evelyn the evening after when she heard about the man with the gun and Leo got to meet her.

As they walked on, they heard a man's footsteps behind and Evelyn clutched tightly to Leo's hand. Leo looked back at the man. The man crossed the street and rapped on a nearby door and Evelyn was able to relax.

Leo said, "You need something to help you relax, but the best I can offer is a cup of tea because you don't do pubs."

"A cup of tea would be lovely, Leo," Evelyn said.

Tea would be good, Leo decided, because he could feel a drop of rain in the air and would be happier with a roof over his head while drinking tea than he would be walking along the street in a shower. He was beginning to know the area well and he was sure there was a place nearby where they could take refuge from the weather and have a cup of something hot. They soon found it.

Leo decided to have a sandwich and Evelyn wanted just tea and they had just given their order when it began to rain. Leo was tempted to mention their timing to Evelyn, but he decided that would be too much of a cliché, so he remained quiet on the matter.

However, he reasoned it might not be such a cliché in 1905, so he said, "That was good timing. Another few seconds and that down pour would have been on top of us."

After doing battle with a gunman, Leo had no fear of a mere cliché.

Evelyn said, "I think it would be prudent to stay here until the rain ends. I think I'll bring my umbrella the next time you drag me around the streets at night time."

"I don't drag, I escort. I don't know why you didn't bring your umbrella, though."

"I notice you don't have one either?"

Leo laughed and said, "Me, a man, with an umbrella, how preposterous."

Evelyn sighed slightly peevishly and said, "Men! Jonas Hanway was the first man to venture onto the streets of this land with an umbrella. Other men laughed, but quickly followed his example when they realised they were getting soaked while he remained dry. Of course, this was back in 1750, before men lost their backbone and Jonas Hanway would not be pleased with us coming in out of the rain for a cup of tea."

"Why, did he get a kick out of people getting soaked in the rain?"

"No, he was opposed to people drinking tea."

"So, you're saying he was a crackpot? One day, men might take to having a handbag, but that doesn't mean I have to follow suit."

"A handbag is a useful item for transporting vital essentials, so it would not serve a purpose for a man to have one because men don't understand what is essential."

"I spotted a woman with a bottle of lemon juice in her bag. How essential is that?"

"A fine example of how little you men understand. Women of today prefer a mild complexion as opposed to looking like a Red Indian. Therefore, lemon juice applied to the facial area helps to retain the required pigmentation."

Leo assumed she was not serious, although she gave him no reason to think this by retaining her most serious expression. He was not convinced, but took a mental note to ask Amelia about it later.

The tea and Leo's sandwich arrived and Leo could detect that Evelyn had a small regret in not ordering something to eat and he lifted one from the plate, leaving three. It was strange that the sandwich was prepared with plain bread where normally he was used to it being pan, but he decided it would be hard to make it with pan bread before the pan loaf was available. There were two slices of bread but cut up into four sandwiches with a generous filling and he took his first bite and said, "Delicious."

Evelyn was not impressed and she said, "Be careful you don't get indigestion."

Leo smiled, moved the plate closer to her and said, "Help yourself."

"Thank you. I didn't feel at all like eating until it arrived."

Leo was surprised and assumed he would need to do some persuading and he decided if she reaches for a second one, he will have to order another one. He mused it must be the same in all era's that a man will place his order and the lady will help him eat it after refusing anything for herself.

Leo took another bite and Evelyn nibbled delicately at her sandwich. The realisation dawned on Leo that a woman sharing a man's meal on an evening out was a sure sign of the relationship between them having reached a point of great strength. It persuaded him into a daydream realm where he imagined what life would be like if he could never get back to prime time and they got married.

He could think of several worse scenarios than marrying Evelyn and he decided they could even be happy together because they appeared to be on similar wavelengths. When he cracked funny, he didn't then need to spend time explaining it, which he has had to do in the past with other women. Evelyn got him each time, even at times when he attempted to bluff her into thinking one way, she would see through his ploy and see things the other way, or as they were.

She smiled and looked away coyly when she caught him staring at her. He could not help staring, though and he held his stare even after she had looked away. He decided she had been through so much at an age when her memories should mostly be happy ones.

He learned more about her than she had told him. He had spoken to Felix and Amelia about her and gleamed a lifetime of knowledge that formed within him the feelings that can only be felt when experiencing someone for a lifetime and he felt he had known her all his life, yet it was just a few short weeks.

He thought he had come to know Laura especially, but he didn't know her at all in the end analysis, otherwise, her departure would not have caused so much shock to his entire being. He had no desire to go through such pain again, had put up barriers to prevent it, yet here Evelyn was, tearing down his barriers and getting through, at times even against his will and better judgement.

He was no longer worried about pain revisiting him and was worried more about pain revisiting Evelyn. If he ever got back to prime time and the kids, how would it affect Evelyn?

He snapped himself out of his thoughts; it had become too much pain. He can deal with pain caused to himself, but not pain he could cause even inadvertently to others.

Felix was making a nightcap drink of hot milk for himself and Amelia when Leo returned. He offered Leo a glass, but the thought of drinking hot milk had nauseating qualities to Leo and he said, "You should mix in a spoonful of Ovaltine with that."

Felix frowned and Leo could see that Ovaltine had not made it to 1905 and he said, "Never mind. I'll make myself a cup of tea."

Felix pondered and lifted one glass and left the other glass of milk sitting where it was. He could detect that Leo needed a late evening discussion and he said, "I didn't get the chance to discuss with you your meeting with Mr Millar. Would you mind if I gave Amelia her nightcap and came back for a chat?"

"I would like that Felix," Leo said.

Felix left the kitchen while Leo put some water into the kettle and got a cup. He was stirring his tea when Felix returned and they went through to the living room and sat down, Felix with his hot milk and Leo with his cup of tea.

Felix sipped his milk. It had cooled down slightly but was still hot enough to do the job he desired it to do and he spoke out at what this job was as he said, "There's nothing like a hot glass of milk at bed time to ensure a sound night's sleep, now, about this meeting with Mr Millar?"

"Yes, he asked me if I would be interested in a proposition."

As Leo sipped his tea, Felix said, "Yes, he mentioned he had a proposition to put to you. I'll not interfere other than by telling you he is a fine and upstanding member of the business world and he will consider you as a person and not as a commodity to increase his bank balance."

"I could see that as I spoke to him. I'll need time to think things over, though."

"I am sure he will be eager for you to take all the time you need. I assume you got all your papers placed in the wall cavity before they tiled the area?"

"Yes, it's all safely tucked away and is waiting for the finder in prime time. I don't know at this point if I'll ever get back, but at least the papers and things will get there, even though they have to take the long and slow route."

"I can understand you missing your children and if you get back to your prime time, we will celebrate here while missing you a lot. However, if you fail to get back, you will need to try to put that part of your life behind you and concentrate on what you have and make a life for yourself here in this time. It will not be easy and you will go through the grieving process for your children, but you need also to think about yourself and your life and happiness here. You can send your children a message through time, and perhaps you already have with the papers you left in the wall cavity."

"I actually did write something for them, an explanation of what happened to me and they will receive it at the same time as they will receive the news that I am gone. However, I became unhappy at leaving such a message because it will still upset them and will in no way remove the fact of never seeing me again. However, I decided on a backup plan."

"It's always wise to have a backup plan in place."

"It's my belt and braces plan. We can use a belt or we can use braces, both separately will do a good job, but both together will give added security and I am assuming you didn't go into the kitchen this morning before the work crew arrived."

"No, as you know, I gathered some old camping things and left them in the attic for Amelia to enable her to make cups of tea during the day. One of the things was a small burner. It can boil a kettle, so I took the kettle, cups etc up there last evening and didn't have any need to enter the kitchen this morning."

"Yes, you told me this was the plan. Last night, before going to bed, I painted a message on the first wall that I'll chip the tiles from in prime time. A last-minute change of mind prevented me from placing the papers inside this wall and yesterday I instead carved out the cavity four feet about the power socket in the kitchen. I did this to ensure I didn't chip the tiles from this area and thought it best to draw my attention to where the documents would be in case I was hesitant in prime time of ripping out the wood."

"So, it was in effect a note to self? You were lucky you didn't receive an electrical shock from the cable running to that socket, Leo."

"I helped in the rewiring of this house, so I know the original wiring went up the wall to the socket and not down and at four feet above the socket, I was perfectly safe. Therefore, I painted the message of 'begin here and rip out' below the socket with an arrow pointing upwards. The tiler's would not pay a lot of attention to this and if they did, they would see where I had boarded up that area and would have assumed the message pertained to this, but will begin tiling where they think is best. The message would not interfere with the tiles and would just mean they would need perhaps to prime the wooden area."

"Would a message survive under the tiles, Leo? When removing the tiles, would the paint not stick to the tiles and some remain indecipherable on the tile adhesive."

Leo frowned in thought for a moment and then said, "Your right, Felix. How stupid. I thought I had everything covered, but I didn't think of that. It was a last-minute decision and I didn't have time to think it all through, as I should have. There is a chance the message might remain on the wall when the tiles have been removed, but I don't like to rely on chance."

Felix took a sip of milk as he pondered and then said, "They left whatever tiles they didn't use, so I would be fine with you removing some tiles and making any needed alterations and then replacing the tiles. Even if we broke a couple in replacing them, there would be plenty left."

"That shouldn't be necessary and even if I don't see the message in prime time, the wood will probably be a puzzle to me and I'll probably rip it out anyway to discover why it's there."

Felix could detect that this problem was not the only issue on Leo's mind and something of great depth was bothering him and he said, "To move away from the wall cavity, Leo, how did the walk with Evelyn go? This was the first since that issue with the man brandishing a gun, was it not?"

Yes, that was the first and she was extremely nervous when we first set out, but not too nervous to prevent her from eating half my sandwich when we stopped for tea and something to eat. She didn't want anything until she saw my sandwich."

"I have been there before."

"We seem to be drawing closer together, Felix. She's good company and she seems to get what I'm about."

"If what you are about is you as a person, then that can only be a good thing and I am on her side because I too think you are a good person."

"I have told her everything, as you know, and she is great about it. We even discussed the possibility of me being sucked back to prime time and she said we are all similar because any of us could be dragged out of this life through death and will not get to say goodbye to those close to us."

"I agree with this as well and she has old head on young shoulders, Leo. By that, I mean she is very wise."

"Yes, I know what it means. But the possibility of being ushered back to prime time has a new significance now, Felix."

"Why, what has changed, Leo?"

Leo set his cup down, took a deep breath and said, "I think I'm falling in love with her."

Chapter 19

Leo became responsible at the colliery for selecting a first aid team to begin training. It was a first time, so was mainly experimental. While Leo was not confident in his ability, others had great confidence in him and it was the hope that it would save lives and that had to impress even those who looked on the miners no differently than they would a shovel, with the view that they can easily be replaced if lost or broken.

The first person he approached, Steve Henderson, was fine with doing a first aid course if it got him away from the office for a while. This caused Leo to strike Steve's name off the list and he told him that if there was not a glimmer of passion on helping the injured and suffering, then Steve didn't have the attitude required for the placement. Steve shrugged his shoulders in a do-not-care-less kind of way and opened his desk drawer to rummage for something as way of indicating that Leo could leave him and go pester someone else. Leo thanked him and left.

Natasha Benson would be eager as long as it didn't interfere with her sharing her lunch breaks with Susan from accounts because they were friends from way back. The new office junior Terrance, who preferred Terry, was enthusiastic and he decided that anything that could be done to help those injured down the mines and prevent deaths, would certainly win his full support and he was eager to sign up for the course.

Leo added Terry's name to the list and he continued from office to office and found another few who were eager to sign up. He then paid his first visit to the actual mine in the hope of drumming up some support there, where the more serious injuries would occur and if he had some first aiders there, that would hugely help.

After getting his full quota, Leo handed the list of names to Mr Weatherford under the gaze of a Field View Camera that looked to Leo as being nothing more than a wooden box with some brass parts. It was innovative tech in 1905, though, and the camera operator busied himself taking many other photographs to commemorate the launching of the collieries' answer to the rising deaths and injuries down the mines.

Mr Weatherford was eager to get his scheme underway. He thanked Leo and told him that it was him (Leo) being in the firm that pushed him (Mr Weatherford) on with it. He saw it as fitting that Leo was a good friend of Felix owing to it being Felix who saved his son from certain death. This was Mr Weatherford's way of giving thanks for his son's life and he hoped the scheme would save many lives at the colliery.

Leo didn't need or require thanks and he was happy to be a part of it. St John's would give training in conjunction with the Red Cross at Trinity College, London. It would be something of a crash course to begin; thereafter each member would receive one-day release each month for several months to receive further training. That was good news; there was bad news too and Trinity College could not take the first trainees for some month. This still left the scheme well ahead of time, though, by quite some time, Clive Weatherford calculated.

Those drafted onto the scheme received leaflets and instruction sheets to get them started. Leo decided, the best way forward, was to gather them all together and at least get to know each other and perhaps set up some training from the leaflets and instruction sheets and Mr Weatherford told them that he had commissioned Leo to organise it all and no one appeared to have a problem with this.

As Leo added the sheet of names to a binder, Steve Henderson arrived with the office boss Ronald Cooper and pointed to Terry. Terry looked up in surprise and didn't appear to know why attention was on him. Leo had an idea, though.

Mr Cooper said to Terry, "Come with me, son." They both left and Steve produced a smug smile and looked around, spotted Leo glaring at him and he raised his eyebrows at Leo and smiled. Leo left and went to Mr Cooper's office. He rapped the door and opened it. He could see Mr Cooper sitting at his desk with Terry standing before him with his head lowered.

"I'm sorry for interrupting, Mr Cooper," Leo said.

"Could you call back later, Mr Lennox, I am busy at the moment."

Leo stepped into the office and closed the door as he said, "That's why I need to speak to you now. Mr Weatherford has signed this lad over for use in the new first aid program, so I need to be here if he is being accused of anything."

"What makes you think he is being accused of something?"

"Is he," Leo asked.

"Actually, yes he is. I have been informed that he stole a rather valuable pocket watch and I am sure you will agree that we cannot allow such things to happen here."

"I agree, of course, but is there any evidence of theft other than one man's word?"

Mr Cooper looked at Terry and said, "Did you steal the watch?"

Terry looked up for a second, then lowered his head again and remained silent."

"I think that speaks for itself, Mr Lennox. Now if you don't mind
—"

"Mr Cooper, yes I do mind. This only proves that the lad is scared stiff, too scared to even deny having any knowledge of this watch. I might know of it, though."

Mr Cooper looked up and said, "You do?"

"Yes, I think I do. As you are aware, I had to compile a list of names for the first aid program and after deciding that Mr Henderson would not make a good trainee, he opened his desk drawer in my presence and I saw a pocket watch. I would suggest it might be the missing pocket watch and might still be there. Would you like to come with me and speak to Mr Henderson and ascertain if I am right or wrong?"

"No Mr Lennox, I will not go with you, but I invite you to come with me."

Mr Cooper rose and left the office, indicating for Leo and Terry to follow him. Along the way, he said, "When we arrive, I need you both to return to your places of work and I'll deal with this."

As they entered the office, Terry went to where he had earlier been and Steve Henderson glared over at him and then looked to Mr Cooper. Leo watched and listened as Mr Cooper reached Steve's desk and said, "I need you to fill out and sign a full report before we can take action. Are you willing to do this, Mr Henderson?"

"Yes, of course, I am, Mr Cooper."

"Excellent, when was the last time you saw the watch?"

"I last had it earlier when I took my jacket and waistcoat off to wash my hands. The watch as normal was chained to my waistcoat."

"So, it was on your waistcoat? Was Mr Brown close by?"

"Yes, apart from me, he was the only one in the room."

"You can sign a statement to this effect?"

"Of course I can, I have nothing to hide, sir."

"No one is saying you do, Mr Henderson. However, just to clarify, could you have left it elsewhere, perhaps in another pocket, maybe even at home, in a drawer?"

"No, I only have one watch and I wear it at all times because it's the only way I have of knowing what time it is."

"I need you to be sure on this, Mr Henderson, are you positive you could not have left it elsewhere?"

"I am one hundred per cent certain, sir."

"And you don't have a second watch?"

"I just have or had that one watch, as I said, sir."

As Leo watched, he could see the way Mr Cooper was playing it and when Steve categorically denies leaving the watch anywhere else, Mr Cooper will ask him to open the drawer. Then he reasoned Steve might have taken the watch from the drawer after Leo had seen it and that would turn the questioning away from Steve and Leo knew who Mr Cooper would then question.

"Mr Henderson," Mr Cooper said, "can you say without a sliver of doubt that your watch was chained to your waistcoat when you washed your hands and that no one else other than Mr Brown was in the general area?"

"I can, and I can also tell you that he was not only in the general area, but was right beside me."

"And you haven't seen the watch since you washed your hands?"

"Not a glimmer of it, sir. Everyone in this office can verify it as my watch."

"Could Mr Brown have since rummaged through your desk?"

Steve frowned, paused to ponder, and then said, "No, he would have been seen by anyone here if he had interfered with my desk in any way."

"Just a couple more questions, Mr Henderson. Can you verify that the stolen watch is exactly as you described it to me earlier and that you don't have another watch, nor or you minding another watch for a third party?"

"It is exactly as described in every way with my initials on the inside of the case and it is the only watch I have or had use of, sir."

"For clarity, we should look in your desk drawer to rule out it being inadvertently left there, so are you sure you didn't leave it there?"

Steve Henderson failed to return a response.

"Can you say without a doubt that Mr Brown could not have left it there?"

Steve Henderson failed to return a response and Mr Cooper opened the drawer, looked inside and said, "Is that your pocket watch, Mr Henderson?"

Once more Steve Henderson failed to return a response.

Mr Cooper said, "I see the chain is broken and that might account for it being in the drawer. In light of this and your sudden inability to give a verbal account, please remove your watch and anything else belonging to you and leave the building with immediate effect. I have no alternative but to let you go. If you prefer, we could leave the matter with the police."

Mr Cooper went to Terry and said, "I apologise profusely for what you have just been through, son. It appears Mr Henderson has taken a dislike to you and desired to cause you problems. Please give it some thought and let me know in due course how we can make it up to you."

"That will not be necessary, sir," Terry said.

"I beg to differ and suggest it is very necessary."

Mr Cooper then went to Leo and said, "Thank you, Mr Lennox. You prevented a gross defamation of that lad's character. I never would have questioned Mr Henderson had it not been for your intervention and while questioning him; I could see him glaring at the young man with obvious contempt and can clearly see what has been going on here. Thank you."

It was Felix, Amelia and Leo for the evening meal with Martha entertaining Harold. Leo was unsure he should tell them about Terry because some people demand there is never smoke without fire, to use the cliché, especially with Terry being unable to deny involvement. Leo understood this, he was similar at a much younger age, and he remembered the teacher coming around the back of his chair and a penknife falling onto the floor. It was summertime and Leo had his blazer off and hanging over the back of the chair, as did most of the other pupils. The teacher insisted the knife fell from Leo's school blazer pocket, but Leo knew he didn't have it in his pocket and had never seen it before.

Leo had to go to the headmasters' office. The headmaster questioned him, and Leo lowered his head in the same way that Terry had lowered his head. Leo could easily have said he didn't steal it and never saw it before, but he was so terrified that he could not make his mouth work with denial and he decided the headmaster would not believe him anyway, so there was no value in a denial.

Therefore, Leo understood Terry's silence, but others might not.

Felix noticed that Leo was not his usual self and when he questioned him, Leo lowered his head and said nothing, at first. He needed a moment to decide on a response.

He raised his head and looked directly at Amelia and then at Felix and told them about Terry.

Amelia was first to give her views and she said, "The poor boy, he must have been so terrified."

"I agree," Felix, said, "It was a break for the lad that you saw the watch in the drawer, Leo."

Leo was relieved that neither came out with the smoke and fire rhetoric and he went on to expose his school days memory of being wrongly accused and realising that neither the headmaster nor the teacher would believe him because they had the evidence dropping onto the floor."

Felix said, "Were you punished for it?"

Leo said, "Physical punishment had been abolished in schools at this time, but they sent for my parents with the intention of telling them I had been found with a dangerous weapon which they believed to be stolen by me. I think they would have expelled me. My parents had their own methods and forms of punishment. However, the boy who owned the penknife admitted to owning it and he dropped it while attempting to get it into his pocket to prevent the teacher from seeing it. He was seated behind me."

Felix said, "That must have been quite an ordeal and I'm assuming by the time the real culprit owned up, your parents had already dispensed their punishment?"

"No, I would have been grounded, as in banished to my room, for a set time, possibly one month or more, but they learned the truth as the same time of learning of the incident because my innocence was discovered before the end of the school day. Neither the teacher nor the headmaster ever apologised, though.

"Life can be so hard for children," Amelia said. "I would not like to need to go through my childhood again."

"Nor I," Felix said.

Leo arrived at Evelyn's house with the knowledge that he would have to tell the whole story to her now. He wished he had a tape recorder and then he could have recorded himself telling Felix and Amelia and would just need to playback the tape to everyone else.

It might not have mattered, though, because Evelyn wanted more information on top of the additional facts and when Leo had exhausted the information he could furnish her with, she frowned in concentration and remained quiet as she dissected each utterance she had heard.

Leo relaxed and was happy with the silence and he was pleased with the way things worked out concerning Terry and the pocket watch.

Evelyn finally said, "I cannot claim to understand this how you will understand it. However, with Terrance no longer losing his job, his life will quite possibly be a lot different for the next decade and a half. This might have spared him the heartache of his family thinking he was guilty, having to leave home and live off the streets, and ultimately becoming dependent on alcohol. However, will it not also lead him on a path that does not have this woman at the end of it who will become his wife?"

Leo pondered on Evelyn's words. He had to agree that with this new scenario and this new life, there is a high possibility that Terry will not now marry Alicia and might find someone else much sooner. He could have an equally happy marriage with another woman. However, if it's not Alicia, then Mike may never be born. Therefore, in helping to prevent Terry's dismissal, he might have delivered Mike to nonexistence.

As he pondered on everything, Leo went from jubilation to total despondency as he realised he might have made it impossible for Mike to be born. He had to put this right.

"Is there anything you can do, Evelyn asked?"

"At this point, no, but I have to think of something."

"Do you know where this woman Alicia lives or even where she works?"

"I only know her name, not her maiden name, just Alicia. It became Brown after she married Terry, but it could be anything now."

"That is problematic. You could enlist the help of the Public Records office or nosey neighbours, but with just the Christian name, it will be hard to trace her. Even if you find out where she lives and can speak to her. This is fifteen years before she is destined to meet Terrance and she might not even like him at his present age."

"We have no way of knowing how many Alicia's there are in this immediate area, Evelyn. She might be outside the area now and could even be living in Australia."

"It doesn't seem possible to find her with just a Christian name. Did you not hear her surname being mentioned?"

"Just Brown, but that will not be any help. With her not being destined to arrive in Terry's life for approximately another fifteen years, I must agree with you that he might marry someone else. I could not check the entire world and must confine it to the local area and hope that if I can find her, we would also need to think of a way of getting Terry and her together. It would mean bringing forward their first meeting by fifteen years, but it's the only way."

"You don't make life easy for yourself, Leo. It would be easier to spin round in a circle and then fire a shot into the blue yonder and go looking for the bullet."

"I'm surprised at you talking this way after that man with the gun. Nevertheless, you're right and I know how hard it will be to find her. I'll not give up, though and will try everything I can think of. Are you sure you don't have a problem with me looking for another woman, though?"

He didn't feel much like it, but for Evelyn's sake, Leo ended his speech with a smile.

Evelyn rolled her eyes and sighed despondently before saying, "You can be quite immature at times." She smiled in a more serious manner before continuing, "I can see, though, that your need for jest is merely a way of dealing with your worries. This Michael must be a very good friend."

"He's the best, Evelyn. I wish you could meet him. I have condemned my best friend to a fate similar to death and have also condemned at least his Father, his brother, sister and his kids to the same fate."

Felix sipped his tea as he pondered after Leo explaining the latest problem about Terry. The living room clock became obvious in the background over the silence until Felix finally said, "Even if you find a woman named Alicia, without other detail such as a surname, you have no way on God's earth of deducing if she is the same Alicia."

"You see the problem. I don't think Alicia is a very common name, and it presents a huge wall to climb. I cannot ask all the Alicia's if they will one day marry a man called Terry because they will not know. If only I had asked, when I last spoke to Mike. He could easily have given me her maiden name and other detail."

"Do you even have the detail of where Terrance lived when he met her?"

Leo shook his head. "I don't think he had an address and lived on the streets, Felix. Maybe he slept at a Salvation army retreat or something."

Leo paused for thought and his eyes lit up with excitement as he looked to Felix and added, "She might have been a Salvation Army worker who took pity on him and that pity might have expanded into something more."

Felix said, "If she is not a Salvation Army worker now, right this minute that will not be of help. We could still contact the Salvation Army and discover if they have anyone by the name of Alicia working with them. Which age group will she be in? I think you mentioned Terrance being about fourteen and in fifteen years he will be twenty-nine, while Alicia might be anything between early twenties and thirties at that time and possibly ten to twenty presently."

"Again we have so many unknown variables, Felix."

"Sorry to extinguish your enthusiasm, but we will find her."

Leo nodded his head in agreement, although he nodded without enthusiasm and he lowered his head in defeat, as the thought of committing his best friend to nonexistence became an even heavier load than it had been and he was sure it would become even heavier again.

Leo could admit to a certain amount of nerves as he rapped on the door and waited until Joe opened it and smiled when he saw who his visitor was. "Hi Joe," Leo said. "I hope I didn't disturb your new son?"

"Not at all, Leo, would you like to come in and see him?"

"I would love to," Leo said and he stepped into the hall and waited until Joe closed the door and then Leo followed him through to the living room."

In front of the fire, there was a filled clotheshorse resting to dry by the heat of the flame. Joe's wife Pauline apologised for the wet baby things and quickly removed them and dismantled the clotheshorse and left it out of sight. As she committed herself to this task, Leo said, "There is no need to go to any trouble, I understand the need to keep above these things. I have two children myself."

"Pauline smiled embarrassingly and Joe said, "You know what women are like, Leo. Pauline, I was telling you about this man, Leo Lennox. Leo, this is my wife Pauline."

Leo smiled and said, "I'm pleased to meet you, Pauline."

Pauline said, "I hope my Joe has been doing an agreeable job on your decorating. Are you related to my Joe?"

This was a question Leo found great difficulty in answering because he was thinking Joe might be his great grandfather, but how could he reveal this to her when he is slightly older than Joe. This would make Pauline his great-grandmother.

Joe motioned for Leo to sit down and as Leo sat on the settee, he said in answer to Pauline, "I wouldn't be surprised." He took an envelope from his coat pocket and handed it to Joe while adding, "This is the promised bonus for an excellent job and a little extra to buy something for the baby. Would you mind if I had a look?"

Joe said, "There is no need because I have already been paid for the work, but feel free to come and see my son."

Joe went to the pram without accepting the envelope from Leo and Leo tucked the envelope in behind a candlestick on the mantelpiece.

The baby was in his pram and if he had not been asleep, Leo might have asked if he could hold him because it's not every day a man gets to nurse his newly born grandfather. It was still amazing to see him in his pram, though. Leo said, "Graham isn't it?"

Joe said, "Yes, we named him after my Father."

The baby's name had earlier sealed it for Leo because he didn't need to rely on an ancestry search to tell him that his grandfather was Graham Lennox and he said, "Graham is an excellent name. What a perfect little man you have, you must both be extremely proud."

"We are," Pauline admitted.

Joe said, "I find that having a son has completed me as a person."

Leo smiled and said, "I felt the same way when my son Peter was born. Anyway, you will have things that you need to do because having a baby can be an extremely busy time. That being the case, it has been a joy to meet you Pauline, amazing to meet Graham and I hope to see you again, Joe. If not, I hope you all have a really good life and perhaps not leave it too late to give Graham a brother or sister."

Leo shook hands with Joe, then Pauline and moved towards the living room door and Joe said, "I'll show you out. Thank you for dropping by and please feel free to call back."

Joe rushed past Leo and went to the front door, opened it. Leo passed Joe and stepped out onto the garden path turned around briefly and said, "It has been an amazing experience seeing your son and thank you again for an incredible job on my house."

They both smiled and Leo left, Joe closed the door and went back into the house.

Leo felt good. He would have enjoyed staying longer, but he came away with the feeling of having family no matter which year he was in. While it was amazing meeting his great-grandfather, it was even more amazing meeting his baby grandfather. He doesn't remember his grandfather who was 74 years of age when he passed away in 1979.

However, he remembers his dad telling him about the old boy and now Leo had met the baby. Being told stories of the family didn't mean a lot to Leo at the time. However, they mean everything to him now and he wished he could remember more than snippets of those stories. It was amazing seeing his grandfather as a baby, though and he aimed to find out much more.

As Leo continued on his way, he called up memories of his best mate Mike. He could see Mike clearly in his mind's eye and could hear his words once more as Mike explained what he had discovered within his family tree:

"Michael's Father was Terrance and Terrance's Father was Michael. As the story goes, Terrance had an appalling life after someone he worked with accused him of theft in his first job and it took him a long time to sort his life out after it. According to my granddad, Terrance was in the job for less than a week. His boss fired him over the theft allegation and his mum refused to believe he was innocent. Soon after that, he left home. I guess he found it hard living with the knowledge of even his family not believing him and he later turned to the bottle. He ended up on the streets, but we Browns are plucky and resourceful and he pulled himself out of it all with the help of the one who would become his wife, Alicia-Jane."

"Of course," Leo said aloud. She was Alicia-Jane, not Alicia! As if an illuminating light switched on over his head, he could see everything more clearly. Not Alicia, but Alicia-Jane - hyphenated! God bless your hyphenated socks Alicia-Jane, I'll be speaking to you soon!

Chapter 20

Life can never be simple, Leo thought as he lay on top of the bed with his eyes pinned to the ceiling and his mind in turmoil. He had it all worked out when he left Joe's house and the fact of the possibility of Alicia-Jane being abbreviated to A.J. even told him who Alicia might be. It was not so clear and positive after the walk back, though, and doubts crept in as other questions came into the scenario.

However, he retained the same determination.

Outside Joe's house, he could see a way forward, and that way was still open even if uncertainty now immersed his hopes in a cloak of uncertainty. He will speak to Terry at work the following day and then pay another visit to Mr Miller's office.

He rolled off the bed and decided to put it all to the back of his mind for now because he had a date with Evelyn. He opened the wardrobe door to choose what to wear and he rubbed his chin and pondered on a shave. Evelyn dislikes the short and sharp bristles of an unshaven face against her soft and delicate countenance and a shave will ensure a kiss. He smiled as he pondered on deciding on a shave just to get a kiss.

He realised this was not the first time he had thought about Evelyn this day. He thinks about her a lot when he is not with her and he finds when not with her that he longs for the time when he will be with her.

It felt strange, he came to this time with Amelia on his mind and now he has Evelyn in his thoughts and he could dare even say in his heart. He could feel a strong bond forging and he would allow it to forge on and increase in strength.

However, as always in every equation, are the kids. He was enjoying his time with Evelyn, but he needed to get back to the kids, although with him now being in the second month away, he felt it was extremely unlikely that he would ever see his kids again and his job would be long gone on the buses.

He chose a shirt, took it from the wardrobe and left it on the bed. He heard Felix coming up the stairs, probably to get ready for an evening with Brenda. He opened the bedroom door and stepped out into the landing as Felix reached the top of the stairs.

"Could I ask a huge favour, Felix?"

"Certainly," Felix said without hesitation.

"I should have asked at the table, but would it be a problem if I invited two young people here tomorrow evening?"

"That would not present us with even a minuscule problem, Leo. This is your home until your own home is ready and you didn't have the need even to ask."

"One, hopefully, will be from Mr Millar's office. I have the full plan drawn up that we spoke off."

"Wonderful! Mr Millar will be pleased. Might I browse it before you pass it over to him?"

"Certainly," Leo said and he raised a finger to indicate Felix pausing a second and he went into his room, returned seconds later with a few sheets of typed paper, handed them to Felix and said, "Browse through them at your leisure. I'll not need them until tomorrow evening. I typed them on Amelia's typewriter to give a more professional appearance."

"Excellent, it's good that the type writer is finally getting some use," Felix said and he took the sheets, glanced at them and smiled before adding, "I'll leave them downstairs for you. Have a pleasant evening with Evelyn."

"You too with Brenda, Leo replied and he went back into his room."

Leo took his coat off in Evelyn's living room and Evelyn took it from him to hang it up. As Leo sat down he called out, I might not be able to get here tomorrow evening, would you like to come over to Felix and Amelia's house?"

"That should not have any difficulty attached to it," Evelyn said as she returned, sat down beside Leo.

Leo added, "You might get to meet my mate Mike's ancestor, Terry. As I told you, I work with him and have invited him over for a while. Mr Millar's junior assistance should also be there to collect the papers I have been working on, although I have to go to Mr Millar's office tomorrow to arrange it."

"If you are going to Mr Millar's office tomorrow anyway, would it not be more prudent to give him the papers while you are there?"

Leo smiled and said, "That would not fit in with my overall plan."

Evelyn sighed and said, "Men and their plans! Would you like a cup of tea?"

"Yes, but not your tea."

"What, may I ask, is wrong with my tea?"

"You have been working all day, so to give you a small break; I'll take you out for a cup of tea."

"You call it a break to have me walking to the tea house rather than the few steps to the kitchen?"

"The night air will do you good."

"You say this after taking your coat off, so should I assume I'll be going alone?"

Leo laughed and said, "No, I'll escort you, madam, but not just yet. Come sit beside me and tell me about your day."

Evelyn sat beside Leo on the settee and said, "It was quite uneventful."

"Is your friend Andrew's love life still on course?"

"I think you mean Edward and yes, everything is fine between him and his girlfriend and he has retained his smile. Did you visit your great-grandfather, the painter and decorator?"

"Yes, I also met my grandfather, although he was sleeping in his pram so I didn't get to hold or cuddle him. It was amazing to see him, though."

"I can imagine, it must have been phenomenal."

"You appear to be coming round to the entire scenario?"

"Why should I not, Leo, it's all part of life, only from a perspective that we are not used to. Although I had problems at the beginning, I believe you because I don't think you would make all this up, there would not be a reason for such deception. Everyone can see the manner of man you are and I have respected Felix's opinion greatly over the years. He is very astute in gauging a person's true character and he is one hundred per cent certain that you are one of the most honest and sincere people he has ever met. He backs your story, which I know he would never do if it was not genuine."

"You speaking like that will make life a lot easier for me and I'm not sure I would believe someone of they arrived so suddenly and gave me a similar story."

"You are a very transparent person, Leo. I must say that I warmed to you the second I first met you, although you had no interest in me."

"You know that Amelia was on my mind uppermost when I arrived in this time. That apart, I soon realised that it would be unfair of me to attempt to build a relationship due to the possibility of going back to my own time when Amelia returned to full health. She has since returned to full health, has enjoyed it for several weeks and has completed her medication. I'm still here so I'm more confident now that I'll not be taken from this time and this allows me to be more open with you on my feelings."

"Which are?"

Evelyn purposefully left an opening for Leo to respond with the full measure of his affection for her, but he was not sure he could offer it in full just yet. He pondered the matter and then said, "I need to be honest, Evelyn, and that means telling you that I am seeing you more and more as being a woman who I wish to spend the remainder of my life with. I have expressed to others my true feelings for you and I should express the same to you. I love you."

Evelyn opened her mouth to speak, but Leo stopped her and said, "Please, let me continue. My thoughts and feelings are not a huge issue in all this and there is still the possibility of whatever force brought me here to this time might at some point return me. If this happens and it becomes obvious that I cannot make it back to you, I'll need to know that you will move on with your life and find someone else to share it with."

Leo could see a tear coming to Evelyn's eye as she said, "I am not sure I could do this, Leo. I have already been through it once and only your arrival in this time gave me the strength to move on after the death of my husband, but if you were taken from me, I don't think I would have the strength to go on."

Leo could see that it was a hard conversation for Evelyn to endure, but he had to carry on with it and he said, "You have to. Remember me if you must, but it's my deepest desire that if we should be parted for any reason, I need to know that you will fight for the life you deserve with a husband and children and many years of happiness with them."

"Is there something you have not told me, Leo?"

Leo looked deeply into Evelyn's eyes, held a hand firmly on each of her shoulders, and said, "No, I have told you everything and nothing remains unsaid. However, some things remain undone and only time will have the full outcome and I don't know what that will be so I have to assume the possibility of the worse scenario and prepare for it."

Leo reached into his pocket, withdrew a hanky and gently dabbed Evelyn's eyes with it. He then handed the hanky to her and gave her a kiss. It was just a quick kiss and he drew the side of her face to the side of his face and brought his mouth close to her ear.

He whispered, "There are things that neither of us may control, but we can prepare for all possibilities and if I am ever taken back to my own time, I'll be made aware of your life and will know and will then be able to live my own life accordingly."

Evelyn said, "I said before that we take the same risk in life and any of us could die at any point in time and be taken from those we love. Tomorrow could see me taken from you and I would expect the same from you that you ask of me. You will also need to move on with your life and, if you can, find someone special to share it. You must not accept anything less."

"I promise you in such a scenario, I'll do my utmost to move on in life and find someone to share it."

"I make that same promise to you while praying that this will not be the case and we will share many years."

Leo drew back to look into her eyes and he smiled and said, "I'll hold you to that."

Evelyn said, "I would expect you to, as I will also hold you to your promise, Leo."

Evelyn had her arm entwined with Leo's as they walked to the teahouse. They chose the long way as opposed to the short because it was a mild evening and there were other people about, which made Evelyn feel safer than empty streets.

Leo had discovered that the police had arrested a man by the name of Timothy Witherspoon for attempted robbery and possession and firing of a gun. He owned up to his crimes and claimed it was the first time and the gun belonged to his late Father. The reason he offered was being out of work and having seven children to feed.

Leo realised this was before the 1911 National Insurance act and understood that things would have been hard for Mr Witherspoon, although he reasoned it would be no harder for anyone else in 1905 who was unemployed with a large family. He was sure Mr Witherspoon's circumstances would not sway Evelyn, but Leo felt some empathy for him in his situation, although he felt he deserved punishment for his crime.

Evelyn rested the side of her face on Leo's muscular arm as they walked along. It helped to ensure her feeling of safety and she knew from experience now that Leo would not be found wanting in a crisis. Leo felt good at her seeing him as her hero.

He was not always a boastful man, but it made him feel well boosted.

They enjoyed the walk and spoke of general everyday matters and Evelyn asked how the matter of the furnishings for the house was progressing.

"Very well," Leo said. "With Joe having finished the wallpaper, I'll be able to move in once the flooring is completed and the furniture has arrived. It will be good to have my own place again. It has been great living at Felix and Amelia's place, but a man needs to have his own space, a little independence."

"I expect you realise you will not have Martha popping in to do all your cleaning and have your evening meal ready for you getting home?"

"I'm well used to fending for myself, so it will not be a problem." He smiled and added, "Feel free to drop-by any time you wish and do a spot of cleaning, though."

"How amazingly kind of you, I must admit to being overwhelmed. I even feel I should return your generous gesture with an offer of dropping by for a spot of work at my house."

Leo laughed and said, "I suppose I could bend to some maintenance work if and when needed."

"In that case, feel free to come any time."

Evelyn felt at ease and Leo could tell she was at ease and the former problem of facing a man with a gun in his hand no longer seemed to have a huge effect on her. She was relaxed and not listening for the sound of footsteps behind them and this was a huge relief to Leo because he was aware that such horrors could remain with many people for a long time.

Their earlier conversation was a huge help too in helping him feel at ease with Evelyn's peace of mind and she seemed content in how things were and this helped Leo feel contented. It was too early to think in terms of wedding rings. He could look ahead, though, to setting up home and going from his house to Evelyn's and calling in to visit Felix and Amelia. If this was his life now, it was shaping up into one with a lot of happiness. He had several financial pokers in the fire to secure more than his future, so he was not only happy but also contented.

He ordered two teas' when they arrived at the teahouse and, learning from earlier experiences, he had drilled Evelyn earlier on to have something to eat and so ordered two sandwiches with the tea. At least, with Evelyn having her own, this would ensure that he would get to eat his entire sandwich.

Evelyn wanted a salad filling while Leo was tempted with the less healthy option of ham. Of course, when the tea and sandwiches arrived, Evelyn decided Leo's was quite appetising. Bang went the hope of Leo getting to eat his in its entirety, although having half of Evelyn's meant that he had the same amount, but with more variety.

He was happy with the arrangement and he had the bonus of Evelyn only being able to eat half of her own, so he had her other half as well. He decided this was fair as it made up for the half she consumed of his the previous time.

During the walk back to Evelyn's house, they discussed the coming weekend and how to fill it. Going to Old Trafford to watch Manchester United would be an acceptable way for Leo to fill part of the weekend, but he realised it would not fill Evelyn with much joy. He suggested getting the train to London and possibly visiting Madame Tussauds and the British museum. These were two places that Leo knew were open in 1905, but there would be other places they could also visit while there.

"I have wanted to visit Madame Tussauds for quite a while," Evelyn said."

"That sorts Saturday out then," Leo said. "Maybe later in the year, I could be persuaded to go with you to Wimbledon for a spot of tennis?"

"I would love that. In return, I might be persuaded to go to Manchester and watch the Manchester football players."

"That would need to be later in the year because they have a closed season which they use to prepare the pitch for the following season. We could go to the opening match in the championship campaign on 2 July against Bristol City."

"I shall enter that date into my diary."

Leo kissed Evelyn on the cheek and said, "You clever woman."

"I suppose I can wear a disguise of some kind to avoid being identified as the world's first woman to watch silly men playing on a field in short trousers. How long does it last?"

"It's scheduled for ninety minutes, forty-five each half."

"Each half of what," Evelyn asked

"Each half of the match, they play for forty-five minutes, then have a break and then play for another forty-five minutes."

"Okay, I suppose I have committed myself to it and so I'll go with you and watch the Manchester football players."

"I assure you that you will not regret it. In my time, lots of women go to matches and there are also ladies football teams."

"Ladies play football? Do they do this openly with people watching?"

Leo laughed and said, "Yes, as brazen as it sounds, and they play to the same rules and wear the same kit as men."

"Kit? That will be their uniform dress?"

"Yes, everything is the same as with the men."

"As you know, there are women who play tennis, but at least they wear proper ladies tennis attire and don't dress the same as the men."

Leo laughed and said, "To fall back on a word I used earlier, brazen is the only word for it."

"You will be aware that Amelia fights for the rights of women to fall more in keeping with what men enjoy, but I don't think I would want equality of rights if it meant needing to dress as a man."

It will not get to that stage – well, apart from women wearing jeans, although some are happy in a shirt and tie. However, women still wear feminine dresses and make-up. The worrying part is, so do some of the men!"

"You jest me."

"I jest you not."

"Men wear ladies attire and make-up?"

"Some. There are possibly men who do the same in this time, only they will do it in secret."

"I suppose we never know what goes on behind closed doors."

"My prime time is open and people feel safe to reveal their innermost desires with the knowledge that they will not be ridiculed – well, not ridiculed too much. The odd head might still turn in the streets, but they seldom receive a brick through their window."

"I think that is a good advancement – not men dressing in a woman's attire, but the tolerance I detect for a different view. I so wish people today could be more tolerant of those who are different from them."

"There is also intolerance and it's not a time of perfection."

"Perfection on an imperfect earth is an impossible hope, do you not agree?"

"I agree within reason. I have witnessed perfection on the football pitch at Old Trafford, but generally, I agree with you."

Evelyn sighed and rolled her eyes at Leo. Leo laughed and said, "Well you have that French Tennis player, what's her face."

"Adine Masson? She is good, but I would not claim her to be perfect, although I did see snippets of perfection when my sister and I went to see her."

"That was not her, my dear, that was the reflection of your eyes coming back at you from the inside lens of your sunglasses."

Evelyn laughed and said, "Do not try to be endearing, it does not become you."

Leo laughed and said, "Okay, point taken."

"Is there a set time for me to arrive tomorrow evening?"

"At Felix and Amelia's, no, you know the time Felix and I normally arrive, so any time from then on. They won't have a problem with you dining with us."

"I would prefer you to arrange it beforehand, so I'll plan to arrive at a later time when you have finished your meal."

"I have already arranged it, even though Felix is adamant that I don't need to ask him or Amelia about such things and just need to mention it to Martha."

"All the same, Leo, I would prefer to arrive afterwards."

"If you prefer, I think I would be the same in your position, so I understand."

Leo was tired when he got home and had decided to go straight to bed. However, he reviewed this decision when Felix asked if he could have a word and they sat down for this word in the living room. Leo could see that it pertained to something of importance and he could further detect that Felix was having a difficult time beginning, so he said, "Is it animal, mineral or vegetable?"

"It's Brenda, Leo."

"Has something happened?"

"Oh my word no, it's nothing like that. Well, when I say that, it could be – or what I mean is –" He stood up and said, "I need to get to the point and I fear I am still a complete bundle of nerves. Leo, I need you to be the first to know because you made all this happen for me, for us, and I'll be eternally grateful to you. Earlier this evening I asked Brenda to become my wife, to become Mrs Bennett. I know we have not known each other very long, but I know she is perfect for me. She accepted, Leo. We are going to be married!"

Leo leapt to his feet as though ejected from the chair with great force and he shook Felix enthusiastically by the hand and said, "That is brilliant news. Congratulations!"

"I had not planned to ask her. I was thinking about it but had not planned to ask, although the conversation appeared to go that way naturally and I did what you once advised and I went with it."

"This news completes my satisfaction on the way today has gone!"

"Am I about to hear that you posed a similar question to Evelyn?"

"Not quite, but we had an amazing talk and might be a huge step closer to that question being asked. You'll need to discuss the house with Amelia and see if she plans to live in Richard's house when they get married."

"I'll have a lot to do that I have not even thought about yet, Leo. I think I need to settle down a shade and try to relax or, what is it you would say, chill?"

"I can understand your excitement, Felix. Don't worry about it, just enjoy it."

"I need a cup of tea."

"I thought you were going to say you need a bottle of brandy!"

They both laughed and went through to the kitchen to put the kettle on. As they left the living room, Felix said, "Yes, I need a bottle of brandy, but will settle for a cup of tea."

As they got cups, sugar etc, Felix added, "I read that article you prepared for Mr Millar and I think it's not only excellent but quite amazing."

"It's just a few thoughts from my knowledge of how things will become in the future."

"I think Mr Millar will be much more enthusiastic over it than you. I realised earlier that I have an appointment in the building adjacent to Mr Millar's premises and I would be very happy to drop it off with him. I need to speak to him about another matter anyway."

"That would be great, Felix, but it's something of a subterfuge. I'm using it to bring his junior assistant here. I need her to meet my mates' great-great-grandfather because she might be his great-great-grandmother."

"Oh, is this the woman named Alicia you were telling me about?"

"To be honest, I don't know for sure. When I left my great-grandfather's house, I had a strange memory of when I heard her name and it was Alicia-Jane. I remembered it just as Alicia. Being Alicia-Jane would give reason to some people addressing her as A.J. and Mr Millar addressed his junior as A.J. and I noticed something very familiar about her. When I later thought about it, it was in the fact that she had some of the same physical characteristics as my mate Mike. She might not be, but I needed to get A.J. and Terry together to see if there is some kind of spark between them."

"If there is and they get together, your friend Mike might be born as their great-great-grandson?"

"It's over fifteen years now before they got married in the original history, so they might have kids before his great-grandfather, but it would be better than them possibly never meeting and Mike and his kids never being born."

"I agree. His father and grandfather would not be born either."

265

"If there is not any kind of attraction between A.J. and Terry, then I'll simply give A.J. the papers and no fowl and no harm done."

"I could arrange for them both to wait in the living room and that would give them time and freedom to chat together and if there is an attraction, it's sure to become apparent before they leave. To extend their stay together, I could arrange to have tea and food taken into them. If they are suited, they will be happy to remain together and carry on getting to know each other."

Leo said, "That could be seen as devious and I like it."

"You taught me well and if it gets them both together in the way you got Brenda and me together, it will have been a good day's work."

Felix completed the final stage of their task by pouring the tea and they carried their filled cups into the living room to continue the discussion.

Leo was first to speak when they settled with their tea and he said, "Are you nervous at the prospect of marriage?"

"Nervous, No, not at all," Felix said, and then quickly added, "Terrified would be a more accurate word. It's not a thing the normal person does every day of the week."

"Even an abnormal person wouldn't do it too often."

"True. There are not too many who begin on such a voyage with the knowledge of a son and daughter and information on the son's time in America and thanks to you, I'll be in the position to change the outcome of that by knowing about it in advance. With having actual dates, I could allow him to travel and experience his failure there and I could arrive when he has learned a valuable lesson and bring him home."

Leo frowned in thought as he said, "That might be risky and he could refuse to come home with pride raising its head."

"I understand that, but it would not be very clever to persuade him home only to be presented with the same problem later in life. He has a desire to prove that he can succeed alone, so I'll need to guide him in the direction of success and let him know how proud I am of him when he succeeds in his venture. However, he will need to face up to failure, so I'll need to teach him that there is a life worth living even after failing at something."

"If I may make a suggestion," Leo said.

"By all means," Felix replied.

"The entire scenario might be averted in a much easier way. I am sorry to tell you this and I pondered on keeping it from you, although I think it might be of benefit for you to know it. It appears that your son will leave for America to seek his fortune there due to you not bringing him into the family business. You had a desire for him to have the pride of creating his own business in the way your Father had done and you feel you failed to. However, although you supplied the finance for him to begin, he was not very successful in other business ventures and decided he could make it in America and make you proud of him. You were proud of him and didn't need him to succeed, but you wanted him too for his benefit."

Leo took a sip of tea and paused to allow Felix to reflect on what he had so far said. Then he continued, "You feel it would have helped you if you had not inherited the business and become a success story on your own merits. You had a desire to impress this on your son to give him the pride of achieving everything alone. However, he was not a businessman of your quality and would have needed your instruction before endeavouring."

"I can see what you are saying, Leo. Indeed, I don't feel successful because my Father created the business and his endeavours alone made it the success it became and I admire people like Richard and my father who created something from nothing, so I can understand how I would attempt to pass this onto my son. I no longer have any enormous ambitions in business and merely desire to take care of what my Father created from nothing and I'll be careful not to expect any more from my children than what I could achieve myself."

"The history books state your son was never included as a member of your staff and it might help to offer him a job and train him to take over the business when you retire. At that, I have said all I need to say and I wish you a peaceful night's sleep and I'm sure everything will go well. Good night, Felix."

"Goodnight, Leo and thank you for everything."

Leo left his cup in the kitchen and climbed the staircase to his room. He was tired and ready for his bed. He switched on the light as he entered the room and closed the door. Nevertheless, at the sound of the door closing, the light went out and the bed, wardrobe and everything he could see dissolved in total darkness.

Leo put it down to the light bulb reaching the end of its life, but he flicked the light switch anyway and the light returned, but the room was empty, bar some things that he had stored in Primetime. Suddenly, he was wide-awake and not at all sleepy, he went back out into the landing and switched the landing light on, and this assured him that he was back in prime time, not in Laura's house, but in his own house, the one he had been renovating in prime time.

Chapter 21

Leo went downstairs and everything was as he left it on Christmas Eve before going to Laura's house with his J.T.R. bag. In the kitchen, three of the four walls were cleared of tiles, although where the entrance to the cellar now had a door that it didn't have before. He went through to the living room. This room too was as he had left it, even the Christmas tree with its flashing lights. He had been away over a month and a half, yet the lights still twinkled with full power. He assumed someone would have come along and pulled out the plug.

He pondered on the possibility of it still being Christmas Eve. There was one sure way of finding out and he went to the kitchen and checked the milk. He raised it to his nose and sniffed. There was not the nasty thickening or foul odour that he would associate with old milk and it smelt and appeared as fresh as when he bought it.

He thought about Evelyn and it was like a depression sweeping over him. Then he thought about Peter and Lydia, tucked up in bed, waiting for Santa. He last parked his car outside Laura's house with his mobile phone on the dashboard. He had the car keys and his house keys in his pocket when he arrived in 1904. However, he didn't see any sense in carrying them around with the house keys being different from 1900s keys for the same house. Therefore, after the first few days, he began to leave them in a drawer in his room along with the messages for Felix and Evelyn.

He checked the radio for the time and it was 11:37. He didn't know for sure because he didn't have a watch and had left his phone in the car, but he assumed when he arrived in 1904 that he had begun his journey through time at about this time, assuming it was now Christmas Eve. He went back into the living room where he last left his laptop, a sure piece of gadgetry that would answer at least some of his questions.

With the need of sleep now having deserted him, he booted up the laptop. He realised his last conversations with Evelyn and Felix had included everything they needed to know. Now he decided he had no reason or purpose left for remaining in 1905. The power that took him back to that time has possibly deemed it needful to return him. It didn't seem fair, though. He was carving out a life in 1905 and fate deemed it right to snatch it away from him.

The date at the bottom right of the booted up laptop suggested it was 24th December. He put his fingers on the keyboard and they began to move, clicking on keys and creating words on the screen in search of answers and having his answers displayed on the same screen.

Some research would kill some time, although he would rather go and see the kids. Without the car or the mobile phone to call a taxi, it would take an age to get there and they would both be sound asleep, so best to leave it until the morning.

He remembered a conversation he had with a work colleague, Alan, who at times drives a taxi to supplement his wages as a bus driver. Alan mentioned there being a couple of drivers booked for the Christmas holiday, but all calls would divert to the driver's mobile phones with the taxi office closed. That would rule out any sense in him going to the taxi depot for a taxi, so without a phone, he would be committed to walking to Laura's house – again!

However, he had the laptop for finding answers and he continued to dance his fingers on the keyboard.

During the following hours, he discovered that Evelyn had kept her promise and married in 1909. They had three children and she appeared to have carved out a pleasant life and was happy. He was pleased about that because she deserved it. He would have liked to share her life, but the main thing has to be her happiness and it helped to know she had a good life and it let Leo know that he had not imagined her in some strange Christmas Eve incantation.

Felix's son survived the Wall Street crash and never even experienced it and took over the business from Felix upon Felix's retirement. That was more good news and he decided fate might have permitted him an extended time in 1905 to allow him to have those last chats with Evelyn and Felix in order to bring these things to pass. There was no mention of Felix's daughter and son-in-law caught up in the hurricane, so they must have avoided it for a second time.

It took a while to find the information he needed, but it was worth the work and he found a photo of Evelyn in later years with her eldest son Leo. This brought a tear running down Leo's face as he wondered if baby Leo got his name from him, although he was far from a baby in the photo and looked to be in his 50s.

As Leo looked closer at the photo and zoomed in, he could see that the necklace around Evelyn's neck was the one he had bought her. He then found a photo of Evelyn and her husband with a baby that he took to be a grandchild, perhaps a great-grandchild.

He then entered the name Michael Brown into the search engine and hovered his finger over the enter button. He had put it off but needed to know if Mike was safe or did the time in 1905 cause his best friend to become a non-entity. The electrical work completed in the house suggested he was fine, but another electrician might have done it.

Leo needed to know, but was terrified of what hitting the enter button would reveal to him.

He rose from the laptop and went into the kitchen and, as the milk was fresh, he decided to have coffee. He purposefully didn't check his email on the laptop because he decided he would need to deal with the past before attempting to deal with the present. He didn't expect anything of a serious nature, more spam than anything else. This got him thinking, though, and he decided it might be best to check on the off chance of something waiting for his attention in his inbox.

He took his coffee back to the living room. He then clicked his email icon in the taskbar and the latest email in his inbox was from Mike to wish him a happy Christmas. He had already read it on his phone before leaving for Laura's house six weeks previously and he smiled at the realisation that Mike was alive, and well and living in prime time! That caused a huge relief to wash over him.

He checked the time on the laptop before closing it down again and it told him that he needed to attempt to get some sleep. He drank his coffee and went up the stairs. He decided to check the room he had left Amelia's furnishings and accessories in, but as he surmised, it was empty, apart from some of his things. With her cellar not sealed off in the new history, she will have gone on to use it for writing until she married Richard and would then have moved everything to their new house.

With Amelia's things gone and the door firmly fixed at the entrance to the cellar, Leo could easily work out that the new history had taken effect in this time and the flux had fully taken effect and he wondered what others like Mike would remember. Would he even be aware of Amelia dying in the old history? Was there another Leo in this time?

If this time didn't include a filled and sealed off cellar, then would it include him going back to 1904? What would be the point with Amelia surviving in the new history? Time, he reasoned, would answer these questions and more.

He went to his room, turned the light on and got ready for bed and realised he at least would be spared having to flush out his chamber pot in the morning. He slipped into bed, lay on his back to look up at the ceiling, and switched off the bedside lamp. It then became too dark to see the ceiling with any kind of clarity.

He still stared up at the ceiling as he attempted to work everything out and would leave the papers and documents that he placed in the wall cavity for another time. He would need to be careful as it will now be over a century old and sudden exposure to light and moisture could cause problems when taking it all from its glass case.

Leo reached underneath his bed for the chamber pot when he initially woke. The sudden realisation that he was now back in prime time filled him with mixed emotions of Evelyn not being here but Christmas smiles with be decking the kids as they drive Laura and Tony crazy. He saw his 1905 clothes draped over a chair where he had left them before getting into bed and it was sad that he would no doubt never wear them again because his business in that year was complete, otherwise he reasoned, he would not be back to prime time.

He went through to the bathroom, then got dressed and went downstairs to put the kettle on. As he entered the kitchen, he remembered the conversations he had with Felix as they prepared a meal or completed a meal that Martha had prepared. He took his coffee into the living room and booted up the laptop. His initial search didn't come up with anything on Martha, although a later search would reveal a connection between Martha and some cousins of Leo who were also the nephew's and niece of the aunt who whacked him on the head with the tin tray.

The tray-wielding aunt worked with Martha's son in the hardware store during her younger days. Martha and Harold spent the remainder of their days together, living over the hardware store. They had one son who got married and had two sons and a daughter. Martha and Harold appeared to have been extremely happy and that made Leo happy.

Surprisingly, Leo discovered that there was also a connection between him and Martha's new husband Harold, but on Leo's Mother's side, strangely. Therefore, before she was married to Harold, she had a family relationship with Leo through his Father and after getting married, she took on a family relationship with him through his Mother. He smiled when he discovered this and decided that Martha intended to be part of his ancestry in any transfiguration.

He decided to send Mike a quick email before powering off the laptop. He thought he should keep it short and just wish him a happy Christmas and perhaps drop in a suggestion that he might call by later.

He then went to a drawer where he kept spare keys, found replacement house keys, and car keys. His wallet and money were in a drawer in 1905, but there was some money in the drawer in prime time, two twenty pound notes, a ten-pound note and a five-pound note. It was there for him to use in paying a friend for some wood he dropped off, but Leo could use it and return it when he gets things sorted out and he pushed the full £55 into his jeans pocket.

He didn't need it, but he decided he would prefer to have it in case he needs to get a taxi and who knows what else will crop up, he decided. With it being Christmas Day again, there will not be many places open to spend it and it might have to keep him going until he gets a new bankcard with his old one being in his wallet in 1905.

Leo left the house on a cold Christmas morning to walk all the way once more to Laura's house. As he walked down the road, he heard the engine of a bus roaring behind him and he began to run to the nearest bus stop. Some bus drivers will be kind; others will take joy in leaving a person stranded.

Leo should have known there would be some buses on, but he works for a bus hire company and they don't rent buses out on Christmas day and he has never had the need of a bus on Christmas morning, so he didn't realise they have a Sunday service at Christmas.

The bus passed him and Leo slowed down his charge forward until he saw the bus pulling in at the bus stop just up ahead and he quickened his charge towards it and thanked the driver as he climbed aboard. He took the money from his pocket and selected the £5, gave it to the bus driver.

"Sorry mate," The driver said, "I don't have any change."

"That isn't even a small problem," Leo said. "Keep the change as a thank you for stopping."

The driver raised a thumb and Leo took his ticket and then took his seat to relax for the journey ahead.

The bus would not take him to Laura's house, but it was a lot better than having to walk all the way and the last half mile or so would not be a problem and he compared the differences to the last time he took the same journey via horse-pulled tram.

The bus was much faster and warmer, much more comfortable. However, all that escaped Leo after the first half of the journey as he turned his mind to the kids. He had thought he might never see them again, yet here he was, on the way to see them again!

When he arrived at Laura's street, he spotted the car sitting outside her house. He briefly thought about his great-grandfather Joe who did such a good job with the decorating and Leo didn't get to live even one night in the house.

He took out his spare car keys and opened the door of the car to get his phone. He would have loved to show the phone to Felix and was sure he would have been mesmerised by it. He decided to open the bonnet as a ruse to give him a reason for leaving the car there and with the bonnet open; he went to the house and rapped the door, his heart pounding.

Laura answered the door and he said, "I couldn't start the car last night and had to leave it there and didn't want to disturb you by telling you. However, I've got it sorted now."

Laura looked beyond him at the car with the bonnet widely opened and had no reason not to accept what he had told her.

She said, "Would you like to come in and wish the kids a Merry Christmas seeing as you are here anyway?"

"I'd love to," he said, and Laura stepped back to allow him entrance.

As he stepped into the hall, she said, "I was wondering why you left your car. How did you get home?"

"I phoned a taxi."

"Did he charge you double time? The double fair began at midnight and it was about 11:30 when you left here, but some would charge double fare before they should."

"No, he was honest and just charged a single fare," Leo lied again and they went through to the living room and Lydia spotted him and ran to him, put her arms around him and said, "Thank you for your presents, daddy. I got everything I wanted."

Leo lifted Lydia into his arms and hugged her, just as he did when she was much smaller.

"I like the things you got me too, dad," Peter said, although he was less enthusiastic with his welcome with being a boy and boys don't show their feelings like girls.

Leo had over 6 weeks to make up for in that hug with Lydia, but he realised it was just one night for her and so he had to hold back and to Peter he said, "That's great! Your ear doesn't seem to be bothering you too much now."

"Magic tablets," Laura said with a smile. Leo reluctantly lowered Lydia back to the ground and she went back to her new stuff.

Leo said, "Is Tony still in bed? I suppose he came home after having a skinful and has slept ever since."

Laura said, "Would you like a cup of tea or coffee, Leo?"

With the offer of tea or coffee replacing an answer to his question, Leo could see that all was not well and he said," I had a cup of coffee before leaving, but would love a cup of tea."

Laura said, "The kids will be fine here enjoying themselves. Come on through and I'll put the kettle on."

Leo followed Laura through to the kitchen and as she filled the kettle and got two cups, she said, "I didn't want to say in front of the kids, but Tony and I had a fight and he stormed out two days ago and I haven't heard from him since. I told the kids he was having Christmas with his old mum."

"People have arguments all the time. He'll be back when he cools off."

"I'm not sure I want him back, Leo."

Leo was unsure how to respond to that. He had come to realise Tony was a good bloke and he loved the kids as if they

276

were his own and he was good to Laura and, while it was hard at first, he would hate to see them splitting up now.

With a lack of verbal response from Leo, Laura added, "I'm beginning to think divorce might not have been the best route for us to take."

"That was your decision; I didn't have a lot of say in it. I had no say at all in it."

"I know, Leo, but everyone can make mistakes."

Leo pondered before saying, "Look Laura, I've just remembered something and I'll have to go so I'm sorry about the tea."

Leo went through to the living room and smiled at the kids as he said, "I'll have to go now but I'll see you both real soon."

He gave them both a kiss and Lydia said, "I love you, daddy." I love you too, sweetheart, you too Peter. Be good for your mum and make sure you eat all your Christmas dinner."

Leo noticed that Laura remained in the kitchen as he made his way to the door and left. He quickly lowered the bonnet and climbed into the car, started up the engine and drove off.

He felt angry; as if Laura was feeling drawn back to him but only on the rebound. If he had not had the past weeks with Evelyn, he might have felt differently, but it took him a long time to get to the stage where he could allow another woman into his heart and his life and he needed to get over losing Evelyn before he could even consider another woman, let alone his ex-wife.

He doesn't often talk to himself, but he punched the heel of his hand on the steering wheel and said, "What kind of mug does she think I am? She can't dump me and then ask me back when things don't go the way she expects. Of course, she made a mistake demanding a divorce, but it's history now and she'll have to live with it in the same way that I had to live with and come to terms with it."

Within a short time he realised he was in top gear and was zooming along past the legal limit for the road. He reasoned that his fury was causing him to neglect the road and he dropped down through the gears and stopped.

277

He needed a moment to compose himself, he took his phone from the dashboard and tapped onto his email, and there was a new one there from Mike. He tapped onto it to read it.

"Leo, I feel bad you being on your own in that huge and empty house. Will you not reconsider coming here for Christmas dinner?"

He smiled, swiped and tapped the screen and put the phone to his ear. It took just a moment for Mike to answer and Leo said, "Mike I just left Laura a moment ago after spending a moment with the kids and I just saw your email, mate."

"As you're not at home, why not spin by here now, mate. I need a hand because the kids are killing me and I can't keep up."

"That's old age. I hear it gets to you like that at your time of life."

"I'm still a month and a half younger than you, old son. Will you come and make an old man very happy?"

"Okay, I'll be there soon."

"Good lad, I'll have a cup and a glass waiting and you can decide which to have first. Have you had breakfast?"

"I said I'll drop by, not take up residence. I've got a proposal for you anyway, mate."

"I'm not sure what to say about that. Do you often proposition men on the phone?"

Leo smiled and said, "I'll tell you about it later. See you soon."

"Great, mate, see you soon."

Leo swiped the phone to end the call and pondered. He would have preferred to have the papers and documents from the kitchen wall before going to Mike's, but he could work around that. He needed to remember that he should not know about Mike losing his job.

Leo didn't have a clue how he would relay everything that has happened as he walked up to Mike's front door and decided he would have to improvise. He would tell Mike everything, he had to, but he would select his time carefully. He realised that Mike would have problems believing him; although he was sure that Mike would know that he would not lie about such things.

Leo didn't need to rap the door and as he approached it, Mike opened it and carried on into the living room, taking it for granted that Leo would enter. He could hear the kids up in their rooms playing loudly and Phoebe was in the kitchen, assumedly tending to the turkey at the early stages of the cooking process. Leo closed the door and followed Mike into the living room.

Mike sat down and directed Leo's attention to a cup of coffee. There was something in a small glass with a chaser in a bottle beside it, and a larger glass with an unopened can of beer. Mike said, "I didn't know if you'd want a beer or something stronger, so I decided on both and you can skip the coffee, mate, your choice."

"I'm driving, Mike."

"Not a problem, you can stay here or get a taxi home."

"When I go home, could you come with me? There's something I need to show you, mate."

Mike gazed at Leo with pretend suspicion and with equally pretend caution he said, "What are you up to, Mr Bond?"

"As I said on the phone, I have a proposition for you."

Mike smiled and said, "Exactly, I'm not used to being propositioned, Mr Bond."

"Leaving James Bond out of it, it's all above board and will change both our lives. I need to show you something first, though."

Mike laughed and said, "Yeah, it's that last bit that worries me."

"Seriously, I need to show you some papers and things from 1905, mate."

"What's this about, mate?"

"I'll tell you everything when you see what I need you to see."

"There you go with the secret agent stuff again, mate."

Phoebe arrived in the room and said, "It's great you could join us, Leo. It's also good that you have decided not to spend all day working on the house."

Mike said, "He wants me to go to the house with him. He wants to show me secret things. Have you got my insurance up to date?"

Mike laughed and Phoebe said, "It would get you out of my hair and let me get on with the dinner if you went to Leo's house now. Sorry, if it seems I'm trying to dump him onto you, Leo, but he can become a pain when he's home all day."

"I understand, Phoebe. As it happens, we could go now and be back in plenty of time for dinner."

"Okay," Mike said. "You've got me all curious anyway. If you go in your car, I could go in mine and then I could drive you back and you could have a few drinks without worrying about driving home."

"You've been drinking, though; will it be safe for you to drive?"

Mike laughed. Phoebe only allowed me to have this one because you were coming. This is the first one I've had all day and have only taken a sip."

Leo rose and said, "Okay, let's go."

"Thank you, Leo," Phoebe said. "You're an angel!"

Mike watched as Leo tapped his fingers on the keyboard of the laptop. He could not understand why Leo brought the laptop into the kitchen first and then got a club hammer and bolster together, but he was sure there was an answer and his former curiosity was developing into him now being intrigued.

Mike said, "I hate to ruin the surprise, mate, but I've seen your laptop before."

Leo didn't reply and carried on reading from the laptop screen. He finally said, "Okay, I don't have soft gloves, so I'll wash my hands to remove any grease that might be on them. Firstly, though, follow me, mate."

He lifted the hammer and bolster, went to the centre of the full wall of tiles, and said, "I have to be careful because everything is in a glass container and I don't want to smash it. Before I get everything out"

"Whatever you say, mate."

Leo said, "It was all a bit rushed with the tillers coming and then I was sucked back."

"Sucked back where?"

"From there to here, of course."

Mike frowned in confusion and said, "Of course, how silly of me, where else? If you're going to chip more tiles out, though, shouldn't you get your work gloves and goggles on, mate?"

Leo tapped the wall along a range of four tiles above the wall socket.

Mike said, "Part of your wall sounds hollow, a bit like my brain, I suppose."

Leo placed the edge of the bolster on one of the tiles that rang solid to his tap, and said, "Here we go, you can close your eyes if you don't want a slither of grout or tile whacking your iris mate." He struck the hammer firmly against the bolster a couple of times in an outward direction from the hollow-sounding tiles until the tile came away from the wall, and then he turned his attention to the tiles that sounded hollow and he began to tap in the opposite direction, using more gentle hammer blows.

Mike stood back after the initial hard blows, but he moved forward again, when he saw that Leo was through to a thin layer of wood. Some of the wood came away with the tiles to reveal a hollowed-out section of the wall and Leo finally put the hammer and bolster down. He looked at the broken writing that appeared under the tiles.

Leo said, "Felix was spot on and my writing is just about undecipherable."

He pulled the remaining wood away and lifted out the glass case.

Mike remained silent and watched as Leo brought the glass case to the old left-behind table and said, "I'll need to wash my hands after I get it opened. Firstly, though -" He lifted a flat head screwdriver from a nearby toolbox and left it beside the glass container.

"How did you know that was there?" Mike asked.

"What, the screwdriver?"

"No, I was referring to the glass container, as you well know."

Leo smiled at Mike and said, "I put it there in 1905, mate."

Mike laughed, but only until he realised that Leo was serious and confusion replaced the laughter. He decided to remain quiet and just watch.

Leo went through to the living room and Mike followed. As they went, Leo said, "The papers inside that glass container have been there for over 100 years and I was worried about the sudden exposure to this atmosphere having a detrimental effect on them. That's why I had to check it all on the laptop."

When they entered the living room, Leo opened a drawer to the desk he used for his laptop, took out some plastic A4 transparent document protective covers, and said, "These should protect them until we get them to where they need to go."

"Where do they need to go?"

"Into these protective covers for now and after Christmas, we'll visit the solicitor to keep it all legal, and then the bank manager to have a place to store all the money they'll rake in for us both."

"What do you mean us both?"

Leo smiled at Mike and said, "We'll see what condition they are in before we have question time, mate."

Leo, with Mike following, returned to the kitchen and placed the document covers on the left behind table beside the glass container. He then went to the sink and washed his hands and as he washed them, he said, I'll use the screwdriver to gently pry the glass lid off. Using a screwdriver might not be perfect, but it's all I have. It should be okay, though and once we get the documents out, the glass container won't matter."

He dried his hands and moved to the glass container on the table. He lifted the screwdriver and said, "I don't want to damage the glass until I get the stuff out, so here's hoping mate."

He used the screwdriver to pry open the lid. He was careful and took his time, prying one section, and then moving the screwdriver along and prying an inch or two along. When he had gone around the entire lid, prying gently until it finally came away from the case. He lifted the lid off and set it down, well away from the case, and then he removed the bundle of newspapers wrapped around the documents and he said, "This is thicker than I remember and I think Felix has opened it up and added some other stuff."

"Felix? You mean the bloke in that photo you have who lived here with his sister back in Victorian times?"

"Yes, but it was in Edwardian times when I met him, 1904 going into 1905."

Mike offered a partial smile and a partial frown and seemed unable to decide which to give dominance to as he became even more confused than before. He said, "You don't have a bottle of something very strong about here, do you?"

Leo said, "You'll find a bottle of concentrated bleach in the cupboard under the sink, but don't drink it all."

Mike smiled and tapped Leo on the shoulder as he said, "Nice one, mate.

Leo said, "I'll get us both a drink in a second. For now, be patient, you'll soon know everything and while it might be hard to take in, it will change our lives hugely."

"I trust you, mate, but I have to admit that I'm getting slightly concerned for your sanity."

"I was concerned in 1904, but it wasn't so bad when I reached 1905."

"Obviously," Mike said. "1905 was a good year for dealing with our concerns."

"I need to ask a question," Leo said. Mike offered his fullest attention and Leo added, "If you hit on a way of buying up things like Man U shares back in 1905 at 1905 prices, would you buy them?"

"Of course, they'd be worth a fortune today."

"Would you buy some for me as well?"

"Without doubt, mate."

Leo smiled and said, "Okay, you can pay me for your shares in a month or two."

Mike frowned in confusion and Leo pushed the glass container away and placed the newspaper on the table, gently unwrapping the contents they surrounded and revealing for the first time to Mike several legal looking documents, stocks and bonds and other papers that defied Mike's understanding as to what was happening.

Leo carefully put each one into its protective cover and then looked more closely at them and said, "Now for the full story, Mike. What I am about to tell you will amaze and intrigue you and you will probably not believe it at first, but I assure you it's true.

283

Are you ready for the single most important story you will ever hear, one that will end forever all your financial problems and will force you to accept that there is more going on in the world than we will ever understand? Are you ready for it all, mate?"

"I'm ready for whatever you have to tell me, mate."

"Okay, here comes the full story."

Mike listened dutifully as Leo told him everything and was happy to share it all. Leo expected him to have many questions and he was pleased that Mike didn't interrupt him at all with a single question and simply listened. Leo decided after some time that he had told him enough to make it all clear to him. He could see Mike didn't just listen; he also mentally dissected what he was hearing. He made judgements as each bit of new information became available to him.

Leo could see understanding eventually appearing in Mike's expression and he remained silent until Leo had finished with the words, "So, now you know everything, mate."

With Leo now silent and awaiting Mike's response, Mike turned away and Leo could see that he was still carefully examining everything and working out finer detail. Leo was anxious to hear Mike's thoughts, but he was happy for Mike to consider everything deeply and Leo had to remember that he had six weeks to come to terms with it all and Mike didn't even have six minutes.

However, Mike finally looked to Leo and said, "I think I understand, mate. I'm confused on reasons, but I understand."

Leo moved to speak, but Mike raised a hand to silence him and he continued, "You obviously got some tiles off without breaking them, and so you were able to dig out that cavity and put those papers in the glass container and seal them up in the cavity. It's easy to make the paper look old and cold tea is one method. It isn't hard to work out how you did it all, but I'm confused about why you would want to. It goes beyond your normal jokes and pranks and I have a problem figuring it out. More than that, I have a problem figuring you out, mate."

"You've got it all wrong, Mike."

"Have I, Leo? Do you expect me to believe that last night you spent time in 1905? I think I have spent all the time on this that I wish to spend and I'll wait out in the car for you. If you aren't out within five minutes, I'll have to assume that you no longer want to join us for Christmas dinner."

Mike left and Leo lowered his head, a reflection of when he could not deny the penknife belonged to him when the teacher passed behind him and it fell to the floor. He needed now to say something to Mike, but his mind and mouth were frozen, closed and inoperable, and he could not muster a word in defence of his claims.

Chapter 22

Leo sat in the living room with his eyes transfixed on the lights of the Christmas tree as they blinked and flashed at various speeds. He should have switched them off, but it required more effort than Leo could muster and all Christmas Day and Boxing Day, they hypnotised him, and continued to blink and flash into the third day.

Leo had never felt like this before, not even when Laura asked for a divorce. He was over one hundred years away from Evelyn and an entire mindset away from Mike and he had no desire or fight left to change anything or attempt to brighten up his life. He had neglected his razor. He wore the same clothes that he dressed in on Christmas morning. He even slept in these same clothes without actually going to bed.

He didn't follow Mike out to the car and had listened as Mike drove off after ten or fifteen minutes. He simply could not bring himself to leave the house, had no desire to interact with anyone and he switched his phone off and booting up the laptop became more than he could manage.

His mind turned to Evelyn and he was pleased that she found someone, pleased too that Felix got married before his original wedding date and Amelia and Richard too had a good life. He decided it would have been best if he had remained in 1905 because now it would be over, no more pain, no more anguish, no more feeling a thick, dark cloud hovering overhead.

He would now be in one of the thousands of graves in the cemetery instead of transfixed by blinking and flashing Christmas tree lights, which he wished, would stop blinking and flashing while going to the plug to pull it out took too much labour. Even putting the kettle on for tea or coffee was no longer worth the effort.

The knock on the front door registered in his ear, but not in his mind.

The front door opening also registered in his ear, but not in his mind.

He saw Mike coming into the room and partially raised a hand in salutation. Mike said, "Are you okay, mate, you either switched your phone off or it's out of charge."

"I switched it off," Leo said, his words automatic and without emotion."

Mike looked closely at him and said, "You don't look good, mate. I think you need a doctor. Have you been sitting here long?"

"I don't need a doctor; I just need to be left alone."

Mike took his phone from his pocket and said, "No mate, you need a doctor. You've gone into depression or have taken a mental breakdown or something. Have you eaten? You haven't, have you? You've just sat there since I left two days ago."

"I just sat down to relax and think. I'm okay. I'll admit that I have been through some emotional problems, but no one will believe me, so there's no sense even mentioning it."

"I believe you, mate."

Leo looked away from Mike and fixed his eyes on the Christmas tree lights.

"No, I do, mate," Mike insisted. He swiped and tapped his phone to bring up a photo and he showed it to Leo. It was a photo of Leo at work in the colliery with Terry. I found this photo on the Colliery website along with the information that Leo Lennox was instrumental with Terrance Brown of beginning a first aid program in the colliery back in 1905. When you disappeared, my great-great-granddad took over from you and headed the program."

Mike put his phone into his pocket to show Leo that he would not phone the doctor. He added, "I'm sorry I didn't believe you, mate, but it was such an incredible story."

Leo raised his hand and tapped Mike on the arm, then grasped Mike's arm and said, "I would have had problems believing it too. I met Evelyn back there. She was amazing. I'll never see her again, though."

"Don't you mean Amelia, mate?"

"Evelyn's brother married Amelia. Felix married Brenda and even Evelyn got married. I was pleased. I didn't want her to be alone. I met family, Martha and great granddad Joe, also my granddad as a baby"

"What do you say we go into the kitchen and see what there is for you to eat?"

"I don't feel hungry."

"You still need to eat. Come on, mate."

Mike began to walk towards the kitchen and Leo rose and followed him.

After staying at Mike and Phoebe's and being banned from all things that would remind him of his experiences of late, Mike spoke to the doctor about slowly reintroducing his friend to life and getting him ready to return to the house and begin making decisions again. The doctor agreed, so Mike told Leo that, he had checked the mail as promised on Boxing Day. As Leo suspected, he had to direct most to the bin. He did have a couple of letters that he reserved for Leo's inspection, one in particular.

Leo read it, it was from Trevor S Bennett who claimed his father was born in this house, and his great-great Grandparents and great-grandparents had lived in it. The name Bennett was a slight giveaway to the great-grandfather being Felix and Amelia, but nothing is ever definite and Trevor had got engaged to be married in July and was wondering if it would be possible to have some wedding photos taken in the garden. Leo immediately got his phone and dialled the number given in the letter.

"Hello, my name is Leo Lennox and I live at 2 Meadowbank Road. You wrote to me a while back and I apologise for taking so long to get back to you, but I have just now been given your letter."

"Hello, Mr Lennox. My dad was born in your house and it's a very special place for me."

"It's a special place for me too, Trevor. Would you mind if I asked a couple of questions?"

"Whatever you need to know, go ahead and ask."

"You mentioned your great-grandfather. Would this be Felix Bennett who had a sister names Amelia?"

"Actually, yes it would. Can I ask how you know?"

"You would never believe me. I also know that Felix married Brenda Paterson and Amelia married Richard Brookes."

There was no response and Leo said, "Hello, are you still there, Trevor."

"Yes, I'm still here, Sorry, I'm just a bit stunned. The story is that my great-grandfather claimed he had a friend from the future by the name of Leo who owned the house in the future and was able to go back in time to when great-grandfather owned it."

"Yes, well, whatever you believe, Trevor, I would love to have you and your bride coming here to have some wedding photos taken."

"That would be amazing and I think we might have a lot to learn from each other. Would it be possible for me to call in and speak with you about it next week or the week after?"

"Of course, drop by any time. I'll genuinely look forward to it."

Leo and Mike arrived at the bank and went into the manager's office without the need of any waiting and the manager bounced to his feet and shot a hand out to greet them with a handshake. He motioned for them to sit down and said, "It has been the privilege of this bank to have dealt with the Bennett account for one hundred and fifty years and it will be an absolute privilege and an honour to help you achieve maximum potential with your finances, Mr Lennox and Mr Brown."

Leo and Mike both decided the manager was slightly over the top with the bootlicking, but they understood the difference the content of the glass case from the wall cavity would make to even the bank and they were happy to sit down and discuss it as the manager instructed his assistant to bring coffee for his prestigious guests.

As the assistant left to tend to the coffee, the manager smiled widely at Leo and said, "We also have documentation from Mr Felix Bennett concerning you, Mr Lennox, and while your account will be to a lesser degree, Mr Brown, it's still extremely substantial and I would suggest you both allow me to organise a financial advisor to –"

"That will not be necessary," Leo said, interrupting. "We will make those arrangements personally."

"As you wish, Mr Lennox, that is perfectly acceptable. Can I say that it has amazed this office that Mr Bennett named you for the first time more than a century ago and had the correct mailing address for you?"

Mike said, "He must have been an extremely astute man, or maybe he took a shot and was spot on? He seems to have been an amazing man, though."

"He certainly does, Mr Brown."

Leo said, "Plus, he was an extremely good cook, much better than his sister Amelia."

The bank manager frowned. Leo and Mike smiled widely.

Leo assumed the man getting out of the rather expensive car was Trevor S Bennett and he assumed the woman to be his fiancée. He was amazed at how Trevor appeared so much like Felix and it was more startling to witness how like Evelyn the woman appeared. It would be amazing, he decided, if the woman was a descendent of Evelyn after Evelyn's brother Richard marrying Felix's Sister Amelia. It would be like history repeating itself.

The man and woman took their time and took in the garden with obvious pleasure as they walked toward the door and Leo had the door open before they could reach it and he extended a hand and said to the man, "You must be Trevor. It's an amazing pleasure to meet you."

"The amazement is completely mine," Trevor said, "You are the double of the Leo in the photos handed down from great grandfather."

"If I can say, you are the double of Felix." He turned his attention to the woman and said, "You must be Trevor's fiancée. You are the double of Felix's brother-in-law's sister Evelyn Brookes."

Trevor and the woman both cast an astonished glare at each other as Leo invited them in. Trevor raised one forefinger to ask for a moment and he went to the car and returned with a doctor's medical bag.

It was a short time since Leo had last seen the bag in 1905, but it still mesmerised him to see it in the present time and he said, "I don't believe it, it's my old J.T.R. bag!"

"That's exactly as my great-grandfather referred to it, a J.T.R. bag," Trevor said. "I was going to ask if you could put any light on it, but obviously you know it, so could I discuss this with you later."

"Of course," Leo said, "It was a gift from my old mate Mike and it got left behind as I was returned to prime time. I'll explain everything, Trevor, but, for now, let me show you inside your great-grandfather's house, which was first owned by your great-great-grandfather Ronald Bennett, who bought the house in 1867."

The house was in an obvious state of disrepair and Leo said, "I'm sorry about the state of the place. I have a crew of workmen signed up to help restore it all to its former glory and it will be completed long before your wedding if you chose to have some photos inside as well as in the garden."

Trevor and the woman remained silent as they entered the house and feasted their eyes on everything. Leo said, "Does it all bring back memories?"

"Yes," Trevor said. "The house came back into family hands during World War Two and I spent many amazing summers here with my brother and two sisters, several cousins also."

That answered some questions Leo had because his information was in the family not owning the house after the death of Brenda a few years after Felix. He reasoned Amelia's survival has changed many scenarios. They went through to the living room and Leo invited them to sit down. He said, "You'll have to excuse me if I appear in any way bewildered, and sorry for repeating myself, but you are the double of Felix."

"I know, I have seen photos of my great-grandfather and everyone says the same thing. Did you mention Evelyn having the appearance of great grandfather's Brother-in-laws sister, was it? I should tell you, though, that this is not my fiancée, Evelyn is my cousin and she loves this house every bit as much as I do and equally has many fond memories of it. My fiancée could not come, but Evelyn would not be persuaded to stay away."

Leo looked at the woman and said, "Your name is Evelyn?"

"Yes," she said, "Evelyn Carleton, I was named after my mother, who was named after her grandmother."

"It's amazing to be in this house again," Trevor said.

"I know how you must be feeling," Leo said. "Come back any time. I have a feeling we will become good friends as your great-grandfather and the Leo you have heard about were. I'll take you on a tour of the house after we talk and get to know each other a bit, but if you would prefer just to wander around without the conducted tour, that will be fine. You will both know the house at least as well as me anyway."

"That's very kind of you," Trevor said, reaching into his pocket for his pen and wallet and taking out a business card from the wallet. He wrote on the back of the business card and handed it to Leo. "I have written my home address on the back and I would love you to come and visit any time. I have my great grandfather's first car in the garage, which I somehow feel you might be interested in?"

Leo took the card and said, "I would be enormously interested in seeing it again."

"Again," Trevor said as Leo looked at the card.

Leo said, "So, the business that Felix's Father began is still going strong? Bennett and Brooks, though?"

Yes, great-grandfather amalgamated with his brother-in-law's firm and they opened a branch in Europe and then another in America."

Leo smiled and said, "I Googled some things earlier, but I have a lot to catch up on. I was aware that your Grandfather took over from your Great Grand Father Felix, but I didn't realise Felix and Richard had amalgamated their businesses into one."

Leo could see how well the business was doing as he arrived at Trevor's house. Then again, he was also doing okay himself and he arrived in a sleek new car that before that he could only dream about. He was pleased that, like his great-grandfather Felix, Trevor was clearly down to earth and he could speak to him as a friend. There was a bell on the door but Leo always preferred to use his knuckles and knock, although, he decided that the house was so large that they might not hear his knock and he might need to ring the bell.

A woman heard and opened the door, greeted Leo with a smile and said, "You'll be Mr Lennox. Trevor won't be a moment; would you like to come in?"

Leo smiled and decided she must be Trevor's fiancée and he applauded Trevor's taste and he saw her as quite appealing to the eye with a rather captivating smile and a most fetching and friendly disposition.

He didn't say any of this to her and simply smiled and followed her. She showed him to a room and invited him to take a seat before she left.

Seconds later, Trevor arrived with an extended hand and Leo rose to shake hands. As they stood shaking hands, a woman arrived and Trevor said, "Leo, could I introduce you to my fiancée, Marian?"

Leo reached out a hand to Marian and said, "I'm pleased to meet you, Marian." He turned his attention back to Trevor and said, "I assumed the lady who invited me in was your fiancée?"

Trevor indicated for everyone to sit down and said, "No that was Dorothy who helps us keep the place as it is."

"Oh, you mean she's your housemaid?"

"We see her more as a friend."

Leo liked that and it smacked of the relationship Felix and Amelia had with Martha, although Dorothy was much younger than Martha.

Marian said, "I need to apologise for not arriving with Trevor when he visited you. I had a pressing family matter to attend to. My mum has not been very well and I was with her."

"I hope she is a lot better now," Leo said.

"She is fine although she doesn't make for a valorous patient and requires more sympathy and understanding than most."

"No doubt it isn't a drain on you to care for her."

"Of course not, she cared for me throughout my childhood."

Leo felt comfortable and at home with Trevor and Marian and he was ready to answer the questions they had for him. He certainly had questions he needed to ask them.

Leo rapped the door and Laura opened it, stepped out onto the doorstep, and closed the door behind her. She said, "Leo, I need to apologise for my behaviour on Christmas day when you came to pick up your car and see the kids. I think I must have been feeling a bit down, but everything is fine now and Tony is back."

"I'm pleased to hear that, Laura, and don't give it another thought. I understand completely. Is Tony at home now?"

"Yes, but why do you ask?"

"No reason," Leo said. He could see that Laura was worried and he added, "Don't worry, Laura. I do understand what you have been through and if you're worried about me saying something to Tony about it, then I can assure you that you worry needlessly."

"Thank you," Laura said and she pushed the door open and they both entered as Tony was going from the living room to the kitchen as Leo arrived in the hallway and Leo stopped and extended a hand to Tony and as they shook hands he said, "I hope you had a great Christmas and an amazing New Year, Tony."

"I've had worse, Leo. Are you here to pick up the kids?"

"Just to see them, I haven't anything arranged."

"If you're not leaving right away, I'm sure Laura could make us all a cup and we could have a chat."

"That would be great, Tony. It wouldn't do the kids any harm to see us interacting congenially together either."

Lydia arrived in the hall and rushed to Leo and he took her up into his arms and kissed her on the side of the face. Peter arrived and Leo decided life felt good, back with the kids and a new love interest who he had arranged to pick up later from the home of his new friend Trevor S Bennett. Who could hope or ask for more.

THE END

oOo

Thank you for reading this

Printed in Great Britain
by Amazon

eac5a070-c10c-4521-ba97-0d312c127bddR02